To my wonderful dad, who taught me that my worth was inherent and divine and who raised me to be strong, work hard, and believe in myself. I love you, Daddy.

CHAPTER ONE

Emma Crawford was a genius.

She watched her mentor, Weston, beam, his hands clasped against the breast pocket of his royal-blue suit, basking in the applause of an audience who were as charmed by him as Emma knew they would be. For months, Emma had prodded Weston to meet with studio execs. He'd been languishing as an occasional guest judge on various Bravo TV shows and as the owner of a popular Polynesian martial arts studio in the Upper West Side. Only she had known that Weston wasn't content. And watching his soft-brown cheeks glow bronze now as he finished the monologue for his first-ever daytime talk show, she knew she'd been right.

As usual.

"Aw, you look like a proud mother hen," Harlan said, leaning toward her so she could hear him over the cheering audience. They were standing backstage, but the screams were so loud they may as well have been in the middle of the crowd. The stage manager didn't have to hype the audience up much.

"Excuse me? Did you say *mother*?" She held up a hand in front of her younger brother's face. Her manicure matched Weston's suit perfectly. "Don't you put that evil on me. I turned nineteen two months ago. In Hollywood years, I'm barely old enough to play a high school freshman."

"Was that a hint about your next role? It was, wasn't it? Just tell me. The crew isn't paying attention."

"No way. We agreed to let Weston reveal both of our next roles, even to each other."

"Which he'll do in approximately four and a half minutes in front of a live studio audience, Ems. Come on. You seriously won't tell me?"

"It's not like you've told me."

"I've given you at least fifty hints. I've been watching a certain sport every day, I took you with me when I tried on cleats—"

She covered her ears. "La, la, la."

"Stop it. You already know." He wasn't really upset, but he wasn't happy about her silence either. If their parents' very public nuclear meltdown and divorce had done nothing else, it had cemented the Crawford siblings' loyalty to one another.

So it was out of loyalty that she gave him a hint. And because she hated seeing the small crease of disappointment between his brows. "No. I'm not playing a high school freshman."

"Which leaves us with two options. Come on!"

"Fine." She narrowed her eyes at him, not in annoyance but in exultation. "The only other thing I'll say is that learning limalama at Weston's studio for the last few months is going to come in pretty handy for all my fight scenes."

"No! You brat!"

"Yes." She folded her arms.

The stage manager got their attention, putting a hand up to his headphones. Weston was prepping the audience for his first guests.

"Well, at least I'll have top billing," Harlan muttered.

"I'll have an action figure," she shot back.

"I already have an action figure."

"From a talking dog movie."

"Oh, shut up."

The stage manager was flagging them while Weston said, "Now let's bring out my very first guests ever: Emma and Harlan Crawford!"

Emma loved a lot of things about the next ten seconds: the raucous applause, the fact that her name was mentioned before Harlan's, crossing Weston's cool white-and-green set, with its potted banyan trees and island backdrop, to get to his white leather couches. But more than anything, she loved when Weston hugged her tighter than her own father ever had and whispered, "Thank you, you wonderful girl," before she sat down. She loved that the smile he gave her reached his eyes in a way he nearly always avoided out of fear of wrinkles. She loved seeing the two men she loved most in the world hug before they all took their seats.

When the applause died down, Weston reached across the couches to grab Emma's hand. "As soon as I signed on to do this show, I knew my first guests had to be Emma and Harlan Crawford. It wasn't just because they're so famous or beautiful, or because they're letting me exclusively reveal their upcoming movies today." Weston pursed his lips over the applause. "I wanted them because Emma Crawford is the reason I'm here with you all today. I tried to tell her I was content with my martial arts and retiring from the public eye. She insisted I needed something more, and since I reminded her that I have been happily celibate longer than she's been alive and flat out refused to date any of the randos she tried to set me up with, my girl got creative."

"That's a polite way of seeing she meddled," Harlan cut in, earning a wave of laughs.

"You know that's right," Weston said. "When Emma found out a new show was in the works, she knew that I was the person for the job, even if no one else did."

A member of the audience screamed, "We knew! We love you!" and everyone laughed.

Weston smiled. "Well, you were right. You and Emma Crawford. My guardian angel. My professional matchmaker."

She looked at Weston, with his closely cropped black hair and

Clark Kent glasses, and tugged his polka-dot bow tie. "You forgot to mention your style icon, Pops."

The audience laughed along with Weston and Harlan. At ten, Emma had starred in a TV show about two tween girls in foster care who were adopted by the same man on Valentine's Day. Their adopted father was played by former-fashion-designer-turned-YouTube-star-turned-actor, Weston Tagovailoa. In the show, Emma's character was reluctant to call Weston "Dad," so she called him "Pops" instead. He called her "Nutmeg," and her adopted sister "Peanut." The show was a huge success, and Emma was asked to be the face of renowned Jacques Clothing's juniors line.

Emma's agent father had brokered the deals, and the show and clothing line remained the best things he'd ever done for her, personally or professionally. The show had lasted another three seasons, and by the fourth and final season, Emma Crawford, Victoria Alba—her TV sister—and Weston had all become household names.

"Style icon? Uh huh. Right," Weston said. "You'd still be wearing nurse's shoes with this sassy jumpsuit if it weren't for me."

"Says the guy wearing the bow tie I bought him."

He patted her hand. "It's a pity wear."

"In front of millions of people? Nice try."

Their banter carried on for a few minutes, revisiting favorite moments from the show, *My Valentines*. Weston looped Harlan in with the finesse of someone who'd been doing this for years. The audience was positively enamored. Weston didn't avoid topics just because they were hard—he asked about their parents' divorce and the effect that had on them, and he turned that into a discussion about the mental health impacts divorce can have on children and parents. Harlan opened up about how he'd been diagnosed with depression last winter after a bad breakup and the strain of his parents' relationship had become too overwhelming to deal with alone. He talked about his time in therapy and how much it had helped.

After the cheers for Harlan quieted, Weston asked him tougher questions.

"Harlan," he said, "you've shown up in the tabloids more and more lately, most recently because of a public argument you had with Dame Catherine." Weston raised his eyebrows at Harlan. "I know how difficult depression can be, but what role does personal responsibility play when you're getting into a courtside fight at a Knicks game with one of the most famous female actors in the English-speaking world?"

Harlan shook his head. Only Emma could see the sharpness to his jaw that he would soften before he opened his mouth. "That wasn't my best moment, but it was also a misunderstanding. A bad joke. We were arguing over a call. I'm a born-and-raised Knicks fan, and she's become a Lakers fan. So I told her she should get back to the old folks' section, and she got understandably angry." Some of the audience hissed; others grimaced. "But you have to understand our history. A few years ago, we were at a big party, and I did something to annoy her. She told me I needed to get back to the 'kiddie table.' So I thought it was a funny callback, this inside joke that she'd get. She clearly didn't remember it."

"In fairness to Dame Catherine," Emma said, "you were nine years old at a Thanksgiving party. The kiddie table was literally where you were supposed to be."

The crowd tittered, and Harlan cringed. "I know, I know. It was in poor taste. I've apologized to her, and I hope we'll be able to move on."

"We all hope so. Otherwise, I think you're going directly to timeout next time you go to a game." Weston winked at the crowd and got a big round of laughs. "Now, how about we mix things up? Liven this party up already?" Screams and cheers met his question. "Who else is dying to know what comes next for Emma and Harlan?"

The roar of the audience answered him. Emma and Harlan raised their hands too.

Weston's eyes narrowed. "Did you two cheat?" To the crowd, he said, "These two *promised* me not to breathe a word about their next roles to anyone—even each other—until I revealed them to the world."

"Which was brutal," Emma said. "Do you know how hard it is to keep anything from a sneaking, spying little brother?"

Harlan pulled her hair. "Shut up, or I'm telling Mom I saw you and Jamal—"

Emma threw a hand over Harlan's mouth, and her words came out in a rush, as if they hadn't rehearsed this earlier. As if this wasn't a publicity stunt Emma's manager had set up with the actor-slash-pop-star in question. "No comment! I have no comment!"

After the squeals died down, Weston's crew brought out a game board entitled "What Will the Crawfords Do Next?" Emma was up first.

Weston picked random people to play a game that involved things like snowshoes, spinning, and shaving cream. It was mayhem, and the laughter in the audience was organic and infectious. Members of the crew shot clues out of cannons into the audience, and the audience then shouted those clues back to the game players, who were trying to unscramble the letters in a word. Finally, one contestant ran up to the game board and slapped her answer onto it. It read:

Valkyrie

Absolute hysteria struck the set. Pure pandemonium. Emma couldn't help but laugh. Her nutmeg-brown waves tumbled in front of her face when she rocked forward. She'd known this would be huge, of course. The Vikings franchise was the biggest thing since Marvel, and fans had been begging for a *Valkyrie* spinoff for ages. But after her nearly year-long hiatus from acting, she'd forgotten how much she loved moments like these.

"You're in a Vikings movie. No big deal or anything," Weston said.

"No, of course not," Emma agreed. "Who's even heard of the Valkyries, anyway?"

Fans screamed and laughed, and Weston chuckled as hard as anyone. "Okay, okay, okay. Now tell us who you're playing."

"I . . . can't say," she admitted, curling into a defensive little ball for show.

"What? No. This isn't what I signed you up for, Emma. I signed you up so that you could give me a big reveal, and this is not enough. Spill."

"I can't!"

"Emma Miriam Crawford, you open that mouth and get to spilling," Weston said, snapping his fingers at her like Pops had.

Emma bit her lip, as if considering what she was allowed to say or not say. "Well, I can tell you that Freyja doesn't know her shield maidens as well as she thinks."

Someone from the audience screamed out, "You're the half-mortal sister!" at the same time that someone else yelled, "You're the Viking warrior from the prophecy!"

Emma pantomimed a zipper across her lips. "Sorry, gang. I'm sworn to secrecy. But I can freely admit that Weston's martial arts studio has played a big part in my preparation for this role."

"That's true," Harlan chimed in. "She's been on my case for months, pressuring me to come with her every morning at five to let Weston whip my butt into shape."

"But you were too busy running in the park—a sure way to get attention from the ladies," Emma stage-whispered to the swooning audience.

Weston asked some questions about when filming would start (January), how much more martial arts she needed to master (all of it—all of the martial arts), and about the casting process. She told a story about the lead actor coming in during her audition, and her having to admit that, because she'd been at university in France since last year, she still hadn't seen the last Vikings movie. He jokingly called out, "Liar!" but she thought he yelled, "Fire!" Without hesitating, she ran out into the hallway and started rushing people to the exits. When the director and producer saw how well she handled pressure—"even when it was misguided"— they offered her the role on the spot.

"You thought he said 'fire'?" Weston doubled over laughing and was still chuckling when he segued to Harlan's game. More people came from the audience, and more mayhem ensued. When a woman covered in shaving cream and feathers placed her sign under Harlan's name, it read:

Offside: The Ethan Tyler Story

Oohs and aahs filled the studio, bringing the audience to a state of reverence every bit as powerful as their fervor over Emma's announcement.

"Ethan Tyler," Weston said, holding a hand up to his heart. "Most of you will remember this story. He was the youngest American ever to play in a World Cup. He scored America's only goal in the final game and was all set to become a huge deal in the soccer world. But instead, he joined the military with his brother, and, well, we all know the tragic end. Harlan, tell us: why this story?"

"When the news about Ethan broke a couple of years ago, it struck me hard. He was only eighteen when he played in the World Cup. He had lucrative contracts coming his way, and he had his whole life in front of him. He gave up fame and renown for something bigger than himself, and his commitment now defines his legacy more than soccer ever could have. His parents gave me a copy of his journal. It's heartbreaking but inspiring. He was half Jewish, like Emma and I are through our mom. His journey to coming to terms with his faith in a world with so much hatred and violence resonated with me pretty powerfully. I hope I'll be able to do Ethan's story justice."

Weston made an Oscar prediction, to which Harlan responded with the proper blend of humility and gratitude, and the crowd with the proper amount of screaming and clapping. With a warm thanks to Harlan and Emma, Weston ended the segment.

During the brief break, they all hugged. "You are amazing!" Emma gushed. "A natural. You're going to be the biggest thing since Ellen."

"Keep sending those vibes into the universe for me, Nutmeg. And thank you." Weston wrinkled his nose. "Now go before I cry off my makeup. We'll catch up at the party tonight?"

Emma and Harlan nodded. They signed a handful of autographs and took a few selfies with fans before the break ended, and then they headed to watch the rest of the show in their dressing room. Emma kicked off her heels and threw herself down on the couch, staring at Weston's smiling face on the little wall-mounted TV. Harlan dropped to an armchair across from her.

"Don't get too comfortable," he said. "I have a car coming in a bit to take us to our next appointment."

"As long as I'm here to watch his sign off." She sighed, checking her feeds. The picture she'd posted earlier of her, Harlan, and Weston backstage already had 200,000 likes. She managed not to look at the comments, which would be filled with bigots and trolls by now, but she had private messages from a handful of friends. She'd get to those later. "You've been cagey about this 'next appointment' all day. Now that I know you're doing the Ethan Tyler story, can't you just tell me what it is?"

"The surprise will be worth it."

Emma looked at the picture of her, Harlan, and Weston again, and she smiled. She watched the rest of his show with that same joy on her face, and when he ended the show, she quoted his sign off with him, in Samoan and in English: *"Alofa atu nei, alofa mai taeao.* Kindness given, kindness gained."

Weston ended every training session the same way. He believed the kindness you put into the universe would come back to you eventually. After seeing the joy on his face—after seeing all her hard work pay off—she couldn't help but think he was right.

CHAPTER TWO

Harlan's surprise was in Yonkers—not a great surprise on the surface. But Yonkers was the home of the New York United Stadium, where the major league soccer team was currently practicing. The team of exceptionally fit, attractive young men.

She'd been in a few professional locker rooms in her day, and although this was nice and NY United was one of the biggest soccer teams in the country, it was also obvious that professional soccer wasn't on the same level as professional baseball or football. The stadium and locker rooms were new, clean, and state-of-the-art, but everything was on a smaller, less-storied scale than she was used to.

The field itself was pristine, with bright-green grass and brighter white lines. The September afternoon was sunny and humid, making Emma only slightly uncomfortable in her loose jeans and T-shirt from her clothing line. While Harlan spoke with the coach, Emma sat in the first row around midfield and watched the team practice.

She was used to athletic men. She'd been surrounded by them for as long as she could remember, especially now that she trained at Riverside Motion on weekday mornings. The big, showy muscles that so many actors developed looked good—really good—but she'd learned there was something even more attractive about muscles that served a purpose. And every muscle on the bodies in front of her served its purpose gloriously.

Never one to merely objectify a body—for long—Emma made an effort to watch what they were doing, to notice what they were capable of, how they used those spectacular forms they'd honed . . .

But the fact was that if this were a movie, the 90s hip-hop standard

"Shoop" would be playing, and her character would be running an ice cube over her lips, because daaaaaaamn.

Pull it together, Emma, she told herself. *Repeat after me: they are men, not meat.*

Okay, she was back, and she was focusing on their skills. One player with quads that could hold up a small house was high-stepping, bouncing a ball from knee to knee while he did so. Another player with a chest that could stop traffic was practicing headers. Yet another had the kind of lean muscles that made him look a coiled spring—always ready to burst into action. He was facing away from her when someone kicked the ball toward him and he jumped into the air and executed a perfect bicycle kick. He was on his feet again in a blink. He wasn't as bulky as some of the other players, but it was like he was designed for maximum efficiency, like his body was meant to be able to run and feint and weave where the other bodies couldn't.

He was a specimen.

The leading lady in her head was biting her lip, waiting for him to turn around and notice her, and their eyes would lock, and . . .

Wait. He really was turning around.

She took in his deeply tanned skin, the light-brown hair that almost covered his thick, dark brows and brown eyes, and the smile that lit up his absurdly adorable face just as a smile was lighting up hers. He flipped his hair out of his face, and she really did bite her lip. She couldn't help it, because he was running toward her.

She squealed and stamped her feet as she held her arms open to him. "LIAM PRICE!" In a flash, he was standing in front of her and she was wrapping her arms around him, feeling those same muscles she'd so appropriately and demurely admired only moments ago. They were impressive.

And was it her imagination, or were his hands completely and totally lingering on the muscles in her back?

Thank you, Weston.

They broke apart, and she put her hands on his rock-hard shoulders, which were damp through his practice jersey. He had a smattering of freckles across his face—more than his sister had, she knew.

He was delicious.

"When did you get so effing hot?" she asked, just short of ogling. She was tempted to make him turn for her, but she wasn't quite that tacky.

"Oh, stop." His ears turned red. "I could ask the same of you."

"Excuse me? I was born hot. This"—she gestured to herself—"has always been there."

He gave her a half smile. "Probably true. Now what are you doing here—" he stopped himself, looking past her and seeming to do some quick mental calculus. "Ah. Right."

A quick peek behind her showed Harlan approaching wearing cleats, a practice jersey, and a strained smile.

Harlan and Liam greeted each other with tight dude-nods and equally tight dude-handshakes. They shared a couple of words about how long it had been, generic congratulations on one another's success, and an almost complete lack of eye contact.

Last year, the Crawfords had starred in a big play in Chicago, where they'd met Liam and Finley Price. Harlan had started dating Finley, but it all ended when he cheated on her and she broke up with him. But Harlan had also helped Liam find his way into professional soccer from his college team. The tension between the two boys was understandable, but also unacceptable.

"No, no, no. This won't do. Liam, Harlan is sorry for screwing up the best thing he ever had with your sister, and it is a regret he will literally take to his grave, if it doesn't actually send him there."

The look Harlan shot her was equal parts fury and betrayal. With a dash of lingering pain.

"And Harlan, Liam is, well, obviously not sorry for his frosty reception or for ignoring you for the better part of a year, despite you having gotten him the agent who has facilitated a great deal of his success. But he respects your regret and knows that losing Finley is the real punishment, so he promises to be friendly again."

Liam blinked a bit too hard a few too many times, but after flaring his nostrils, he nodded. "She's right. It looks like we're going to be seeing a lot of each other for the next few months, so we can let the past stay in the past."

Emma looked between the two of them. "What do you mean?"

"The studio and the league planned a PR move for me to start training with New York United," Harlan said. "All I knew was that they had a hotshot international player on loan for the season who would be my trainer and guide to all things soccer. I didn't know it would be you."

"And I didn't know that you were the actor they wanted me to work with," Liam said.

Emma wanted to shake them both. "And I didn't know that Misha Ng was violently allergic to tulip pollen until I sent her flowers and her hands blew up like Goodyear blimps, and then I realized she was, and oh my gosh, enough already. Finley's happily past all of this, okay? Try to keep up, boys."

They both gave her versions of a sheepish grin. Liam's was real. Harlan's was a practiced fake.

"Are you ready for practice, Harlan?" Liam asked.

"Let's get to it."

Both boys waved at Emma as they ran onto the field together. She watched long enough to see that Liam and Harlan were playing nice, but that it would take months for Harlan to resemble the rest of the men on the field. She pulled out her phone and took a selfie with the guys practicing in the background. After a bit of editing, she tagged the guys and the team and posted it. A notification buzzed on her phone, followed by a calendar reminder and another notification. She dismissed each before texting her manager.

Drew, you're right. I need an assistant.

Almost immediately, Emma's phone rang. She took a deep breath before answering. "Hi, Drew."

Several months ago, when Emma decided to return to New York and to acting, she got in touch with manager extraordinaire Drew Nevin. The woman was a shark without being cold-blooded, which Emma appreciated. She worked well with Emma's agent father too. Emma's upcoming movie was proof of that.

"Emma, hon, let's talk about *The Weston Show*."

"Okay."

"One of the PAs patched me in so I could see the segment. You were good. Charming, delightful, everything fans have come to expect from you. The fire drill story delivered, but next time, play it out a bit longer. Talk about the facial expressions of the people in the room, linger on how things seemed to go still and you were processing a hundred things in a moment—stuff like that. People eat it up."

"Good feedback. I'll practice it more before I tell it again."

"Good. Now let's talk about Harley. You know I love your brother, and it's a big part of the Crawford brand, how you two come as a package deal, but he's not the star of your show. You can't always defer to him."

"Did I?"

"You let him be too big a part of your interview. He interjected a lot more than you did. People want to see both of you, but when the spotlight is on you, keep it there. If he tries to take it, then be a bigger part of his interview. It's not about taking over; it's about making sure you're seen."

"Got it."

Drew gave her a few more notes, and Emma paid dutiful attention. They talked a bit about assistants, and when the call ended, she jotted Drew's notes into her journal app before flipping back to social media. She scrolled through her feed until she reached a post from her former costar on *My Valentines*, Victoria Alba.

It was a picture of her on the Stanford campus with her bandmates, standing in front of Rodin's *The Gates of Hell* group sculpture. Vic was in *The Thinker* pose, while the other three mimicked *The Three Shades* at the top of the sculpture. Her caption read, "Rodamn, this thing is beautiful." The post went on to explain that her band was performing that night at her alma matter. Because heaven forbid anyone forget that the actor-turned-critically-acclaimed-singer-songwriter had graduated at nineteen from Stanford University.

Emma looked up the Dante quote (just to confirm, of course—she'd read *The Inferno*) and commented, "Kind of hard to abandon every hope with y'all slaying like this."

See? Vic wasn't the only famous and intelligent woman in the world . . . even if her "Rodamn" comment was hilarious.

Ugh.

Before Emma could shove her phone in her bag, a reminder buzzed: "Improve Your Mind, Loser."

She pulled up her eReader without even considering dismissing it (as she only sometimes did). She was ten chapters into a biography about Audrey Hepburn, but it was a welcome change from the other "Improve Your Mind, Loser" attempts she'd made over the past few months. After quitting her advanced French tutorials last month, she'd switched to Spanish and was progressing decently. She'd avoided documentaries since finishing the one on construction accidents (a documentary no New Yorker should ever, ever watch). And no matter how hard she tried, she couldn't bring herself to finish the biography on Tolstoy that Lin-Manuel had given her for her birthday. Now she'd have to avoid him for months and hope he forgot all about it.

After another chapter, her fingers found their way back to social media and the feed for *The Weston Show*. The episode wouldn't air until tomorrow, but the excitement online . . . Wow. He was definitely going to be the next Ellen. Thanks in no small part to her.

"What are you smiling at?" Harlan's voice said from beside her.

She did a quick double take. Harlan and Liam were both showered and changed. Liam's hair was slick and messy enough that she wanted to run her fingers through it.

Damn, he was cute.

"I invited Liam to come to Weston's party tonight," Harlan said.

"Good thinking, Harley." She stood and looked between them, her eyes having to raise a few more inches to reach Liam than her brother. Neither of them moved. "I know you're both very pretty, but could we all stare at each other in the car, instead? Let's go."

She turned and started for the locker room when Liam put a hand on her elbow. "Maybe best not to go through there. Naked jocks and all that."

"What, are you afraid they'll say something to me?"

"Not even a little. Those guys are all bravado and fragile egos. I'm afraid you'll say something to them, and we won't win another game this season."

"You know me better than I thought. Lead on."

Harlan hung back enough that Emma knew he was making an effort with Liam, but that he was nowhere near comfortable yet. Maybe she shouldn't have been so cavalier earlier when she'd mentioned Finley. Harlan had had a tough year. While he'd stopped seeing his therapist since she'd been back, self-help books littered his condo. They were the reason she'd basically told him what her next project was, even after swearing to Weston that she wouldn't. They were the reason she'd left the Sorbonne after only a year. They were the reason that, as hard a time as she gave Harlan for cheating on Finley, she still wished her friend had forgiven Harlan and taken him back. Harlan had never been happier than when he'd dated Finley. Emma had never been happier than those months in Chicago either.

As the three trekked through the stadium, Emma linked her arm through her brother's. Harlan was the most important person in the world to her, and what was happiness if not helping the people she loved most be happy?

CHAPTER THREE

Emma was applying eye shadow when she heard a knock at the door of Harlan's Upper West Side condo in the newly renovated Highbury Lane building. For years, Highbury's location just north of 96th Avenue had been a turnoff for most wealthy New Yorkers, but recent gentrification meant that the area was no longer taboo to the rich and famous. When England's most famous couple bought the top two floors the month after Harlan moved in, Highbury became the hottest new spot in the Upper West Side.

"Liam, is that you?" she called from her vanity when she heard voices. "Come in here and talk to me. I'm bored."

She was halfway through her second eye when both boys showed up in her bedroom. Harlan pulled up a chair from her desk while Liam leaned against the door frame, his arms folded in a way that made his biceps fill the crap out of his sleeves. He was watching her—studying her, really—and the crystal jars, baskets, and palettes organized on her vanity. She leaned close to the mirror with one eye closed and one hand holding a brush inches from her face. "What?"

"I'm just watching. I was already in college when Finley started wearing makeup, so this is new to me."

"Emma's mastered the art of achieving the right balance of makeup for every event," Harlan said, sounding like a cheesy commercial. Then came the jab. "Probably why she still has a line of lip gloss at Target."

If Liam weren't there, she'd remind Harlan that her clothing-and-makeup line were the reason her net worth eclipsed his. Instead, she stuck out her tongue.

"Oh, right, from *My Valentines*," Liam said. "I was, what, like sixteen when it ended? But I watched every episode. I had to see what happened with Victoria. And you."

Emma put down her hand, straightened up, and opened her eye, each movement perfectly executed to convey maximum meaning. "I'm sorry. You cared more about *Victoria* than me?" She stuffed her makeup brush into the appropriate jar. "Freaking men. Of course you were more interested in the girl who *developed* first."

A smile crept up one side of Liam's face. "I was more interested in what would happen with her character's music career, but why would it bother you either way?"

The most perfectly saucy response sprang to the tip of her tongue, but she caught a shadow of a V forming between Harlan's brows. Watching her and Liam flirt would be awkward, even without the lingering tension between the boys.

Emma returned her gaze to the mirror, ran a finger over the sides of her lips to fix her lipstick line, and smiled. "Because I was the better actor. Obviously."

"No dispute here," Liam said.

The three made their way downstairs, where a car was waiting for them.

The show had rented an exclusive nightclub for the after-party. Emma had already danced with some beautiful men and some fabulous women, including Misha Ng. Misha had been Emma's best friend on *My Valentines* for the last two seasons, and they'd stayed in touch over the years. They weren't pour-your-heart-out friends, but more let's-go-to-a-party friends, and that worked for Emma. Mostly.

Emma and Misha were on their way to the bar when Emma caught a glimpse of a lightly streaked brown bob and shift dress she would love on anyone else. Unfortunately, they belonged to the last person she wanted to see tonight: Kelly Bates.

"Kelly alert!" Emma whispered in Misha's ear. "Kelly alert!" But the music was too loud, because Misha stopped and looked at her.

"What are you talking about? There's an Amber Alert? Here?"

"No," Emma said through gritted teeth. "Kelly . . ." She gestured with her head in Kelly's direction.

"Oh, hell no." Misha bolted behind Emma and pushed her in Kelly's direction with a "Good luck!"

Emma stumbled toward Kelly, whose overly plucked eyebrows raised heavenward. "Dear Emma! What a sight for sore eyes you are. Weston told me that you moved into Highbury Lane, but I've never seen you there. Is it the same Highbury Lane where I've lived for years? On 100th?"

"Right off of Central Park, yep. Do you really live there?" Emma asked, although she knew very well that Kelly did. It had been her only concern about moving in with Harlan.

"Yes, I bought my condo years ago, before Manhattan Valley was in fashion. Most of my neighbors have sold their units for ten times what we bought them for, but I won't. It's home. I could never leave. Not for all the money in the world."

Emma braced herself, knowing that at any moment she'd hear mention of Kelly's niece, Vic. Because everything in Emma's life always came back to Victoria Alba. The Peanut to Emma's Nutmeg. Weston's other "daughter."

"Victoria was so sad that she couldn't come tonight. Did you hear about that accident when she was boating? How she went overboard without a life vest and would have drowned if her manager hadn't been there to save her?" Kelly clutched her chest with all the fear and anxiety of an overly concerned aunt.

"I saw that on E!," Emma said. "What a relief that she was okay."

"Relief? I'll say it was a relief and a million times more. I don't know what I would do without her. And what would the world do without her? One of the most accomplished musicians of our day. Do you know she's tied for the most Grammy nominations of any musicians her age? Not that either of us are surprised. We've known what a treasure she is for years, haven't we? There are so few celebrities with Victoria's depth of feeling and thought. She called me yesterday while she was reading . . . Oh, how do you say it? Kirkguard?"

"Kierkegaard," Emma corrected. She had learned about the Danish philosopher in her Intro to Philosophy class last year.

"Right. She was telling me about the difference between hope and acceptance, and talking about the courage it takes to believe in something compared to resigning yourself that it will never happen. It was something like that. I didn't understand. She said it's the theme of her next album, and I felt so out of my depth, all I could say is that I can't wait!" Laugh lines appeared all over Kelly's face. "What could I even say? Can you imagine?"

Two years ago, Emma had been filming a movie in a swamp in South Carolina, and the cast had taken out rowboats for fun one night after filming. While she was rowing, her hand had gotten too close to the rickety wooden boat, and an inch-long splinter had driven itself under her fingernail. The pain was excruciating. Sickening.

Kind of like this.

"Kierkegaard would inspire anyone," Emma said. "Kelly, if you'll excuse me, the little girl's room is calling. We'll catch up later!"

Kelly was still saying her goodbyes when Emma was out of earshot. She weaved through the press of eager bodies until she reached the restroom, where she exhaled in relief. Kelly was hard to take in any dose, but every mention of her niece's depth and accomplishments made Emma feel so vapid. It's not like Emma hadn't read Kierkegaard or written angsty, allusion-filled poetry. She had. But Kelly had a way of talking to Emma as if she and Emma were in equal awe of Victoria, as if Emma could never aspire to that sphere of thinking, let alone that plane of nirvana-esque enlightenment.

Emma looked at herself in the mirror, at the glitter in her eye shadow and the sequins on her midnight-blue dress. It was gorgeous. *She* was gorgeous.

Who needed the depth of oceans when you could out-dazzle the stars?

When Emma returned, she found Weston at his table with some of his friends and cousins. He happily made room next to her when she joined them, and she reveled in the light in his joyfully crinkled eyes as they roamed the club. The place was packed with Weston's family, friends, and staff, and their family and friends and friends of friends. Four of Weston's cousins were on the dance floor teaching the crowd a traditional Samoan dance. She'd rarely known Weston to smile with so much meaning. He always seemed to be half restraining himself, like he was afraid of letting people see the real, deep emotion that lay just below his beautiful surface. And yet, here he was, twice in one day, with wrinkles around his eyes.

"I think this is the happiest I've ever seen you," she said.

"You did a good thing, pushing me to go for this. So I have something for you." He pointed to a girl about Emma's age on the dance floor with Weston's makeup artist, Marcus. She had a naïvety about her, with her big round eyes, cupid mouth, and shoulder-length auburn curls. "I found you an assistant."

"That girl? She looks like Dorothy first stepping into Oz."

"That's closer to the truth than you think. She's Marcus's cousin, and she's been helping out on the show this week as an intern. She's almost as wide eyed as she looks, but she's a hard worker and she isn't connected to anyone outside of him in this town, so you wouldn't have to worry about her spilling your secrets. Plus, Marcus vouches for her."

"What's her name?"

"She's calling herself Winter White."

"Ew, Weston, no."

"I know, I know," he said. "She's a little too easily persuadable, Marcus tells me, but that's another reason I think you two would work well together. She can keep you grounded, and you can keep her from wandering into traffic. Figuratively speaking."

"Because it's you, I'll talk to her."

"I knew you would." He kissed the side of her head—a more fatherly gesture than anything her own father had done in years. "Now I need to get my butt on that dance floor. You coming?"

She saw Liam walking over to the bar, where more than a few actors were congregated. One of the women, who was famous, beautiful, and twice Liam's age, leaned toward him and looked to be whispering in his ear. "No," Emma told Weston, "you go ahead. I'll find you later."

CHAPTER FOUR

Emma was on her feet before Liam had even backed up. She pressed through the throng, barely pulling her eyes away from him long enough to smile at friends. When she was almost to him, she heard him say, ". . . flattered, but no."

The woman raised a glass to him. "Your loss, sweetheart," she said.

Liam shrugged—literally lifted his shoulders—and called out to the bartender.

"What's your poison?" Emma asked as she slid between guests to stand beside Liam.

"I'm not interested—oh, hey." He put his cool hands on her bare shoulders, his relief palpable and pulsing through his gentle touch. "I'm so glad it's you. I have never been hit on so much in my life. Help me, Emma Crawford. You're my only hope."

"Princess Leia, *Star Wars: Episode IV*, 1977," she said as he removed his hands. Not that she'd minded them there.

"You remember the game!"

The game was a favorite of Liam and Finley's—watch a terrible movie with friends and call out any allusions, references, or blatant rip-offs from other media. To win, you had to basically be a human IMDB. Which Liam and his sister were. Emma and Harlan had played it with the Prices last year in Chicago. When they'd all been happy. "Of course I do. I could have won if I hadn't gone easy on you."

"False. Finley went easy on me. You just weren't good enough."

She dropped her jaw in as dramatic a fashion as she knew how and whacked his shoulder with the back of her hand. "Excuse me? First, I can't be trusted around naked men—"

"Not quite what I said—"

"Then I'm not as hot as Vic—"

"Definitely didn't say that."

"And now I don't know enough Hollywood trivia?"

"That one, I said."

She sat on a bar stool. "You are not easy on a girl, you know that?"

"Do you want that? Someone to go easy on you?" He took the stool next to her. It was a little quieter at the bar, and they didn't have to shout to hear each other.

"No, not really. But I wouldn't mind at least a little blatant flattery."

"Isn't that a contradiction?"

"Of course not. I'm not saying I need constant blatant flattery, but a few well-placed compliments that gush like geysers can do a lot for a girl's ego."

"I don't think your ego needs much."

"Dude!" Her jaw dropped all on its own this time.

"No! Not like that. I'm not saying you're full of yourself; I'm saying you've earned the confidence you have. You're intelligent, funny, a skilled actor. . ."

"Painfully hot," she supplied.

His lips quirked into a half smile. ". . . and more. All of which I think you know."

She ran a hand through her hair. "I do know. Which is the only reason I can take your particular brand of honesty."

"*Particular brand*?"

"Yeah, you know, you're a truth bomber. You drop little truths so casually, like everyone is self-aware and as capable of handling them as you are."

He paused, and she had the sense that he was thinking about what she'd said, actually processing it and not just paying lip service. His eyes were on the counter. "I hope I only do that with people who can handle it."

She nudged his arm with hers. "I'm sure you only use your powers for good."

He smiled. "Thanks."

The bartender asked if they wanted to order anything. When Emma tried to order a margarita, the bartender laughed. "Try again, Ms. Crawford," he said. She grumbled out her request for a Diet Coke.

"I'll have a milk," Liam said.

A milk.

"Just say it," Liam told her.

"I have nothing to say. Not a word." She pursed her lips.

"Why is it that when people get sober after their fifth DUI, all the world applauds, but if someone simply chooses not to drink, whether it's for health, like me, or for self-control or religious purposes, they're a weirdo?"

Liam's mom was an alcoholic, among other things. Her abuse had taken a serious toll on Liam's sister. Finley hyperventilated just smelling beer. Liam seemed comfortable enough being surrounded by alcohol, but his refusal to drink it made Emma wonder about what Liam wasn't telling her. "You have every reason not to want to drink. I don't think you're a weirdo."

"Not even about the milk?"

"No, the milk is super weird, especially when you could have ordered a hot chocolate."

He scrunched his nose. "Do you think they have hot chocolate? Dang it. That sounds really good right now. This place is freezing."

"Only because you're not dancing."

"No, that's my gift to the world. I'm not much of a dancer."

The bartender gave them both their drinks, and they spun around and sipped while they watched the dance floor. Despite Liam's almost jarring lack of deference to her, he was easy to talk to. They hadn't known each other particularly well last year, but Emma had fought for Finley's friendship, and the two had become even closer. At least, until she'd moved in with Harlan.

Her brother hadn't been in a place to handle Emma and Finley's friendship. When he'd catch her video chatting or texting with his ex, when he'd see her smiling at her phone, he would grab a self-help book from a bookshelf or dining room table and hole himself up in his room for hours. So Emma had been forced to decide: Finley or Harlan. Her best friend or her only real family.

She chose Harlan. It was nothing outright. She didn't ghost Finley out of nowhere. But she delayed her responses to texts. Shortened them. Made less back and forth. By late summer, they were texting a couple of times a week, but it was nothing like it once had been. Finley was either too gracious or too self-conscious to ask about it. Emma mourned the loss of her friend, but it was the lesser of two evils. Because hurting Harlan wasn't an option.

So Emma hurt herself instead.

Don't think about it. It doesn't hurt as much as it would if it were Harlan.

That was right. She straightened up and looked at Liam, drinking his milk. "How does it feel to be back in the country?" she asked him. "Do you miss playing in England? What does being 'on loan' mean?"

"In reverse order: it means that the team still owns rights to me, but that NY United pays my salary for the duration of the loan. I do miss playing in England; I like the speed of life there and the fact that on Arsenal, I get to train with some of the world's best football players—soccer, I mean."

"Wait, I thought you played for West Ham. Did you get traded to Arsenal?"

"Yeah, my agent and I thought West Ham wasn't taking advantage of me enough at the end of last year, even after I moved up from the developmental squad. Arsenal's a better team. And loaning me out gives me a lot more opportunities." Liam's tone was friendly enough, but his shoulders were hunched, making him look closed off. Was he afraid of what she'd ask next?

"So you're glad to be back in the good ol' US of A?"

His shoulders relaxed. "Yeah, there's so much space to move and breathe here. And I've really missed the food."

"I didn't think English food was that bad."

He took a drink and licked a spot of milk from the corner of his mouth. "Not normally, but I have a reputation on the team for culinary fearlessness. Right after I signed with Arsenal, a bunch of the guys went to Scotland for a weekend, and the veteran players dared all the rookies to try haggis. I was the first one to do it. I just ordered some deep-fried haggis balls, popped them in my mouth, and went on with my day."

"How were they?"

"Disgusting. Like vomit covered in dirt. But everyone had made such a big deal about it that I didn't want to give them the satisfaction of throwing up in my mouth. Especially when it already tasted like throw up. After that, they started talking about how I have an iron stomach. Ferdinand, the team's star, was super impressed, because he can't stomach anything. So now, instead of getting to eat fish and chips, I have to try the cow-tongue stew."

"Why don't you just tell them it's disgusting and you want to eat something that doesn't suck?"

"I'm guessing you don't follow Arsenal on social media, do you? Pictures and videos of me eating weird crap are a part of every road trip now, and they get a ton of buzz every time. The team asked me to keep it up while I'm on loan, but I've managed to convince them that US cities don't have too many exotic choices. So instead, I'm highlighting the foods that cities are known for. Last month, I had Cincinnati chili, which is basically chili on spaghetti noodles. That's a freaking five-star meal after you've eaten liver, let me tell you."

"That's bonkers. I feel a little bad complaining about having to get 200 milligrams of protein every day so I can gain ten pounds of muscle before January."

"Whoa. That's real work. What are you doing, drinking raw egg whites?"

"Every ninety minutes. They have one in the bar for me."

He made a face. "So other than that, how does it feel for you to be back in the States?" Liam asked. He called it the *States* instead of *America*, something she'd only ever heard immigrants or children of immigrants say. Liam's dad was Brazilian, and he'd been a famous actor before his untimely death.

It was easy to forget that Liam's heritage meant something on a day-to-day basis. Liam and Finley would have grown up hearing different words for things. Their dad spoke Portuguese to them in their home. What had all of that meant for Liam? Being mixed race? Having part of his identity come from another country, when the person who gave him that identity was gone? Being half Jewish in Hollywood was hardly noteworthy. Neither was being the child of a bitter, public divorce.

"Emma? You still in there?" Liam was waving a hand in front of her face. "I lost you for a minute. What were you thinking about?"

She looked down to see that his milk was gone. She stirred her straw through the ice, looking at the way the club's lights were holding a mini rave in her glass. "Sorry, I guess I was—" An excited cry from the dance floor pulled her attention, and she looked over to see Weston in the middle of his cousins and friends, dancing with a little more reserve than the others, but still. He was dancing, and he was happy. All was right with the world.

Emma took a long sip of Diet Coke. "Being back in *America*," she emphasized, "is just fine. I liked the Sorbonne, but did you know that there are people in France who don't follow American gossip? I had classes with people who'd never even heard of me. How could I stay in a country with such heathens?"

"That sounds very distressing."

"Extremely."

"So is that why you came back? The twenty percent of people who thought you were just like them?"

It wasn't why, of course. She'd come back home because Harlan needed her. He'd wrapped up filming on *Robolords* last December, and he'd flown to France the next day, staying in the hotel next to her apartment for an entire month. He hated that he'd done that movie. He'd dated his costar, and they'd broken up during filming, which had created such deep fissures on set that TMZ had picked it up. Their dad had flipped. "The only drama the paparazzi should report about you is the kind that you control," he'd always told them. Harlan had stayed in France to escape their dad's anger just as much as he had the fallout from his nightmarish ex.

When January had rolled around, Harlan was still in France, even though his next film was about to begin shooting. She'd only managed to convince him to get on his flight to LA by saying she was taking a leave of absence from the Sorbonne at the end of the semester. She'd told him she missed him and acting too much. It was time to come home.

He'd cried when he hugged her before getting on the plane. That's when she'd known she made the right choice.

And when she was being honest with herself, she had to admit that the Sorbonne and her acting hiatus hadn't been the escape she'd wanted them to be.

"The twenty percent anonymity is eighty percent of why I came home," she told Liam. "The other twenty percent is because I didn't know what I was trying to escape anymore. I wanted to get away from my parents and everything that fame had done to them, but distance didn't change anything. It just made me miss the things about acting that I love. And the people I love more."

"I think I know what you mean."

"Really? Did you miss Finley a lot?"

The corners of his eyes tensed. "I always miss Finley."

Okay, he was definitely defensive that time. Why? "She's the best, so I get it. She's so proud of you for chasing your dreams. You should hear the way she brags about you. You set a really good example for her."

"Did she say that?"

"Yes, but in about a thousand times more detail. Have you met your sister? She worships you."

His head was shaking, but he didn't get a chance to respond.

"Are we drinking to Emma's success?" Harlan asked from behind them.

They both swiveled on their stools to face him. Neither Harlan nor Liam looked particularly thrilled to see the other. She was going to have to work on this.

"What success is that?" Liam asked. "The Vikings movie? Congratulations, by the way. Kára is my favorite Valkyrie from the comics. I can't think of a better 'wild, stormy one.' "

"Someone's letting his nerd flag fly," she said, bumping his firm shoulder with hers. "But if you're baiting me for info, sorry, sucker. No spoilers."

He dipped his hand in her drink and splashed the remains of her

Diet Coke on her face. Before she could debate dabbing her face to save her makeup or retaliating with an ice cube down his shirt, Harlan said, "I was talking about Weston's show. Emma here was responsible for this."

"Really? How so?"

Emma pressed a napkin to the Diet Coke sprinkles on her forehead while she looked at Liam. "Oh, I'm sorry, maybe you could ask that again without the incredulity?"

Liam smiled. "I like how you do that. The way you say 'Um' or 'I'm sorry' or 'Excuse me' at the beginning of a sentence, but you don't actually mean that you're hesitating or sorry."

"No, nor should I be." Emma threw her crumpled napkin at his face. He caught it. "Now, let me educate you on how I orchestrated this whole thing. I stayed with Weston when I first got back to New York while Harley finished filming in LA. I could tell something was lacking for him. So I asked around and found out that a new talk show was in the works, but the host they'd wanted dropped out. So I put a bug in the producer's ear, as well as Weston's, and voilà! *The Weston Show.*"

"So . . . you told him to apply for a job opening?" Liam asked.

"There's a little more to it than that," Harlan said, and although she couldn't tell if Liam was serious, she knew without a doubt that Harlan was. His knuckles were white.

"I'm not trying to be dismissive, just trying to understand what it means when you say she's *responsible* for this."

Emma put her glass down on the bar harder than necessary. "Maybe talking about her like she isn't here is a bit of a douche move, don't you think?" she asked them.

She looked at Harlan. "I don't need you to speak for me. But thank you," she said, softening her tone for him. To Liam, she spoke a bit harder. "And hey, Captain Truthbomb? I didn't audition for Weston or interview Michael Strahan to understand how to navigate daytime

TV as a person of color, if that's what you're getting at. Weston has successfully hosted three separate Bravo shows. I trusted his abilities. But I also didn't simply talk to my sewing circle for all the hot gossip. I talked to the producer and a network executive. I helped them see that the best way to launch a successful show isn't to create a copycat of Ellen or Michael Strahan, but to innovate. Weston's Twitter presence is practically nonexistent, but his YouTube channel has fifty million followers. His could be the first talk show to reach teens and Gen Z. Teenage girls are the number-one trendsetters and adopters of emerging technology and reaching that demographic could change the future of daytime TV. The show obviously agreed, seeing that they made an extremely lucrative deal to partner with YouTube and release exclusive content to his subscribers."

She was huffing, her chest heaving from her rant. No one could give an impromptu impassioned speech like an actor.

"I stand corrected. I'm sorry," Liam said. "You deserve all the credit Harley is giving you."

She stared at him, hardly believing how easily he'd swallowed his pride and conceded. Her own pride kept her from registering her surprise. "Yes, I do. I'm a damn genius."

"You're right. Well done, Emma." He looked up at Harley, whose arms were folded over his chest. "I think I'm going to call it a night. My 6 a.m. wakeup call won't answer itself." His smile was sweet and apologetic, the way it stretched tight and lifted to one side. "I'll see you at practice tomorrow."

He squeezed Emma's shoulder as he walked past, and his hand was warmer than it had been only a few minutes earlier. Or maybe she was the one who was cold now. Harlan took the seat that Liam had vacated. "I don't know how you talked to him for so long. He's insufferable."

"He's really not, Harley. He just doesn't feel the need to flatter me, and he can actually admit when he's wrong. Don't you think that's kind of nice? You two were friends once. Don't let your past determine your future."

"Whoa, that was kind of profound."

"I know." She pulled out her phone and tweeted out the wisdom. "We should pay someone to stitch that on a pillow."

CHAPTER FIVE

"First question," Emma said to the girl Weston wanted her to hire as an assistant. "My stylist here thinks that it's time for me to add in some auburn lowlights to get my fans ready for my role in *Valkyrie*. I think I should just let hair and makeup take care of it once we start filming in the fall. What do you think?"

The wide-eyed girl was sitting on a stool across from Emma, who was in a salon chair while her stylist tapped his foot behind her. Misha Ng, who had been bored enough to join them after her own haircut, was sitting on a stool near Emma.

"You're making this part of your interview?" Misha asked. "Babe, you know those hacks on set don't care how your hair holds up. They'll bleach you out and paint on some tacky red that fries your hair right off. Trust the pros, not . . . I'm sorry, New Girl, but who are you?"

"Winter White," the girl said, wringing her hands together in her lap. Emma could see Misha trying to catch her eye, but Emma wouldn't look at her friend. "Your stylist seems like he's really, really good. Just look at this place! I feel like I'm in some sleek café in Paris."

"Which means . . .?" Emma prodded.

"That . . . you . . . should listen to your stylist?"

"Good. I agree, even if I like to give him a hard time." She blew her stylist a kiss in the mirror, and he swatted the top of her damp head softly with his comb before separating and pinning sections of her hair. "But you called yourself Winter, was it? No. Your legal name is Brittany Smith," Emma said. "Rule number sixteen of Hollywood: don't change your name to something that typecasts you before the interview has even started."

Brittany nodded fast. "There are rules?"

Misha snorted.

"Oh, Brittany, yes," Emma said. "I hope you're a quick study, because if you get this job, I'll drop little nuggets like that on the regular."

She pulled out a notepad and wrote that down.

"Good girl," Misha said. "She can stay."

"I'm honored you're considering me, Ms. Crawford, but I should tell you that I may not be able to commit to the job for long—if you offer it, of course," Brittany said, her cheeks flushing prettily. "I just interviewed for a meteorologist job at a station back home last month, so I'm waiting to hear back. They said they really liked the footage from my college station. Can you imagine if I got it?" She beamed, like the future she was imagining as a weatherperson was something to be happy about.

Emma's stylist held a hand against his chest, his mouth forming a perfect, disbelieving O.

"So this was back home? Where is that, exactly?" Emma asked. If it were a big market—LA, Atlanta, Chicago—it wouldn't be the worst thing.

"St. Martin's, Ohio. But the station serves Cleveland too." How the girl managed to say this so brightly, without a hint of despair, was almost heroic.

Her stylist had composed himself, but Misha didn't have his tact. Her tongue was sharper than a pair of scissors. "Was your mother a weatherperson in St. Martin's, and she died tragically young? It's sweet if you want to honor her memory, but I'm sure she wouldn't hold you to it from beyond the grave."

Brittany's smile faltered. "No . . ."

"So . . . you dreamed about this when you were little?" she continued.

Emma tutted, and at the same time, a shake of a head in a chair next to her caught her attention. The man looked to be in his mid twenties and was alarmingly pretty, with bright-blue eyes and a decent fake tan. He was also familiar. Lose the blond streaks that he was hopefully here to lose himself, and she could almost place him.

"It's not like I've been offered the job yet." Brittany shoulders drooped like a balloon with a leak. "But it is a really good job, you know. It's the number-one station in Ohio."

Emma shot daggers at Misha in the mirror and smiled warmly at Emma. "Handling Misha's brattiness is the second part of your interview, Brittany, and you're killing it. Good for you. You should feel free to chase your dreams, whatever they are."

Brittany returned Emma's smile more hesitantly than before. Which was kind of appropriate. Being a weatherperson in a tiny market was the type of dream someone *should* doubt, at least someone with Brittany's looks.

She was certified farm-fresh, no question. But she was exceptionally pretty, and her natural auburn hair was the exact shade that women paid thousands of dollars to get—Emma's lowlights were a testament to that. With makeup and wardrobe help and some acting lessons, she could get a job on a soap opera in a snap. And perhaps with enough time she could star in some Lifetime movies. Or she could train with Emma and get a role on a Netflix or CW show as a hot ninja! Then she would have a nice, comfortable B-list career that would one day have her laughing at ever having dreamed so small.

The warmth Emma felt last week at Weston's inaugural episode returned, filling her chest like a cozy fire in winter. She wanted that feeling again, and she knew exactly how to get it. She wouldn't simply hire Brittany as her assistant—she would make her a star.

"All right, Brittany. Are you ready for your next question?"

———————————

Emma finally let Brittany go after they learned that they'd both had the same first crush as five-year-old girls: the cartoon fox from the animated Robin Hood. That had settled it for Emma. She'd sent Brittany away with a promise that she'd call soon, and the other girl had practically bounced out the door.

"She's adorable. Like a little kitten falling out of a tire swing. But, Ems: a *weatherperson*?" Misha shook her head while the stylist was peeking under the foils. "I can't. I can't!"

"Be nice. She has a lot of potential. Can't you see her as a soap star with that dreamy look of hers? Tell me you see it," Emma said.

"I see it," the guy she'd noticed earlier said. Emma hadn't paid any attention to him since that initial flash of recognition, but she swiveled toward him now. Some of the blond had been toned down (thank goodness), and his hair was getting trimmed. "Sorry, I normally wouldn't admit to eavesdropping, but I just so happen to act on *So the Night Falls*. You probably haven't heard—"

"That's how I know you! I watched *So the Night Falls* all summer a few years ago when I was in between movies. Are you still with Lucia? I *need* you to be with Lucia."

"Lucia's in a coma, I'm sorry to say."

"Nooooo!" Emma shook her fist in the air.

"But I visit her every afternoon. There's a sexy nurse trying to get in the way, but between you and me, I don't think she'll have much luck."

"I'm glad to hear it. It's . . . Bryce Elton, isn't it?"

Bryce's eyebrows lifted a hint. "Yes. I can't believe you know who I am. I know you, obviously. I don't live under a rock."

"Um, excuse me? Rock people are a huge portion of my fan base."

"My mistake." Bryce's stylist was cleaning up his neck line, and Bryce was motionless, except for his blue eyes, which looked like they

43

were dancing. "I'd like to help Brittany, if you're serious about trying to get her into soaps."

"Ohmygosh, please! Give me your number, will you?"

She expected him to pull out his phone and text his number to her, but instead, he reached into his pocket and handed her a business card.

Okay, then.

"Thanks," she said. "I'll be in touch."

"I look forward to it."

Bryce's cape was pulled from around his shoulders, and a moment later, he was gone.

Misha looked at Emma. "Did the universe literally just bend to your will?"

"What can I say? We're tight like that."

By the end of the week, Emma had a new assistant who had been thoroughly vetted by her manager, Drew. Drew declared Brittany's was "the least exciting background check I've ever seen." This only made Emma like Brittany more. The girl was naïve, but she wasn't ignorant, and by all accounts, she had a great work ethic without being tainted by ambition. Emma would teach her everything she needed to know.

"I get it now," she told Harlan and Liam while they played *Top Chef* one afternoon in Harlan's state-of-the-art kitchen. A rep from Harlan's film had visited practice only the day before and had been concerned with Harlan's slow progress and his "reluctance to submit to Liam's instruction." Emma overhead the rep insist that Harlan spend more time getting to know Liam personally so he could trust his coaching. So Harlan had invited Liam over.

The fact that Liam had accepted was proof that he was making good on his promise to Emma to get along with Harlan.

"What do you get?" Harlan asked.

"Do-gooders, you know? The Bonos and Angelinas of the world. Helping Weston and now Brittany? It feels kind of amazing."

Liam looked up from his sandwich, his eyebrows raised teasingly. "You're comparing helping refugees and starving children in war-torn Third World countries to helping people go from rich to super rich?"

"No, wise guy, I'm saying that after feeling this much satisfaction doing such a small kindness for two friends, I understand why people would make huge sacrifices to help people in need. I'm not saying I know exactly how they feel; I'm saying I get it. Keep up."

"Okay. Okay." He looked at his crumbling bread. "How are you guys making your sandwiches look so . . . sandwichy?"

"Master Chef," Harlan said, stirring the potatoes and corned beef in his frying pan.

Harlan's assistant had ordered an array of groceries for them, and they each had thirty minutes to make the best sandwich. Harlan would probably win with his corned-beef-hash-and-egg sandwich, the jerk. It smelled delicious. Liam was equally sure to lose with a Monte Cristo sandwich that he'd made with toast instead of frying the whole thing, to say nothing of the cheddar cheese. Meanwhile, Emma's ahi tuna sandwich was a firm seven out of ten. Her tuna was good, but her wasabi mayonnaise was a little too heavy on the wasabi. She hoped it was on the edible side of sinus burning.

She and Harlan had been obsessed with cooking shows since she'd moved into his place. In fact, Harlan had given Emma cooking lessons from a famous chef for her birthday. It was as much a gift for him as her, seeing as the lessons were for two people. On the first night, Emma had surprised them all when she'd made a very respectable apple-and-cheddar scone. Harlan's had been hard, like day-old bread. He'd tried the recipe three times more the next day until the scones were the perfect amount of crumbly.

After every class, he did the same thing: practiced and perfected each recipe. Emma didn't. It was the same when they'd taken tap and gymnastics and art classes as kids. Emma always got good faster than Harlan. He worked harder until he was better. It wasn't competition, just how they were wired.

Harlan's electronic assistant gave them the one-minute warning. "Time to start plating those meals," Alexa said in a voice Emma found a bit sultry for a robot.

"*Plating*?" Liam said, looking around and accidentally wiping powdered sugar on his cheek. "Is that seriously what you call it? That's not pretentious or anything."

"Oh, right, because you've never eaten at Per Se," Emma said, drizzling the wasabi mayo over the top of each sandwich.

"You know some of us aren't stupid rich, right? No, I have not eaten at Per Se."

Harlan looked up from where he was straightening the hash on his last plate. "I know your mom blew most of your dad's money, but you have the third highest contract on NY United. You're kind of rich."

The top of one of Liam's sandwiches was sliding down the plate. He stabbed a toothpick through it. "I've had that contract for a month. To most people, yes, I'll make a crap-ton of money in the next year. But it's not guaranteed, and I don't have a backup. I dropped out of college for soccer. If I blow my knee out next week, that could be the end, so I'm saving every penny I can. I'm certainly not spending a month's worth of grocery money on a meal at a restaurant where they pride themselves on their *plating*."

"We call that a Go to Hell Fund," Emma said as Alexa announced that time was up.

Harlan called out to their assistants. Sean and Brittany appeared in the kitchen a moment later, sitting along the far counter.

"What do you mean?" Liam asked.

"It's when you save up enough money that if something happens on set with a handsy costar or an entitled director, you can knee them in the junk and say, 'Go to hell.' Keeps you from ever feeling like you have to make decisions for money."

"That's brilliant," Liam said, and he looked like he meant it.

Emma winked before grabbing both of Harlan's plates and turning to their assistants. "Brittany, Sean, thank you for coming. We'll keep this anonymous, so Liam can't accuse anyone of favoritism. He's a broke famous professional athlete, so he needs all the help he can get." She glanced over to see him chuckling.

Brittany was delighted, tasting each plate with the sort of eager dedication that Emma was already coming to adore. "Oh, that's unexpected," she said when she got to Liam's sandwich. She looked like she was studying the bite she'd just taken, moving it around. "I thought the Monte Cristo would be fried, but toasted is a good option for people who, um, who don't like the taste of egg and butter."

Liam groaned. Emma shushed him.

After Brittany and Sean tried each sandwich, Emma's was declared to be the prettiest but her wasabi mayo had given Sean a coughing fit. The baby. He probably couldn't handle horseradish. Harlan's was declared the overall winner, to nobody's surprise.

"So what have you won?" Brittany asked Harlan. Sean was already back at work—managing Harlan's social media, from the looks of his screen. But Emma hadn't turned the reins over to Brittany fully yet. Brittany had a meeting with Drew later in the week, where she'd get extensive instructions about her job. In the meantime, Emma had Brittany shadowing everything Sean did and following Emma around carefully, including to her morning workouts at Weston's studio. Muscles were in, and if Emma was going to make Brittany a star instead of a weatherperson, the girl would need to tone up.

"Emma has to make me dinner for the next week," Harlan said, flashing his dimples in a way that tended to turn Emma's friends into simpering puddles of goo.

Brittany was no exception. She giggled.

Emma shot her brother a glare meant to scare his dimples away. Instead, it brought a glint to his eye. "Harlan just hasn't found a cook yet."

"I can help you, if you want," Liam said to Emma, mercifully pulling Brittany's attention from Harlan. "Considering I was the actual loser and clearly need the practice, it feels fair."

"She can't ask you to do that. Besides, don't you have a game Friday night in Jersey?" Harlan asked.

"I'll buy everyone a hot dog at the game," Emma said. Liam cocked his head to the side. "Obviously, we're coming. Do you think Jersey will scare me off? After that joke of a sandwich you made?"

Liam flashed the half smile he seemed to have made for her. He leaned against the counter, picking up one of Emma's ahi sandwiches and taking a big bite.

And started coughing. And coughing. He stuck his face in the sink and drank straight from the tap. "I'm not the only one who needs the practice," he croaked.

"You just can't handle spicy food," Harlan said to Liam. He took a bite. "The tuna is perfect, Ems." He swallowed, and his eyes watered.

"Oh, shut up."

Liam and Emma did the dishes while Harlan had a call with his manager and Brittany shadowed Sean.

"Brittany seems nice. How do you think she'll be as an assistant?" Liam asked.

"Considering my last assistant sold my data to the paparazzi for ten grand, leading to a scandal that destroyed my brother's mental health, I think she'll be a dream."

"Is that what happened? I thought your phone was hacked."

"I was wrong. But it serves me right for taking pictures of Harlan in the act. I meant to blackmail him into never doing anything so stupid and self-destructive again, but . . ." She handed Liam a rinsed plate, unwilling to look him in the eye. Disgust at the memory, at her complicity in her brother's attempted cover-up, filled her gut and throat like heartburn.

"It wasn't your fault. You trusted the wrong person." Whether he meant her old assistant or her brother, she wasn't sure. But at least he wasn't going in for the kill: if Harlan hadn't cheated, there would have been no scandal, no breakup, no broken heart, or mental breakdown. "I'm sorry it hangs over you. I'll go easy on Harlan."

"Thanks." She gave Liam another plate to load. "But as for Brittany, I'm obsessed with her. She's adorable and sweet and naïve, and she doesn't ask me gross questions about actors, and I'm pretty sure she's never even seen drugs, let alone been to a party that serves them on a literal silver platter."

"*Silver platter*? You didn't—"

"Ew! No thank you." She handed him a glass. "But you're not really surprised, are you? Finley told me that the paparazzi used to follow you guys when you were out with your parents. And then, well, she told me about everything with your mom." Just mentioning Deirdre Price made Emma feel sick to her stomach. After a car accident killed Liam and Finley's dad, their mom had become an addict and a child abuser. Finley had the scars to prove it. If Liam had them, too, they weren't visible on his back and arms like his sister's were. It didn't mean he hadn't been hurt by her, though. It didn't mean she hadn't damaged him in other ways. "After seeing what we've seen, you can appreciate what a delightful change Brittany is."

"No question."

"And it feels good, honestly. After helping Weston, I feel like I have a new outlook: I want to help more people, and Brittany is one of them. You've seen her. She could make it in this business."

The dishes were all loaded, and Liam wrung out a dishrag before cleaning the countertops. "What does she want to do?"

"Well, she *wants* to be a weatherperson in Cleveland, if you can believe it."

"Cool. I'm sure you have tons of connections that could help her."

"Are you for real? You can't think I'm going to help her become a weatherperson in Ohio. I said I want to *help* her, not condemn her to a life of misery."

Liam frowned. Lips turned down and everything. "But you said that's what she wants."

"She's twenty-one and graduated from St. Agatha of the Ohios or whatever. She came out to intern on Weston's show because her cousin is his makeup artist and because she couldn't find a job in the cutthroat world of local news."

"Emma—"

The way he said her name stiffened her spine. It was disapproval. No, disappointment. "Don't *Emma* me. She loves soaps and wanted to be a soap star all through middle school. I'm helping her achieve her dreams. I already have someone in the industry willing to help me, okay? So if you'll excuse me, I plan to help my new friend and would appreciate you stuffing your condescension—" His frown stopped her. She sighed. "What?"

"You think I'm being condescending by disagreeing with you? I'm trying to be a friend. It sounds like you're pushing your goals on her when she doesn't aspire to this life. This business can destroy people. She's completely ignorant about what really happens around your world, and she's even more unprepared for it. She's never even seen drugs? What's she going to do when a director or actor pushes them on her? Or pushes themselves?"

"I'm not going to feed her to the wolves; I'm going to teach her how to avoid them."

"She's not you, Emma. She doesn't have your resources or your confidence or your backup."

"My *backup*?"

"Yeah, Finley told me you've always had your dad at every casting call and meeting with you. I know he's a jackass, but he's also kept you safe in ways I think you take for granted."

"*I* take it for granted? I've been hit on by men over twice my age since I was twelve years old. I've had to beg my dad to come to most of those casting calls and meetings. And do you think he's been on set with me every day of my life? Do you think I've never been alone with a director? Believe me, I take *nothing* for granted."

He tossed the dishrag into the sink and slumped against the counter. "You're right. I shouldn't have said that."

"Damn skippy."

"But, Emma, every reason you just listed is another reason I think you should reconsider your plans for Brittany."

"So women should just give up? They shouldn't even go into acting because of the chance for harassment? Screw the matriarchy, huh?"

"No, women shouldn't give up. But women who *don't want this life* shouldn't be pushed into it. No one should be."

"I hate you a little bit."

Harlan yelled to them from the other room, telling Liam the driver was there to take them to practice. Liam called back that he'd be there in a second.

"I don't want you to hate me," he said, his voice soft and low in a way that made her almost take back her words. "Just think about what I'm saying?"

She pursed her lips. "I'm thinking about stuffing this towel in that pretty mouth of yours. Is that the same?"

"No. But I'm glad you think my mouth is pretty."

She smiled in spite of herself. "Fine. I'll think about it."

CHAPTER SIX

Riverside Motion was Emma's happy place. Weston's show had been on the air for over two weeks, and it trended on social media every day. He already had three GIFs, including one of him raising his eyebrow at the camera with an "Mm-hmm" that everyone she knew was using. His success only seemed to fuel his fire in the studio.

"Are you serious, Crawford?" he snapped at Emma while she was sparring. "I've seen you do a better grab-and-lock during a sale at Barneys. Get it together."

Emma wiped sweat from her brow and pushed herself harder, grappling with her partner. If Weston weren't barking in her ear, she'd coast, which was why she only trusted her fitness to him. She'd gotten lazy in France, doing yoga consistently enough, but without ever breaking a sweat the way she should have.

Weston told Brittany to get her power from her flow before moving on to his next victim. "Elton, I know you're new, but when you begged to join my class, I assumed you'd at least show up."

Elton? Like Bryce Elton? Emma had texted him yesterday about meeting up for breakfast after class. She hadn't expected him to join them. She risked a look back and noticed that Brittany and Bryce had been partnered together. When had that happened? Bryce winked a brilliant blue eye at her before responding to Weston.

"Yes, sensei," he said.

"What do you think this is? *Karate Kid Six*? Stop sucking up and start dropping that butt."

It was the magic of Weston that his words were met with determination instead of grumbles. Limalama had a dance-like quality and a subtle essence that embraced both power and fluidity. Weston expected his students to move with the stealth of assassins and the grace of dancers.

After class, Emma helped Weston put the gear away and prepare for his next group of students. He only taught the two morning classes Monday through Friday, while the other instructors took the classes through the rest of the day. Emma wouldn't have woken up at 4:45 a.m. for anyone else in the world.

Weston wiped his sweating face with a towel while Emma chugged water. "When I told you to hire Brittany, I thought she'd handle dry cleaning, social media, and your calendar. I didn't expect you to turn her into a project. Why do I get the feeling Bryce Elton is part of some master plan for Brittany's future?"

"Because you're very wise." She'd told Weston about her conversation with Liam from the other day, and he hadn't been quite as dismissive about Liam's concerns as she'd expected. But he'd also agreed that no one could prepare Brittany better than Emma could, so she'd forgiven him.

"Well, good luck, Nutmeg. And remember to watch that elbow, or I'll knock you on your tail next time."

"Yes, sensei," she said, and he whipped his towel in her direction.

Emma joined Brittany outside, where it was mild and the sun had yet to rise. Wispy white clouds were painted across the early morning sky. Brittany was looking up at them. "It's a nice morning," Emma said.

"I think it'll be a beautiful day. Cirrus clouds are a good sign, and these ones are barely moving." Brittany breathed in deeply and smiled. Her face was still red from class, and a light seemed to glow from within her. "That class was so good, but so hard! How can Weston possibly be in his fifties? Do Samoans not age, or is it just him?"

"Okay, rule number, I don't know, four," Emma said. "Don't ask questions like that. Like ever, not even to me."

Brittany's eyes went saucer-like. "Oh, I didn't mean anything—"

"I know, which is why I'm trying to help. When it comes to comments about race, ethnicity, sexuality, identity—watch yourself."

"Okay." She nodded her head around like she was trying to find a better pocket of air. "Okay, thanks. There really is a lot to learn, isn't there?"

"You have no idea."

Brittany's forehead creased a little more with each nod. "Right, sorry. That was so stupid of me."

Emma wanted to kick herself. She was talking to Brittany like she'd talk to Misha—not that she would ever try to teach a woman of color about racial sensitivity. But she was being too familiar with Brittany, too casual in her advice. "It wasn't stupid of you, and it was wrong of me to imply otherwise. You're learning. *I'm learning.* I should never have told you not to ask me questions," she said, Liam's reminder buzzing in her head. "Ask me whatever you need to. Just . . . we all have to think about what we're saying, okay? Thoughtless words can stop a career or hurt a relationship before it even starts."

Brittany's forehead creases deepened.

"Another rule: don't crease your forehead. Or frown too much. Or squint. Premature wrinkles are your enemy." Emma smiled, and Brittany exhaled in visible relief.

Bryce came out of the studio after making them wait for another twenty minutes. He'd obviously showered, but he'd changed back into workout gear. Clean workout gear. And were her eyes deceiving her, or had he put on foundation?

Oh, brother.

"Hey, Bryce."

"Emma, Brittany," he said with a nod. "It's great to see you both again." He shook both of their hands like they were in some kind of a board meeting instead of leaving the gym, where they'd just trained together for the last hour. "Shall we?"

The three walked to Emma and Weston's favorite café, L'Orange. It was a kitschy little vintage restaurant that served the best eggs Florentine in the city. The owner was an old friend of Weston's, and she always kept a table for them in a nook away from prying eyes. But Weston wasn't with Emma today, and their nook was taken. Still, the owner smiled when she saw Emma and sat them at a cozy table several feet away from a window with light, sheer curtains. After a few minutes of looking at the menu, they placed their orders with the server.

Brittany asked Bryce about how he had gotten into acting, about his role on *So the Night Falls*, and about soap operas in general. He gave them an earful, telling them story after story about how he'd been discovered, about something that had happened on set, about the lines he'd ad-libbed, times he'd helped a castmate, or times a script had been changed because of his input. To hear him talk, he was a writer, director, actor, and humanitarian all in one.

They had their food by the time Brittany was able to ask her next question: "Is it hard not to fall in love with your costars? Soap operas are so romantic and dramatic all the time."

"Truthfully, I think I fall a little in love with every person I act with. Acting draws out such depth of emotion from people. It's stunning to see my costars use their past, their *pain* to create a thing of beauty."

Brittany put a hand over her heart. "Wow. Is it like that for you, Emma?"

"Uh, no. Not even a little. Even when I have good chemistry with someone on set and we're around each other all day, as soon as I'm out of character, it's completely different. I fall in love with their character for my character, maybe, but not for me."

"You're right, Emma. That's exactly what it's like," Bryce said. "The person you're playing and the person they're playing call to each other . . ."

Emma had to tune him out before she rolled her eyes into the back of her head and they got stuck and she had to get rushed to the ER. The tabloids would read, "Emma Crawford's Superiority Complex Breaks Her Eyes, Sends Her to Hospital." Or something less flattering and more inflammatory because she was a woman in power.

Besides, Bryce was here because he agreed that Brittany had the right quality for soaps, and Emma shouldn't fault him for being a little starstruck around her. So what if he had showered and changed back into workout clothes, so as to maintain some falsely casual appearance? So what if he was grandstanding a little too much? He was here to help, so she could smile when he gave Brittany the number for his acting coach and pretend to blush when he complimented Emma and overused her name.

"You bring so much charm to your roles, Emma," he said, echoing the first review that came up when someone searched for Emma online. She thanked him and sipped her tea, turning her attention out the window at the first polite moment. She watched a couple walking their matching teacup poodles. The dogs' tiny legs took twenty eager steps for every one step of their owners. When they passed, Emma saw the glare of a camera lens through the sheer curtains. She groaned.

"Don't look now, guys, but we have company."

Bryce spotted the paparazzi immediately. "Not paparazzi. You have to be kidding me." He pursed his lips and then turned back to Brittany. "Anyway, I think Brittany embracing her vulnerability on screen would be really powerful," Bryce said, finally seeming to remember the point of their little get-together. "Do you want to come with me to the set next week and see how the magic is made?"

Brittany gave him her signature wide-eyed nod and asked if Emma could come too.

"Of course! It would be a thrill to show you around, Emma, if you'd like to come."

"Sounds fun. I'll just have to check my calendar."

When Brittany reminded her a few minutes later that they needed to leave for their next appointment, Emma could have kissed her. Bryce promised to get them the details for the tour of the set before the end of the day.

When they got outside, he leaned in to hug them both. A bit longer than necessary, in her mind, and she had a feeling it had something to do with that photographer and the fact that Bryce had decided to shower and change . . .

Yeah, he'd definitely set this all up.

"Rule time," Emma told Brittany as they walked down the stairs to grab the subway back to Harley's condo. "When you're meeting with someone you don't know well, *always* schedule another meeting right after it."

"And I did, just like you asked. But . . . why, exactly?"

She wanted to say, "Because of that!" but if Brittany didn't see what *that* was, she didn't need to jade the girl. "Because it's more efficient. You're already out and about, so make it work for you. You know."

Brittany wrote it down, word for word.

Emma's next appointment was meeting her trainer, stunt coordinator, fight coordinator, and stunt double. She wouldn't work with any of them, except her trainer, for the next couple of months, but it was important that she knew their expectations of her and that she show them just how much of her stunts she would be able to do. They showed her a few simple fight sequences, and she picked them up fast enough that they were all impressed. Which meant that she could keep going to Riverside Motion every morning.

Filming would be primarily in Virginia in just over three months, so Emma had to bulk up fast. She'd been lifting weights for a couple of weeks and eating more protein than she'd ever thought was possible. She was already up two pounds, but they wanted her to gain at least eight more pounds of muscle before filming started in January, and her diet-and-workout regimen was even stricter than Harley's. In addition to her limalama with Weston, they wanted her powerlifting with her trainer for two hours a day, six days a week.

She was tired just thinking about it.

When she and Brittany arrived home later that morning, Emma's dad was at the condo with Harlan and what looked like an endorsement contract. They walked into the dining room, and Emma was immediately tempted to walk right back out.

"Emma, good to see you. Is this your new assistant?" her dad asked.

"Yes, this is Brittany Smith. Brittany Smith, meet my dad-slash-agent, Pierce Crawford."

Emma's dad stood and shook Brittany's hand. Brittany smiled at him a little too long. Their dad had that effect on women. He was every bit as good looking as Harlan, with the same dimples and hazel eyes, but aged to perfection, or so the tabloids said. His thick brown hair had light streaks of gray in it, as did his neat beard. Emma's friends frequently lost their minds over him.

One good thing Emma could say about her dad was that he didn't like them too young. Another was that he was one of the best agents in showbiz. If he weren't her dad, she'd have been thrilled to have him representing her. As it was, she just wished that he cared more about *her* than about her next role.

"How did the meeting with the trainer and coordinators go?" her dad asked. Her calendar was shared with Drew and her dad. Privacy was a luxury she hadn't known much of.

"Good enough. They're really happy with the martial arts, but they've added hardcore powerlifting, which we knew they'd do when they offered me the role," she reminded him.

"Are you getting enough protein? When I was here Sunday, you didn't eat once in three hours. Just because you've signed a contract, don't think they can't cut you for not meeting their requirements. If you don't think any number of girls would jump to take your role, I've failed you."

You've failed me in more ways than I can count.

"We talked about it today at my weigh-in. The trainer gave me a schedule, and Brittany has already ordered everything we need for it."

Brittany smiled and gave Emma's dad an efficient nod.

"So, Harley, how are things going with Liam?" Emma asked, changing the subject. The more attention her dad paid her, the worse things tended to get. Her every flaw—real or perceived—would be magnified under his lens. "Are you guys getting along yet?"

"Why wouldn't you get along?" their dad asked Harlan.

"He dated Liam's sister last year in Chicago," Emma said. "Remember?"

"That's right, when Harlan begged me to help Liam secure some tryouts in Europe," their dad said, as if Harlan could forget calling in a favor from their dad. He'd held it over Harlan for months. "Too bad you screwed that one up. I like the Prices. Liam is just like his dad—keeps his head down, his nose clean, no scandals. You two could learn a lot from that family."

"It's not like we're embroiled in drugs and drama, Dad," Harlan said through gritted teeth.

"No drama, really? Tell me about your fight with Dame Catherine again? Or how about the tweet you sent last night to that rapper about his sneakers? You called them 'the wrong kind of nasty, just like your face,' didn't you?"

"Harlan, you didn't," Emma said in a tone too chiding for the moment.

Harlan reared back. "What the hell is this? Are we going to parade each other's mistakes around for judgment? You can't possibly want that, Dad, considering how much we know about you, right, Emma?"

"Harley, don't—" Emma said.

"Why not, Ems? Didn't you find a no-name scamming on Dad around the set for weeks when you were eleven, offering to sleep with him in exchange for professional consideration? How long was it before he started representing her?"

"I thought you had enough sense to keep your mouth shut," their dad said, looking at Emma with a kind of quiet disgust he should have reserved for the mirror.

Emma didn't respond. Her pulse was hammering too hard for her to keep her voice steady, and he sensed weakness quicker than a shark sensed blood in the water. Stupid Harlan. Why couldn't he just swallow his damn pride? Yet she was the one who'd turned her dad on him in the first place, trying to escape his notice. Stupid, stupid Emma.

"What's your point, Harley?" their dad asked.

"I picked a fight, Dad. Let it go. We don't air the skeletons; we bury the damn body. Isn't that what you've always said?"

Their dad looked furious, but he didn't argue, only because Brittany was there and Sean was in the other room, Emma knew. If he hadn't had an audience, he'd have blown the place to hell.

"That's enough, Harlan. Calm down," their dad said, condescension saturating his voice.

Harlan's face was so red he looked like he'd just run a marathon. "Whatever you say, Dad. You're the boss." He got up and stormed out.

Their dad methodically stowed his laptop, notebook, and pen in his bag, as if he wasn't a red-hot volcano ready to burst. He stood to face Emma. "You need to handle him."

Anger and injustice roiled in Emma's gut, and her words spilled out before she could catch them and bottle them up. "Me? He's your son, Dad, not to mention your client."

"He's also eighteen and your little brother." He stabbed a finger in the direction of Harlan's room. "He's not my responsibility. He's a liability."

"Yeah, but he's also a paycheck, right? That's why you keep us around?"

A shift next to Emma reminded her that Brittany was there and probably horrified, if not scared out of her mind.

"Grow up, Emma. I taught you better. Or maybe you weren't clever enough to catch on. What was it *The Guardian* said? 'All dazzle, no depth.'"

He walked out of the condo, leaving Emma standing in the middle of the dining room, her chest heaving with the effort not to scream or cry or flip over the table. She couldn't believe he'd talked to her like that in front of her own assistant. She felt exposed, naked, like her skin had been peeled off to reveal a hollowed-out corpse. "The only thing he taught me was how to look out for number one." Emma balled her hands into fists, gritting her teeth so tightly, they hurt. "And I wasn't it."

CHAPTER SEVEN

When Liam showed up at the condo early that evening, Emma and Brittany were at the dining room table. The light from the panoramic windows reflected off of Emma's phone screen. Emma had been quiet since the conversation with her dad, and Brittany hadn't done more than ask a few questions. The minimum she could get away with, Emma imagined. She understood the feeling.

"Sorry to interrupt. Is Harlan around? He asked me to stop by after practice. Said he wanted to hang out."

"He did?" Emma asked. Her throat felt gunky, filled as it was with repressed emotion. "You two really *are* getting along better these days."

Emma's speaking seemed to open the door for Brittany to do the same. Her words came out fast, like she was so eager to talk about something other than Crawford family drama that she couldn't contain herself. "Why wouldn't you two get along? Is it because Harlan dated your sister?" She covered her mouth with her hands. "Sorry, I shouldn't have said anything. I heard them talking with their dad earlier." Her voice dropped, as if just mentioning Emma's dad would fill the room with a poisonous gas that would kill them all.

Liam sat down at the table across from them. Emma saw his glance jump to hers and his eyes tense slightly, as if he was trying to read the room. "Everything with me and Harley is in the past. Reconnecting with the Crawfords has been the best part of my move to New York."

He looked at her when he said this, a softness to his voice that would have caused a pitter-patter in her chest, if she weren't still fuming about her dad. Instead, Emma found herself appreciating that Liam hadn't placed any blame on Harlan. Especially as Harlan was probably listening from the kitchen. He came in a moment later, acting like he hadn't heard anything. "Oh, hey. You came," he said to Liam.

"Thanks for inviting me over, although I guess you're expecting me to cook dinner now, huh? I hope you guys like bratwurst cooked in a frying pan, because that's pretty much all I know how to make. Along with all manner of other meats cooked in a frying pan. Also cereal, if it's a cheat day." He blew his lips out in a raspberry. "Don't you just miss cereal sometimes?"

Emma half-smiled, but Brittany and Harlan laughed. Liam's presence was like the sun blasting through gloomy storm clouds. The lingering tension scattered like leaves in the wind. Harlan looked at Emma, and they smiled at each other. Harley seemed lighter than he had all day. Maybe longer. The stress that so often pulled his shoulders up disappeared, and he settled into the chair. Emma had the urge to hug Liam for his kindness to her brother.

"Harley, how much meat do you like?" Liam said, standing.

Harlan jumped up. "Were you being serious about frying brats in a pan? That's what the grill is for."

Harlan came back a few seconds later, holding the brats protectively as he walked through the dining room and out toward the patio.

Liam joined the girls at the table, his half smile firmly in place. "I seem to be out of a job. What are you two doing?" Liam asked.

"Brittany has officially taken over my social media. I'll still write up some of the posts, but she's going to take care of everything else."

Emma watched as Brittany pulled up a picture and started editing, filtering, and cropping. Emma gave her some feedback, and Brittany took it in stride. Then Brittany saved it in the drafts to post later in the day, when engagement was typically higher.

"I didn't realize how much effort goes into your posts," Liam said.

"Pfft. You should have been here when I was writing the caption. There's a reason I only post three times a week."

"So let me get this straight: you're erasing flyaways in this picture, yet you posted a picture a few weeks ago of you eating a donut with Boston cream on your nose."

"Uh, yeah. This post is for a charity event. My picture has to make people want to read the caption, but it can't distract from the message or the charity. That donut picture was self-serving, content for fans. And do you know how many pictures I had to take before I hit the perfect blend of goofy, relatable, and hot? Like, fifty."

"You pull it off in real life every day." His eyes twinkled, and he leaned across the table with his hand out so he could better see the picture. Emma extended the phone closer to him, and his fingers grazed hers, sending a spark up her arm and straight into her gut. "I bet you could have used the first one."

Emma held his gaze, wishing that Brittany weren't in the room. She kept her conversation neutral, but their hands were still holding the phone between them, and their fingers were touching. "If I were a guy, maybe. But I'm a woman in Hollywood. Do you know, I was once caught making a weird face pre-sneeze, and because I had a double chin in the picture, fan sites were talking about me 'getting fat'? My publicist at the time called me and said I needed to learn how to sneeze better."

"You should post a video of you sneezing. I bet you have an adorable sneeze." He looked at the picture of her in her sexy red dress once more before letting go and sitting back in his chair.

Her chest felt warm, and her cheeks glowy. "It's as adorable as the donut picture, if that answers your question. And . . . you follow me on social media?"

"Of course I do." His half smile was delicious. "How else would I know where to get my donuts?"

Harlan came back then with a plate of bratwursts in one hand and a pair of tongs in the other. "Who's ready to eat?"

Liam looked at Harlan. "I'll get the dishes."

Emma was about to follow when she heard Brittany's phone ring. Britt's cheeks flushed a deep, splotchy red that would look awful on camera. "Sorry. Do you mind if I take this somewhere private?"

"Go ahead." Emma pointed to her room.

Liam returned from the kitchen with plates, silverware, and a vegetable-and-hummus tray Sean had ordered, and the three started eating. Emma wasn't hungry, but she needed the protein, so she ate as much as she could. She could feel Liam's eyes on her, but each time she looked at him, she had the sense that he'd just looked away. The corner of his mouth kept pulling upward, and every time she saw it, she felt a frisson of electricity pass between them. Could Harley sense it? She hoped not. She didn't need to explain whatever was going on to her brother. Not that there was anything to explain.

When they were done eating, Harlan suggested a Mario Kart tournament. Brittany was just returning to the room, so Emma told the boys they'd join them later. Emma watched Liam following her brother before turning to Brittany, whose tomato complexion had dulled to a pretty, warm peach. "Everything okay?" Emma asked.

"Yes. I-I can't believe it, Emma. It was the station. In St. Martin's. They offered me the job! They sent all the details in an email that they said should be in my inbox already."

"Well," Emma said with false brightness, "what are you waiting for? Let's take a look."

Brittany opened the email, and Emma blinked at the salary. When she'd first heard that Brittany wanted to become a weatherperson, she had looked up the average salary. The number had seemed abysmal . . . until Emma discovered what the average national income was. She knew she was beyond rich, but she hadn't realized just how big the gap was between her and her fans, which, until a few weeks ago, had included Brittany.

Brittany had a degree in meteorology, which meant that she'd be hired as a meteorologist. That title meant the station was offering a better-than-average salary. Emma didn't know anything about benefits, but it all sounded rather generous. Almost as generous as what Emma was paying her. Probably more generous than the first few years of acting in soaps would be.

But she'd read up on the plight of meteorologists, especially female ones. Long hours, a low salary cap, isolating schedules, harassing emails from male viewers (all of which the station would require her to answer). And heaven forbid she ever get pregnant. No. This wasn't about where Brittany was starting, but where she would end. With Emma's guidance, she could have so, so much more.

"What should I do? They want an answer in two days."

"You'll answer them tomorrow afternoon, then. Call, obviously. Not email. That will show them that you respect their offer enough to answer them promptly and politely. You'll thank them for their generosity, let them know how flattered you are, but then tell them about the opportunities in Hollywood that you want to see through."

Brittany's hands fell. "So you think I should turn them down?"

"Wha—I'm sorry. I assumed you were asking how to best turn them down. But if being a TV meteorologist sounds like the most fulfilling, exciting job you could ever have, then you should take it."

"I don't know if it sounds *that* exciting. But it is a good offer, isn't it? Santino said it was."

"It is," Emma admitted, though she didn't know who this Santino person was. "It's surprisingly good. They obviously know that you have real talent and potential, and they think that offering you such a good package will help them snag you before you can make it big in Hollywood. And you should know, your first few years in soaps won't make this much. So if you're looking for security, then you should take their offer." Brittany nodded. "But if any part of you wonders what it would be like to do more, to be more, to be seen on TVs in New York and Paris and Beijing, not just in Ohio, then . . ." Emma held out her hands. "I can't make the choice for you, Britt. But I'm sure you'll make the right choice, whatever it is. And even if you're in Ohio, we'll stay in touch."

More than anything, these last words seemed to strike Brittany. Her lips tugged down, and she fidgeted with a slight crack at the corner of her phone, picking at it with her thumbnail.

"Thanks, Emma."

"Britt, why don't you head home? Talk it over with Marcus. We can talk tomorrow, okay?"

Brittany gave Emma a quick hug before saying goodnight. Emma sat back down at the dining room table, deep in thought. She pulled up her Instagram and created a new post. It was a picture of her and Brittany trying on dresses earlier in the week. They were both wearing absurdly sparkly, ill-fitting red dresses and laughing at each other when the dressing room attendant snapped the shot. "A good assistant is hard to find," Emma typed. "A good friend is even harder. But it's always blue skies with my girl Britt @winterwhite, whose future is bright."

She didn't reread the post, didn't obsess over perfect wording or precise grammar. She hit send and walked into the other room, where Rose Gold Rosalina was ready to kick some Mario Kart butt.

CHAPTER EIGHT

"So what happened with Brittany last night? She get sick or something?" Harlan asked the following evening. Brittany had been so off that morning at Riverside Motion that Emma had insisted she work from home instead of coming over to the condo. Brittany had agreed and had been working dutifully all day. Emma's messages and ever-changing calendar were proof of that.

"Or something," Emma said as Liam walked into the kitchen.

Harlan had invited Liam and his housemates to come over after practice. Because the guys lived less than a mile away in Harlem, the easy distance had brought them running. Especially after they'd heard about Harlan's cooking skills. And video games.

Emma told Harlan and Liam about Brittany's offer and how Brittany had felt about it last night. She'd hoped that another good workout would make her sweat out her anxiety over Brittany's decision, but even two straight hours of grueling lifting hadn't made a dent.

"I hope she has the smarts not to take it," Harlan said. "She's too pretty to stay local like that. She could be so much more."

"What do you mean, she could *be* so much more? Acting won't improve the quality of her soul. If anything, I'd say acting would put it in jeopardy," Liam said.

Harlan groaned. "Oh, come on. You know what I mean. I'm not saying that actors are better than other people. I'm just saying that there's more out there than Ohio."

"More for whom?"

"Objectively, I'd say pretty much anyone," Harlan said.

"Anyone who isn't content in Ohio and who wants it enough to prepare and go after it themselves, maybe. Emma, you've obviously helped her become more self-assured and socially aware. But whatever happened yesterday with your dad completely spooked her. She was still a deer in headlights when we were talking, and that was hours later, wasn't it?" he asked Harley, who nodded. "How do you think she'd react if she knew about my mom or the details of your parents' divorce? The drugs, the multiple affairs? Can you imagine if either of you had told her even a small bit of the crap you've seen on set or at parties? She would spontaneously combust."

Harlan was shaking his head. He didn't care enough to get angry, but Emma flexed her hand, and the knuckles cracked. "Liam, I know you think you're helping, but who are you to decide what she gets to do or what she's capable of?" Emma's words came out reedy, but as hot as dragon's breath. "You act like I'm throwing her into the middle of the ocean without a life preserver. But at least I have faith in her ability to swim. I believe in her. I'm giving her *more* options. That's what women have fought for since the beginning of time. Maybe you could stop trying to limit those for her, okay?"

"I'm not talking about options; I'm talking about information and preparation. I would say the exact same thing if she were a starstruck boy from Iowa. I don't want to see anyone—let alone Brittany—subjected to the kind of abuse that's so rampant in this industry."

"You sound pretty patronizing, dude," Harlan said. "Emma didn't tell her what to do, and you admitted yourself that Brittany's already grown in the few weeks she's worked with Emma. If she takes the job, great. She made her choice. But if she decides to pursue acting, who better than Emma to help her learn to navigate our world?"

Liam held up his hands. It was supposed to be a peace offering, but she wished it was a sign of surrender. She already knew him too well though. "You have a point."

"But you don't concede," Harlan said.

"Neither do you guys," Liam said. He drummed his fingers on the table. "Is that okay? Can we call a truce and agree to disagree on this?"

"Yeah, truce," Harlan said.

Emma said nothing. She was thinking about the picture she had posted last night, the picture that had a million likes, along with hundreds of comments speculating what movie @winterwhite was going to be starring in, comments about how hot she was, about how her skin and hair were unreal, about how Emma and Brittany were all sorts of goals: hair goals, friend goals, fashion goals, even teeth goals.

Emma hadn't hesitated for a moment when she'd posted that picture, but that didn't mean she knew why she'd posted it in the first place. Not really. She wasn't sure what impact it would have on Brittany. She didn't know what impact she wanted it to have. Was she being manipulative or supportive of her new friend?

The question gnawed at her stomach worse than a crash diet.

"I've decided not to take the job," Brittany told her when she came by the condo that evening, while the guys were in full video game mode. Whatever had made Brittany so off this morning seemed to be all but forgotten. Her under-eyes were a little dark, but she looked fine otherwise.

"You're not?" It was both what Emma had feared and wanted to hear. If this was her doing, not Brittany's, then Liam was right: she hadn't given Brittany more options, but rather forced her into the options Emma wanted for her. "Are you sure? You seemed so happy yesterday when you found out." She should say more, she knew, but this was as much as she could get out. Because relief was making her throat thick and sticky.

"No, I'm sure. You were right: I was flattered, and it felt like a dream come true. But then I realized that it's okay to have more than one dream. You've shown me so much in the last few weeks. And I have a new dream now."

"You do? Because of me?"

"Actually, Bryce helped me realize it."

"Bryce? What do you mean?"

"He texted me last night. He said that he'd been thinking of me and couldn't wait to show us around the set this week, and he hopes that one day, he and I will share the set." Brittany's warm, peachy glow returned with a glorious vengeance.

"He did?" She had to give him credit: he'd said he'd help Brittany get into soaps, and he was following through.

"And he already scheduled me headshots with his photographer for tomorrow, and he put in a good word with his acting coach, who agreed to let me in his class!"

"Britt, are you sure this is what you want?"

"Well, I was torn last night. I thought I wanted the job back home, and obviously Santino and my family were ecstatic. My little brothers were screaming on the phone, and even my older sister seemed proud of me, and she's a lawyer in Chicago. But after Bryce's message and after what we talked about yesterday, I started thinking that maybe there really was more out there that I should experience." Brittany's glow increased to radiant.

Relief swept over Emma like a sea of fans breaking past the barrier at a premiere. Emma hadn't pressured Brittany into her decision after all, which meant that she had no reason to feel guilty or to second-guess what she'd meant by posting that picture. If Brittany was going to stay, Emma'd make it more than worth her while; she'd help Brittany achieve her wildest dreams. The power dynamic would shift so that they were peers and friends, and Emma's influence would be simply due to Emma's greater experience, not a debt Brittany owed. A friendship of choice, not of convenience or location or position. And in five years, who knew? Maybe they'd be going to a premiere together, maybe they'd be video chatting from their closets in the morning for wardrobe advice. Maybe they'd be lifelong friends.

"So you're happy with this choice?"

Brittany nodded. "But do you think you could help me figure out how to turn the job down?"

They spent the next twenty minutes practicing what Brittany would say, and then Brittany spent the next five minutes repeating those words on the phone to the station manager who'd offered her the job. Emma couldn't hear the other side of the conversation, but the strain on Brittany's face made her gut twinge. When Brittany finally said goodbye, she looked pale but resolute.

"It's for the best," Emma said. "And besides, when you're famous, they'll be able to point to your face on a billboard and tell everyone in St. Martin that they almost hired you once."

Brittany smiled at that. "I'm going to text Bryce and tell him."

Emma looked at her phone at the same time and saw a text from Finley: *Who is this Aleki person, and why is he hitting on you all over Insta? Also, he's gorgeous. Well done.*

This was followed by a GIF of Jason Momoa flinging his hair and another GIF of someone with hearts popping out of her eyes.

She squelched the hundred possible responses to Finley's texts, knowing she'd give something more bland and less authentic tomorrow, but she was doing it for the right reasons. And that mattered. She flipped over to Instagram to numb the pain of her regret and found the comment in question. It was from Weston's nephew, Aleki Hale. His mom was Weston's sister, and his dad was a producer in LA. He and Emma had known each other through social media for years and through Weston, by reputation. He was every inch the young Jason Momoa that Finley thought he was.

He was also a terrible flirt, which Emma unabashedly loved. He commented on all of her posts, usually with absurd compliments on the goofiest of her pictures. The donut picture from weeks ago had earned her an only slightly inappropriate haiku about the merits of Boston cream that she couldn't stop laughing at.

She saw his comment from her post with Brittany: "Are you trying to kill me with this hotness, Crawford? Cuz ded."

Emma typed a quick response: "Success! Hahahaha!" She heard Brittany clear her throat and looked up.

"Everything all right there?" Emma asked.

"Good. Great." Brittany looked so happy that Emma's earlier doubts evaporated completely. "But can I ask you a question? Some of your celebrity friends have messaged me since you posted that picture— which was so amazing of you, by the way! My family almost died of shock when they saw you call me your friend!"

"You *are* my friend, silly. Now what was the question?"

"Well, a few of them have been messaging me, and they asked for, well, for nudes."

"Oh my—" Emma groaned, muttering a long string of obscenities. "Who?"

"Tom, Blair, and two Chrises."

Emma growled. "Right, got it. And how did you reply?"

"Well . . ."

"Please don't tell me you sent a shot with your head in it."

"I haven't responded yet."

Emma exhaled her relief. "Britt, what did you do when skeezy guys texted you for nudes back home?"

"I blocked them."

"Then do the same now."

She spluttered. "B-but . . . they're famous."

"Right, and they're also douchebags."

Brittany's brow darkened, like she was having a hard time understanding how these beautiful, influential men she'd admired could be such utter scum.

"Okay, you ready for another couple of Hollywood rules? These apply to texting, messaging, social media, email, your personal camera, all of it. Are you ready?"

"Of course." She put down the phone and grabbed her notebook.

"Never, ever send a nude with your head in it. Ever."

"No . . . head . . . Got it," she said, looking up from her notebook. "Why?"

"Because then the scuzball asking you for nudes can't turn around and exploit, bully, harass, or otherwise publicly shame you. Do you understand? Same as high school and college."

Brittany nodded, writing down every word, even though she had to already know it all. "O . . . kay. What's the other rule?"

"No nudes, Britt. Not even to your boyfriend. Because phones get hacked, relationships end, and dudes can be the worst. No. Nudes."

Brittany stopped writing mid-word. "Sorry, um, why didn't you say that first?"

"Because I can't guarantee that you'll take the 'no nudes' advice, which is obviously the more important rule. But rule number three? Someone asking for nudes doesn't care about you. Shut it down and move on."

Brittany put down her notepad. She looked like she'd just learned that unicorns didn't exist. "You must think I'm so naïve for thinking these guys would be better than the guys I went to high school with."

Emma scrunched her nose, feeling a surge of affection. "I love that you believe the best in people. You'll meet some of the most influential, wonderful people in the world in this business. But you'll also meet some crappy, terrible jerks who use people and spit them out like gum. Stay away from anyone who asks you to do things that they wouldn't gladly discuss in an interview. So many people look up to stars and hold us on a pedestal without wondering if we actually deserve it. You're already learning that the pedestal has to be earned, not assumed. That's a good thing, Britt. Never beat yourself up for learning."

"Thanks, Emma. I don't know what I'd do without you."

Emma squeezed Brittany's hand. "Good thing you have me, then."

CHAPTER NINE

Headshots were a rite of passage for all actors. To Bryce's credit, his photographer, Katsu, was good. He set Brittany up in an alley against the mint-green brick wall of his studio, and the coloring suited her brilliantly. The day was cool and overcast, and the lighting was ideal. The trick to headshots wasn't to look airbrushed or unattainably beautiful—it was to look like you on your best day. Beauty alone was overrated. To stand out, Brittany's headshot needed to highlight what was unique about her look, while still looking professional.

It was an art.

"She looks amazing," Bryce said to Emma as they watched Katsu direct Brittany to put an arm over her head and narrow her eyes more.

"But she doesn't look like *her*," Emma said.

"You're right. You're exactly right. She looks too . . ."

"Serious."

"Far too serious." He asked Katsu to make her look flirtier, and Katsu nodded, instructing Brittany to bite her lower lip, to lean forward, to raise her eyebrows.

"This is all wrong," Emma said. "We need less coquette and more ingénue."

Brittany's eyes popped in clear confusion, but she was still biting her lip.

"Perfect." Katsu snapped a dozen shots in an instant.

Once Katsu understood Brittany's personality, the rest of the shoot was magic. An hour later, they were huddled around his desk, looking through the photos on Katsu's computer. As expected, the pictures of a naïve Brittany were perfect. Bryce favored the sexier options, and Emma couldn't necessarily blame him. Brittany was stunning.

"I know it isn't her, but think of all the roles she could get as a temptress with that red hair and pout," he said, practically drooling on Katsu's screen.

"Which she could still get, thanks to the little lip bite in this one. And if Britt likes it, she can add it to her short list. We'll want five or six, anyway. But we need to capitalize on the Brittany Smith look. With her eyes, she could be cast as the girl next door or the heroine in a horror flick or the average Jane who gets a princess makeover—"

"Oh, I love those kind of movies!" Brittany said, prompting an indulgent smile from Emma.

Bryce nodded. "Yeah, you're right. The way those doe eyes pop will really make her appeal to directors. You really know this business."

Maybe he was agreeing with her because he actually agreed with her. Maybe her arguments were so compelling that Bryce couldn't help but see reason. Maybe he really believed in Brittany. Maybe he was so smitten with the girl that any compliment someone gave her could only be met with nods.

But if they were in a movie, Emma would slap his face, grab his collar, and shout, "Pull yourself together, man, and have your own opinion!"

They weren't in a movie, though. More was the pity.

They helped Brittany narrow down her choices, and she ended up selecting five of the six headshots Emma thought were best. This, Emma told herself, was not an example of undue influence so much as a credit to Brittany for deferring to Emma's wealth of experience. Emma had been acting since she was a little girl. She'd made the top ten of almost every major "20 Actresses Under 20" list since she was twelve years old. It was natural for Brittany to go with Emma's picks.

"I'll touch them up and have them printed for you by next Friday," Katsu told Brittany. Before they could make arrangements for Brittany to pick them up, Bryce offered to do the honors.

"It's the least I can do," Bryce said.

Technically, the least you could do would be nothing, Emma wanted to say, though the voice in her head felt more like Liam's than hers. She smiled at the thought, at the idea of the argumentative banter that would follow such a comment—

Wait, why was Bryce smiling at her? Oh, shoot. She was smiling because of that stupid thought about Liam, and he was clearly misinterpreting her.

"Thanks, Bryce. That's really good of you."

"It's my pleasure. Brittany told me about your next appointment, so I'll see you both tomorrow on set."

"I can't wait," Brittany said, almost squeaking.

When they walked to the subway, Emma congratulated Brittany on remembering to schedule another appointment.

"Of course! I listen to everything you say. I want to make you proud, Emma."

The look on Brittany's face made Emma's heart twinge with protective affection. "You're an angel, Britt."

"Let me get this straight," Harlan said that night while Emma pored over messages and sipped on a protein shake. They were sitting on the couch watching *Master Chef*, but she kept missing things, which she knew bugged Harlan. "You hired Brittany to be your assistant, yet you were too busy helping her launch her career to get to actual work today, so she's sending you things to address now, when you should be able to rest? Kind of a stupid move, sis. Didn't they teach you that in college?"

It was a throwaway line. It wasn't meant as a jab. Yet the mention of college made her blood boil in her veins. "Yeah, and how's that GED working out for you?"

"I took the test last month, and you know it." Harlan snapped. "Why are you so touchy about this college thing, anyway? We don't need degrees to do our jobs. We're not all sanctimonious brainiacs like Victoria Alba."

"I know that. It's not like I'm competing with Vic," Emma said.

"Whoa, you sure about that? I think I struck a nerve."

He had, of course. On paper, there was no reason why the two girls shouldn't have been friends. They had similar life experiences and tastes; they'd shared tutors for the first two years of filming. But, although Emma had been the breakout star of the show, the more serious critics had always praised Vic's performance over Emma's. While Emma's portrayal was hailed as "charming" or "delightful," Vic's was "subtle" and "nuanced." Emma was a fireworks show. Vic was a poetry reading.

When Vic proved to be the better student—despite the fact that Emma was, in fact, gifted—it made Emma want to give up on school altogether. She had thrown a fit to her dad that she wanted a new tutor.

She hadn't actually wanted a tutor.

She'd felt self-conscious and had wanted his attention. She'd wanted him to tell her that she was brilliant and creative and that he was proud of her. She'd wanted him to say no—to tell her that she was just as smart as Vic if she was willing to work her butt off the way Vic did. She wanted him to set a boundary like he would have years earlier. She wanted him to care more about her as his daughter than his meal ticket.

But he hadn't asked a single question; he'd simply taken care of it. The next week, she'd gotten her own tutor and had managed to get ahead again, but it was nothing to Vic, who'd skipped two grades before the show ran its course. And after the show ended, Vic left acting to pursue her degree and—oh, yeah—to become an acclaimed indie singer/songwriter with a record number of Grammy nominations for someone her age. No big deal.

Emma knew it wasn't fair to either of them to compare, and even with everything her parents had put her through, she wouldn't have traded her life for Vic's. Discovered when she was four, pimped out by her parents for more and more roles. They fought over her money, treating themselves with lavish houses, cars, and vacations while Vic worked constantly. Emma had heard rumors of the impossible expectations Vic's parents put on her and about their anger if she didn't exceed every one. The day Vic turned fourteen, her aunt Kelly helped her file for emancipation. When it was granted, she moved in with Kelly. She started pursuing other avenues the second *My Valentines* ended, each more meaningful than the last.

What had Emma done after the show ended? Starred in a few teen rom-coms, played the daughter of the president in a disaster movie, performed a play in Chicago, and—oh, right—she'd dropped out of college.

Fireworks.

So, yes, Harlan mentioning Vic bugged her. But what bothered her most was that she would still be in Paris studying French literature or psychology or maybe history if not for him. And sometimes—in her lowest moments—she resented him for it.

Shut your stupid mouth, she told herself. *The one person you can count on in this whole world needed you, and you're complaining that you didn't get to stay in France? You're lying to yourself. You were alone and isolated. You didn't know French as well as you thought. Your roommate was like a demon sent specifically to torture you. You found out your parents' divorce was finalized on* Oh Là Là. *When Harlan showed up, begging for you to come home, it wasn't some big sacrifice. It was a relief. You came running gladly.*

"Yeah, maybe I'm still touchy about Vic," she said, trying to push down her self-flagellation. She rolled off the couch to the floor and started stretching. All the working out lately meant that the muscles in her body were permanently screaming at her. "I don't know what it is about her, but I just don't like her. There. I said it."

"I get it. She's always seemed like a stuck-up brat to me. But don't tell Weston."

"Oh, I'm sorry, did I get a brain transplant? Of course I'm not telling Weston. He thinks we were always friends."

"You know, I read an article about her last month after that incident on the boat when she almost drowned? I guess she's been doing all sorts of soul-searching, and there's speculation that she's planning an acting comeback. She's supposed to be in New York at the end of the month."

"Please don't say she'll be staying with her aunt Kelly." Emma bent an arm behind her head and tugged on her elbow, stretching her sore triceps.

"Ask Weston. He and Kelly are still close."

"He'll try to get us to hang out."

"But this way, you'll have weeks to come up with an excuse."

She texted Weston.

A moment later, he sent his response on Marco Polo. She pulled up the video, which showed him in the writers' room. The people behind him looked to be on break. "Nutmeg, so glad you asked! Yes, Vic is coming into town in a couple of weeks, staying with Kelly. Kelly said she'll probably be here through the end of the year. I'll get everyone together. A dinner party, nothing big. Bring Harlan and that adorable Liam Price he's always hanging with. I know they're both straight as boards, but don't tell me that bromance isn't the cutest thing ever.

Brittany can come. Bryce too. He's kicking butt in class. I'll invite him tomorrow. Oh, and you should know that a surprise guest will be here next week—someone I think you'll be excited to meet. I'll bring him too. You'll be glad of it, promise. Much *alofas!*" He ended the video.

"That brat!"

Harlan was watching *Master Chef* again. He paused it. "What?"

"He has a *surprise guest* coming, which is obviously his sneaky, underhanded way of making sure that I can't get out of the party for Vic. He knows I'm a sucker for surprises, and if he's trying to set me up, the guy must be amazing."

"It'll be his nephew, Aleki, I guarantee it. He's been talking about you two falling in love and making 'beautiful mixed-race babies' since you were, like, sixteen. He's hardly going to set you up with someone else when Aleki's single." Harlan pressed play and watched the contestants try to make Greek bread.

Emma threw out her legs as wide as they could go and stretched, pulling up Aleki's profile on Instagram. He'd posted a picture of himself surfing last week in LA, where he was an intern for Weston's agent. He had hundreds of comments, some of which were almost pornographic. So naturally, Emma had commented, "PHOTOSHOPPED." To which he'd replied, "Blocked and reported." And she'd written, "JK you are so pretty omgeeeeee," and he'd said, "Status: unblocked, unreported, but unloved," and she'd sent some crying face emojis, and they'd gone back and forth for days. She looked at their exchange, smiling.

If Aleki Hale were in town, she'd be there, even if the room was full of the Vics and Aunt Kellys of the world.

To prove her maturity, she texted Vic: *Weston tells me you're coming to town. How exciting! Can't wait to catch up.*

There. Simple, supportive, and carefully crafted so as not to invite a lengthy, drawn out text thread.

Vic's response popped up on Emma's phone just before bed: *Thanks, Emma. I'm excited to be coming home. The recording studio is starting to feel too much like a tomb. Is it weird that I'm leaving LA to finally get some sun? :-)*

Vic's text was cute, fun, completely inoffensive. Emma replied with a "hahaha" but didn't crack a smile.

CHAPTER TEN

Bryce's tour of the studio where *So the Night Falls* filmed was about what Emma had expected. A few soundstages, lots of interchangeable sets on wheels, lighting, microphones, cameras, and crew everywhere. What was unique was the sheer speed at which everything moved. One of the scenes Emma watched only had two takes. Two! Given that *So the Night Falls* filmed about 250 episodes each year, it made sense. But it was hard for Emma to wrap her head around cramming an entire episode—sometimes two—into a single day.

Not that she would be staying all day. She'd been there for thirty minutes and was already eager to leave. The cast and crew had been cool, asking for selfies and congratulating her on her upcoming movie. She'd taken pictures with everyone who'd asked and knew that, by the end of the day, she'd be tagged in dozens of photos.

This kind of thing was good for her brand. She'd had Brittany live tweet as they'd watched an episode of the show earlier in the week in anticipation of the tour, and she'd been met with tens of thousands of retweets, favorites, and comments. It was a good experience for Brittany, who was getting better at understanding Emma's voice. And best of all, she'd trended that day for something other than *Valkyrie*. Twitter had gone bonkers when Bryce responded, saying that he was a fan of hers, but he only had eyes for Lucia. She'd responded, "CANCELLED," which had prompted thousands of comments like, "I AM DEAD," and "I would ship them so hard!" and "I know Bryce isn't actually dating Lucia, but I will literally die if I ever see him publicly with someone else, especially a F***ING CRAWFORD."

Emma had never realized how seriously people took their soaps.

"What do you think?" Bryce was asking Brittany.

"I love it!"

"Then would you want to run lines with me later?"

"Me? Yes! That would be amazing! I did a lot of theater in high school, but it's been a few years, so I'll be rusty. Don't laugh too hard, okay?"

"I make no promises." Bryce's eyes sparkled as he spoke to her. Or did they do that with everyone?

In his element, Bryce was a different man. He was confident, comfortable with the cast and crew, and barely obsequious at all. He was almost charming. And when he announced that he'd talked to the director and had arranged for Brittany to be an extra for the next few days of filming ("if Emma could spare her"), Emma almost liked him.

"I'm sorry for not running it by you, Emma, but I felt I had to jump at the chance. For Brittany. I hope that's okay." He said this as if Emma was Brittany's mother instead of her boss.

"Emma?" Brittany asked with the enthusiasm of a child asking if she could get two scoops of ice cream. "Would it be okay? I'll get to everything you need during breaks and tonight, and I'll talk to Drew at lunch—"

"Brittany, I trust you. You should stay! Act! I'm only sorry that I won't be able to watch. You know I have . . ."

"Your appointment with your trainer, I know. I understand completely! Are you okay without me for the rest of the week, though? I feel like since I got this job, you've been doing more for me than I have for you."

Most people who Emma knew would say something like this with an underlying sort of insincerity. They would pay lip service to their concern and to their duty, while not-so-secretly hoping they could get whatever they wanted. Brittany meant it. Emma could tell by Brittany's body language. It wasn't just the way she focused on Emma as she said it, but the way she planted her feet firmly facing Emma, instead of with her body twisting toward Bryce and the set.

"I love your work ethic, Britt, and like I said, I trust you. Act your butt off for the rest of the week, have fun, and get to whatever you can in your downtime, okay? Just keep me posted."

Brittany squealed and gave Emma a hug before bouncing off to wardrobe.

Emma shot off a quick text, and then looked up at Bryce. "This is really cool of you. When you said you wanted to help Brittany, I didn't think you'd do so much. Thanks for your help."

"It's my pleasure." He leaned against the door frame next to her, folding his arms. They were only a foot away, closer than they needed to be, but he was speaking quietly. "You're right about her. She has a quality that I think the camera will eat up."

Emma's phone vibrated with a call, and she pulled her lips into a frown. "Oh, shoot, I have to take this. Can we talk later?"

He waved her toward the door. "Of course, go. I'll text you and let you know how she does."

Emma answered the phone with a "Hey, can you give me a second?" She flashed Bryce a smile that he returned in full force and then followed the exit signs until she was outside. "Thanks for the escape call," she said quietly. "Harley wasn't answering his phone."

"No problem," Liam said. Emma could hear the sound of the locker room in the background. "He's talking to someone from the film. Sounds like they have some ex-military guy who's going to train Harley on the technical stuff. But why didn't you just tell Bryce and Brittany you needed to go?"

"You don't understand—these situations have to be finessed. If I'd just left without risking being late, it would have seemed rude. Or

Bryce would have wondered if the meeting was a last-minute excuse. But this way, everyone saves face. Get it?"

"If you say so. How'd it go?"

She pulled a hat, sunglasses, and scarf out of her bag and walked toward the subway as she told him what Bryce had done for Brittany. "So I'm going home to meet with my trainer, but after that, my day is suddenly wide open, and I'm super bored just thinking about it. What are you and Harley doing later? Want to meet up?"

"Harley mentioned an appointment later, but, um, I have to get back to my place to watch a recording of New Jersey before tomorrow, and then, well, I sort of have this whole ritual the night before a game. It's . . . weird."

"Color me intrigued. Text me your address, and I'll meet you there later. Moral support." Her words were met with silence. "Unless that will completely mess up your karma. Will it?"

"I don't know, honestly."

She'd wanted him to say no easily, to say that it would be a welcome change, that being with Emma would help him get out of his head or focus or do something magically helpful. But he hadn't. Was Emma pushing her presence on him when it was unwanted? When *she* was unwanted?

The thought made her blood slow in her body, turning her limbs colder than the biting morning air. She pulled her cardigan tighter around her. "You know what, don't worry about it—"

"I think you should come."

They'd talked over each other.

"What, sorry?" Liam said.

"Nothing." Had he said what she hoped he'd said? "I interrupted you. What did you say?"

"Oh." Liam paused again. She knew him well enough by now to

know that he wasn't so full of confidence that he splashed it all over people with every step he took. But he wasn't hesitant either. He was cool-headed, comfortable with himself and his opinions—he often took a stand, and when he did, he was convinced of his own rightness.

Right now, he was none of those things. He was distinctly, adorably flustered.

"Yes?" Emma prompted as she flew down the steps to the subway.

"So, yeah, you should come over."

Emma felt her blood rush again, hot and fast.

"I've been off my routine so much lately. If anything, you'll probably be a good luck charm."

"Well, well, well. You looking to get lucky, Price?"

His pause was just long enough to make her wonder if she'd said the wrong thing. But when he started chuckling, Emma's pulse quickened. "Emma Crawford. What am I going to do with you?"

"It was an honest question," she said in a falsely innocent tone. "I don't want a team of angry men holding me responsible for a humiliating loss to New Jersey tomorrow night."

"Oh, believe me. They'd forgive you."

She swiped her card through the reader and pushed past the turnstile, a small smile on her face. "Because I'm even prettier than Vic?"

His laugh was breathy. "You are such a brat."

"A little blatant flattery, Price. Would it effing kill you?"

"Come on, you know you're prettier than Vic."

Ha! "But does Baby Liam?"

"Um, what?"

"Baby Liam. You know, the Liam who obviously had a crush on Baby Vic and not on Baby Emma. I remember when you came on set, you know."

"Please tell me you're lying."

"I'm not. Sorry, pal." She leaned against a pillar and waited for the subway. Halfway through her second season, Gabriel Price had arranged a visit to the set for his son's birthday. It was probably only a year before he died. She had known Mr. Price through Harlan, who had starred with him in Harley's first film. He was kind and handsome and had taken Harlan under his wing. So she had been excited to learn that he and his son would be visiting the set. His painfully cute son, it had turned out. Emma had swooned just seeing the older boy. Mr. Price had given Emma a big hug, and she'd waited for Liam to hug her or shake her hand or wave a bit shyly, but Liam had had eyes only for Vic. He hadn't even said hi to Emma; he'd just waited for Vic to finish her scene and then had told her what a big fan he was. "Okay, I admit that I didn't remember last year when we met. My memory was jogged."

He groaned. "How?"

"I was going through Vic's social media a couple of days ago and found a 'Flashback Friday' picture with the two of you from the day of your visit, and it all came back. I wish I would have remembered it last year. I would have teased you so hard."

"Well, you're famous for your maturity."

"Says the guy whose crush was so enormous, he couldn't even acknowledge my existence at the time, let alone my superiority."

"I'm acknowledging it now, okay? I don't even follow Vic. I should find that picture—"

"Don't bother. I'll screenshot it and send it to you."

Her dad had always said that he could hear a smile on the phone, and he was right: she was hearing Liam's loud and clear. "Looks like someone doesn't want me following Victoria Alba."

"Oh, shoot, just getting on the train. Signal's fading. Were you saying something?"

"You are such a brat." The laughter in his voice was lower than normal, and it made her shiver. "Listen, practice is starting, but I already texted you my address. So . . . I'll see you soon? I'll grab us dinner."

"Okay. See you soon."

———————

A few minutes before four o'clock, after a training session that convinced Emma that the muscles in her legs had been replaced by pouches of lava, Emma's car dropped her off in Harlem just outside of a restaurant called Fat Bob's Burger Palace.

"This can't be right," she said.

"The address is twenty yards ahead in that construction zone, see?" Her driver pointed forward through the windshield. There was a sidewalk shed set up that she could walk under, but there were so many pipes and exposed beams and wires, and the parapet looked a little shaky, and the whole thing was a deathtrap and . . . and . . . Dammit, she never should have watched that documentary about construction accidents. Stupid Emma.

"And you can't get me any closer?"

"Not without a forklift. Sorry, Ms. Crawford."

She frowned at the scene ahead. "You've been driving a long time, haven't you?"

He nodded.

"Have you . . . ever heard of a beam suddenly falling down and killing someone? Or someone walking through a puddle at the same time that a live wire falls into it and they get electrocuted, or—"

"You could just walk in the street."

This is New York. Someone will hit me with their car and keep driving like it's a regular Thursday afternoon, she thought, but she'd admitted enough of her fears for one afternoon. Her manager retained the car service, and although the drivers all signed strict nondisclosures, she also knew that for a price, most anyone would say most anything.

"I'll do that," she said. With a bracing breath, she put on her sunglasses, stepped out of the car, and watched the driver pull into traffic. Vehicles zoomed past her, going way faster than was necessary. And why were so many people honking? She stood with her butt backed into the barricade, watching traffic while her hair whipped against her face from the steady stream of cars. The intersection light was changing, which meant her window to sprint twenty yards was fast approaching. She wished now that she'd worn sneakers instead of cute flats. She hadn't wanted to dress up too much, because it wasn't like this was a date, but she'd wanted to look sassy and flirty, because, well. It wasn't *not* a date. Cute flats had felt like the right balance.

She hadn't known she'd have to race with traffic. For her life.

The light turned red, there was a lull before the cars turning made it into the lane, and Emma made a break for it. Her thighs had ached before she'd even started moving. Bursting into action was torture. The lava that had taken up residence in her thighs exploded, melting her legs and threatening to sink her into the concrete. She clutched her bag to her side, pumped her arms, and sprinted past the chain-link fence and noisy machines.

It only took a few seconds—four, maybe five at the most—but when the construction ended and Emma reached the sidewalk alive, she doubled over and panted.

Which was when she heard the snap of a phone.

She felt shaky with adrenaline and fear, and she wanted to grab the person's phone, throw it on the ground, and stomp on it. She popped up and looked around to find the source of the clicking.

"When you said you were coming over, I didn't think you'd run all the way from 100th," Liam said, taking another picture.

"You could have warned me that I'd have to face the gauntlet to get here." She exhaled a loud, annoyed breath.

Liam was wearing that quirky half smile he so often seemed to wear around her. "And you didn't take the sidewalk because . . ."

"Death. Because it leads to death, okay? And I'm a huge fan of being super alive and not remotely crushed by a falling sidewalk shed, thanks. Now are we going inside or what?"

"Actually, I was just going to grab some burgers at the place down the street. It's part of my ritual."

"But you said to meet here at four."

"Which gives me three minutes. I'm a fast runner too." The quirk in his lips was teasing, and it was stupid for her to be annoyed and even more stupid for her to feel self-conscious that he had risked not being home when she showed up. It didn't mean he didn't want to see her.

Right?

"I'm never late," she said, still huffing and wanting to kick herself as soon as the words were out. Why did it matter that he know she was ultra punctual?

He rubbed the back of his neck, looking at her. "You know, that doesn't surprise me."

"Why do you say that?"

"My dad always said that punctuality is a sign of respect."

The day grew warmer all of a sudden. "You think I'm respectful?"

His ears went red. "Not of my dinner surprise, but yes, otherwise, you seem like a very respectful person."

"You already said you're getting burgers. What's the surprise?"

His lips pulled to one side. "It's not a surprise if I tell you. Come on. Time to participate in the pregame ritual of your dreams."

She looked down the wreck of construction that she'd just avoided. "Where are we going?"

He followed her eyes. "You're serious about being afraid of walking through the construction, aren't you?"

She didn't answer.

"I won't make you walk underneath the Scaffolding of Death. Come with me."

She looked at his outstretched hand, at the creases on his palm. Under his watch, she caught a flash of a round, circular scar that looked like someone had once stamped out a lit cigarette on him. His mom. She'd seen the same brands all over his sister's back last year.

She slipped her hand into Liam's, glad her sunglasses would hide the wetness in her eyes.

CHAPTER ELEVEN

Liam pulled her into a dry cleaners. They were met with a blast of hot air, though it wasn't cold enough outside to need quite so much heat. Emma fixed her hair and watched with naked curiosity as Liam talked to the African woman behind the counter. She wore a brightly colored dress and an air of total disinterest. Liam asked her something in another language, and her eyes shot to Emma before returning to Liam's. She asked a question, and Emma caught the word *famosa* in it.

He nodded and continued in Portuguese. When he finished, the woman shrugged and gestured to the two of them, pointing through the shop.

"*Muito obrigado,*" Liam said.

"*De nada,*" she said with a wave.

Liam led Emma through racks of clothing and industrial cleaning machines. The smell of chemicals was stronger as they walked farther back. Liam waved to the workers he passed and uttered a few greetings—which were met with the same disinterest the woman up front had shown, though Emma doubted they could even hear Liam over the noise—before they reached the back door and pushed out into the dank alley.

"Was this all just a ruse so you could show off your bilingualism?"

"Obviously."

They walked through the narrow, grimy alley, stepping over rank mystery puddles that Emma suspected were mingled with human waste, at the very least. *Vive la* New York.

"I met Fauzia and her family a couple months ago. They're from Mozambique, which was a Portuguese colony. I thought they'd like speaking Portuguese with a customer, but they don't care too much. They were more impressed that I'm a pro footballer."

"They didn't look *that* impressed."

"They really didn't." He gripped the back of his neck. "Anyway, it's probably not that novel to speak Portuguese when everyone you work with and live with speaks it too. But it's still cool for me."

"And so you, what, made up some story about how we needed to use the alley so I could dodge some obsessed fans?"

"No, I told her *I* had the obsessed fans. Even though she gives me the 'football discount,' she didn't believe me. She said you looked like the famous one, but we could use the back door to the alley anyway."

"You must think I'm so stupid to be afraid of a construction zone, but I watched a documentary, and now I have dreams about driving or walking through construction zones and random things crushing me. I even get anxious driving under overpasses. I keep thinking they're just going to break away at the moment I get under, and *BAM*! No more Emma."

Their feet crunched on the alley grit. "I don't think that's stupid at all. I'm afraid of loads of stuff."

"Such as?"

"This is a no-judgment zone, right?"

"I wish I could make that promise, Liam."

He laughed under his breath, and she loved the way he looked both vexed and amused at the same time. "I'm afraid of bees . . . anything that stings, really. I'm not allergic to anything, and I've never actually been stung or bitten beyond mosquitoes. But the *idea* of it terrifies me. When I was a kid, I went to the bathroom once and saw a fly in there and refused to drop my pants to pee, because I was so sure the fly was going to—get this—'bite my bummy.' That's a direct quote. I know this, because my dad was recording Finley doing somersaults when I screamed from the bathroom and came running out, crying, 'Don't let the fly bite my bummy!'"

A peal of laughter left Emma's mouth, and she clutched Liam's forearm, bumping his side with hers. He was so strong and warm, and the cords of muscle in his forearm flexed under her grip. "I will pay literally all of my money to see this."

"Not a chance."

"But it's so adorable! You were, what, twelve when this happened?"

"Ha ha. She was two, and I was five, smarty-pants."

"Aw, I want to pinch your cheeks."

"Get in line behind the fly."

They had made it to Liam's destination: the open back door to none other than Fat Bob's Burger Palace.

"Really?" she asked.

"Trust me."

It only took a minute for Liam to pay for the burgers he'd already called in, and Emma was glad of it. The place was grungy. Not filthy, but worn down. The black-and-white linoleum floor had faded completely in places. The dingy countertops were chipped. The sign looked like it was from the '80s. A permanent cloud of grease had permeated the air.

Weston would tell her she was letting her bourgeois show. He'd tell her to look past the façade and admire what made the place special. He would tell her to close her eyes, clear her senses, and try to feel the restaurant's very essence.

So she did. She closed her eyes and listened to the sound of burgers on the grill spitting grease, the sound of people laughing and talking, the sound of the cash register and of the cashier yelling to the kitchen. It sounded happy. Thriving. She breathed slowly. If this were a rom-com, this was the moment where she could take a deep breath and cough on the grease in the air. But instead, she let the smell in, and she had the sense that Liam was right. The place smelled good. She hoped he'd ordered onion rings, not that she'd let herself eat more than two.

She opened her eyes again, and only a few seconds had passed. The cashier was handing Liam his change and the bag, and Liam was leading her back outside, to where the rickety sidewalk shed loomed large.

"We're not forcing one another to face our fears, are we?" Emma asked, trying to sound light.

Liam shook his head and took her down to the crosswalk, where they could take the long way back to his place. She smiled thankfully at him and took the bottled soda he handed her while they walked. She looked at the label.

"Grape Fanta? This is pure sugar. My trainer would lose his mind."

"I know. That's why I got you diet." He clinked his bottle against hers.

"So this is Harlem, huh?"

"How do you like it?"

She looked around, her eyes spotting everything that felt distinct from the Upper West Side, where she spent most of her time. The sidewalks were cracked and pockmarked with wear. Cars lined the narrow streets, the occasional Mercedes or Lincoln Continental interspersed with the Cadillacs and Honda Civics. Up ahead was what passed for a park in Liam's neighborhood: chain-link fence, asphalt, and a run-down playground that her mother would say was as likely to give a kid tetanus as a good time, but then, her mother had never taken her to a playground.

The basement of the unit next to the playground advertised a "Medical Practice."

Liam's voice sounded in her ear. "Stop."

"Stop what?"

"Stop looking at this neighborhood like it's going to give you a disease."

"I'm not," she said, not sure if she was lying or being honest, even as she said the most honest thing she could think of next: "I'm wondering what it would have been like to play at a playground."

A man pushed a tiny boy on a swing, ducking under him as he gave a big push. The boy's squeals of laughter punctuated the air, answering Emma's question. "Do you wanna go?" Liam asked.

Her eyes shot to his. Was he teasing her? But no, the look on his face was serious. He was offering to go to a playground with her. She shook her head, pressing her arm against his as they walked. "Maybe next time," she said.

"You're on."

They passed an open braiding center and a closed jazz bar. Two kids, maybe seven and eight, ran out of the braiding center and darted past them in high-top sneakers. The smaller kid tried to chase what looked like his older sister, who was carrying a basketball. The door to the salon was propped open with a chair, and a woman paying at the desk shouted after the two kids to "get back here or face the consequences." She looked upset, but it wasn't the kind of deep-rooted rage that Emma had seen on her dad more times than she could count. It was more tired annoyance. Her "these kids'll be the death of me" eye roll to the cashier showed a hint of indulgence, a far cry from the apathetic, painkiller-dulled glances that had been the hallmark of Emma's mother's looks for almost as long as Emma could remember. What would she have given to have her parents care more about what she was doing than how much she was making?

They were past the salon now, but Emma glanced back down the street, where the older sister was dribbling the ball and her younger brother was trying to steal it from her. Their mom was marching to catch up with them, calling their names. The kids laughed as they ran farther down the street.

The feeling of Liam's hand on her elbow brought her head back around to face forward.

"Watch your step," he said softly.

"Thanks." She stepped carefully, her next words born more of habit than sincerity. "Wouldn't want to fall down one of these potholes."

"Right. That's what I thought."

At the end of the street, they crossed at the light and then headed back down to Liam's townhouse. The mahogany paint on the stairs was chipped and worn. She watched Liam's Adidas shoes fly up the steps, followed by her Jimmy Choo flats.

Liam was one of eight players who shared the townhouse. The team rented out a few properties to its players, but Liam told Emma he liked this one best. And it was nice enough. It was big and bright, with parquet flooring and white walls and doors. The wrong shade of white, but still. The fireplace was a nice touch along the far wall of the main room, where a huge TV had been mounted on the wall. There was a bit of a smell, but then, eight guys lived there. At least some of them were bound to have questionable hygiene.

She wondered what Liam's room was like. Was it messy? Did he throw his clothes on the floor? Did he do his laundry? She already knew that Fauzia next door did his dry cleaning. That gave her hope, at least.

Not that it mattered to her. But if he were secretly a huge slob, that would suck. For someone. Someday.

The kitchen was like something out of a movie: piles of dishes everywhere, empty protein containers and milk cartons left out on the counter. The remains of a package of steaks had a handful of flies swarming on it. She shuddered.

"Dude, Luis, this is disgusting!" Liam yelled through the open back door. "Come clean up your crap!"

Emma looked out the window to see four of Liam's roommates huddled around a grill in the tiny paved backyard, drinking what she knew must be protein shakes, along with a few beers. She'd met all of them the other night at Harlan's place, and they seemed cool enough. Luis nodded to Liam and told him he'd clean it up tonight.

"They're pigs. Sorry about the mess. We'll go up to the roof."

Three flights of stairs later, they were on the roof, which wasn't much quieter than the kitchen had been. The guys' voices carried up to them, but the separation was nice. She joined him at a small wooden table with a closed umbrella. The sun was low enough that the surrounding townhomes provided shade. The late autumn afternoon was cool, and Emma wished she'd brought a bigger jacket.

"So you mentioned you don't drink because of health reasons," Emma hazarded. "But I noticed a few of the guys had beers. It's not a team requirement?"

"No. Kelechi and I are the only teetotalers. His is for religious reasons, though."

Liam's leg bounced beneath the glass table. She put a hand on his shaking knee. "I think if my mom had done to me what yours did to you and Finley, I wouldn't want to be around alcohol too much."

His knee slowed a little. "I don't care if other people drink. I care if *I* do."

"What do you mean?"

"I can't risk becoming her," he said before his bouncing leg lifted him up out of his seat and away from the table. He ran a hand through his hair, not quite making eye contact with her. "I'm going to run downstairs and grab a water. Do you want one?"

"Yeah, sure. Thanks."

"Great, I'll be right back."

Emma's eyebrows tugged together as she stared at the roof door. She picked up her cold soda and started fiddling with a corner of the purple-and-white label that had peeled up. It was stubborn, but she dug a nail underneath and slowly peeled layer after layer off the bottle, depositing each in the paper sack that carried their cooling dinner. She let her thoughts drift until she heard the roof door open again. Liam's messed hair was back in place.

"Sorry that took so long." Liam handed her a bottle of water and sat next to her.

"You had to touch up your makeup. Been there."

His smile was more relief than amusement. Which meant he didn't want to keep talking about drinking or about his mom. But Emma wasn't ready to switch topics entirely. The last ten minutes had stirred up some emotions that she so rarely confronted, let alone had the chance to talk about. She didn't want to drive Liam back downstairs, but who else could she talk to? And what was the point of them hanging out if they couldn't talk?

"I have a weird question," she said, wishing Liam's shoulders didn't pull up at her words. "Did you notice that mom back there who was chasing her kids down the street?"

"You mean the way she watched them like what they did mattered?"

So he'd noticed it too. "Yeah, her. Do you think it was real?"

"*Real*?"

"Yeah. I mean, what if it was just an act? What if she doesn't actually care and it just looked that way to us because we're outsiders and don't know them? What if she was putting on a show for the people at the salon and she knows just the right way to smile in public so people don't suspect that she hits her kids or that her nightly cocktail of Xanax and Chardonnay has numbed her so far beyond caring that even that small effort to pretend for an hour was more face time than she's put in with them all week?"

Liam pulled out the burgers and—thank the stars—still-warm onion rings and put them on the table. Emma shoved a whole onion ring into her mouth and bit down. It helped erase some of the bad taste in her mouth.

"I see what you're saying." He rubbed his wrist beneath his watchband. Was that his only scar? How messed up was it that she even had to wonder? "But the kids were laughing, almost teasing her. I think they were running from their mom because they knew she'd chase them, not because they were afraid she'd hurt them. If they were afraid, I don't think they could have run like that; they wouldn't have wanted to risk what was coming."

Emma turned silent. She didn't want him to end there. She didn't want him to just change the conversation or walk off again. She wanted to dig in the way he always did with her. She wanted him to open up.

"I keep thinking about you not having been to a playground," Liam said. "When I was little, our house in Chicago had a playground in the backyard. My dad would play a game he called 'Bear Chase the Bunny' when he got home at night or on weekends when he wasn't filming. He'd chase us all around the yard and up the ladder and down the slide. We were the bunnies." His speech didn't flow as comfortably as it normally did. If anything, it felt like every word was an effort. "I remember running past Finley once to get away from my dad and accidentally bumping her to the ground. She skinned her knee in the grass and started crying, and my mom yelled at me from the patio to stop being a bully. I ran and hid under the slide. I felt sick."

"But it was an accident."

"Yeah, but I felt sick because I was mad at Finley for being so weak and ruining the fun, and I was afraid I'd get in trouble. My dad scooped up Fin and made sure she was okay, and then he carried her over to me, where I was hiding under the slide. I was nervous and upset at Finley and sad because Dad'd been gone for weeks and we were having so much fun and now I was sure it was over. But instead of yelling or sending me to my room, he told me to come out. When I did, he gave me a hug and said, 'It's okay. I know you love your sister.' Finley was still crying, and he told her that it's okay to cry and have fun at the same time, and then he picked her up and set her on his shoulders, and they chased me together, Finley laughing through her tears." Liam's voice caught on the last word, and he cleared his throat.

"You're the best brother in the world to her, Liam."

"She deserves better," he said, and the way he stared at his onion ring made her drop the question on her lips.

"Well, I deserve this burger in my mouth right now," she said, because he had opened up, and as much as she would love to know more—so, so much more—it had been hard for him, and he had done it anyway. He had done something hard for her.

Liam's eyes met hers, and he smiled.

She unwrapped her burger and—stupidly—almost gasped. He'd ordered her all-time favorite: jalapeños, bacon, avocado, pepper-jack cheese, and mustard, all wrapped in lettuce instead of a bun. But she'd never told him this. He'd asked someone. She couldn't imagine him asking Harlan, and she didn't think Brittany had ordered burgers yet. Had he asked Finley?

She sniffed, blinking quickly to keep herself from being stupid and crying about something as silly as avocados and bacon and . . .

"Jalapeños too strong?" Liam asked.

"No. They're perfect."

———————————

Liam's ritual was simple: burgers and grape soda, if he could get it. Strawberry or lemon-lime if he couldn't. He'd already watched a recording of the opposing team before she'd arrived, so now just one item on his checklist remained: watching kung fu movies.

He'd only been on the team since July, but in the past two months, most of his teammates had joined in watching the movies, so he didn't have to watch them on a tablet in his room anymore. They sat on the floor and crowded Emma on the couch—though, in fairness, she supposed she was the one crowding them. Luis, of the fly-infested steak packaging, sat beside her, with Liam on her other side. She squished as close to Liam as she could without sitting on his lap. Not that that would have been the worst thing. A few times, she'd caught him looking down at her out of the corner of her eye, and she'd looked up at him, and they'd shared a smile that she didn't even understand herself, let alone whatever unspoken language they seemed to be communicating in.

But she liked it. A lot.

When her phone rang around 8 p.m., they were just starting their second movie, *Shaolin Soccer*. She hopped up from the couch and took the call in the kitchen.

"Hey, Harley. What's up?"

"I just had dinner with Dad and need to forget what an ass he is. Where are you?"

Crap on a cracker. "Where are you?" she asked.

"The Boathouse. And who do you think picked up the check?"

"He sucks, Harley. Don't beat yourself up for trying to give him a chance to be decent."

"Are you home?"

Liam had just walked into the kitchen, and she pointed at the phone and mouthed *Harley*. He got close enough to touch. "I have an idea," she said. "Why don't we meet up at Liam's? I ran into him earlier, and he mentioned that he has this ritual of watching kung fu movies the day before a game. Why don't we crash the party?"

"Do you think he'd mind?"

Liam's face was a blank slate.

"I don't think so. I'm already out, so I'll meet you there, okay?"

"Okay. I'll be there in thirty."

She put her phone in the pocket of her cardigan and put a hand on his warm, firm chest. "He just had dinner with our dad, who was an A-list a-hole, as usual. Do you mind that I invited him over?"

"If you want him here, then he's welcome." Liam was too articulate not to say exactly what he meant. And the meaning of those words made her stomach flutter. He reached up to her leather teardrop earring, his fingers grazing her ear and neck in a way that made her shiver. "But is there a reason you don't want Harlan knowing we were already together?"

"Why do you ask?"

"I'm just wondering what you're going to tell him about . . . us. Hanging out. What should I tell him?"

"It's none of his business."

"So you don't want him to know?"

She was normally such a good people reader. Why couldn't she read Liam's face right now? Why couldn't he say what he really wanted to say?

Why couldn't she?

"He's not in the right place to worry about that right now." She let her hand fall from his chest, and he instantly leaned back. She caught his pinky finger with hers before he could back away fully. "But that doesn't mean we can't still hang out."

"Okay."

"Are you ready to get back to the movie?"

He put his hand on the small of her back and followed her into the room.

A couple of Liam's teammates had shifted onto the couch, so Liam pulled up a chair for her. She shook her head and sat on the floor in front of the chair. A moment later, he sat in the chair behind her. After a small hesitation, she leaned against his legs, the skin on her back in a perpetual state of tingling. When she rested her head against his knee, he started playing with her hair, and she sighed.

They sat like that until Harlan showed up a half hour later, when she sat forward and Liam dropped her hair. Harlan joined Emma on the floor. Just like that, the moment was over.

CHAPTER TWELVE

Emma's and Harlan's seats were near the middle of New Jersey's stadium, three rows back. Soccer was different than other professional sports she'd attended. They played thirty-four games from March to October, and then playoffs ran through November and December. She wondered if the comfortable schedule accounted for how they could run nonstop for over ninety minutes. The stadium was small but almost impossibly loud. She suspected the overhangs around the top of the stadium were responsible for the noise. The sound felt like it was swallowing the stadium up. Both teams' benches were on the same sidelines—Emma and Harlan were closer to the visitors' side. Close enough, in fact, that she could see the way Liam opened and closed his fists as he geared up for his penalty kick around the fifty-minute mark.

Emma had never liked soccer all that much, but when that New Jersey player had pushed Liam down and Liam had rolled around gripping his ankle, Emma had never cared more about a sporting event in her life. She'd wanted to rush the field and roundhouse kick the guy in the face.

"It's mostly show. You know that, right? Soccer players are better actors than most actual actors," Harlan said.

"You don't know that. Is he favoring his right leg?"

Harlan said something, but she didn't hear him. She didn't pay attention to the way the players were lining up or the ear-splitting screams in the stadium either. Her eyes were glued to Liam's back.

When he ran and kicked, she shouted louder than anyone. She held her hands up to her face. "Go in! Go in!"

The goalkeeper dived and barely managed to deflect the ball with his right hand. The United fans in the crowd groaned, while the home fans screamed for joy.

Liam's coach waved him off the field as a replacement came in. Emma could see the sweat and discouragement dripping from his face.

"How has he been playing this game compared to others?" she asked Harlan. "Did we jinx him last night by going over?"

"Come on. Don't tell me you believe in all that superstitious crap."

"No, but if a *player* believes in them, then they matter psychologically. A changeup could throw them off. Maybe I—maybe *we* shouldn't have gone over."

What a stupid slip. She saw Harlan's calculating face working from the corner of her eye, but she kept focused on the game.

"How did you beat me to Liam's last night, anyway?" Harlan asked.

"I was just about to go shopping. And the traffic gods were kind to me." Why was she lying about this? Why didn't she want Harlan knowing that she'd been hanging out with Liam?

"Well, sorry I ruined everyone's night," he said. "One of the guys said that you'd been having a great time before I showed up."

Harlan's presence had been a wet blanket over a firework. His mood had killed the fun they'd been having—and not just for Emma and Liam. He'd kept on whispering how stupid he felt, getting up and pacing before sitting back down again. It had been distracting and annoying, and even though nothing had really been happening with Liam, she couldn't stop wishing Harlan had gone home instead.

Which was terribly disloyal of her. "Stop it, Harley. You didn't ruin anything. Don't spiral over this. Dad's not worth it."

"It's not just Dad. I can't stop thinking about everything that happened with Finley. And then Viola," he added of the girl he'd dated during filming last fall and through the winter. It was far longer than he'd dated Finley, yet Finley's was the name he said first. If Emma had to guess, it wasn't Finley he couldn't get past, but who he'd been with her and who he'd become in the end—a cheater, like their dad. "And then there was Kalyn in the spring, and things with that girl Hannah fizzled out before they could even start. Every time I date someone, it turns toxic. What's wrong with me?"

She turned in her chair. "Nothing. Listen to me: you are not the problem. You're the freaking best. Anyone who doesn't realize that doesn't deserve you. You need to let yourself move on."

Emma had seen a therapist last year for a few months in Paris. She hadn't been depressed or anxious. She'd just been sad and lonely and had needed to talk to someone who could help her understand and work through her feelings. What she'd realized through the process was that people often put their issues in convenient boxes to hide the bigger issues that lay beneath. For Harley, that box was spelled F-I-N-L-E-Y. He'd crammed all of his issues so tightly in that box that it was almost impossible to see past them, let alone to find the root of his problems, none of which were Finley.

It bugged.

"I think what's hardest is seeing how similar she and Liam are. He's become a good friend, but it's hard having so many reminders of her all the time."

It really bugged.

"Harley, have you thought about going back to your therapist? If these emotions are resurfacing, then maybe you should talk to her about it again. She helped so much last time."

"That's a good idea. Maybe I will," he said. He plunged his hand into a bag of peanuts and started cracking and discarding the shells. "But I need to ask you something."

"Anything." Liam was going back in the game, and Emma watched him run out to the field.

"You don't *like* Liam, do you?"

Her eyes jumped to Harlan before her brain could catch up. "What? Where did that come from?"

"I just need to know."

She didn't swallow, because that would be like showing her hand. She held his gaze, making sure that she had the right look of openness in her eyes, the right curl of amusement in her lips. "Why do you need to know?"

"Because if you like him, I think you should watch out. He's a runner, Ems."

"What do you mean?"

"I mean that he splits when things get hard. When things went bad with his coach at Notre Dame, he bounced. Last year, some of the West Ham players were being dicks, and Liam pushed his agent to move him to another team. Luis told me all about it. His contract with Arsenal isn't any better than what West Ham was offering."

"I don't see the concern. He didn't like his college coach, and he didn't like his teammates. People have left jobs for less."

Harlan's gaze sharpened. "Fine. If you don't want to believe me, then at least remember that he's only on loan from Arsenal, okay? He'll be back with the team at the beginning of next season. Soccer over there is basically royalty, and the money's ten times better than it is here. You heard him the other day talking about how he has to take every advantage he can now while he's a healthy commodity." Harlan wasn't wrong, and she hated him a bit for that. "I don't want to see you hurt."

"He doesn't have the power to hurt me," she said, even as a prick in her heart told her otherwise.

"Are you sure?"

She hadn't realized how much she cared about Liam until she had to lie about her feelings to her brother. But the real torture was still to come. Because if Harlan was this upset about the idea of Emma and Liam dating, that could only mean one thing: she could choose her happiness or Harlan's, but not both. And because it was Harlan, the choice was already made. "Baby bro, what's with the third degree here? Listen. I adore Liam. We're friends. But we both know I prefer baseball players." She winked, like the movement wasn't physically painful for her, and the suspicion fell from his face.

"That's a relief. I don't think I could handle another Price-Crawford scandal. Though the paparazzi would love it."

"When you put it that way, let me reconsider. No press is bad press, after all."

"Ha ha," Harlan said.

They returned their attention to the game. She watched with a heavy lump in her throat as Liam scored the game-winning goal with four minutes to spare.

Looked like she hadn't jinxed him after all.

After the game, Harlan and Emma watched and cheered while the team jumped around and the big players gave interviews, including Liam. When he was done, he jumped the fence and ran up to them. He gave Harlan a quick hug before holding his arms open for Emma. She wanted to squeeze him, to hug him so tightly that the scent of his sweat would last all night. She wanted to give him the kind of hug that she could revel in for weeks, the kind of hug that would soothe her regret and soften her anger at the unjustness of a world where she had to put her brother's happiness above hers. She wanted the kind of hug that would help them both move on.

But instead, she released him quickly and didn't meet his eyes, even though she felt them burrowing into her.

"Um, thanks for being here, guys," Liam said. "It means a lot to me."

"Wouldn't have missed it," Harlan said. "We still hanging tomorrow? Bring the guys over, and I'll grill something."

Liam's eyes flicked to Emma's, so she put on the most passive expression she could muster. The V between his brow formed and disappeared so quickly, she could have imagined it, if the sight hadn't made her heart ache. "No, I'll have to miss tomorrow, sorry. But I'm sure the guys would love to come over. Text Luis or Kelechi." Someone called his name, and he looked back and waved. He was grinning when he looked back at them. A grin that should have been hers. "Thanks again for coming. I'll see you Monday."

With that, he hopped the fence and returned to his team, leaving Emma to watch him go.

At Riverside Motion on Monday, Emma's punches were harder, her kicks more precise, and her focus was laser sharp. She'd spent all Saturday shopping with Weston for new appliances for his loft. It was the break that she'd needed, and she'd found herself feeling more generous toward her hurting brother. She'd surprised him with a new set of cast-iron pans, which had led to him inviting Liam's housemates and a couple of old friends over Sunday afternoon, after Emma got back from a photo shoot. He called it the "First Annual Great Crawford Cook-Off." He won.

But as much as she thought she had a handle on her emotions, her aggression in class told her otherwise. Weston barked compliments to her and challenged the rest of the class to keep up with her. When they went to breakfast later at L'Orange, he asked about it.

"I've known you since you were ten years old, and I've never seen you so on fire. Who broke your heart?"

She speared a bite of egg onto her fork and dipped it in hollandaise sauce. "Stop it. No one broke my heart. Why would you even think that?"

"Because the more hurt you are, the more you express yourself. Limalama is your tapestry, and you were painting a pretty violent image today, Nutmeg. Want to talk about it?"

"Not really."

"Well, you just keep that heart of yours open and ready, okay?"

"Why? When does Aleki get here?"

"Next weekend." He tapped the table. "I'm as transparent as glass, aren't I?"

"More like crystal. I love that about you."

His spinach, steak, and egg bowl was almost empty. "Well, you can thank me in ten years when you two are married and the proud parents of Little Weston and Little Westina."

"Names subject to change, of course."

"Probably not. Don't think I haven't noticed how flirty you two are all over Insta." He stirred his tea with a dreamy sigh. "You two would make the most beautiful babies."

"Uncle Weston has baby fever, huh?" She leaned back into the vintage yellow chair. "For someone with no interest in relationships, you sure are a romantic."

"Guilty."

They walked out to the street after paying their bill. As always, Emma left a generous tip.

"You never want servers to talk with their friends about how cheap you are," Emma's dad had told her and Harlan years ago. "A big tip won't bankrupt you, but it'll increase the chance that the server says something nice about you when TMZ comes calling." Her dad may have been a rotten snake, but he wasn't wrong. She added that advice to the list of things she needed to tell Brittany.

Emma and Weston walked out to the street, sunglasses and hats in place. Emma told him all the latest updates from Brittany: filming was going so well!, they liked her so much they gave her three lines and put her in an extra scene!, Bryce was an angel!, he wondered if Emma could stop by filming this week to see how far she'd come! So could she please be there?

"And? Are you going?"

"I may as well. Bryce texted me the time Britt will be filming her scene, and the only thing I'll miss is a protein shake. I'll just double up later."

Weston's face swiveled toward hers as they were stopped at a light with a dozen other pedestrians. Emma shuffled to keep warm. "You've been home for almost four months now. Are you happy about it?"

"Sure. Why wouldn't I be?"

"You took a break from all of this for a reason. I just want to make sure being home, being back in the limelight, is what you want."

"I wouldn't make a life-changing decision for anyone, Weston."

"Oh, Nutmeg, you and I both know that's not true. You would give me a kidney if I complained of back pain."

Why did that simple statement make her throat feel swollen and achy? "What's the point of having two of something if you can't share?"

Weston looped her arm in his. The day was cool, so while she was wearing a light jacket, Weston's warmth was nice. "You don't have to sacrifice so much for people to love you. You're worth loving all on your own. The right people will always see that. Anyone else doesn't belong in your life."

Weston's words replayed in her head long after she got home. After her shower, after a quick lunch, and all the way to the studio, where Brittany would shortly film her lines.

It was a beautiful sentiment, what Weston had said. Touching and inspiring. The kind of sentiment to frame on a wall and memorize in one's heart.

She wondered if it was true.

CHAPTER THIRTEEN

Emma arrived just in time. The crew was changing up the scene with an efficiency that Emma had never seen before. With how much filming they needed to get through, there wasn't time to perfect the lighting or even the lines, let alone to get the emotion exactly right in each scene. Getting the story out on time trumped all.

When Brittany's scene began, Emma watched raptly from behind the camerawoman. Bryce's character was visiting his girlfriend in the hospital, and he'd made his way into a break room for coffee and a moment of privacy to cry alone.

In the background, Brittany walked through a prop door into the break room, looking like she'd been up all night. She poured herself a cup of coffee, and while Bryce was whispering a prayer, hands clutched around the creamer, Brittany tapped him hesitantly on the shoulder.

"I'm sorry to bother you, but could I borrow the creamer?"

Bryce looked at Brittany with surprise, following her gaze to creamer he didn't realize he was holding.

He sniffed and handed it to her. "Sorry about that. It's been a tough few months."

"Don't I know it," she said, taking the creamer with a stifled yawn. Then she smiled at Bryce and patted his arm with her free hand. "But you know what they say: It's always darkest just before the dawn."

Brittany used the creamer and exited the break room, leaving Bryce to return his head to his hands. A moment later, Bryce received a phone call from a nurse. The sun broke through the window and illuminated his smiling face.

Lucia was awake.

End scene.

Emma clapped, but she was the only one to do so. Of course. The cast and crew all did this 500 times a day. But as everyone resumed their positions for the next take, Brittany looked like she was glowing from within. She had done well, and she felt it. As well as Emma could have hoped. These three lines would lead to so many more.

After two more takes, the director dismissed Brittany and Bryce in order to move on to the next scene. Brittany squealed and ran to Emma, who gave her a tight hug.

"You were brilliant, Britt! I'm so proud of you!"

"Thanks! It felt amazing," Brittany gushed.

Bryce directed them back to his dressing room, explaining that they could take a break there while they waited for his next scenes. "I won't be finished filming until five or six at the latest, if you want to get dinner somewhere tonight," he said. "To celebrate Brittany."

The way he added celebrating Brittany felt more like an afterthought than a plan. "Oh, we're definitely celebrating Brittany. My house tonight. Seven o'clock. Don't be late."

After an afternoon getting manicures, trying on clothes, and (fortunately) catching up on work, Emma and Brittany welcomed their guests to Harlan's humble 3,000-square-foot condo. Harlan (thank the stars) was all smiles and laughter, getting people drinks, showing them to the different rooms where they could find food (kitchen), video games (main room), poker (dining room), and karaoke and dancing (the rarely used pool room—both Crawfords sucked at pool). It wasn't a big party—maybe fifty people, but it was last-minute. Weston came with Brittany's cousin Marcus and a few friends. Jamal—the pop star Emma's manager had set her up with as a publicity stunt several weeks ago—was there with his sister, Kimmie. Jamal and Emma's friend Misha seemed enchanted with each other. A few of Harlan's castmates from his last movie showed up, as did Liam and his housemates. She hadn't realized Harlan would invite them. After Emma and Liam's awkward bro hug after his game Friday, she wasn't sure how she felt seeing him at all.

Emma and Harlan's friends didn't know Bryce, but everyone played nice together. Maybe it was because of the way Bryce stayed next to Emma and Brittany all night like a loyal puppy. Maybe it was because he was almost ethereally pretty, like a delicately featured elf from the Lord of the Rings movies. But instead of being starstruck by all the A-listers, he seemed to revel in the attention. And he couldn't stop commenting on the party Emma had thrown together. And "thrown together" was exactly the right description. She would be embarrassed under other circumstances, but she had told herself that the party was about Brittany, not about showing off her hostessing skills.

Not that Bryce seemed to notice. To him, it was spectacular, all of it.

Of the food (which was out buffet-style, instead of being served to the guests): "This is delicious, Emma," Bryce said, standing between Emma and Brittany with a plate of stuffed mushrooms, bacon-wrapped figs, and avocado crostini appetizers.

"You just have to know the right people," she said. The food was from a canceled wedding. Hopefully, no one noticed how fancy the cake was.

"And you have to have excellent taste," he added.

Brittany popped a mushroom in her mouth. "Mmm. They're really good, Emma! The mushrooms are a bit too earthy, though. I don't think I like them, come to think of it."

Of the atmosphere (of which there was none—no lighting and no DJ, apart from Jamal's sister's iTunes): "It's absolutely effortless, from top to bottom," Bryce said.

"I think the word you're looking for is *slapdash*," Emma said.

119

"No, it would take weeks to put together just the right blend of lights and sounds. It's so soft and inviting."

"And yet it only took us asking Alexa to set the lights to 'elegant,' isn't that right, Emma?" Brittany said, forcing Emma to hide a smile.

Of their guests (two of whom were making out against the pool table while Liam and two of his housemates were actively playing pool): "You have great friends."

She shoved the pair off of the pool table and told them to get a room. But not hers. "They're reprobates, Bryce."

"Oh, no doubt. The best friends always are," he said.

"Emma, were those chandelier lights always broken?" Brittany asked.

For all of his fawning, though, Bryce was quick to tell everyone how well Brittany had done all week. Emma watched him tell the guests in the dining room (who were picking out all traces of carbs) just what a natural Brittany was. And then he announced it was time for a surprise.

From a satchel he'd put in the corner, Bryce pulled out an envelope with Brittany's headshots. He beckoned Brittany to him in the middle of the room and took out each of the headshots in turn. They were perfect.

"The camera really loved her, just like Emma had predicted. She's beautiful, of course. Anyone can see that. But she has a . . . *je ne sais quoi*. An *it* factor that you can't put your finger on."

"I think it's the flax-and-protein shakes of Emma's I'm sneaking," Brittany said.

Liam laughed.

"It's not some protein shake," Bryce insisted.

Emma didn't know if Brittany had been earnest or teasing—she could never quite tell with the girl. But it was certainly deflection. Brittany didn't crave attention like so many actors. Bryce may have had good intentions, but she would have expected him to understand

Brittany a little better by now, especially as they'd spent days together on set.

"She's a natural talent," Bryce continued, "and this won't be the last we see of her, I guarantee it. Emma knew. All along, she could see her potential."

His hands were clasped and pointing to Emma. Not Brittany.

Well, this was awkward.

Did he expect applause? For people to raise their glasses and toast her, when this party was to celebrate Brittany? Yes, she loved the spotlight, but she wasn't a straight-up tool. How could she fix this without embarrassing both Bryce and Brittany?

Her eyes jumped to Liam, who seemed to sense her internal struggle. He raised his glass of milk and smiled. "To Brittany, with her excellent taste in employers, natural talent, and vast potential. May your star continue to rise."

Bryce opened his mouth, but his words were swallowed by calls of "To Brittany."

The awkwardness disappeared, along with half of the room's drinks. And the more her friends got into their drinks as the night continued, the less anyone remembered Bryce's display. Emma was glad of it. In her darkest moments, she still wondered if she had pressured Brittany into making the right decision. But when Brittany pulled her over to the karaoke machine to perform the Spice Girls' "Wannabe," her doubts vanished. Brittany sang and danced with joyful abandon, and when Emma worked the room, Brittany was right there with her.

After hours of karaoke, dancing, and schmoozing, Emma escaped to the balcony. The cool night air nipped at her nose and made her hug her arms around her chest, but she felt like she was lit from a fire within. Brittany was so happy. Emma hadn't ruined her life by convincing her to turn down that job. All was well with the world.

A light breeze ruffled her hair, and Emma put her hands on the railing and squinted out at Central Park. Lights illuminated the various paths, and she tried to make out Central Park's Great Hill while she listened to the only other people out on the balcony: Weston and Liam's teammate, Kelechi. They were in a spirited debate about, of all things, the fastest way to enter ketosis, so the body would burn its own fat as fuel.

Is that what passed as conversation in real life? Not that her life wasn't real . . . but was it? She'd been in France for ten months, and sure, she'd hung out with people. People who mostly wanted stories about the Hemsworths and to tag Emma in photos to get more followers, people who wanted to brag that they were friends with a star. Not many of them had cared to actually get to know her. Fewer believed that she'd earned her way into the prestigious school. Still, she preferred those people to the ones who hated her without ever talking to her, like her demon roommate, Carina.

She didn't let herself think of her roommate often. Carina was a judgmental hag who'd decided without ever having a conversation with Emma that her very existence was frivolous. She was constantly in the middle of a provocative phone call with her mother or sister about the pitfalls of consuming media, the fickleness of social currency and fame, and the puppets who worshipped pop idols. She railed against the women who willingly entered a corrupt system just to complain and cry, "*Moi aussi*! Me too!" when they didn't get the job they wanted.

It wasn't the first time Emma had wanted to punch someone, but it was the first time she'd had to physically restrain herself from doing so.

"You look deep in thought," Bryce said.

Emma looked around to see that Weston and Kelechi had taken their debate back into the condo. She was alone with Bryce. "I thought

I left you and Brittany on the dance floor. You seemed to be getting along well."

"Oh, we were. Britt's a good girl. Sweet."

His tone made her stand up taller. "And she's loyal and fun and works harder than almost anyone I know."

"Yeah, yeah. She's all those things. Like I said, a good girl."

Why did Emma sense a "but" in that sentence? Why did he sound so dismissive, so patronizing? *A good girl.* As opposed to what? To whom?

"She's the best," Emma insisted.

Bryce stood next to Emma with his back against the rail. He had his arms folded in that way guys did to make their biceps look bigger. Ugh.

She kept looking out at the park until Bryce grabbed his phone. "Here, take a selfie with me."

"Why?"

"Because, if you don't post it, did it even happen?"

"Fair point." She looked at Bryce's screen while crossing her eyes and sticking out her tongue. Bryce's face changed from a smoldering look to duck lips. He took several pictures, and when Emma relaxed her face, he kissed her cheek. Emma pulled back a millisecond too late. She could still feel his too-soft lips on her face.

"What are you doing?"

Bryce kept the phone up. "You know what I'm doing. Hold still." He lunged in for a real kiss.

He took a picture at the exact moment that Emma stuck her hand between their faces.

She caught a glimpse of the finished product: Bryce's lips and nose smushed against her firm open palm, her profile showing a flared nostril and dangerously glinting eye.

"Did you just tell me to *hold still* so you could make a move? What the hell?" she asked, wiping her palm on her jeans. She wiped the feeling of his lips from her cheek as Bryce rubbed his nose.

"I could ask you the same thing. I was just taking a picture, Emma. Why are you being so dramatic?"

"I'm not being *dramatic*; I'm telling you that I don't want you to kiss me, let alone on camera."

"Calm down. Obviously, I'm not going to post anything now that I see how freaked you are about a simple kiss. I thought you wanted me to."

The steam issuing from Emma's ears could have powered a locomotive. "You thought I—" She stopped herself and inhaled deeply. "You thought wrong. And please stop telling me how to feel."

Bryce gave an angry shake of his head "You've put out signals for weeks, inviting me to work out and to brunch and to party. What else was I supposed to think?"

"You mean, apart from thinking about how to follow through on your commitment to my friend? Nothing. You were supposed to think *nothing*, unless it was about her."

"You think I did all of this for *Brittany*? For that basic Midwestern bumpkin?"

"Yes, but only because of the overwhelming evidence: you told me you wanted to help her, and then, oh right, you helped her. Repeatedly. Gee, how could I be so confused?"

"You're right: I did help her. Over and over again, I went out of my way to help because *you* wanted me to."

"Excuse me? I never asked you—"

"Not outright, but you didn't offer to do any of it yourself, did you? Like you couldn't have called up any daytime TV show and set up an audition for her? Like you couldn't have arranged acting lessons or headshots? No, you let me because you wanted me to be involved. Because you want *me*."

Emma felt like gagging. "Wrong. I could have and would have done all those things myself, in time. I let you help because you eavesdropped on a job interview, literally inserted yourself into a situation that had nothing to do with you, and because you obviously wanted—"

"You! I wanted you! I did this for you!"

"Then you made a huge mistake," she said.

He folded his arms and exhaled in angry puffs, looking her up and down. His face had contorted into an ugly, bruised thing.

"It's time for you to leave."

"Fine. You're overrated anyway." He began his march for the sliding glass door.

She laughed. "Ouch. Sick burn, Bryce."

"No, you know what? You're worse than overrated, because you're not hot enough to get away with being such a stupid, shallow bi—"

"Shut your mouth." Her voice was as low and menacing as she could make it and still be heard. "And leave. Now."

He looked like he was debating something—knowing his penchant for overacting, she was waiting for him to spit in her face, at which time she would kick his junk into next Tuesday. She was almost excited by the idea. But instead, he chose better and left without another word.

She was shaking with adrenaline and anger. Her fists were balled so tightly the muscles in her right hand were cramping. She shook out her hand and rubbed her palm deeply until the cramp subsided. She exhaled a long, shaky breath and turned back around to look over the park, to follow a single lighted path with her eyes.

She was such a fool.

How could she have trusted her friend's career to Bryce Elton? How could she have believed that someone in this business would ever do something nice, with no ulterior motive? Did people in real life even do such things? Would a stranger in Chicago overhear someone on the train talking about looking for a job and offer to help?

No way. People were people. Fame only enhanced whatever was already there. The Bryce Eltons of the world were always looking for ways to scam women. His small power only brought out his natural douchebaggery. But there was scum everywhere, at every level.

Why couldn't he have tried one more thing so she could have had an excuse to punch his teeth in? So she could have erased that smirk from his stupid face when he'd called her stupid and shallow?

Shallow.

She hated the word so much, and she hated him more for calling her that. For somehow finding the one thing she feared about herself and for slapping her in the face with it.

Emma put her elbows on the rail, dropped her head into her hands, and massaged her temples until the slimy sense of shame coating her throat and lungs had calcified.

When she returned to the party, most of the guests had cleared out. Harlan was talking with Jamal's sister, Kimmie, on the couch in the main room, Brittany and Marcus were singing karaoke to Katy Perry's "Roar" in the pool room, and Liam and Weston looked to be in deep conversation across from each other in the dining room, where cards and chips were scattered around the table. She took the open seat next to Weston, laying her head on his shoulder. He rested his head against hers.

"It was a nice party, Nutmeg. Brittany seems happy."

"Does she?"

"Of course she does. Why wouldn't she? After everything you and Bryce did to help her? No, she's happy. Her karaoke selections are proof of that. But where's Bryce been?" Weston asked. "I haven't seen him in a while."

"I saw him sneak out about a half hour ago," Liam said. "Unlike Brittany, he didn't look happy. Any idea why?"

She didn't have to look at Liam's face to know that he suspected something. She closed her eyes and yawned. "I'm sure he has an early morning and got mad because he stayed up too late or something. He's kind of a prince when it comes to that stuff."

"That's one word for him." Liam spoke quietly, but it was loud enough that he definitely wanted to be heard.

Weston's head shook against Emma's. "You're too cynical, Liam. Bryce has a good heart," he said. Emma opened her eyes.

"I've never been called *cynical* before." Emma sniffed in disbelief, and Liam's eyes widened. "Ms. Crawford, do you have something you'd like to share with the class?"

"The only reason you haven't been called cynical—to your face—is because your friends have never seen you interact with stars. We bring out your cynical side."

"Don't say 'we.' It's not everyone. Not you."

"But you admit it."

His eyes narrowed, probably at the playful way she'd checked him. She could kick herself. Harlan's words about Liam leaving in a few months sounded in her head. Could she really let herself start something with him just to watch him go? "I admit it. And I admit that I think Bryce is a snake. I don't think he was bending over backward for Brittany out of the goodness of his heart. He wants something out of this, I guarantee it."

Weston laughed. "So, so cynical."

"Maybe I need to take a page out of your book," Liam said. "What is it that you say at the end of each show? 'Kindness given, kindness gained'?"

Weston said the Samoan phrase, but nodded.

"That's nice," Liam said. "But I think we can believe that, promote that, and it still won't change the fact that some people are out for themselves."

"I agree," Emma said.

"Oh no! You too?" Weston asked. "Don't tell me Liam is pulling you over to the dark side."

Liam caught her eye, and even though she felt uncomfortable under the weight of his gaze, she didn't look away. She didn't want to. "No. I don't think Emma's that easily persuaded. What she does, she does for herself. Or Harlan," he added with a smile that he must have thought would soften the blow of his words. Is that really what he thought of her?

Was it true?

"The list of people she'll go to the ends of the earth for is a little longer than you might think," Weston said. His fond tone was the balm her soul needed, and it was exactly the reason she would sacrifice anything to keep his faith in her.

"No need to try to convince Liam of my virtues, Weston," Emma said. "I think his opinion of me is pretty well cemented at this point. As it is of Bryce, the aggressively ambitious turd-face."

"Maybe your list isn't that long," Weston teased.

She put her head back on his shoulder, a falsely light note to her voice. "No, maybe not."

CHAPTER FOURTEEN

"Don't you think it's strange that Bryce has just disappeared?" Brittany asked while she and Emma were sparring. She lunged at Emma, who let Brittany grab her around the shoulders. "I know he's been at work all week, because I've texted with some crew members, and they say he's been in a terrible mood. And he was texting me so much last week, but this week, it's like I stopped existing the day after the party. What could have happened? Do you think—is it something I said?"

Emma executed a flawless whipping technique, snapping her left arm upward and hitting Brittany's face with the back of her open hand softer than Weston would have encouraged. Brittany grunted and swung at Emma, who parried her attack with one hand and drove her other hand into Brittany's throat. Softly. Brittany coughed.

"Don't even think about blaming yourself," Emma said. "Actors are fickle, Britt. Whatever is going on in Bryce's head has nothing to do with you and everything to do with him. Maybe . . . maybe he was using you and dropped you when he didn't get what he wanted."

Brittany frowned. Emma tackled Brittany, but Brittany freed herself by executing an elbow strike to Emma's face. Emma responded with a palm strike to the base of Brittany's head, followed by a counterclockwise spin and a forearm strike to Brittany's face. Brittany stumbled, and Emma brought the back of her hand across Brittany's cheek far softer than she would on another partner.

"Why would he use me? What could I possibly have to offer him . . . other than . . . the obvious. Which I didn't yet."

"That's exactly the point. If he didn't want you because it was too much work, then he isn't worth your time."

"But he's been so sweet! You should have seen him when we were on set together. He was so nice. One time when he went to get himself a tea, he brought me one too. He forgot that I don't like tea, but it was still so nice of him to think of me. And whenever we ran his lines, he told me how great I was at helping him stay in the scene. And then he said all those nice things at your party. About, you know, how beautiful I am."

Emma half expected Brittany to explode into a cloud of hearts when she slapped her.

"I think Bryce has done everything we could have wanted for you, Britt. Now's the time to move on and find new opportunities."

"But . . . I like him."

"Then I need to introduce you to someone better. A hundred some-ones better. Maybe one of Liam's teammates."

"None of them are as gorgeous as Bryce," Brittany said, looking twitterpated even as Emma shoved her elbow into the girl's gut. "Unless we're talking about Liam. He's so hot!"

How the girl could giggle while getting slammed into the floor was a mystery.

Brittany's concern over Bryce ghosting her became a full-blown preoccupation by the weekend. Harlan had traveled with Liam and the team to Atlanta for an away game, so Emma had insisted that Brittany sleep over while he was out of town. She didn't mind being alone, but she liked being with friends a lot better.

At least when said friend wasn't obsessing.

"Look at this: he's tweeting from Las Vegas! He's at the Bellagio 'with his boys.' He won big at the blackjack tables . . . but, oh no! He lost it all playing roulette. He has a hashtag that says . . . 'maybe don't always bet on black.' That's funny."

"It really isn't." Emma looked up from her daily Spanish study app that she was only a week behind on. Give or take. "Why are you scrolling through his tweets, Britt? I thought you were moving past him."

"I am! I totally am. I'm just bored, so . . ."

"Then learn Spanish with me."

"I already know Spanish. Santino and his family moved from Mexico when he was a kid. His parents didn't speak much English, so considering we were together for six years, I figured I may as well learn it."

"Wait, you speak Spanish? And who's Santino?"

"My boyfriend through high school and college," Brittany said, and Emma realized Brittany had mentioned him before. Brittany continued her obsessing. "And just two hours ago, Bryce went to a Brazilian grill for dinner. Says he can't pronounce the name, but he can sure eat the food."

"Has he talked about the bathrooms yet?" Emma said. Brittany threw a pillow at her from the couch. "What? He's live-tweeting everything else about his day."

"Well, then you'll be happy to hear that there are only two more updates: he says he's clubbing at Eleven, and he's dancing with KeyAra."

"Who's KeyAra?"

"That lifestyle YouTuber? She does hair-and-makeup videos, but she also goes shopping in, like, cat makeup, and one time, she recorded herself getting busted for shoplifting in a sexy nurse's costume. Poor Bryce. He must be hating it. He's too sweet for her."

"Don't count on it."

The following morning after a butt-kicking workout, Brittany was back on her phone, pouring over Bryce's Twitter and Instagram. Brittany showed Emma wannabe artsy pictures that Bryce was taking and captions and tweets that hinted at some big things happening, some life-changing things, and Emma was tempted to smack the phone out of Brittany's hands at least a dozen times.

"It's a good thing we're going to get massages, because then you'll have to put your phone down," Emma said on their way to her favorite day spa in the Upper East Side. She normally had her masseuse come to her, but she needed to get Brittany out of her head. Yet Brittany hadn't look up from her phone their entire way from Harlan's condo through Central Park. Emma couldn't take it anymore. She stopped in the middle of the sidewalk, stepped in front of Brittany, and shook the girl's shoulders. "Britt, I feel like an old person talking about *the problems with these damn millennials right now*! You're killing me. Put down your phone. It's autumn in New York. Look around, smell the falling leaves, live a little, et cetera. Bryce is old news. You're too fabulous to be following some guy's life instead of living your own."

Brittany frowned but dropped her phone into her bag. "You're right. I'm sorry. I've never had someone do so much for me and then just ignore me like this. I must have done something wrong, Emma, but I can't think of what it is, and it's making me sick."

"I promise, you didn't do anything wrong. Bryce just isn't who he pretended to be." This was the moment she should have told Brittany everything and let her friend mourn what she thought about Bryce but also move on from his douchebagging ways. But Emma didn't want to hurt Brittany's feelings after putting Bryce in her path in the first place.

Brittany's nod was as reluctant as it was unconvincing. "I'm sure you're right."

Emma linked her arm in Brittany's and peered through her sunglasses at the beauty of nature and the smiling faces of . . .

"Oh, crap. Pick up your phone, Britt. Now, now, now." Emma pulled out her own phone and shoved it in front of her face while Brittany was scrambling in her bag.

"Wait, why? What just happened?" She was frantically digging in her bag when the person Emma wanted to avoid spotted them.

"Emma? Is that you?"

Emma put down her phone and pasted on her best fake smile. "Kelly. What a surprise to see you."

Kelly laughed. "The bigger surprise is that we don't run into each other every day! I thought I saw you last week, but it must have been someone else, because I called out, but the girl didn't turn. Oh well. Where are you two headed?"

Emma was glad Weston wasn't with them. His caring presence would remind Emma about the eating disorder that had blacklisted Kelly from modeling and Hollywood. His hand on her shoulder would keep her listening to Kelly out of a sense of obligation, and hours could easily pass before Emma had the opportunity to extricate herself from the woman's fawning.

Thank goodness Weston wasn't with them.

"We're off to get massages. But we're running la—"

"Oh, I can't believe I didn't tell you already! Did you know that Victoria is coming into town?" She looked at Brittany. "My niece, Victoria Alba. Emma was her costar in *My Valentines*." She looked back at Emma. "She'll be here tomorrow night, and she's going to be here for months, you know! She thought she would take a break from recording, but she's going to try recording a totally new conceptual album here, and well, who knows what else? Maybe she'll try out acting again! Or, ooh, Broadway. After that terrible scare she had on the houseboat when her manager saved her, I just haven't felt right about her being gone for so long. I've been begging her to come home, and she said she thinks it's time to. Isn't that wonderful?"

That houseboat accident was certainly playing in Vic's favor. As if it wasn't enough to be an acclaimed singer/songwriter, she now had the distinction of having a near-death experience. Tabloids loved that crap.

Vic was evidently smart enough to capitalize on the fact.

"You have to come by when she gets back into town. Promise me you will. It would mean so much to have both of you girls back together again."

Kelly was about to wax nostalgic—Emma could see it in her eyes. So it was against her better judgment that she punished Future Emma by saying, "Of course! In fact, I think Weston is planning a dinner party."

"Oh, that's right! That will be lovely. But you know, we'd love to have you—"

"I can't wait!" Emma interrupted. "I'm so sorry, but we really have to get going to our appointment. Talk soon!"

"So good to see you, dear!" Kelly was saying while Emma pulled Brittany along the path.

"Always have an appointment," Emma said.

"It's very effective," Brittany said.

———————————

Sunday night, Harlan returned.

"I come bearing curry with cauliflower rice," he announced, hefting a takeout bag. "And a tired soccer star."

Liam followed him into the room, where Brittany was watching the Weather Channel and Emma was working on a post. She'd send it to Brittany when she was done. Brittany, it turned out, was at her best late at night. While Brittany was working with Bryce on *So the Night Falls*, Emma woke up each morning to find that her assistant had spent hours making up nearly everything she had missed during the day. The timestamps were at hours Emma didn't even believe in. But Brittany insisted, and Emma was too relieved to have an assistant she could trust.

Harlan deposited the food on the coffee table and left everyone to fend for themselves when he flung himself on the opposite end of the couch from Emma. He grabbed the remote and changed the channel.

"Hey, Brittany was watching that," Emma said, not looking up from her post.

"Oh, sorry, Britt," Harlan said. "I just assumed it was background noise. Do you mind if I change it? Mario was at the game and interviewed me and Liam. It's supposed to air tonight."

"I don't mind at all," Brittany said.

Liam sat between Emma and Harlan and started opening containers.

"Liam, how was the game?" Brittany asked.

"We won, so it went well enough," Liam said.

"He's being modest," Harlan said, taking the container Liam offered him. "He got three assists last night."

"It's an overrated stat. The only one that matters is that shot that hit the crossbar and deflected away from the friggin' goal."

Emma finished the post, forwarded it to Brittany, and set down her phone. "You know, self-pity is a wildly attractive trait," Emma said. "Do go on. You're getting hotter by the minute."

Liam dropped his head and shook it with a low laugh. "I want to throw this bag at you so bad."

Emma kicked his leg with a bare foot. "Don't even think about it. It would be like a scene from one of your kung fu movies. A plastic knife would get lodged in my throat, and a fork would stick in the center of my forehead." She pantomimed getting stabbed in both places.

"No way. Because I'd be aiming both at that sassy mouth of yours."

She nudged him again, and he grabbed her foot, holding it softly but firmly in a way that sent a shiver from her toes up to the top of her head. She was anticipating a tickle fight that she wouldn't mind in the slightest when Harlan shifted visibly on the couch. He cleared his throat, and Emma pulled her foot back from Liam's grasp. She tucked it underneath her butt, leveraging the movement to reach for a takeout box and plastic fork. How could she let herself flirt like that?

She couldn't look at Liam's face. But a moment later, in between bites, he was asking Brittany about her week, and Brittany told him about her new acting class—the one Bryce had recommended.

Emma had managed to keep Brittany away from Bryce's profiles most of the day, and she was determined to maintain her streak.

"Did you guys know Brittany is fluent in Spanish?" Emma said. By way of distraction, it was not subtle. "I was doing my daily Spanish practice—"

"You're learning Spanish?" Liam asked.

"She has a daily plan to improve her mind," Brittany said. "She reads nonfiction books and scientific articles and is learning Spanish."

"And how's the plan working out for you, Ems?" Harlan asked. "Is it even weekly at this point?"

Emma imagined throwing a knife into Harlan's throat. "How do you say 'Shut up' in Spanish?" Emma asked Brittany.

"*Cállate.*"

"Right. Harlan, *cállate* your stupid mouth."

"Calm down. I'm only joking. You're the one who thinks this stuff is necessary. I think you're plenty impressive as you are."

"Yes, I am," she said. "And now you may all continue praising my virtues. Proceed."

Why couldn't she look at Liam when she said that? Why did Harlan have to care who she dated? Why did Liam have to be leaving in January? Why did he have to be here at all if they couldn't smile and flirt and tease? Stupid Emma. Stupid Liam.

She looked up at the TV and saw an image of . . .

No.

He couldn't have.

"Um, hey, Britt, would you run to the kitchen and get me some water? I have a tickle—" Emma was saying, but Brittany had noticed the shocked stares on Liam and Harlan's faces. She looked at the TV, at the breaking news from E!

Bryce Elton Marries KeyAra in Vegas Chapel O' Love.

"Unmute it," Brittany was saying in a half whisper, half shriek, which Emma hadn't realized people did in real life. "UNMUTE IT."

Harlan unmuted the TV.

A picture flashed onto the screen of Bryce and KeyAra with their tongues down each other's throats, followed by another picture of them holding hands bearing matching gold wedding bands. They both looked drunk, although not stupid drunk. Bryce was wearing a powder-blue tux, and KeyAra a sheer, white minidress. Her bouquet was surprisingly understated, tasteful even . . . an odd contrast to the network's black censor bars over the woman's breasts and butt.

The anchor was describing their whirlwind romance in a script Emma could have written herself: Bryce and KeyAra had met on Friday night, had spent all day Saturday together "falling deeply in love," and by the early hours of Sunday morning, they had known they were soul mates and were eager to pledge their lives to one another.

Emma's script would have included a lot more gagging and eye-rolling, but the major events were all there and in the right order. KeyAra had followed Bryce to New York, and the pair would ship her belongings out sometime in the foreseeable future. The anchor seemed confident that this would only boost both of their careers. In fact, they'd evidently already released a video on YouTube about their wedding that had thirty million views. It was a how-to guide to throwing a last-minute wedding, and Emma imagined it featured an uncomfortable amount of mutual groping.

Emma opened her mouth to make any of the ninety-four snide comments that had come to mind in the last few seconds, but a glimpse of Brittany's face made the thoughts crumble like a dry biscuit. Her wide eyes were red, her face was white—making her few freckles stand out all the more—and her hands were clasped over her open mouth. "No," she was whispering. "No."

Emma knelt by Brittany, putting a hand on her friend's shoulder. "He isn't worth it, Britt. Remember? We've talked about this. He isn't as sweet as we thought, or he'd never have run off on you with no explanation just to marry the next woman he saw."

"No," she said. "It can't be like that. He's different, Emma. He must . . . he must really love her. He must see in her everything he couldn't see in me." Brittany stood. "I'm sorry. I need to go. I can't be here."

"Britt, no, stay! You don't want to be alone right now—"

"Yes, I do. I'm sorry, Emma." Brittany ran from the room. A few seconds later, the door to the condo opened and closed.

"Stupid Emma!" She threw herself back onto the couch, burying her face in her hands. "How could I let this happen?"

She was waiting for Liam to drop a truth bomb that would explode all over her and sink her farther into the ground where she belonged. But he didn't. Instead, he said, "Brittany forgot her bag. I'm going to run it out to her and then call it a night. See you tomorrow, Harley. Bye, Emma."

Liam grabbed the bag and left almost as quickly as Brittany had. She almost would have preferred the truth bomb.

"Why are you beating yourself over this, Ems?" Harlan asked when they were alone. "You didn't do anything wrong."

"Didn't I? I'm the one who exposed Brittany to all of this in the first place. I convinced her to give up that job in Ohio. I introduced her to Bryce, encouraged her to pursue acting, and now she's heartbroken."

"Stop for a second and look at this rationally, okay? You helped her see that there's more out there than being a local meteorologist. You helped her network and found her an opportunity. You didn't make her fall for Bryce or make him run off to Vegas for a quickie wedding—"

"I'm more at fault there than you think." She told him about how Bryce had cornered her last week, insisting he'd done everything for her because she wanted him to.

"He said that? He said he did all of that because you wanted him to? Man, that dude needs a punch to the teeth."

"Believe me, I've fantasized about it all week."

"What a douchebag. I'm sorry, sis. But it's still not your fault. Brittany's a big girl and can make decisions for herself. And Bryce is a loser who probably can't spell the word *consensual*, let alone use it in a sentence."

"Should I have told Brittany? After he hit on me and ran off like that, should I have let her know what a manipulative prick he is?"

"To what end? So she could feel like he rejected her twice? No, it would only make her resent you for coming between the two of them. What she doesn't know won't hurt her."

"Except she already is hurt."

"Yeah, but not by you. Do you want to lose the best assistant you've had in years? I wouldn't risk it."

She went to bed that night with Harlan's words playing on repeat: if she told Brittany, she'd lose her.

She knew all too well what happened when people learned things they didn't want to hear. Look what had happened when her mom had learned about her dad's affairs.

No, everyone had skeletons in their closet. She could keep hers locked up tight if it meant keeping Brittany as a friend. The truth wasn't worth the risk.

CHAPTER FIFTEEN

Emma loved visiting Weston's set. He was so high in demand now that even a quick break was a feat, but he'd sworn that he'd always make time for her, and the following Wednesday, he did. She sat with him in his office-slash-dressing room, which was far bigger than their dressing rooms on *My Valentines* had ever been.

"Um, hello, could you be more fancy? Look at this! Nadège hand-made you a suit herself and sent it to you as a congratulations gift? You're killing me, Weston."

Only Weston could look humble instead of utterly pleased with himself. "We're old friends from our Jacques days."

"Well, send your old friends my way, will you? I could use some."

"Nutmeg. You have been gloomy every morning this week, and now you're bringing that dark cloud to my office? Spill."

A stab of guilt ran through her. He'd worked so hard to get here, and she was cluttering up his life with her worries.

"It's no biggie. I'm worried about Brittany, because she's so upset about Bryce."

"I warned you about how impressionable she is. She's a quick learner, but she doesn't have any life experience to give her wisdom yet. Marcus told me that her life has been like a postcard. She has a good home, a great family. School was never a problem—she was the homecoming queen but evidently immune to all of the bullying and eating disorders that TV warns you about. She's only ever had one real boyfriend, and they broke up just after graduation. She's a kitten, sweetie. She was destined to fall too hard for someone—or something—the second the opportunity arose. But that doesn't mean she can't shake it off. Who better to help her do so than you?"

"Maybe you're right. Harley agrees with you, at any rate."

"Well, if your little brother agrees with the president of the Emma Crawford Fan Club, you know we're onto something."

Emma sat back in the cushy armchair. "You're right. I just don't like seeing Brittany hurt."

"You have a candy-coated shell, Emma Crawford," Weston said. "It looks hard at first glance, but it melts fast and is sweet as can be."

"Great, now I want candy. Thanks a lot, Weston." She reached for a bowl of sugar-free mints that he kept on his desk, but he swatted her hand away.

"Not until you improve that high kick. I was embarrassed for you this morning."

———

Emma kept waiting for something to snap Brittany from her funk. And on Thursday, she hoped it would finally come. Brittany's episode of *So the Night Falls* was airing—the one where she had speaking lines. They'd already watched the scenes where she showed up as an extra, but it had been hard to spot her in the crowds of people at the fake hospital. But this would be different. Emma knew it. Misha, Jamal, Kimmie, Liam, and some housemates joined Harlan, his assistant Sean, Brittany, and Emma at Harlan's condo. Liam and his housemates all came wearing white T-shirts with the words "Brittany Smith Fan Club" screen-printed on them. Brittany broke into her first grin of the week.

"You guys didn't have to do that for me!"

"Yeah, we did," Luis told her. "You're going to be famous one day, and we need to make sure that we're on your list of people you knew and liked before you were famous. Hence, the T-shirts."

"*Hence?*" Emma repeated. "Luis, are you trying to sweet-talk my girl?"

Luis's cheeks went red. "What? Me? No. Shut up." He mumbled something in Spanish, and Emma saw Brittany smile to herself.

"You know she's fluent in Spanish, right?" Emma asked.

Luis got up and walked into the kitchen, his teammates laughing at his departure.

"Okay, everyone shut your traps! The show is starting!"

Like any soap opera, decades of context underscored every scene, and virtually none of it was necessary for comprehension. When Simone kissed Rhys, Kimmie threw popcorn at the screen, and when Killian crawled out of the hole that Taysom had left him in, everyone cheered. But when Bryce's character, Robbie, whispered his urgent prayer in the hospital break room, everyone fell silent. Brittany's lip was trembling just watching Bryce.

Then, in came Brittany herself. Her skin was translucent, and she had a soft glow that made her look like a guardian angel. The scene was even better than Emma remembered, and Brittany even more captivating. When she told Robbie that it's always darkest just before the dawn, she noticed more than one person watching with baited breath. After Brittany's exit, everyone applauded.

"You were amazing!"

"Fantastic, dude!"

"Seriously, that was so good! You stole the scene!"

Brittany's glow returned as she basked in their warmth and good-will. "Thanks. You guys are too kind."

"No, you're just that fabulous," Emma insisted.

The party disbanded shortly after—it was a miracle that so many of their friends could show up on such short notice—but Brittany seemed closer to herself for the rest of the day. And that was more than worth it.

By Friday night, Emma was in such a good mood that she got dressed for Weston's dinner party without remembering just who it was for. In fact, she forgot the whole way to Weston's Midtown loft. But when she, Brittany, Harlan, and Liam stepped onto the elevator, the smell crashed into her like a wave.

Emma sniffed. "Is that . . . bergamot and musk?"

Brittany nodded. "And something else too. Maybe ginger?"

"Nutmeg," Liam said. "Why?"

Emma exhaled in resignation. "It's Calvin Klein One. I can't believe I forgot that we're going to see—" The elevator doors opened. "Kelly!" Emma cried as the woman pulled her from the elevator, practically suffocating Emma with affection.

"Emma! My sweet, darling girl! It's so wonderful to see you! It's been so long."

"We just ran into each other last week."

"I know, but to live in the same building and to never see each other?"

Yeah, you've mentioned that before. "Well, Highbury is big," Emma said, but Kelly wasn't listening. She squeezed Emma into another hug.

"I love getting your updates every week," Kelly said. "Your post about the donuts is my favorite. Do you remember the one? You had a spot of cream on your nose? Or was it jelly on your cheek? Hang on, let me check." She pulled out her phone, put in her thumbprint, and switched to the other thumb when her phone gave her an error. "I'm always doing that. Now just hold on." She looked through her apps for Instagram, swiped to another screen, and then another, only to come back to the first screen and find it.

"It's really okay. I know the picture you're talking about."

"Do you? Good. Did you read my comment? What did I say? Let's see here . . ."

She was scrolling through the comments. All 1,980 of them.

"Actually, I think I do remember it!" Emma lied. "It was so sweet of you!"

Kelly brightened and put her phone down. Mercifully. "Oh, I'm so glad you liked it. I said something like, 'Boston cream? More like Boston *dream*!' And then I added that little smiley face with the heart eyes? But I wasn't sure if it made sense, because you're not from Boston; you're from New York. I deleted and rewrote it maybe five or six times, but I couldn't think of anything better, so I finally decided to rewrite it and hope you knew what I meant."

"I did. And it put a smile on my face."

"Oh, that means so much to me! I love getting to keep up with you on social media."

Emma looked around in a panic, desperate for someone to save her. Instead, her eyes found Vic. Victoria Alba, in the flawless flesh, with her thick black hair, soulful brown eyes, and lips that had actual memes about them. She smiled at Emma with a look that conveyed a warmth and graciousness Emma couldn't fake right now if she tried.

Maybe Vic really was the better actor.

Emma's attention snapped back to Kelly. "So, Kelly. Tell me how you are. It's been so long."

"I've been seeing a new nutritionist, you know. Did I mention that at Weston's party? Dear Victoria found me the best nutritionist in Manhattan. Monique is a miracle worker. I have so many sensitivities I never knew about, but Monique is relentless. Did you know I may be lactose sensitive? I never knew! I've had a glass of milk before bed almost every day since I was two years old. But not anymore. Monique had me cut out all dairy. Because of the lactose, you see. I cut it out for months, and now, if you can believe it, she wants me to start introducing small amounts of lactose *back into my diet*. She said she wants to see how much I can tolerate. We started with butter, and it turns out I can eat it."

"That makes sense. Butter is fat, and lactose is sugar. So butter couldn't have more than negligible traces of lactose in it."

"Oh no. Butter has lactose because it comes from cows."

Emma's smile hid her firmly gritted teeth.

"But I'm still not sure about yogurt or most cheeses. Unless it's part-skim mozzarella. I have that every day as my morning snack."

"But—"

"And the best part is that I've been reintroducing ice cream, and it hasn't caused almost any problems."

Someone had shoved a wrench in the wheels in Emma's head. Her brain was malfunctioning. "But . . . you know ice cream has a lot more lactose than cheese or yogurt . . ."

"Chocolate is best, although I had some pralines-and-cream that was good too. Vanilla isn't sitting with me as well, though Victoria said she doesn't see how vanilla ice cream could cause me problems when the others don't."

"Your niece is smart. You should listen to her."

Kelly's laugh was more incredulity. "*Smart*? I'd say she's more than smart! You know she already graduated from Stanford, don't you? Finished in two and a half years. The dean said he'd never seen someone so famous work so hard, and you know Natalie and Gerard both went there, too, don't you, and they're famous for having left Hollywood to pursue their degrees. But as well as they did, it's nothing compared to my Victoria."

Emma's teeth were clenched so hard she had to be cracking a tooth. "I'm thrilled to hear it."

Ten minutes later, Weston came by and stole Emma away. Kelly smiled at Weston. "I'm sure I've occupied Emma long enough. She's probably tired of listening to the stories of an old has-been."

Emma patted Kelly's arm. "Oh, stop. It's always good to see you, Kelly."

As Weston walked her from the living room through the spacious, minimalist loft, she bit her tongue. Weston didn't like anyone talking badly about anyone, although he never stopped her outright. He put up with everything she did. But she knew if she opened her mouth, a torrent of irritation would rush through the loft like a flood and wipe everything else away. A poor way to repay a man she loved better than her own father.

"You've been kind, Nutmeg," Weston said. "And I have a present for you because of it." He was directing her to another small group, where she saw a wave of dark-brown hair with natural sun streaks resting atop a body that could inspire a sculpture. Weston put his hand on the young man's shoulder, and he turned around, every inch the Adonis he was in his pictures. In fact, he was even better looking, because the wicked twinkle in his eye had never quite come through in pictures the way it came through now.

"Aleki Hale," Emma said. "In the flesh."

Aleki's smile was as playful as she'd hoped it would be, and his wide-set brown eyes practically danced. "Emma Crawford, as I live and breathe. Look at you: you're a goddess."

"Guilty."

Weston patted both of their cheeks. "Enjoy."

Aleki stepped away from the group he was talking to, which included—Emma realized with a twist in her stomach—Liam. She glanced to see him looking at her with an expression she could only call thoughtful. But he said something to Brittany, and the two of them started for the kitchen.

"So you're staying with Weston for the time being?" she asked Aleki. "How long will you be in New York?"

"A couple of months, most likely. I'm an associate agent now, so I can work from anywhere."

"Ooh, well aren't you fancy."

"I hear you only deserve the best, so . . ."

She laughed.

Aleki sidled up next to her, folded his arms, and leaned his head toward hers. "Okay, time for you to give me the rundown. Tell me about everyone. Who's who? Who do we like? Who do we pretend to like?"

She side-eyed him. "Are you setting me up? What did your uncle tell you?"

"He told me that yours is the most important opinion in the room, so I'd better pay attention to it. He also told me that—"

The door to the elevator opened, and half of the loft turned to see who stepped out.

"Crap on a cracker," Emma whispered.

"What? Who is it? Oh . . . don't I know those two? Whoa. That's a lot of leather and skin for a dinner party."

So this was KeyAra. The pictures on E! hadn't done her justice: she was even more of a Kardashian knockoff than Emma had expected. Her hair was dyed black and straightened to within an inch of its life. Her skin was tanned into a sort of ambiguous brown that fell somewhere between Liam's and Aleki's coloring and was positively unnatural on a white girl with teal contacts.

Somehow, this girl had twelve million followers on YouTube— twelve million people who watched her videos for makeup-and-fashion advice. And now relationship advice.

"Leather and Skin over there is KeyAra, a lifestyle YouTuber. I don't know much about her. But the guy still wearing full set makeup is her new husband, Bryce Elton—a soap star. I know more than enough about him. The two met in Vegas. A week ago." Emma's eyebrows told the rest of the story.

Aleki's eyebrows responded. "And came back married. Okay, then. I take it we don't like them."

"We're reserving judgment on her. But he's a manipulative, social-climbing snake."

"And why did my uncle invite him?"

"Because you know how he is: he sees the best in everyone, and I don't want to shatter the illusion. Bryce ambushed my interview with Britt last month. He offered to mentor her in the ways of the soap opera to save her from a life as a weatherperson in Ohio. She worked for her college station and caught the local news bug, but she's past that now. Anyway, Weston thought Bryce was a sweetheart for offering to help her."

Aleki looked as skeptical as she could have hoped. "I know guys like him. He wanted something from her, and when that didn't work, I bet he quit her like sugar."

"Something like that."

"So, what? Should we feel bad for the wife?" Aleki asked as Weston spoke to the pair with a welcoming smile. Whatever Weston said prompted an explosion of laughter from KeyAra.

"You're a flirt, aren't you?" KeyAra said loud enough for the neighbors downstairs to hear. She grabbed Weston by his suit lapels. "Well, you're two weeks too late, so you'd better stuff those pretty words back in your mouth, Mister Weston, because I won't be swayed: I belong to Mister Brycie now." She released the lapels and smoothed them down.

Emma's eyes found Harlan's. He was standing with Jamal's sister,

Kimmie, who'd arrived shortly after they had. Harlan widened his eyes, and they both looked away from one another before either of them started laughing and set off the other. Liam and Brittany made their way over a moment later. Brittany was pale and shaking and quite possibly on the verge of throwing up.

"This was unexpected," Liam said on Emma's other side.

"You think?" she muttered. She held out a hand to her friend. "Britt, come with me. You have to meet Weston's Great Dane."

"No," Brittany said, hugging her arms across her chest. "I need to see this. I need to get it through my head that he chose her over me. And I can see why. Look at her: she's gorgeous and cool and funny, and no one can take their eyes off her."

Emma looked at Liam, who seemed to be trying to connect the obnoxious woman in front of them to the description that Brittany was giving, and his brain was getting the same error as everyone else's: *does not compute.*

Aleki took a step toward Brittany. "I just realized why you look so familiar. I used to date this girl from . . . where was it?" He looked to Emma, who quickly mouthed, "*Cleveland.*" Aleki's eyes dropped back to Brittany's. "Cleveland! Her college station was legit. I know this is a long shot, but did you do local weather at any point?"

The heavens parted, and Brittany's face brightened like the sun. "Seriously? Yes, I was the meteorologist for Cleveland College my junior *and* senior year. Well, I wasn't technically a meteorologist yet. Wow. I can't believe you saw me."

"Yeah, I did. You were great. I remember telling my girlfriend how charismatic you were. What was that catch phrase you would always say at the end?"

Brittany cocked her head. "Um, I think it was, 'Back to you, Raul.'"

Aleki gave Brittany a big nod. "Right, 'Back to you, Raul.' Classic. Such delivery."

Emma hid a laugh.

"Come sit with me. I want to hear all about the high-stakes world of local meteorology."

Brittany laughed. "Oh, stop it. It's boring."

"It's not if you're telling it." Aleki guided Brittany to the table, where Weston was calling everyone to dinner.

Liam hung back with Emma. Or was she hanging back with him?

"Bryce is sure looking your way a lot for someone who just married his soul mate."

"I hadn't noticed," Emma said.

"Did he hit on you at your place the other night?"

"Why do you ask?"

"Just a hunch. I saw the way he acted at Brittany's party. For someone giving a toast to the guest of honor, he sure managed to make it about the wrong person."

"Well, we both know how much I love attention."

"Not like that. And I saw him conveniently disappear in your direction during the party. He left without saying a word to anyone shortly after that. And when you finally came back, you looked . . . I don't know. Not upset, more thrown."

She looked down to realize she was wringing her hands. She released them. Emma Crawford didn't wring her hands over anything, even something as sweet as Liam's concern. And why did he have to be concerned when he was leaving? When Harlan was so very in the way? "You seem to be keeping close tabs on me, Liam." She said it too lightly, too sarcastically, and Liam backed up. His face cleared. Exactly as she intended.

"We're friends. I care what happens to you."

She patted his arm like an aunt would, like the feeling of his skin didn't make her ache for more. "That's sweet, but remember that I already have a brother, okay. I don't need a second one."

Liam looked toward the table. If he was hurt, he was hiding it well. And how awful was she for wanting this charade to hurt him as much as it did her? "I think we're both full on the sibling front. Should we join the party?"

"After you."

CHAPTER SIXTEEN

Because Emma and Liam were the last to the table, they were stuck with the last two seats. And because Emma had stupidly followed Liam instead of leading the way herself, he got first dibs.

There was an open seat next to Kelly at one end of the table and another next to KeyAra opposite them.

Emma's mother had rediscovered Judaism last year, after moving in with her Orthodox boyfriend in Florida the second the divorce was finalized. The couple had visited over the summer and taken them out for Chinese food. When Harlan joked that pork fried rice was a way to lure Jews into hell, the boyfriend said, "Well, actually," and told them about Gehinom. It was the part of the "world to come" where wicked souls were sent. It wasn't like the Catholic version—no fire or brimstone—but rather a place where souls waited and evaluated their lives in order to be purified and ascend to the heaven option.

And boy, was she evaluating her life now. Liam sat beside Kelly and Vic, leaving Emma to take the last empty seat next to KeyAra and, by extension, Bryce.

Weston was welcoming everyone to his home, being charming and kind and adorable, as always. At least, Emma imagined he was. She couldn't say for certain, because KeyAra was talking over him, commenting on the place settings, on the ombre apple-candle centerpieces, on the chandelier, and the view. She kept leaning over to Bryce, slapping his arm, and pointing to something in Weston's loft and saying, "Ooh, he fancy."

"Mr. Brycie, look at this china. It's exquisite," she said, flipping the plate up and taking a picture of the bottom. "And now our china will be exquisite too." She gave a pursed-lip smile that she must have picked up from watching reruns of *America's Next Top Model.* "Not that you need much help, Mr. Brycie. Your apartment is for reals gorgeous."

Bryce kissed KeyAra's hand. "My lifestyle may not be enough for every woman, but I'm glad that the *right* woman can appreciate it."

Her mom's boyfriend had been wrong. Hell was real.

When dinner was served, KeyAra's questions for Weston through "Mr. Brycie" continued. "Ask Weston what this little sausage thing is called," and "Ask Weston if we can take some of this sauce home. I want to slather it all over . . ."

Emma tuned in to Kelly and Liam's conversation across the table to save herself from hearing what KeyAra wanted Weston's sauce for.

"My gluten sensitivity is so tricky," Kelly was telling Liam. "I never know what foods will set it off."

Liam was looking at her plate. "Aren't you worried about the bread?"

"Oh no, sourdough never gives me problems."

Emma could tell from the kink in Liam's neck that he was about to look up, about to make eye contact with her. She looked away before he could.

Her eyes shot down the table. Harlan and Kimmie were talking in low tones with their heads close together. Kimmie wore a smile even sexier than her navy dress, and Harlan was hanging on her every word.

Don't screw this up, Harley, Emma thought before giving her traitorous thoughts a shake. She liked Kimmie. She wanted something to work out with them. But she loved Harlan, and if anything went south, she'd support him, no matter what. Just like he would support her.

Another glance down the table showed Brittany smiling in between Aleki and her cousin Marcus. She seemed almost comfortable. But Emma caught the girl's eyes dart toward Bryce more than once.

Poor thing.

A sound like two eels fighting pulled Emma's attention back to her surroundings. KeyAra was kissing Bryce. But not just kissing him. Her lips had his in a death lock that Emma was sure would lead to Bryce having to get an emergency lipectomy.

She shuddered.

"Mmm, Mr. Brycie. Your lips are like candy."

Bryce's smile was coy and nauseating. "I may not be much to some women, but it's nice to know that the *right* woman finds me attractive."

KeyAra laughed and assured "Mr. Brycie" of his stunning beauty. Emma pitied the girl. Because Bryce's little running comments had nothing to do with KeyAra and everything to do with Emma.

When the main course of grilled lamb chops was served, the conversation at Weston's end of the table shifted. Marcus brought up the name of a producer who had recently been outed as a serial harasser. Weston was shaking his head, saying how the man had betrayed and harmed so many people. "Power turns people into their truest selves. Good people take every opportunity to do good; bad people take every opportunity to become monsters. From everything I'm hearing, Harold is as big a monster as anyone."

"It brings up such a brutal question," Marcus said, "of the role of victims. They don't owe anyone anything. But what do we owe them? How can we empower them with a voice? If we could provide a space for them to speak up, think of—"

There was a knock on the table, and Emma looked to see that Kelly's glass had fallen, and her drink had spilled. It was spreading across the table, reaching KeyAra's place setting and still going. KeyAra jumped up, as if it were acid instead of ice water falling on her leather miniskirt.

"Oh, I'm sorry. I'm so, so sorry," Kelly said. The hand covering her mouth was trembling. She stared at the water's path in horror, looking too thrown to act. Vic was already on her feet, dabbing at the tablecloth with her and her aunt's napkins. Liam was only a beat behind her.

"It's no problem," Weston said, walking toward the kitchen. He returned with towels. Emma stood and helped now, too, and in a quick minute, it was like nothing had happened. The white tablecloth barely looked worse for the wear.

Kelly apologized profusely before excusing herself. Victoria followed her.

What was that about?

Dinner continued, while KeyAra made a fuss about the effort of dry cleaning leather. When Bryce told her that he'd gladly buy her a new skirt, KeyAra clapped and kissed him too loudly. "Mr. Brycie, how did you know gifts are my love language?"

Bryce put his forehead to KeyAra's. "When it's the *right* woman, you just know."

Emma closed her eyes and exhaled slowly. She would give her right ovary for this night to end already.

It was an honest-to-goodness relief when Kelly returned a few minutes later and KeyAra scraped up enough tact to stop kvetching about the five drops of water that had hit her upper thighs.

The conversation was still focused on the producer, Harold Hawkins. Kimmie was talking about the impossible situation that victims were placed in and what a disservice society put on victims by expecting them to speak up instead of expecting the harassers to stop harassing.

"It goes back to one fact: If you want to stop rape, DUDES GOTTA STOP RAPING," Kimmie said.

Everyone nodded.

Victoria cleared her throat. "It's true, but until that happens, those of us coming up in this culture have to be smart." She put a hand on her aunt's. "Aunt Kelly has given me a lot of advice over the years, and I don't think I could have survived even this long without it." She looked at Emma. "Do you remember what she told us during our third season on *My Valentines*? That was the year we got boobs," Victoria told everyone.

"Some of us more than others," Emma said, and Victoria smiled with a small head shake.

"Anyway, she said there are a lot of bad people in this industry, and we couldn't predict who could hurt us, but we could make it hard for them. She said to think of it like defensive driving. If someone else hits you, it's always their fault, but if there's a way to avoid getting hit, you take it. She said to watch the eyes of the crew around people in power. If they avoided looking at the person, there was a good chance that person is bad news. And she said to never, ever go to a meeting without someone you trust completely. Maybe it's your manager or your assistant, your publicist, even your favorite wardrobe artist. Whomever. Do you remember any of this, Emma?"

Victoria's dark eyes were sweet and vulnerable, and Emma wasn't annoyed by the depth of their beauty in that moment.

"Actually, I do. I hadn't remembered who it came from, though. I thought it came from my dad. Or Weston."

Harlan laughed darkly. "You think Dad cared about you getting taken advantage of? Ha." The truth of those words hit a little too close.

"I'm flattered that you would hear such good advice and think of me," Weston said. "But I've heard Kelly give that advice before. That's all her."

Kelly's eyes were trained on the water stain. "Victoria has always been so sweet. Not many up-and-comers would listen to an old has-been like me."

"There's no one whose words I trust more in this world. You gave me everything I have."

Kelly squeezed Vic's hand. "To hear her, you'd think I somehow rescued her, when she's the one who saved me."

Emotion tickled Emma's nose, and she looked away from the display toward Harlan. He was watching Kimmie stir her drink. Weston and Aleki were smiling at each other. Marcus was patting Brittany's shoulder as she gazed longingly at Bryce, who was in a staring match with KeyAra.

She didn't know who Liam was looking at.

Weston said some nice words about the respect he had for everyone at the table, and he invited them all to break their diets for the night to try the best crème brûlée cheesecake he had ever made.

KeyAra hissed. "Ooh, is there any chance you have something with chocolate? I don't do cheesecake."

"I have a Black Forest gâteau—"

"That sounds like cherries. I hate cherries."

"Or several different kinds of gelato."

"Great! I'll just go into the kitchen and make myself at home. Thanks, Westie." She winked at him and headed straight for the kitchen.

The flash of Weston's dimple was the only evidence that he was amused by the situation. He excused himself to follow KeyAra.

"Mr. Brycie!" KeyAra called out. "Are you sure you want to leave Weston alone with me?"

"Excuse me," Bryce said to the table, as if anyone was paying attention. "My bride beckons."

Aleki coughed, and that was the only excuse Emma needed. She kept her head down as Bryce left the table, hoping that he would miss her silent shaking. But as soon as he turned the corner into the kitchen, the laughter she was covering exploded from her mouth.

She looked down the table at Aleki, who was grinning openly at her. "Emma Crawford!" he stage-whispered. "How rude!"

"You are trouble," she said.

His jaw fell open in feigned shock. "What do you mean? I just choked on a piece of ice. Why are you looking at me like that? I really did."

She narrowed her eyes at him but didn't say more. When she looked back to her side of the table, Vic and Liam were watching her. Neither looked happy.

Surprise, surprise.

When KeyAra, Bryce, and Weston all returned to the table, Weston asked KeyAra how she liked being a lifestyle YouTuber.

"Oh, it's the best job in the world. All you have to do is have a great camera and microphone, killer makeup skills, a flare for the dramatic, and a face like mine." She pursed her lips and smiled with her eyes. Smizing seemed to be the signature move of the couple soon to be known as BryAra.

"That's not all there is to it," Bryce said. "She spends hours a day shooting and editing, and she's always reaching out to new brands about partnerships. She gets sent thousands of dollars in merchandise every week, and she turns down more opportunities than she could keep up with. She's a business savant."

Maybe KeyAra really was as business savvy as Bryce was describing. Emma knew there was a lot more to KeyAra's job than putting on lipstick and sitting in front of a camera for fifteen minutes. But Bryce was a little too eager to convince everyone of how proud he was of his wife, and Emma was a little too exhausted to keep this fake smile on her face for much longer.

People had no idea how hard acting really was.

"Mr. Brycie is sweet, but he's also right." KeyAra looked across her at Vic and then at Emma. "You know, the three of us could come up with enough content to get every major brand in fashion knocking down our door. Can you imagine? People would be *obsessed* with our videos. Vic, you're, like, the hottest deep chick I've ever seen in real life, let alone on TV. I could just apply makeup to you, and you could say all the profound things you write in your songs, and people would lose. Their. Minds." She punctuated each of the final words with a clap.

"Sorry, I have an exclusive with Jacques until I'm twenty-one," Emma said, preempting whatever KeyAra was about to say about her.

"Do you actually wear their stuff? I mean, their clothes are pretty fab, but, like, you're not wearing their primer right now, are you? Their formula is totally off. They shouldn't have used both iron oxide *and* mica. Makes it pill."

"I haven't noticed that problem." Emma didn't know why she was lying. The pilling was her biggest complaint with Jacques's primer. But she'd made a lot of money from her partnership with the brand, and to hear this surprisingly insightful comment from someone who made Emma want to shove pencils in her ears was, well, no. It was just *no*.

KeyAra squinted, her eyes roving Emma's face for the tiny little balls of primer that would totally be there, if Emma weren't wearing a different brand. As it was, Emma's makeup was flawless.

"Hmm. Maybe I got a bad batch."

"Maybe," Emma said.

"Anyway, they haven't branched out into sheet masks yet, so unless they have that in the works, they're in for a rude awakening. Good thing you only have two years left on that contract." Emma didn't answer, and KeyAra didn't stop talking. "Now, Vic, how much will it take to get you on board, hmm? I won't take no for an answer."

"Oh, I couldn't possibly. I wouldn't know the first thing about giving fashion or makeup advice."

"You are so cute. *I* know about that stuff. Come on. Just say yes!"

Another signature move of the BryAra power couple: not knowing when to take no for an answer.

The conversation quickly devolved into a series of demands and rejections.

KeyAra: "I have the wildest idea: Let's go clubbing!"

Everyone: "No!"

KeyAra: "How about I just record, like, a couple of minutes with everyone right now."

Everyone: "No!"

KeyAra: "I'm so tired, Mr. Brycie, why don't you rub my feet while Vic plays us something."

Vic: "I don't have my guitar."

Aleki: "Uncle Weston, don't you have one in your room?"

Emma (in her head): *No!*

And so on.

CHAPTER SEVENTEEN

Harlan decided to go out with Kimmie that night, and Brittany and Marcus were close enough to walk back to their place in Hell's Kitchen, so that left Emma and Liam to share a car to the Upper West Side together.

"Can we just talk about how I was a model of restraint tonight?" Emma asked as soon as her back hit the leather. "Between Kelly's absurd diet and KeyAra's absurd existence, I can't believe I didn't blow up. I literally almost lost it at least a dozen times."

"Yeah, you were the very picture of self-control," Liam said.

"I really was. There was only that one time, when Aleki laughcoughed like that? I couldn't hold it in anymore. How did you handle it all night?"

She rolled her head against the back of the seat toward him. He was staring out the window. "I just listened."

"But wasn't it intolerable? Kelly kept talking about her gluten sensitivity *while she was eating bread*. I just can't listen to it anymore. And don't even get me started on KeyAra. I could go off."

"KeyAra isn't a person; she's a brand. There's a guy on Arsenal who's exactly like her. He's a benchwarmer and not getting any better, but he's super good-looking and trendy and has become this big online influencer. He's leveraged his fame to make the team keep him around. KeyAra's savvy like that. She knows exactly what she's doing."

"You're right, and she's using her *savvy* for evil instead of good."

"Can't argue there."

"Oh, hello. Is the cat finally coming out to play? I was wondering if you'd let yourself be candid for even a second."

161

He turned to face her. "Yes, KeyAra's persona is obnoxious. She's a calculated facade, and she gladly makes money off of it. But Kelly? Come on, Emma. She's a sad, broken woman. I feel awful for her."

"So do I! My heart aches for her. Every cheat day, I feel a spike of fear about how easy it is to go from headliner to footnote. But she still has a good life—a better life than most of the world. She's still wealthy—she always talked about how saving half of everything she earned was the best business decision she ever made. She has Vic, who obviously doesn't find her the least bit tiresome. She has good friends—"

"And yet she still struggles with her self-image, and she can't do the job she loves most in the world, not because she's not good at it, but because of something that happened before we even hit puberty. The world has told her that the core of who she is unworthy."

"You're reading too much into this, Liam. Yes, Hollywood cares about appearances as much as it cares about actual talent. Maybe even more. But you're forgetting that Kelly had a couple of bad movies before she ever went to rehab for her eating disorder. Remember *Meet the Krubskies*? Or the remake of *My Stepmother Is an Alien?* I agree that she was talented, but Hollywood is fickle even when there's no backstory."

He leaned back, letting Emma watch the stream of cars and street-lights pass through his window. "I know what you're saying. The same thing happened to my dad. A couple of bad movies, and suddenly he's on a cable sci-fi TV series instead of sitting with his former friends at the Oscars. But is that all that happened to Kelly?"

"She's a profoundly silly woman. Maybe people on set agreed. You can feel sorry for her and still acknowledge that possibility, can't you?"

He didn't answer.

"Dude, can't you just let yourself not like someone sometimes?"

"I didn't care for Aleki."

Emma popped her eyes out. "What? How could you not like him?

He's intelligent, charming, knows exactly how to include people, he's steady—"

"He's not remotely steady."

"And you can make this judgment after the five seconds he spoke at dinner tonight?"

"No, I can make it based on the thirty minutes I talked to him before Weston introduced you guys, based on the fact that he could have distracted Brittany any number of ways, but instead he chose a lie that would devastate her if she found out, and the fact that he laughed at Bryce and KeyAra in front of an audience the second their backs were turned. The world is like reality TV to him."

"By that logic, I'm as much of a joke as he is."

"Your ability to make any conversation about you is almost stunning."

His words hit her like a punch to the gut. "Wow. What a douchey thing to say."

Liam slammed his eyes closed. He looked like he was in pain, and Emma was glad of it. He took two, maybe three long breaths. "You're right. That was douchey of me, and it's not what I meant. What I meant was that my logic doesn't apply to you, because you also did some really nice things tonight. You went to Weston's dinner party because you love him, despite knowing how much the guests would annoy you. You made sure Brittany was looked after. You were sweet with Kelly, even though I know how badly you wanted to talk to anyone else."

"If it was that obvious, I couldn't have been that sweet."

"Only because I know you. And because you've mentioned how annoying she is a time or two."

"Guilty."

"I shouldn't have said you make conversations about you. That's not true. But I don't want you to internalize someone else's flaws just because you can relate to them. I think Aleki is kind of a joke. Yes, you laughed after he did, and I thought it was rude. But I also know how much more there is to you than that single moment."

How had he managed to be a tool, apologize, and come off so mature and measured that she couldn't even let herself stay mad at him? Why couldn't he just be a jerk so she could stew in her anger for even a minute?

She studied him, his smooth jaw, slightly crooked nose—from a break?—the dark slashes of eyebrows that framed his eyes. She liked everything she knew about Aleki so far. But Liam was right about one thing: Aleki wasn't steady. Not compared to Liam.

"What?" His brow wrinkled.

"Does the weight of being perfect ever exhaust you?"

"You think I think I'm perfect?"

"I think you feel like you have to be. You always have to think everything through, you have to have justification for a bad opinion of Aleki or even KeyAra, and your justifications make perfect sense, even if I disagree with your conclusions. You're so reasonable about everything. So committed to kindness. You set a high bar." She'd meant to sound snarky. Not earnest.

The lights outside kept illuminating different sections of his face: the way his lips were pulled tight, the way his eyebrows were laced together, the way he was staring at her, unblinking. "I wish I were half the person you're describing."

"Oh, come on. You're a choirboy. Perfect teammate, perfect friend, perfect brother."

He scoffed.

"Name one bad thing you've ever done. No, I mean it. I'm not talking about speeding or skipping classes. Something you regret."

He looked away now, his eyes reflecting the steady stream of lights outside the car. "Did you know that after my dad died, my mom came home wasted and broke Finley's jaw? She found Finley watching one of my dad's old movies because she missed him so much, and my mom lost it. The guy she brought home turned out to be an off-duty officer, and that's the only reason Finley wasn't hurt worse."

Emma nodded.

"Did you ever wonder why Finley was alone?"

"You had a soccer game out of town—"

"I lied. The soccer game was a two-hour bus ride we took the next morning. I stayed at a friend's house because I couldn't handle being home for another minute. I didn't know if my mom would be home or not. I hoped she wouldn't be. But I was so tired of the yelling and the screaming and the hitting that I—" He squeezed his eyes shut. "I just left her there."

Emma pictured the small cigarette burns that covered Finley's shoulders and back, sure that what Liam was remembering was so much worse. "Liam, that's not on you. It wasn't your job to keep her safe—"

"Then whose was it?"

"You were so young—"

"I was seventeen, Emma. I wasn't a kid. I was all she had, and I abandoned her, even though I knew she had it worse than I did." His face looked like an open wound, red and throbbing. His tears left an angry trail down his cheeks.

"You can't beat yourself up over this. Pain isn't a competition. She would never blame you for trying to protect yourself—"

"She should. If she knew what I did, she would." He covered his face with one hand as sobs burst from him.

Emma grabbed his free hand from where it was balled in a fist on his leg. She smoothed out the tight muscles and threaded her fingers through his, kissing his hand before covering it in hers. "She wouldn't,

Liam. You aren't to blame for what happened. You could as easily have been asleep already or in another room when your mom came home and found Finley. The officer stopped her as soon as he saw what was happening. You couldn't have done any better than he did, and if you'd been there, your mom would never have gone to prison, because no one would have known. You protected yourself at a time when you were hurt and scared and sad, and you were both saved in the process."

Liam sniffed and dashed the tears on his face with his free hand. "She worships me, and I've done nothing to deserve it. I've chosen myself over her time and time again. When my mom came back into our lives last year, I was too relieved that I was in Europe to think about what my absence would do to Finley. Do you know how easily I could have come home? I didn't have practice or tryouts for three straight days, but I didn't do it. All I cared about was that I wouldn't have to see my mom. I hate her. I hate what she did to us. Finley's trying to learn how to forgive her, but I don't want to. I want her to rot in hell."

Emma slid her finger under Liam's watchband and felt the burn mark branded into him. She touched it softly with the pad of her finger. "I don't blame you. But Finley is strong, and she knows that you love her unconditionally."

"Unless my mom is around."

"No. That doesn't change your love for your sister. You have a history of serious trauma, Liam. Maybe you need to process that still, but that doesn't mean that you're not an amazing brother. Finley told me about all the times that you *did* jump in to protect her, how you physically restrained your mom. And knowing you, I'd bet there were times that your mom wanted to hurt someone, and you drew her anger to yourself, didn't you?"

Liam's chest heaved, and he bit his lip before giving a short nod.

"Your mom is the only one at fault here. You have to see that."

He squeezed her hand, and she squeezed back. When his eyes finally met hers, they were dark pools of sadness and hope, and she wished that she could take away every bad memory, every hurt and tear that his mom had inflicted upon him. "I've never said any of this out loud." His words were as fragile as a thin layer of ice over a puddle. "I've been too afraid of how people would look at me if they knew."

Emma's heart felt like it was expanding in her chest. She was the only person he'd trusted with his greatest shame. "And that's why you try not to judge other people too harshly."

Liam's mouth twisted, like he was trying not to cry again. But he nodded.

"If anyone judges you, I'll bury the body. Deal?"

A ghost of a smile appeared on his face. "Deal."

Emma asked her driver to drop them off at Liam's townhouse before taking her to Highbury Lane. When the car pulled up to his row of brick buildings—construction be damned—Emma stepped out of the car with Liam. She folded her arms around him softly, but his return hug was tight, and the way he held her, the way he breathed her in like she was oxygen . . .

"Thanks, Emma," he whispered into her hair, and her eyes closed at the feeling of his shaky breath and pounding heart.

"Anytime."

CHAPTER EIGHTEEN

For months, Emma had managed to live in the same building as Kelly and hardly ever see the woman. But now that Vic was in town, they seemed to be drawn together like magnets. Weston had asked Emma to show Aleki around Manhattan, so he was with her when they bumped into Vic and Kelly at Emma's favorite coffee shop.

"On your six," Aleki said, looking directly behind Emma. "We have a Vic and Kelly incoming. Are you ready?"

"To hear about Kelly's phantom sensitivity to Kona coffee beans while she sips on an espresso? No. Do we have time to sneak out the back?"

"We don't have our drinks."

"Do we really need them?"

"Yes." He put a hand on Emma's head and shook it lightly. "You can do this. I'm imbuing you with all the strength in my severely under-caffeinated body."

"Boo. You're buying now."

"I take it back. Let's sneak out."

"Ha."

The line was long enough that Vic and Kelly couldn't see them immediately. At least, they wouldn't have been able to if the six-foot-three Aleki didn't keep standing on his tiptoes, peering over the crowd, and then reporting everything he saw in an exaggerated whisper.

"You won't believe it," he whisper-yelled. "Victoria grabbed a menu and is looking at the breakfast sandwiches. At four in the afternoon!"

"For shame," Emma said.

"Oh no, Kelly is pointing at the menu and—what's this? Yes, it looks like she's asking questions."

"Hmm."

"Still asking questions."

Their names were called, and the barista handed them their drinks.

"She's *still* asking questions . . . whoops. No, she stopped."

Emma took a sip of her green tea "Okay. Why the *whoops*?"

"Because they just spotted me."

"Aleki Hale. You will be the death of me." Emma started toward the two women.

"We just met, and you're already talking till death do us part?"

She elbowed his rock-hard stomach in lieu of shushing him. He looked delighted by the turn of events. Her thoughts turned to Liam's words from last weekend—not that Liam had made a single appearance in person or text since then. How had he said it? Aleki watched the world like everyone was in a reality TV show.

Liam wasn't wrong.

"Hi. Fancy meeting you two here," Emma said. "Weston asked me to babysit Aleki for the day. I guess he was throwing tantrums at the studio because he missed his nap."

Kelly's tittering was loud enough that, if most of the patrons weren't already watching the reunion of Emma and Vic, they'd have started. "*Throwing tantrums* . . . you make it sound like he's a little boy!"

Emma leaned in, smiling conspiratorially. "I knew you'd pick up on that."

"Victoria, have you thought anymore about my offer?" Aleki asked with a playful expression, his eyes roving Vic's face.

Vic blinked, but it lasted a fraction of a second too long, as if she was annoyed by the reminder. She looked at Emma before looking back at him. "I have. But I don't think now's the time for me to make a change. I told you before: I'm taking a break, not looking to get into a new partnership."

Emma looked at Kelly, whose eyes were bouncing back and forth between Vic's and Aleki's.

"You know how to reach me if you change your mind," Aleki said with a tight smile. "We'll see you both later."

He put a hand on Emma's back, and the two of them left the warm coffee shop and stepped outside into the chilly midafternoon air. The day was overcast, and Emma was already wearing a hat, but she put her sunglasses on, too, and zipped up her jacket to her chin. Star camouflage at its finest. Fifth Avenue Roasters coffee shop was on the east side of Central Park, a twenty-minute walk from Harlan's condo, but Emma's fitness regime had taken over her life. She couldn't let herself off easy, and opting for convenience on even little things was a recipe for disaster. Her trainer had been brutal that morning at her weigh-in. Emma had lost a pound, which meant she still had seven pounds of muscle to go. Her trainer had added two extra protein shakes a day, plus snacks. He'd sent a new meal plan directly to Brittany, who promised she'd have everything ready for Emma by that evening. He'd added more weights too. She needed to be deadlifting 190 pounds by filming in January.

Worst of all, her dad had found out. The studio must have told him, because he and Drew had scheduled a conference call with her not an hour after the crappy weigh-in. Her dad had drilled into her head how she needed to take her role more seriously. "You know, Victoria Alba would be just as good a Kára as you could be. If you aren't careful, the role could be hers in a second, and no one would even remember you'd been cast."

"I don't know that we need to go that far," Drew had said. "You're a superb actor, Emma, and they cast you for a reason. Martial arts is about mental toughness as much as physical toughness, right? So is your training. Channel that every time you have to wake up in the middle of the night to down a protein shake. You're strong. You can do it."

The memory of her dad's words were like a slap to the face. Why couldn't he have brought up someone else? Why did it always have to be Vic?

But his words had had their desired effect: she was more committed to the training and eating schedule than ever. She wasn't going to screw up an opportunity like this. She had less than three months until filming started. She could handle it.

"You're deep in thought," Aleki said. "You didn't even ask me what that was about with Vic back at the coffee shop."

"Sorry. I was just thinking about my new training schedule," she said, popping a handful of nuts. "What was that about?"

"Last week at Uncle Weston's, I tried to talk to her about me representing her if she makes her return to acting. Her current agent doesn't represent actors, whereas I'm learning to do both. So it would be a perfect fit."

"She seemed pretty disinterested."

"Tell me about it. I can't understand why, either. She knows the agency's reputation, and Weston can vouch for the fact that I've been trained by one of the best agents in the industry. I'm a hard worker. Committed. Dead sexy. What isn't to like?"

"Vic values her independence, which makes sense, given everything she had to go through to earn it. I imagine that entering into any sort of agreement or partnership is difficult for her." There. That was so generous a response that even Liam couldn't have faulted it.

"That feels like a nice way of saying she's inflexible and resistant to change. How did you work with her for so long?"

Whoa. Was this a landmine, or could she actually be candid? "Honestly, I never got to know her that well. She was pretty closed off. I got the feeling that her education and career were more important than relationships to her. She was super driven. I always looked like a lazy sack compared to her, even when I was working ahead or was up late memorizing a last-minute change in the script. It was never as much as Vic was doing. Ever." Her voice had gotten firmer, her tone sharper. Shoot. She'd just shown her hand, hadn't she?

"Didn't that get old? Always having to be around someone too dedicated to perfection to just be a human every now and then?"

Or maybe he understood better than she thought. Echoes of her conversation with Liam swirled in her mind. Maybe if she'd heard from him since then, she'd be more generous now. "It was exhausting. I felt like I was in constant competition with her, but she didn't even do me the courtesy of acknowledging that I was in the race. The first season, I would go to her dressing room sometimes and ask if she wanted to hang out, play cards or video games, talk—anything. We were both so young and still new enough to all of it that I'd hoped we'd be real friends, you know? But she was always doing something more important. If I had a crush, she had a calculus exam. If I had a grudge, she had a German tutor. Nothing was ever enough. I sure as hell wasn't. Eventually, I just gave up altogether."

"What was the point, right? What's the point of trying and trying with someone who keeps rejecting you?"

His tone and words halted her mid-nod. "You know her from LA, don't you?"

Aleki squinted behind his sunglasses.

"You guys have run into each other, and this isn't the first time you've tried to convince her to sign with you."

"You got me." He reached into her bag of nuts and took a small handful. "My agency started sending me VIP passes and invitations to parties as soon as Weston's show was announced and they realized that our being family could work in my favor. They promoted me from intern agent to associate agent. I met Vic at a party in the spring. She actually approached me, if you can believe it. She was asking me a million questions about agenting, talking about how she wanted to return to Hollywood but wasn't sure how to do it. We saw each other at a lot of events after that. When I told my boss, he gave me the job to land Vic. It hasn't worked out like I'd hoped."

"Yeah, she has that effect on people. But buck up, buttercup. You're now part of the elite club of people who aren't good enough for Victoria Alba."

He knocked his cup against hers. "I'll drink to that."

A week after their late-night discussion, Emma had yet to even hear from Liam. Harlan saw him every day at practice, but when Emma asked about him, Harlan just joked about Liam pulling a Running Man.

It hurt.

Liam had confessed something so personal that she had assumed it would bring them closer. It had made her wonder if they could stay close, even after he returned to England in January. But instead, he'd bolted.

On the other hand, Aleki was more present than ever. She'd admitted to a nearly decade-long competition with Vic, and he was only there for her more. His presence was the distraction she needed from thoughts of Liam. Aleki's habit of taking joy in absurdity was infectious, and Emma was able to speak more candidly than she did with anyone but Harlan. Her brother was only too happy with the arrangement.

"I've missed this Emma," he said after the two returned from a charity dinner late one evening. Aleki had gone as Emma's plus-one, while Harlan had taken a reality star he'd been Snapchatting with for the last week. They kicked off their shoes when they got home, and

Harlan fired up the Cooking Network before texting Sean to get him sleep aids from the pharmacy. It was only midnight, thankfully, so his assistant may not have even been asleep yet.

"You mean the Emma who slays it in slinky sequin dresses while raising money for refugee relief?"

"No, bozo. The Emma who doesn't question her place in the world. Ever since Chicago, you've been different. You looked like you had fun tonight. It feels like you're coming back."

If she had been different, wasn't that a good thing? Wasn't it growth to reevaluate who she was and where she belonged? And yet, Harlan was her biggest fan. If he welcomed the old Emma back, there was a reason. "Maybe I am."

"Good. I like Aleki."

"Then you should ask him out. Now toss me the remote. I can't watch more cooking shows, man."

"No. This is my house. You can move out if you have a problem with my TV choices."

She threw a pillow at his head. "So, why didn't you take Kimmie to the dinner tonight? It seemed like you guys were hitting it off at Weston's."

"We were. But I realized we're not as compatible as I thought. She's just not the right girl for me."

"Was this before you went back to her place or after?" Annoyance tinged her words.

"I take it back. New Emma is still here, sanctimonious as ever." He turned the volume up on *Iron Chef Junior*.

"Asking a question hardly makes me sanctimonious."

"That question does."

"Fine, how about a different question. Does Kimmie know she's not the right girl for you? Does she agree with your assessment of your incompatibility? Or is she sitting at home, wondering why you were calling and texting her for weeks and suddenly, she's been ghosted?"

Harlan sat up, his face turning red. "Where is this coming from? Is this really about me, or is it about Liam's obvious lack of interest in you?"

Emma was leaning back against the couch, but she still felt as if she were rocking backward. "What are you even talking about? There's nothing between Liam and me, and you're deflecting." She was about to rip into him, but the hollow look in his eyes calmed her tongue. She took a deep breath. "All I'm saying is that I don't want to see you fall back into your old patterns where you think a relationship is going to save you." It wasn't what she'd wanted to say. She'd wanted to tell him that his old patterns of using girls like disposable hand towels was perpetuating his cycle of self-hatred, but even she could tell how judgmental that would sound to him. And they never judged each other. They accepted each other, skeletons and all.

"I don't think a relationship is going to save me. But how am I supposed to know if a girl is right for me if I don't test out the relationship?"

"Maybe it's time to take a break from girls." *Or maybe it's time to stop treating girls like cars you can test drive and return.*

"Eh. Maybe. Maybe not." He sat back in the armchair and picked up his phone. "Man, what's taking Sean so long? You'd think there aren't a hundred 24-hour pharmacies between 34th Street and here."

"It's hard to find good help," she said, knowing the sarcasm would be lost on him.

"That's the truth."

Since Weston's party, Brittany had thrown herself into her work with such determination, she hardly seemed like the same person. Emma came into the kitchen one morning to find Brittany and Sean sitting on opposite ends of the bar, drinking their Diet Coke and Red Bull, respectively, while furiously typing away on their laptops.

"Britt, I didn't expect you here so early."

"Sean got me in touch with this huge network of celebrity assistants, and I realized I haven't been doing nearly enough, Emma." She looked distant, and Emma noticed the Bluetooth earphones in her ear. "Yes, that's right. You charged Ms. Crawford for the elite package, yet she posted about it on Instagram, which we both know is worth well over the $1,100 you've charged her. And yet, L'Eau Spa reached out to me just this morning offering a free spa treatment with no strings attached. I imagine they'll be very grateful when she posts about it next week. I wonder what people would think if she likes it even more than Serenity." She paused, her lips puckering tightly. Then her eyes popped. She took a slow breath, and Emma was sure it was to calm herself. "I'm so glad to hear it. Once the bill is settled, I'll schedule Ms. Crawford's next appointment. Yes, I could talk to her about a picture with a mask on. We'll write a caption that makes you both look good. Excellent. Thanks for your time."

Sean nodded at Brittany, while Emma stared at her assistant as if she were a stranger.

"Wow," she said. "That was impressive."

Brittany panted like she'd just run a marathon. "Thanks! That was scary. But I was talking to Natalie, Kirsten's assistant? She gave me the script she uses almost word for word. I cut out the cursing, but that's the third time it's worked this morning! It gets easier each time. And good news: I've had your charges canceled at Postino, La Belle, and now Serenity. All you have to do is post from each place next time. Can you believe it? Natalie told me that she does this for Kirsten, and they never pay for anything."

"Well, I don't need to be too much like Kirsten, okay? I don't like my feed getting too cluttered with ads. I already have some sponsored posts—"

"Right, I have those scheduled. Sean helped me create a calendar to make your feed more consistent content-wise. If we alternate a workout post, a 'real life' post, and a sponsored or freebie post each week, it should spread them out enough to keep the page's personality authentic."

"And mine."

Brittany beamed. Emma half expected to see a tail wagging behind her assistant. "I promise, the Emma Crawford brand will be intact."

Emma went to the refrigerator when she noticed the eggs, ham, and spinach on the counter under a heated cover. "Did you make me breakfast?" She'd already had her first shake of the day, but she had a lot of pounds to go.

"You and Harlan still haven't found a cook, and your trainer was very insistent about the exact proportions of your meals, so I thought I'd make it as easy as possible for you."

"You sure have." Emma took the plate and fork and joined Brittany at the counter. "So how is the acting class going?"

"It's good. But I'm so busy that I think I probably need to quit."

"Britt, no. You can't quit, and you don't have to be *this* busy. Getting comped is nice, but I can pay for the stuff I buy. And we can hire a cook. Or we can call for delivery—"

"That's my job, Emma. Speaking of which, I noticed that you've eaten at a few places that aren't on your list, so I've updated your favorites. Natalie and Sean have told me how much of my job relies on anticipating your needs, so I promise I won't let you down."

"You haven't let me down, Britt. You always rise to the occasion."

Brittany took a call and Emma listened to the assistant who, barely six weeks ago, couldn't speak to Harlan without squeaking like an eager mouse. Now she was telling TMZ that "Aleki Hale is the nephew of Emma's mentor, Weston. While they're having fun together, Emma and he are just friends."

Her little girl was growing up.

————————————

Much to Emma's dismay, the next morning, Weston's martial arts studio was overrun with undesirables. Not only had Bryce made a reappearance—no doubt hoping to cling to Weston's ever-rising star—but he'd brought his wife. She came in wearing a skintight leopard-print '80s-style leotard, dragging Vic along with her.

"Honey, if I have to be here at 5 a.m., you have to, too," KeyAra told Vic.

Since when had these two become friends?

Vic gave Emma a smile that she would think was sheepish on anyone else, but was probably meant to convey her gratitude for the opportunity to spend time strengthening her body-soul connection with cherished friends. Ugh.

"I didn't realize you came to Weston's class," Vic said.

"Haven't missed since I moved back to New York," Emma said, stepping back and forth and swinging out her arms and legs. Class wouldn't start for a few minutes, but she'd had another late night with Aleki, and she felt especially stiff.

"How is it being back?" Vic asked.

"Fine. It's home, you know?"

"Do you miss France? University?"

How was she supposed to answer this? If she said no, she'd seem like an uncultured, fame-hungry ignoramus. But if she said yes, then she'd seem like she was living her life on someone else's terms, that supporting her brother was somehow a sacrifice.

"Yes and no. The time was right for me to be there when I was, but now it's time for me to be back here. Who knows what next year will bring?"

Vic nodded, like what Emma had said was wise instead of cryptic, inane, and born of an insecurity only Vic could inspire.

"I hated being at Stanford," Vic said, copying Emma's movements. "I missed Aunt Kelly. I missed my band. I missed life. I didn't connect with almost anyone while I was there. I felt like I was a museum exhibit more than a person. I'm not as famous as you, but still, people always wanted to take selfies with me and have me record their voice mail message. It was humiliating. And then there were the people who thought I was just a phony there for a publicity stunt, including my roommates. I moved into my own place halfway through my first year and maxed out my course load so I could focus on studying and get out of there as fast as possible."

This was the most personal Vic had ever gotten with her. And it was so close to everything Emma had experienced that empathy and understanding rushed through her like adrenaline. "I know exac—"

"All right, all right, all right!" Weston called into his wireless fitness microphone. "Get those lazy butts moving. I'm talking to you, Crawford. You think a late night babysitting is going to buy you some kind of free pass in my class, you think wrong."

Emma saw Vic studying her out of the corner of her eye. For the first time in Emma's life, she wished Weston had been late.

When it came time for sparring, Weston paired them up by skill level, as he often did. And for the first time in her life, Emma felt like being paired with Vic wouldn't have been the worst thing in the world.

After class, Emma, KeyAra, and Vic went into the changing room together. KeyAra talked about how hard it was, how hot everyone was—Weston, all working it in his spandex like some ancient God, how delicious and manly Mr. Brycie was when he was dripping sweat, how Vic's legs were works of art, how obscenely distracting her own body was, even to her.

Emma didn't know whether to be offended or relieved that she didn't make KeyAra's list of "people and things at martial arts that are hot." KeyAra rushed out of the changing room ahead of them, eager to see her husband, and Emma caught up to walk with Vic.

"Hey, I keep thinking about what you said about your experience at Stanford," Emma said.

Vic waved her hand in the air. "Oh, don't. Forget about it. I was being dramatic." Vic said, her expression even more dismissive than her words.

What just happened? Hadn't Vic opened up and admitted something personal for the first time in the nine years they'd known each other? Maybe Vic thought Emma would judge her or wouldn't understand. But she did. Perfectly. "Well, I wanted to say that I-I kind of know what you mean."

"Yeah, college was a trip, wasn't it?" Vic said. "Off topic, how are things going with Aleki? It seems like you two are really hitting it off."

Emma's chest stung with the pain of burst hope. What was she thinking, expecting things to be different between them after so long? Yes, Vic had finally shared something vulnerable. But it had been a statement, not an invitation. Something to show that, in spite of her perfection, she, too, was relatable and had known isolation. Vic was too good for Emma and her drama. She didn't want to be friends. Why couldn't Emma get that through her head?

"Aleki's cool. We're having fun together," she said, unwilling to give Vic an iota more information than that.

"Are you? So glad to hear it."

"That's right, I forgot you two know each other," Emma said. "From LA."

"He told you that?"

"Sure. We talk."

Vic closed her eyes tightly, a clear marker of annoyance. Vic had been out of acting for too long, if she didn't realize how clearly she was broadcasting her emotions. "What did he say, exactly?"

"That you were shopping around for an agent who could represent you if you return to acting—"

"He told you I'm returning to acting?"

"Uh, everyone has told me, including your aunt. You know it was in an interview recently, right?"

Vic sighed. "I can't believe you read that."

Emma's spine stiffened. "I didn't. Harlan told me about it. Listen, all Aleki said was that it doesn't sound like you're interested in committing to him right now, okay?"

"He's right, I'm definitely not interested in committing to him." Vic was so obviously upset, and Emma so obviously had no idea why.

"Cool," Emma said, because there was nothing else to say. "I've gotta run, and I'm sure KeyAra is waiting for you. See you later, Vic."

Vic didn't even bother saying goodbye.

The entire way back to Highbury, Emma stewed. She couldn't believe that she'd tried to open up to Victoria Lorena Alba, of all people. Her nemesis. The steak to Emma's sizzle.

She wouldn't make that mistake again.

A buzz on her phone drew her attention: her daily "Improve Your Mind, Loser" reminder. She scrolled to the bottom of the recurring event and stabbed the delete button.

The day was looking up already.

CHAPTER NINETEEN

Harlan had always hated Vic out of loyalty, but even Emma found his animus a little over the top. He was cooking steak and shrimp on his spacious terrace while Emma choked down a hardboiled egg. Sean and Brittany were working on their laptops at a table, where the patio heaters were blasting. Liam was expected any minute. He was heading out of town for an away game the following day, and Harlan wasn't tagging along. For as much as Liam was staying away from her, he and Harlan had become thick as thieves, and it worried Emma. Harley was becoming a bit codependent, turning Liam into a security blanket more than just a friend. In fact, he'd dragged Liam along to his *Today* show interview earlier in the week, and she was willing to bet that either Liam or Emma would join him on his next interview too.

She wished she knew what was going on with Harlan. He was energetic and active and seemed happy enough. But he was also moodier and more self-indulgent. More, she hated to admit, like their dad. He would lose his mind if she told him that, though. She couldn't even hint about him seeing his therapist again without him getting pissy. And she understood why: he needed her for unconditional love and support. And if supporting him meant listening to him badmouth Vic, she could handle it.

"She's always been holier-than-thou," he was saying after she described their awkward exchange that morning. "She never took breaks when I came on set. Do you remember that? I'd come to visit, and we'd hang out in your dressing room or get lunch with Weston, and no matter how many times we invited her, she'd never come. Remember?"

"Yeah, I remember. It was so weird," she said.

"Not just weird. Petty. It was her way of telling you that you were beneath her. She's always sucked. I don't know how you put up with her for all those years." He glanced at his timer and poked at the shrimp. The smell of salty steak and buttery seafood was making Emma's mouth water, and she wasn't even hungry.

"Her music is overrated too. I'm not saying she's hot, but if she were less attractive, no one would know her name. She certainly wouldn't have been nominated for so many Grammys."

This was perfect—Harlan could say everything the devil on Emma's shoulder wanted to say, letting Emma listen to the angel on her other shoulder as she came to Vic's defense. "I don't know. Her voice is pretty amazing."

"You have a good voice. I don't see you walking around the town making sure everybody knows what an amazing singer you are. You could have been just as big as Vic, if you wanted. I bet she doesn't even write her own songs."

"She takes pictures of her notebook—"

"Because copying something into a notebook is an insurmountable difficulty? Come on, Emma. Weston has gotten into your head too much. Vic needs to get taken down a peg. We should do it. In fact, I will. I'll post something—"

"What? No. Please don't, Harley."

"Why not? And don't use Weston as your excuse."

Why couldn't he see how badly him calling out Vic would hurt Emma? "Because she's not worth it. A feud would only sell her more albums. Yes, she's uppity and self-righteous, but if we start calling out every actor and musician for that, we won't have a bridge left to cross."

Her use of the plural—we—was the right move. She wasn't pointing a finger or warning him; she was thinking of them. The Crawford brand. Harlan shrugged, but didn't push it further.

The patio door opened, and Liam stepped onto the terrace from the condo. He was wearing a thick cable-knit sweater that made her want to curl into him. She hugged her arms tighter around herself.

"Hey. I hope it's cool that I let myself in," Liam said, as if he hadn't ignored Emma for the last week and a half. As if he hadn't bared his soul to her and hugged her like she was the most important person in the world. "No one answered, so I assumed you guys were out here."

Harlan held out his arm, and the two slapped hands twice in some kind of high five handshake she hadn't seen before. "That's why I gave you the code. We were just talking about Emma's old bestie, Vic," Harlan said.

Liam didn't catch Harlan's sarcasm. "She seems really cool."

Of course he thought Vic was cool. She was as perfect as he was. "What you're really saying is that she remembered you, huh, lover boy?" Emma said. At Harlan's look of confusion, Emma explained about Liam's crush and the time he visited the set with his dad. Liam's ears were red, but he didn't look fussed otherwise.

Harlan punched Liam's shoulder. "And now you're finally getting your shot with her. Score!"

"Yeah, it's not even a little like that," Liam said.

"Why not?" Emma asked. "She's a little too reserved for my tastes, but she seems like she'd be perfect for you."

He looked her right in the eyes now. But what was that look? Accusatory? Defensive? "You think Vic is my type?"

Harlan answered, and Emma pulled her eyes from Liam's to look at her brother. "Nah, she's too vanilla."

Liam grabbed a skewer and jabbed it into a perfectly cooked shrimp. He blew on it before taking a bite. "Wow, dude. That's really good."

"Ooh, Harley, is Liam avoiding the conversation?" Emma asked. Why wasn't he denying it? She *needed* him to deny it.

"Definitely avoiding the conversation."

"Definitely," Liam said, smiling. "I don't need to walk across a field of landmines. So I'll just admit that I think she's nice and leave it at that."

"See, Harley?" Emma said, giving Liam's muscled shoulders a shake. "I predict a spring wedding. Congratulations!" She wanted to see Liam's expression, but it would ruin her exit, so instead, she made a beeline for Brittany, whose head was in her laptop.

"Hey, are you getting excited for tonight's acting class?" Emma asked, sitting next to her. The heater above them pulsed with warmth.

"Are you sure I should be going?" Brittany asked. "Everyone in the class has more experience than me. I'm not sure I'm advanced enough for it."

Last time Brittany had made objections, it had been on account of work. Now, it was about experience. "Of course—I believe in you, Britt. But where is this coming from?"

"I want to make sure I'm respecting everyone's time, yours included. That's all."

Harlan came over a minute later with the meat, and Liam and Sean had the dishes and sides. The men joined them and started dishing up. Sean worked while they ate. The guy needed a life outside of Harlan.

"Harley, man, this smells amazing," Liam said. "You're like the next Bobby Filet."

Harlan and Emma laughed. Sean snorted, his eyes on his phone. "Did you say Bobby *Filet*, like the world-renowned chef?" Harlan asked. "You know his name is Bobby Flay, right?"

"Duh," Liam said. His ears were tomato red. "Of course I know his name is Bobby Flay. It was a pun, because you grilled filets."

"Nice try, pal," Harlan said. "A very noble effort."

"I do what I can."

Harlan put the rarest steak on his plate. It was so red, blood was dripping from it.

Brittany stared at the steak. Her eyes didn't go lunar-eclipse wide, but her shock came through loud and clear. "Why is that steak still bleeding?"

"Because Harley is gross," Emma said. "He doesn't know that pink all the way through is the only way to eat a steak. Right? Listen to Brittany. She's from the Midwest: she knows steaks."

"Oh, I really don't," Brittany said. "My parents are vegetarians. I didn't start eating meat until tenth grade, when I started dating Santino. So I'm more familiar with tacos al pastor than porterhouse steaks."

"You've mentioned Santino before," Liam said. "Are you two still in touch?"

"Yeah, all the time," Brittany said, taking the medium-well steak Harlan offered her. "He's a news producer at the local station. Kind of like a scriptwriter? We just talked yesterday when he told me they hired"—she straightened—"the weatherperson. She went to Toledo College and majored in communications, but she didn't actually study meteorology. I watched the recording. They're in for a rocky start." She smiled, but Emma knew it was forced by the way her chin pulled down a bit too far. "Santino's still really close with my younger brothers. He's like the big brother they wish they had."

"That must be hard, being away from your family," Liam said.

"It is and it isn't. Living in New York is like a dream come true, especially with Marcus. And I'm getting to know so many amazing people, and getting to work with Emma means the world to me. I can't imagine not knowing her."

"I know what you mean," Liam said. His smile was too warm for the moment, let alone for all the push and pull they'd had of late. Why did he have to smile like that now, when she was mad at him and confused by him? She wanted to take that smile off of his adorable face and shove it . . . back in his adorable face.

"Let's not go that far," Harlan said. "She snores loud enough to wake up the neighbors."

"I hate you," Emma said.

"My brothers and I fight like this all the time." Brittany's eyes were fixed on the skyline past Central Park. She looked far away.

"Hey, Liam," Emma said. "You have a couple of away games coming up, right? Back-to-back in Chicago and Cleveland, if I remember right."

Liam nodded.

"Brittany, you should go with him. Take a break, go visit your family for a few days. You can even work from home, if you're worried about abandoning me." She bumped the girl's arm.

"Are you sure?" Brittany looked like a helium balloon struggling against the thin piece of ribbon that tethered it to earth. When Emma said yes, Brittany would float into space.

"I'm positive, Britt."

And there she went.

When Brittany left for her class, Harlan sent Sean out for low-carb ice cream from a place in Riverside, which left Liam, Harlan, and Emma to clean. They had a cleaning company come in semiweekly, but when Liam was around, the Crawfords were extra-domestic. Or at least Emma was. She didn't want him to think she was too spoiled or shallow to even load a dishwasher.

The three brought the dishes into the kitchen, and Harlan went back out to wipe the table and clean the grill—because, after a recent tour of the *Chopped* set, he was committed to caring for his grill as carefully as Marc Murphy did. That left Emma and Liam in the kitchen to do the dishes as they had so many weeks ago.

"That was thoughtful, what you did for Brittany," Liam said, rinsing a dish in the sink. "It shows how well you know her."

Not that well, she thought. She never asked Brittany about her family. It wasn't a topic she brought up with anyone. So few of her friends' parents were still together, let alone happy about it. She knew more about her friends' sober companions and therapists than she did about their families. What did that say about her? About her world?

She took the plate from Liam and loaded it the way she'd seen him do before. "It wasn't that big of a deal. She's been working herself harder and harder the last few weeks, and whenever I give her time off, she finds new jobs to undertake for me. Sean put her in touch with the *assistant network*."

"And that's influencing the way she does her job?"

"Oh, yeah. She trusts everyone, so she gets persuaded pretty easily." She closed her eyes hard before opening them and leveling Liam with a preemptive gaze. "Before you say what I know you're going to say, yes, that is a risk for anyone entering this industry, which is why I'm slowly showing her the ropes and toughening her up. Okay?"

"Okay." He rinsed another plate and passed it to her, and another after that. They continued in silence until he cleared his throat. "Can I ask . . . how does Harlan seem to you?"

The little hairs at the nape of her neck rose. But as defensive and wary as she felt, a part of her felt relieved too. She wasn't the only one who noticed. She wasn't the only one who cared. "Why do you ask?"

"Never mind."

"Wait, why would you bring that up and then dismiss it immediately?"

Liam's nostrils flared. "Why do we always answer questions with questions? Why can't we just trust each other's intentions?"

"Trust has to be earned."

"And I haven't earned it?"

"Oh, I don't know. Where have you been for the last week and a half?"

Liam rocked back on his heels. "What do you mean?"

"You realize you just answered my question with a question, right?"

He pinched the bridge of his nose. "I don't want to fight with you, Emma."

"If anyone's looking for a fight, I think it's you, and I think it's because you feel guilty for ignoring me."

Liam opened his mouth, then closed it before backing into the counter with a heavy sigh. "You're right." He rubbed his wrist. "I felt ashamed. You've seen the ugliest part of me. I didn't want you to look at me differently."

She closed the dishwasher and leaned against the counter next to him, the storm in her chest calming. Her arm touched his. "Then let me see you. Don't run. Talk to me. You've proven you're good at it."

He dropped his hand from his wrist and let it fall next to hers. Their hands grazed, but Emma didn't take his, as much as she wanted to. She felt too vulnerable for such a gesture.

"I'm sorry I said you were looking for a fight," Liam said. "We were never allowed to talk back to my mom. We couldn't even ask her questions after my dad died. I think the second I was able to express a contrary opinion, the power got to my head. You put up with it better than, well, pretty much anyone." The tremble in his voice made her want to open her heart and tuck him inside of it.

"I may have been a little more defensive than I let on," she admitted. "My dad uses every weakness against me. Sometimes, I worry that you're going to do the same when you challenge me on something."

Liam shook his head hard. "No. I would never do that to you. I like that you disagree with me."

"You do?"

"Yeah. It makes me feel like you trust me with your thoughts and that you respect mine enough not to just dismiss them."

Why did this make the back of her eyes sting? "I could never dismiss anything you say."

Liam's eyes wrinkled in a smile so deep, it reached her soul. "But a little blatant flattery couldn't hurt, right?"

She laughed, biting her lip in that way she only did around him. "Obviously." Then her smile fell. "As for your question: I don't know what's up with Harley. I think he's past his depressive episode, but he's becoming self-destructive. He's defensive, he snaps at me if I challenge him on anything, he picks fights indiscriminately, and he's slipping back into some crappy habits with girls. I don't know what to do."

"I've noticed."

"I know why I haven't called him on it—I can't. But you're Captain Truthbomb. Why haven't you?"

He ran his hands through his hair, mussing it in the process. "Because you said he's in a bad place right now. I don't want to make things worse. But how do we help him become his best self if he needs acceptance at all costs?"

"Who gets to decide what his best self is? You? Me? Isn't he more likely to become that person through love than through judgment?" She shifted so she was looking at him instead of standing beside him. She scanned his face, and his big, brown eyes were like open books. The tension that normally permeated their disagreements had vanished. They weren't fighting or even debating. They were trying to understand each other. The difference was tangible.

"Judging an action is different than judging a person, though. When Brittany has said something unknowingly offensive, you've corrected her because it's the right thing to do, right? Is it different here? If Harley is being self-destructive, isn't helping him see that a kindness?"

"In Brittany's case, it's clear. She doesn't know what she doesn't know. But I'm not a moral authority who can look at Harlan's life and objectively decide what's right and what's wrong. I couldn't do that to him even if I wanted to. Could you?"

"I don't know. And I don't know if he'd accept it from me if I did."

"And now you know what it's like to sacrifice your pride for Harlan Crawford," she said, wishing she were teasing.

"I'm already well-acquainted with that pleasure."

She looked up to see a wry smile twisting his mouth. She wanted to ask him what he meant, but he spoke again before she could. "Thanks for trusting me, Emma. And for calling me on my crap. I never knew how much I needed to be challenged before I met you."

"Well, that's just silly of you. But I'm happy to oblige anytime." He leaned his head so it was resting on hers, and her eyes closed, and she would have happily stayed like that all night. All year.

"I should get going," he said all too soon. "But thanks for talking to me. And for putting up with me being scared and stupid."

"Back at you."

Liam took slow steps to the front door, and Emma followed him, wishing he would stay longer. "And hey, you're not the only one who needs to be challenged. It's good for me too. On the rare occasion that I need it."

"Very rare occasion," Liam said, pulling the door open.

"Extremely."

His shoulders shook at the same time that he breathed out a laugh. He turned when he was out in the hallway and started walking backward. "Good night, Emma."

"Good night, Liam."

She closed the door behind him and pressed her head against it. She felt like her heart was smiling. The glass door to the terrace opened, and Emma stepped toward the kitchen when Harlan met her in the hall. He was holding a grill brush and a rag covered with char and grease. "Where's Liam? Did he leave without saying goodbye?"

"Shoot. That's my fault, Harley. We sort of got in a fight, and he left right after. I'm sure he would have said goodbye otherwise." It was near enough to the truth that she didn't feel guilty for lying, especially since she was sparing his feelings.

Harley threw the grill brush to the ground, and Emma recoiled against the wall. The brush bounced off of the light wood floors and clanged into the white wall opposite her, leaving a trail of black char.

"What the hell is wrong with you, Emma? I have one really good friend in this world, one person outside of these walls I can trust. Are you *trying* to sabotage that? I can't understand you. You claim to be here for me, but then you pull little power plays like this to prove that you can. I get it. You win, as always. Thanks a lot."

He stormed through the condo. Before she could process what had happened, before she could even close her fallen mouth, she heard his bedroom door slam.

Fire erupted in her chest. After everything she had done . . . after the countless ways that she had sacrificed . . .

The urge to do violence was overwhelming. She wanted to grab that grill brush and shove it down his throat. She wanted to take his fancy meat tenderizer and start smashing the appliances. She wanted to take his new grill and throw it off the balcony, just to make him scream. No, that was stupid. That could hurt someone. She could kick his soccer ball through his TV. Or cancel the Cooking Network. Or fire Sean behind Harlan's back. Or call him out on Twitter for being such an unbelievably selfish prick. Or talk to Finley right outside of his door.

Or better yet, she could call Liam back right now and make out with him in front of Harlan just so she could revel in her brother's pain.

Her hand cramped, and she realized she was clutching her fists too tight again. The pain brought awareness, a flash of rationality. Was she really willing to ruin her friendships just to punish her brother?

The rage in her chest spilled into her limbs, searing her nerves.

Yes. She would scorch the earth around him, even if it took her with him.

She had to calm down before she did something stupid. She had to . . . She had to . . .

She had to get out of here.

She pulled out her phone and saw a missed text from Aleki. He was going clubbing. It was only eleven. Early enough that she could still blow off the steam bubbling inside her, late enough that her trainer would kill her for not getting enough sleep. Her fingers flew across the screen: *I need a driver and a security guard, STAT.*

Brittany's response was almost immediate. *Done and done!*

Her next text was to Aleki: *I'll be there.*

CHAPTER TWENTY

Emma changed into a black dress and black heels, and put on a hell of a lot of black eyeliner. She left her hair out and a little messy. She looked fierce and unstoppable.

Her driver dropped her off at the nightclub, and the security guard Brittany had arranged escorted her out of the car, up to the bouncer, and into the club. Inside, it was loud and chaotic. The lights pulsed in time with the frantic beat. The dancers threw their bodies into every movement with abandon. She looked at the faces and saw her own intensity mirrored back at her. It wasn't joy; it wasn't rage. Just pure energy. This was exactly where she needed to be.

Her security guard wasn't as tall as they usually were, but he looked like he could crush a skull with his bare hands as easily as she crushed a can of Diet Coke. That was all she needed, really: enough intimidation to keep the creeps away. She didn't want to have to watch her step. She wanted to stop thinking, stop fighting, and just enjoy herself with no guilt, no second thoughts, nothing. She was a live wire in search of an outlet, nothing more.

Aleki approached with his reckless grin, and her pulse sped up with his every step.

This is what she wanted.

"Shoot, girl," he said, looking her over. "You look absolutely lethal."

"You don't look so bad yourself," she said.

He had on jeans and a black T-shirt that showed muscles that went on for days. And his hair . . . People could write songs about his hair. Maybe she would, if she got her fingers into it. He offered her his strong, smooth hand, and she let him pull her out to the dance floor.

Dancing with Aleki was exactly what she'd hoped it would be. Fun and flirty—so, so flirty. Attentive without being too serious. Hot without getting too intimate. Their bodies moved in perfect sync, their breath mingled, their bare skin touched over and over.

Songs changed, fast to slow and back again. She didn't know how much time had passed. Minutes, hours. She was too entranced. A server brought Aleki a drink and then another. Emma didn't pay much attention, didn't take breaks or sit down to recharge. She lost herself to the music, to the dancing, to the energy that surrounded her and filled her hollow spots. She couldn't remember why she'd been so mad earlier. She couldn't bring herself to care about Harlan or her dad, about Liam or Vic. There was no doubt, no questions of loyalty or love. Her awareness of self melted into the room, and she became part of a unit so much bigger and more alive than anything she'd ever experienced. She didn't know where she started or where the throng of people surrounding her ended.

Until she felt a hand forcefully grab her hip. She was jolted back into her body, and she looked around in shock. It wasn't Aleki's hand, and it sure as hell wasn't hers. The hand was firmly and slowly creeping forward and down to a place no hand had a right to be.

Instinct took over. Emma was back in Weston's studio, practicing takedowns. The movements came as easily as they did in class—easier, even, because there was no holding back. She shifted her weight to the balls of her feet to accommodate her heels, and then she followed each brutal instinct all the way through until it was done. She drove her elbow with full force into the offender's gut, spun around, and grabbed his throat before hooking his knee with her foot, pulling his legs out from under him, and smashing him to the floor. His back hit first, followed by his head. He looked dazed.

Good.

"You don't get to touch me," she seethed, crouching over the stranger. She was dimly aware of a phone pointed at her. She didn't care. "Got it?"

The guy was clutching his throat, his eyes bugging out like a cartoon character starving for air. He was acting like he couldn't breathe, when she knew for a fact that he could. She was nowhere close to actually choking him, although she wanted to so badly, the effort of keeping herself from crushing his windpipe was almost painful. The adrenaline pumping through her veins made her feel all-powerful, even while disgust and fury churned in her gut. Only a few seconds passed before Emma's security guard was pulling the guy to a stand. Aleki helped Emma up and put a hand on her shoulder.

"Are you okay, Ms. Crawford?" the guard asked, pinning the guy's arms tightly behind his back.

"No, I'm not. This douchebag just groped me."

The music was still playing, and even with the handful of people around them watching and filming, most people were still dancing. It wasn't like in the movies, where the overhead lights flipped on and the music abruptly stopped and everyone caught every detail. A few people rushed up to Emma, asking if she was all right. One girl was talking to her security guard, who was still gripping the offender. But soon, Aleki had flagged down club security, who walked the group over to a small office in the back. When the door closed, the driving beat just outside quieted to the point that Emma wondered if she was hearing her own heart drum in her angry chest.

Security took down the details and told the guy—Layton—to shut up when he tried to deny he'd done anything. Evidently, the woman talking to Emma's security guard was a fan who'd been filming Emma most of the night. She'd happily sent him the video for proof. Emma didn't know if she should feel relieved or concerned by the breach of privacy.

Security said the guy would be blacklisted from every club in New York by morning. Then came the kicker: they asked if she wanted to file charges.

"Um . . ." She looked at Aleki, who grimaced and held out his hands in an "I don't know" gesture. "I don't know yet. Do I have to decide now? Can I talk to my attorney?"

"Yeah, you can talk to your attorney. We'll report it to police anyway, and we'll send this guy's info to your security guard so you have it."

Layton's blond-bearded face contorted. "This is bullsh—"

"You're gonna want to shut up," Emma's security guard said. "We have you on video."

"I thought it was my girlfriend, man! There are, like, a thousand people in there. How was I supposed to be sure who was who?"

Emma felt the fire reignite. It roared to life in her chest. "Here's a pro tip: if you're not sure, *you don't go near their crotch.*"

"Whatever. I barely touched you. You're lucky I don't sue you for assault. I'm pretty sure I have a concussion from your little psycho move back there. You on steroids there, She-Hulk?"

Aleki laughed incredulously. "*Sue?* Are you for real, Layton? Getting publicly called out and humiliated for sexually assaulting someone isn't a good look. Claiming that you're the real victim on top of that? Good luck. If your 'girlfriend' is real, I'm betting this is the last you see of her."

Layton told Aleki where he could stick the advice and exactly what he thought of Emma Crawford as an actor and a person. Club security informed them that they were adding everything Layton said to the statement. That shut him up.

There was nothing left for Emma to do, so her security guard snuck Emma and Aleki out through the back, where Emma's driver was waiting. The three piled into the car, with the guard in front.

It was over so fast, she could almost wonder if anything had happened at all. And really, had anything happened? A dude had groped her in a club. Didn't a million women have the exact same story?

"I'm sorry I ruined your night," Emma said.

"Don't say that," Aleki said. "You didn't ruin anything. If you hadn't been assaulted, watching you take that jackass down would have been the highlight of my night. Assault aside, to be clear."

"We're clear." Emma rested her head against the door. This night was supposed to be an escape. They'd been having so much fun, until Layton and his hand had ruined everything. "What do I do, Aleki? Am I overreacting? Do I press charges?"

Aleki's sigh was slow and labored. "I don't know. I get your hesitation. The media will dissect every part of the night. They'll talk about your dress, about how much skin was showing, about if you were inviting this. If there's a picture with you and a drink in your hand, it'll turn into an issue of your judgment and if you can even say what really happened."

"I'm not even buzzed. I took like four sips of your drink."

"And I can vouch for that. But you know they won't stop there." He kept talking, telling her the countless ways the events could be twisted to reflect badly on her, to make Layton the victim. She could see the headlines now: "Spoiled Starlet Ruins Man's Life Over Mistaken Identity."

She massaged a pressure point in her hand, trying to slow the headache rampaging through her brain. "How could something so simple on the surface have so many hidden pitfalls?"

"Welcome to Hollywood."

Emma took a shower when she got home, a long, hot one. She didn't feel the shame she'd always heard people talk about; she only felt anger. She felt like the universe had betrayed her by allowing a creep like Layton to ruin what should have been a fantastic night. She felt like she didn't teach Layton a big enough lesson.

She felt confused.

The stories she'd heard about assault didn't match up with what she was experiencing. She felt a little more vulnerable than she had a few hours ago, but no guilt. No one was ever "asking for it," let alone her. And no amount of careful planning could control the Laytons of the world. And she had been careful. She'd gone to an exclusive nightclub with excellent security and her own guard. She didn't even have a drink, so no one had the chance to slip her something. And yet that hand had still . . .

She shuddered and turned up the heat.

How was she supposed to feel? She'd heard so many women talk about the deep sense of shame they felt. She knew shame, and she wasn't feeling it now. But she couldn't compare her small ordeal—a creep trying to grab her crotch—to what so many women had experienced. Maybe this wasn't even really assault. Maybe she really was making too big a deal of this.

Besides, she'd dropped that tool like a box of rocks. A grim smile overtook her at the memory, at the feeling of her elbow driving into his gut and the way she had felt his breath forcefully expel against her hair. She had knocked the wind out of him with that elbow. She replayed each movement in her head in slow motion: the perfect sweep of the legs, driving her hand into his throat. Squeezing.

She should have squeezed harder. She should have made him beg for air, for his stupid, worthless life. She slammed her palm against the side of the shower. Again. Again. Her palm was bright red and stinging, but she couldn't stop herself. How could he have done that? How could he have thought he could just touch her like that? Why couldn't she have had some sense of what was about to happen and have dropkicked him before his hand had crept down her . . .

This time when she struck the shower, she closed her fist. She screamed and dropped to her knees on the tiled floor. Pain exploded in her hand, traveling up her arm and through her chest like acid. It melted everything in its wake, including her bones, her organs. It was so hot. And the pain . . . She doubled over, her stomach seizing as she threw up. Her stomach was empty except for a bit of water, so it was mostly bile and stung her throat. She watched the shower water rinse the rancid vomit, watched it swirl around the drain before disappearing through the tiny holes.

She stayed on her knees, letting the water stream over her and her throbbing right hand. It had begun to swell, and her heart was hammering inside where she was positive she'd broken a metacarpal. Weston had warned her about a boxer's fracture when she'd first started training with him in May. And it had finally happened.

How could she have been so stupid? What grown damn woman went around punching a wall? What was wrong with her?

Calm down, stupid, she told herself. Her rage and self-loathing had gotten her nowhere. It was time to calm the hell down. She forced herself to slow her breathing, to stop the panting that was only making her panic harder. She counted to five on her exhale, five on her inhale, shaking the whole time, but she did it. She repeated the effort for several breaths until she could increase to six seconds, seven, ten.

Good, now stand up.

She rose and turned off the shower. She clutched her hand to her body as she opened the shower, draped a thick towel across her back, and stepped onto the plush mat. Where she'd been sweltering only a moment ago in the shower, now it was like stepping into a New York winter. She crouched down, huddling under the towel, shaking from cold and pain and maybe even shock. The pain was still so intense. Shouldn't the shock be numbing it by now? Is that what shock even did? That was stupid. She wasn't in shock. She was just so cold. And the humidity in the bathroom was so oppressive, it was hard to catch her breath. And there were those weird lights flickering. Not flickering, just sort of floating. No, blurring. She blinked hard, but the room didn't get clearer. Opening her eyes was getting trickier. And when had the room gotten so quiet? She opened her jaw, trying to pop her ears.

Maybe she should lie down, rest for just a minute until the pain subsided. Her head was both heavy and weirdly light, and the room kept spinning and spin—

————————

She was lying on something soft. She was cold. Her eyes wouldn't open, were too heavy to open. She was so tired and—

————————

Her eyes fluttered open. Where was she? Why was she on a bathmat? Naked? And holy hell, why did her hand feel like it had been slammed in a car door and set on fire at the same time? Why was it so swollen?

Her memories slammed into her like her fist against the shower wall. The club. The hand. The shower. Her stupid, stupid fist.

She must have fainted from pain or exhaustion or shock, maybe. She didn't know. But she had to get up and get . . . where? What did she have to do?

Focus, you dumb slut!

Don't slut-shame, she thought and instantly started laughing, hard and hysterically. What was wrong with her that she called herself names as motivation? Why did it work so well? And what did it say about her that she could both shame and defend herself in subsequent thoughts? She was laughing so hard, tears were pouring down her cheeks and pooling in her ears.

"Okay, focus you glorious goddess, you," she said. "And stand up."

She rolled over and planted her left hand in the soft white mat to brace herself as she rose as slowly as possible. When she got halfway, she kept her head level with her hips, making sure the blood didn't drain from her head too quickly and cause her to faint again.

Her hand hurt so badly she could cry.

She made it all the way to a stand and gripped the counter to keep from swaying. She could hardly see her naked form in the steamed mirror. She would need, clothes, right? For . . . where did she need to go?

"Focus, numbnuts. Goddess. Whatever. You have a broken hand and just fainted. You need to go to the hospital. Call 911. No, go wake up Harlan."

Her brother! Her brother was home. Harlan: the one person who always had her back. She pulled her robe from its rack and slid it awkwardly onto her left side before tugging it gingerly over her right. She jostled her hand in her attempt and tears sprang to her eyes. She felt like she'd been stabbed with a hot poker.

With effort, she was able to pull the robe all the way on and tie a sloppy knot. She left the bathroom and went down the hall to Harlan's room.

The door was open, but she knocked and said, "Harley, wake up. I need to get to the hospital." She took a step into the expansive master suite, knocking louder on the door as she passed. "Harley? Wake up," she said. She flipped on the light.

His bed was empty.

It was four o'clock in the morning, and her stupid brother was gone at the moment she needed him most. She had no one. No one to call. No one who cared about her.

She was totally, completely alone.

Emma sank to the floor and sobbed as she told Alexa to call 911.

CHAPTER TWENTY-ONE

By 6:30 a.m., Emma was at Mount Sinai Hospital, alone, lying on a hospital bed in her bathrobe, hopped up on morphine, and hooked up to an IV. She was being treated for exhaustion and dehydration, and the doctor was waiting for the X-ray to confirm if the fifth metacarpal in her right hand would need to be reset or not. But at least her hand didn't hurt anymore. In fact, it felt light, like it was going to float up to the ceiling. Which wouldn't be surprising, considering how puffy it was. She should fill it with helium and watch it fly away.

She snorted. She wasn't high—they didn't give enough morphine for that—but she was so effing tired, and when Emma got tired, she got punch-drunk. Everything was funny. Serious topics made her giggle. If she were at home, she would tuck her feet behind her head and roll on her back around the room like some kind of windup toy, like she used to when she and Harley got home from filming around the same time (thank you, child labor laws). They'd be so tired that they could barely hold their heads up, but they knew neither could sleep until they'd caught up with each other. They were always at their silliest then. Some of her best memories with Harley were from those late nights.

And now one of her worst memories with him was from another late night.

The betrayal she felt at him not being there was deep. He had stormed out of the house simply because Liam hadn't said goodbye, and she had taken the fall willingly. She'd texted Harlan after she was admitted to the hospital, and nothing. She couldn't imagine where his bitterness had driven him. To a girl, no doubt. An ex or a future one. A one-night stand, maybe.

He was pathetic.

As soon as the vicious thought entered her mind, guilt engulfed her, which only made her angrier. How dare she feel guilty for being mad when he'd abandoned her out of spite? He didn't know she'd need him tonight, but to just go MIA, when she was available for him twenty-four hours a day, even on another continent? It hurt.

The nurse came in and told Emma that the doctor would be in shortly with the results. He told her to rest while she could, and she lied and said she would as soon as he was done checking her vitals. She wouldn't sleep. Even with the morphine, she couldn't turn her brain off now, no matter how hard she tried. Too much had happened in the last eight hours.

She flipped on the TV and scrolled through, stopping when she came across a rerun of *My Valentines*. It was the episode where Weston took her to buy tampons for the first time, and they both bought all the wrong things, all while Emma's character was cranky because of her cramps, new hormones, and the fact that she didn't have a mother who cared enough about her to teach her about her body.

Meanwhile, Vic's character was hiding an adorable puppy she'd found in the room she and Emma shared. It was just like the puppy that her biological parents had bought her for Christmas when she was five, right before they'd died. But when Emma got home with a box of adult diapers instead of pads, she found her shoes pulled out of the closet and thought Vic was trying to sabotage her the way she had when they'd first moved in with Weston, back when they were afraid he'd only keep one of them.

The two girls had a huge fight, and it wasn't until Emma was curled up in bed crying that night that she discovered the truth. The puppy crawled into bed with Emma and licked her tears until she started laughing. Vic came over and told her everything, and the two girls hugged and cried together. When the puppy howled, Weston burst in wearing silk pajamas, a sleep mask on his forehead, and wielding a baseball bat. The girls saw that he'd come to save them from whatever threat he'd imagined, and they jumped off the bed, ran to him, and hugged him tightly.

The episode was the season three mid-season finale. It was the turning point for each of their characters, the moment they realized they weren't three individuals living in the same house but rather a real family. Because they weren't alone anymore. They would always have each other.

She was crying when the doctor came in with the results. Emma changed the channel before muting the TV. Crying was okay in a hospital, but watching reruns of yourself was never okay anywhere.

"Ms. Crawford," Doctor Zaltzman said. She had big, fabulous glasses that magnified her brown eyes so they overtook her lined face. The woman was probably only in her late fifties, but Emma wasn't around a lot of non-celebrities. Seeing wrinkles and no signs of fillers or Botox . . . it was weird. The doctor looked at Emma. "I'd hate to see the other guy."

"Ha."

"You have a boxer's fracture, a break in your fifth metacarpal, just at the neck." She pointed to the spot right below her pinky on her own hand. "It was a clean break; no need to set the bones. The nurse will be in momentarily, and we'll fit you for a cast. You'll have that for three weeks and then move to a splint for another couple of weeks."

The nurse came in, and the two carefully wrapped bandage tape around Emma's wrist and thumb, then they moved on to separate her last two fingers from the others before putting on the cast.

An hour later, Emma was casted up, her morphine was cut off, and she was getting a discharge lecture from a hospital staff member.

"Because you fainted, we can't legally release you on your own, so you'll need to call someone to pick you up," the woman was explaining.

"I'll have a car come get me."

"No, Ms. Crawford, you don't understand. We have to release you to someone who'll watch you in case you lose consciousness again. It's a liability issue. Your parents are listed as your emergency contacts. Who should we try first?"

Emma's laugh sounded like the last notes of a dying music box. "Neither. My mom moved to Florida, and my dad wouldn't show up unless it was with a contract."

The woman tapped her pen against her clipboard. "We need the name of someone we can release you to."

She picked up her phone to see that Harlan still hadn't responded. She'd texted Weston a bit ago, and he hadn't responded either. No surprise. He was already done teaching at Riverside Motion and would be in the thick of prepping for the day's show. He always turned his phone off when he was busy, but she could call his assistant and . . . and what? Take him away from everything he'd worked so hard for? Make him look bad to studio executives by forcing him to neglect the show so he could monitor her for twenty-four hours? He had to film today. He deserved a real chance to make his show a smashing success. She refused to take that away from him.

"Can you give me a minute to track someone down?"

The way the woman's mouth pulled down in pity made Emma want look away. "I'll come back in five. Better yet, I'll give you ten."

"Y-you're not going to tell anyone about this, are you?" Emma asked. Her nose and eyes stung, but she had to ask. She couldn't see this show up on TMZ with the rest of this nightmare of a night.

The woman's pity was in full force now. "No. Even if I weren't bound by confidentiality, I wouldn't talk about this to anyone. Take your time."

When the woman left, Emma called Brittany, the natural choice. Brittany answered after the sixth ring, and she sounded like death warmed over. "I'm so sorry I'm not there yet, Emma," Brittany explained. "I went out with some people from my acting class last night, and they convinced me to try sushi, even though seafood always makes me sick, and I know I shouldn't have, but I tried the eel. And the tuna. And calamari—"

"Oh, Britt, you poor thing. You're sick. You don't have to apologize," she said, a lump making her throat stick as she tried to swallow. "I'm taking the day off, and I was just calling to tell you to, as well. Hang in there, hon. I'll check in on you later."

Brittany thanked Emma and abruptly ended the call. She was probably throwing up. Emma rested her back on the hospital bed, staring at her recent texts and calls.

She tried Aleki. No answer. He was probably still asleep. It was barely eight in the morning, after all. Misha had just left to shoot a commercial in LA, and Jamal was in Atlantic City for his mom's birthday.

Who else did she even have?

She looked at her favorites and saw the third one down: Finley Price. The ache in her chest felt like it was being pried open just seeing Finley's name. She wished more than anything that they lived next door still. She wished they were still close, that their friendship hadn't been one more thing she'd given up in the name of loyalty. It was so unfair. So blatantly unfair. And with every text that Finley sent her, with every generic, late response Emma sent, the ache grew wider and deeper.

Finley would have been on the next plane out. It wouldn't have done Emma any good in the moment, but just knowing that someone cared enough to come running . . . She didn't even know what that felt like anymore. It had been so long since she'd come first. To anyone. Even to herself.

She stared at her phone, pulling up her contacts. There was one more person she could call. One person who she desperately, frantically wanted to answer.

But what if he didn't? What would that rejection do to her?

Trust, she thought.

She hit the call button before she could talk herself out of it. She closed her eyes, pleading with the universe as the phone beeped.

He picked up on the first ring.

"Hey, Emma," Liam said, his voice sounding so warm that she could cry with affection even more than relief. He must have heard her quiet sobs, though, because his words rushed out: "What's wrong? Are you okay?"

"Can you pick me up?"

"Of course. Where?"

"I'm at Mount Sinai Hospital. Ask for Holly Golightly, and they'll show you to my room."

"Mount Sinai? Emma . . ." He exhaled into the receiver. "I'm on my way. But . . . are you okay?"

"I broke my hand," she said, lying with the truth. "I fainted after, so I have to be released to someone I know."

"I'm so glad that's all it is." He didn't say the words so much as breathe them. "I'll be there as soon as I can." She heard a rustling, like he was already moving. Like he cared enough to come running. For her. "Thanks for calling me."

"Thanks for answering."

A knock on the door roused Emma. Had she fallen asleep? She didn't remember almost anything after talking to Liam, so she must have. A glance at the clock showed that thirty minutes had passed. "Yeah, come in," she said.

The door opened, and in walked Liam. He was wearing Adidas shorts, shirt, and shoes—he looked like a walking advertisement for the official sponsor of Major League Soccer. She was about to say so when she noticed the intense look in his eyes.

"Hey," she said instead. Her eyes felt like they were caked with sand, and her voice sounded like it had been run through with a cheese grater. "Thanks for coming. I tried to convince them that I could call a driver, but they insisted it was hospital policy after someone faints."

"You were going to hire a car? Emma, come on. Why wouldn't you want help?"

Because no one wants to help. "I just didn't want to inconvenience anyone. It's so early."

Liam walked toward the bed. She scooted over to make room for him. He sat down facing her and took her casted arm carefully in his hands, holding it like any movement would break her worse. "So what happened? Luis told me that you had an incident at a club last night. Did this happen there?"

"It's already on TMZ?" He nodded, and she groaned. "No. The club thing—it was stupid. An entitled loser tried to get handsy."

"*Handsy*? Did he—"

"Nothing happened. I made sure of that," she said. And although she hadn't felt any shame in the early hours of the morning, she felt some lying about it now. But that was stupid. Why did it matter who she did or didn't tell? She didn't owe an explanation to Liam or anyone else.

Liam didn't look satisfied, but he dropped it. "I'm sorry that happened."

"Nothing happened."

"I'm still sorry." She looked at the way he was holding her cast. He held it like her pain mattered to him, like her feelings were precious to him. Yet, he didn't treat her with kid gloves. The juxtaposition was perfectly, patently Liam. "So the broken hand came after the club? But not from your alleged takedown of the handsy loser?" She eyed him. "Yes, I read the post. And I looked it up on E! too."

"It wasn't from that. I slipped in the shower."

"You slipped onto your fist? This is a boxer's fracture, right? A guy on my team in college punched a concrete wall after a game and fractured his fourth and fifth metacarpals. After his surgery, he had a cast that looked just like this. Although, his wasn't hot pink."

"Pity for him."

Liam was still cradling her arm. "You know you can always talk to me, right?"

"There's nothing more to tell."

"Okay." He took her thumb and first two fingers in his hand, stroking them. Her hands were ice-cold, and she shivered at the sudden heat. He kept her uninjured fingers covered until her shivering subsided. "Better?" he asked.

She nodded.

"Does that mean I can sign your cast now?"

"Yeah, but too bad you don't have a Sharpie."

"They gave me one at the front desk." He pulled one from his pocket, popped the cap off, and licked his lips. "Is it embarrassing that I've been debating what to write from almost the second we got in the car?"

"Super embarrassing. Everyone knows that the first thing that comes to mind is usually the best."

His ears went red.

"Um, what was the first thing you thought of writing?"

"Nothing." He shook his head a bit too hard. "'First comment.'"

She laughed. "That's good. You should write it."

"No, it's stupid. I haven't been able to think of anything good, and it may go down as my greatest shame."

"It doesn't have to be funny, you know. Just whatever you feel." She hadn't meant to drop her voice, but it was quieter, and he was nodding like what she'd said was profound instead of a stupid throwaway comment.

"Okay." He started writing. She hadn't known he was left-handed, especially because he wore his watch over his left wrist. He must have worn it there to hide his scar.

His hand moved deliberately, softly. He was so tender with her. Her heart rate increased until it was as fast and shallow as it had been last night. Her head swayed just as Liam finished.

"Whoa, you okay? Do you need to lie down?"

"No, I'm just tired. I haven't slept yet."

"Let's get you home so you can sleep. Do you want me to stay, or would you prefer Harley? I can stay, no matter what Harlan does. If that's okay."

She blinked slowly, her thoughts feeling increasingly foggy. "Harley's mad at me. He's not coming."

"What? No, Emma, he's here. I picked him up on the way."

Hope swelled in her chest but stopped at her throat. He'd answered Liam's call but not hers. And besides . . . "If he's here, where is he?"

Liam looked at her cast. "He was talking to one of the interns. I think he wanted to go visit some sick kids, make their day."

She should have burst into tears. She should have wept until she needed another IV. But instead, Emma felt like she was leaving her body, like she was watching this scene play out from another room. This was one disappointment too many to process. "He's using this as a publicity stunt? I've had the worst night of my life, and he's just down the hall, posing for photo ops? I can't believe he's all I have."

"He's not all you have."

"Yes, he is. That's the way it's always been, and it's the way it always will be."

"No, Emma. You have so many people who love and care about you."

"Liam, come on. *So many people*? My parents literally could not care less about me. At least when they were married, I was a pawn they could use to hurt each other. Now that they're divorced? I get weekly forwards from my mom. She doesn't ask about me—she doesn't even send me my own email. She writes to both of us, because the effort to send two separate emails is more than she can spare. But at least we get weekly reminders from her that we don't know our heritage and that we can thank our dad for ruining all of our lives. And speak of the devil, the last two conversations my dad and I have had, he's told me that I'm a mediocre actor who could be replaced by Victoria without fans even noticing because I'm so lazy and shallow. And that's nowhere near the worst thing he's ever said to me.

"Weston is the busiest he's ever been. Between his studio and his show, I see him, but I'm not his priority, nor should I be. He's finally settled and doing what makes him happy. He deserves better than to have me come into the space he's worked his whole life for and dump my baggage all over him. Brittany—I love her, but let's face it: she's paid to be my friend. Who else do I have? Celebrity friends who call me when they want to party but forget about me the rest of the week? A best friend I abandoned? An aunt and uncle in Chicago? Fat lot of good that does me when I need a ride home from the hospital. Harlan is all I have, and even he was too mad to come see me this morning. Don't you find it pathetic that we've only really known each other for two months, yet you're the one person who came to help me?"

Liam shook his head, his lips pulled down. "No. I didn't find it pathetic. I was sad, because I knew you were hurt. But, Emma, I felt special that you asked me. I thought—" He paused and cleared his throat. "I thought it meant that you know how much I care."

The icy detachment that had taken over Emma's body melted in a flash. Her limbs thawed, and she realized he was holding both of her colds hands with his warm ones. The warmth from his hands spread up her arms and into her chest. "Liam—"

"Emma!"

The door flew open. It was Harlan.

CHAPTER TWENTY-TWO

Harlan burst in. "One of the nurses back there told me about some sick kids who needed cheering up. I knew you wouldn't mind, but I'm sorry it took so long to get here." He rushed to her bed, pushing Liam out of the way in the process, and hugged her tightly. "I'm so sorry I wasn't here for you, sis. I was a jerk last night, and I shouldn't have just left. Do you hate me?"

The hug was nice, but she couldn't ignore how hollow his apology rang. She had no doubt it was sincere, but his well didn't run as deep as it once had.

Don't say that.

Why not?

"I really needed you."

"And I'm here, so Liam, you can take off. I know you need to get going—"

Please no.

"I'm not going anywhere," Liam said, as if reading her mind. "They discharged her to me. I can miss one practice to make sure Emma's okay."

"So they can discharge her to me instead."

"I already signed the papers, Harley. I have to watch her for twenty-four hours. The last thing I need is Emma passing out and suing me for neglect." He winked at Emma. "Besides, don't you have to meet with your trainer and the ex-Navy Seal guy?"

"I'll move them to tomorrow."

Emma rubbed her head. "Can you two just shut up and take me home? I haven't slept in thirty-six hours, the painkillers already wore off and my hand is killing me, and I really don't want to hang out in my robe in front of you guys for a minute longer than I have to. Cool?"

Harley and Liam looked at each other with a tension she hadn't seen in months. "Cool."

———————————

Emma woke around six that evening with no memories of anything after she had crawled into her bed the second she'd gotten home. She could smell tomato soup and grilled-cheese sandwiches, and the smell was enough to rouse her completely. She stretched, popped a couple of ibuprofen, and awkwardly changed into some jogger pants and an oversized sweatshirt. Then she looked in her vanity mirror.

She was sickly pale, and she'd seen dead rats with better hair. She grabbed a brush, tried to tug it through some knots, but gave up before she was done. She was being stupid. It didn't matter what she looked like now. Harlan had seen her in the rough a million times, and Liam—if he was even still there—had seen her this morning.

Besides, he'd probably left already. It wasn't like he needed to be there.

She cradled her hand to her body and opened the door, where voices carried to her from the kitchen. She padded her bare feet down the pale wood floor, hearing Harlan, Liam, and . . . more.

Brittany, Weston, and Aleki were sitting around the bar in the kitchen with Liam, while Harlan served them all Emma's favorite comfort food in the whole world: grilled-cheese sandwiches with tomato, avocado, and bacon.

The smell filled her with nostalgia. When their dad was a producer—before he became their agent—this was his go-to meal to make when he was home for dinner and wanted to be domestic. Once she and Harlan started acting, he made it less and less, until, when Emma was ten or eleven, he stopped making it altogether. He had moved on from being a family man long before the divorce.

But before then, when he would make it, their mom would wander into the kitchen, snag the spatula, and spank him with it, and he'd pull her into a long kiss. She would tease that his grilled cheese was the other reason she'd married him, and no matter how much Harlan and Emma asked, she'd never explain what the first reason was. Emma understood the innuendo now, and it made it even sadder to think of just how much they'd cared about each other once. How much they'd cared about the family they'd created.

"There she is!" Harlan called, seeing Emma. "The woman of the hour."

Everyone clapped and cheered.

Emma raised her cast. "If I'd known what a noble reception I'd receive by breaking my hand slipping in the shower, I'd have done this ages ago."

Weston jumped up from his chair and put his arm around her. "I'm so sorry I wasn't there for you this morning, Nutmeg. I had my phone off and missed your text, but you know you could have reached me."

She sank into his embrace. "Thanks. But I had it taken care of."

He released her and put his hands on her cheeks. "You don't always have to be the heroine, you know."

"I'm not letting some man swoop in and steal my thunder," she said.

"No, you are not." His eyes wrinkled behind his thick-rimmed glasses. "I'm glad you're okay."

Aleki threw out his arms, gesturing for Emma to take the stool next to him. He draped his arm around her affectionately. "Harlan called me at noon and told me about all the excitement I'd missed at the hospital this morning. I hadn't realized you were keeping the party going," he said with a squeeze. Then to the others: "You wouldn't believe how badass this girl was last night."

"Yeah, I heard about some incident," Harlan said. "What happened?"

"So we're just out dancing, minding our own business. Emma is shaking her hips, fierce as Beyoncé, and suddenly, this blond hipster doucheface grabbed her hip and started—"

"Started to spin me around," Emma said, holding Aleki's gaze. She didn't want anyone knowing how the guy's hand had traveled.

Aleki nodded. "But Emma wasn't having it. She pulled out some legit limalama magic." He proceeded with only minor embellishments, but he was a natural storyteller. He described Layton and his absurd blond beard and mimicked him getting slapped around all over the dance floor. Weston was smiling proudly at all the right parts, Harlan was laughing, and Brittany was awestruck. Only Liam looked concerned. And maybe a little hurt. Was it because she'd been with Aleki? Or because he was worried about her?

"It was awesome," Aleki said when he picked himself up off the floor (after pantomiming Layton's bug-eyed gasping for breath). "I've never seen anything like it."

While the others marveled at Emma's takedown, she tried to let their words fill the hole in her chest that the last twenty-four hours had created. Aleki's retelling had been funny and engaging, and she could easily imagine recounting the story on late-night TV some time. Interviewers and fans would flip for a story like this. She could milk last night on the press circuit for weeks while she was promoting the new movie. It fit her brand and the promotion plan perfectly. Drew and even her dad would be all over it. And judging by her missed calls from each of them, they were waiting to hear every detail.

But was that all last night was? Could she reduce it to a story for laughs as easily as Aleki had? Could she shrug off the feeling of that hand—

She shuddered.

"Everything okay?" Weston asked. "Is your hand hurting?"

"Yeah, but I just took some ibuprofen. It'll kick in soon. But what do we say about stuffing a sandwich in my face? I still have seven pounds to gain, after all."

By eight, the group retired to the main room. Brittany left early, on account of her stomach still being off. But she gave Emma a big hug and signed her cast right on the palm with a big heart. Weston followed Brittany out, seeing as he had a 4 a.m. wakeup call at Riverside Motion waiting for him. He hugged Emma before leaving, and on her cast, he wrote, "You'll always be my heart, Nutmeg." She was almost embarrassed by how much it meant to her.

Her phone rang, and Drew's name and face appeared on the screen. "Excuse me, gang," she said, pushing up from the couch with her left hand. "I need to get this."

She took the call in her room. "Hi, Drew."

"Emma, honey, where have you been? Are you okay?"

"Broken hand—a boxer's fracture, they call it."

"*Boxer's fracture.*"

Emma heard the sounds of typing in the background.

"I like it. Sounds tough. Now I need details. Everything that happened last night. I assume that's how you got the fracture?"

"No, I got that slipping in the shower early this morning."

"Oh no. I can't use that. Are you sure it didn't happen last night? Maybe you just didn't notice? No, never mind. We'll call it a training accident. Hitting the showers is part of training, after all." Emma didn't bother agreeing. If Drew had her mind made up, the matter was settled.

Yet, her next words were soft. "How are you feeling after last night? I already got the rundown from the guard, so you don't have to tell me anything more than you can handle right now. Are you okay?"

The guard. Of course Drew had gotten a report from the guard. Drew's company kept the private security firm on retainer, just like the car service. His loyalty had been to Emma's safety, not her privacy. That, he freely gave to Drew.

"It's not a big deal. I can talk about it."

"Why don't you think it's a big deal?"

"Because I took care of it. Yeah, it sucked, and I felt completely, totally violated. But so did his windpipe when I was done with him."

"*So did his windpipe* . . . damn. That's hardcore." Emma waited to hear clicks from Drew's keyboard, but they didn't come. "Do you feel like this is something you want to take a public stand on?"

Emma didn't answer.

"That's a question, not a judgment."

"I mean, a stranger groped me, Drew. It's not like I was raped."

"Emma, it's as big a deal as you feel like it is. This is your body, not just your career. If you want to move on this, we should. We should file charges and take this to the press."

"You mean incorporate it into the Emma Crawford brand?"

"Sure. Show that you champion women's rights and enforce them. Be a leader."

Emma heard another call coming in. This one was from her dad. "Drew, my dad is calling."

"Talk to him and call me back. He probably he wants to make sure you're all right."

Emma couldn't even laugh. She switched calls. "Hi, Dad."

"Emma? Are you okay?"

She never expected to hear those words out of his mouth. A sob escaped her throat. "Not really."

"You should eat something."

"I have. Harlan made me one your grilled-cheese sandwiches—"

"A sandwich, Emma? No, you need protein, not carbs. You're supposed to be bulking up for this role, not fattening up."

She had no words. No tears either.

"You can't just go off the rails every time you have some minor upset."

The words found her. "*Minor upset?* Dad, did you hear that I was assaulted at a club last night?"

"*Assaulted?* You're overselling it. I talked to Drew, and she forwarded me the video. Someone grabbed you, and you beat the hell out of him. Good for you. But you're lucky if he doesn't sue. You need to play this smart."

Emma heard a ringing in her ears. She stared at a spot across the room until her eyes lost focus. Her dad warned her how this could look in the media, about how her reaction could jeopardize her career, just because she was the subject of some unwanted attention, when millions of women had it so much worse. Some champion of women's rights she would be, throwing a fit over being touched wrong in public.

She didn't know when she stopped listening, and she didn't know when he'd morphed into talking again instead of berating her.

"I talked to your trainer, and he'll be by tomorrow to create a new training plan. This throws a wrench in everything. If I find out you aren't taking your weight gain and training more seriously, I'll cancel your contract myself."

"I'm trying, Dad." She hated the pleading note in her voice. "You have no idea how hard I'm trying. I'm making protein shakes with cream, flaxseed, and raw eggs and waking up sometimes twice a night to drink them. I snack on nuts, choke down six meals a day, plus more shakes. I don't know if I can keep this up." Why was her voice shaking now, of all times? Why did the back of her throat ache just thinking about swallowing one more handful of almonds?

"Emma, listen to yourself. You're complaining about having to gain weight for the role of a lifetime. Do you know how entitled you sound? How do you think fans would react to hearing this?"

Emma squeezed her eyes shut and put her cast to her forehead. The cast felt so clunky, and she felt so stupid having to wear it at all. "I know. You're right."

"Yes, I am. You had a rough night, and you've had your time to relax and recover. Now it's time to suck it up and be the professional I know you can be."

"Yes, sir."

Emma pulled a shake from her mini fridge and drained it while she dialed Drew. If she took a moment's break, her dad's words would fester and decay inside of her. Drew answered on the second ring, asking about the conversation with her dad.

"I'm not going to make what happened in the club an issue. I'm not going to file charges. I need to focus on my career."

"Is that what he— Emma, are you sure that's what you want?"

"I'm sure."

Drew paused. She was probably typing something. "Well, okay. I can see where you're coming from. It would be a departure from what your fans expect. They'd love you just as much, don't get me wrong. You'd lose some, and you'd gain some. But if you're sure this is what you want, I'll support you."

"Thanks. It's what I want."

"Good thing is that you already have the line down: you felt violated, just like his windpipe when you were done with him." She laughed lightly. "We can make this direction work, if it's really what you want." Another pause. "Okay, yeah, we'll just add this story to your repertoire. Tell it right, and it'll make your fire-drill-interview story look quaint." Emma heard typing again. "Yeah, I can go with this. Why don't you think about it a little tonight, and we'll chat tomorrow?"

Emma got up from her bed. She was tired and didn't want to protest or insist for another second, but she also felt like she was languishing in her room. "Okay."

"And, Emma, I am sorry about your hand. I talked to your trainer, Jason. He said this kind of thing happens and he can find a way to work with you—"

"I just drank a shake, Drew. Don't worry about me not making my weight."

"Oh. Okay. Attagirl. We'll chat tomorrow."

"Talk to you then."

Emma tossed her phone onto her bed and crossed over to her vanity. She looked into the mirror, and her gaze became deadly. She was no one's victim, certainly not Layton's. She had made that douchebag beg for mercy, and she would do more to the next guy who tried. She remembered the feeling of pure power that had electrified her in the moment she'd taken Layton down. Her muscles had been energized, her mind as clear and focused as a laser. She had humiliated him.

Aleki had characterized Layton perfectly: he was hapless and weak. Emma had done that to him. She had brought him to his knees—lower—until he was begging for air.

If this was a survivor story for anyone, it was him. And he was lucky she'd let him survive.

Emma left the room and spent the rest of the night laughing with her friends and eating everything she wanted, including some things she didn't want. Any other day, she would say she was punishing her body.

But tonight, she felt like she was triumphing over the rest of the world. When Aleki flirted, she flirted back. When Liam cast her concerned looks, she shrugged them off, ate another handful of candy, and kept doing whatever the hell she wanted. His concern was no good here.

She could take care of herself. She'd proved that much last night.

CHAPTER TWENTY-THREE

Late the next morning, Emma was headed downstairs to the gym to meet her trainer. When the elevator stopped on the fourth floor, Emma braced herself. But instead of Vic or Kelly, it was KeyAra. The woman gave Emma a pursed-lip smile, and Emma made a snap decision. She held open the elevator door.

"Are you coming from Vic's?"

"Mm-hmm," KeyAra said. "You know, I've been meaning to pick your—"

"Ooh, sorry," Emma said, stepping past KeyAra. "I was just on my way to chat with Kelly and Vic now. See you around!"

The elevator door closed, leaving Emma alone on the fourth floor. Harlan's condo was on the eleventh floor, which had only three occupants on it. But the units on the four lowest floors belonged to those who'd refused to sell out when Highbury Lane became the most exclusive complex in the Upper West Side. The remodel here included the hallways, but not the eight units to each floor. Emma walked the hallway to unit 4D as if it were a plank. She knocked, waiting for the push that would send her careening to the bottomless depths.

Kelly answered, and Emma took the plunge. "Emma, what are you doing here, dear?"

"I'm meeting my trainer in the gym in a few, so I thought I'd stop by and see how you two are doing." Emma smiled like this was the most natural visit in the world, instead of merely the lesser of two evils, even if one of those evils was a twenty-second elevator ride with the stunningly insufferable KeyAra.

"Well, come in, come in! Vic is just on a phone call in her room with her manager. Come, have a seat. You know how those phone calls are."

Emma followed Kelly into the condo, which was maybe half the size of Harlan's spacious three-bedroom. The rooms were pretty, open, and dated, with lots of dark wood, warm accents, and older appliances. Emma noticed two bedrooms and bathrooms off of the main living space. Emma wondered if Kelly had given Vic the master suite.

Kelly led her to a rich-brown leather couch, which Emma sank into. "Can I get you anything? Vic made a lovely cheese plate for me last night. She wants me to experiment with more cheeses than just mozzarella, but I've told her not to jump the gun. Oh, but I haven't asked you about your broken hand, you poor thing. How is it? Are you in pain?"

"No, I'm fine, thanks. It was just a bad fall."

Kelly's demeanor changed, almost as if some of her silliness had faded. Emma had always thought Vic resembled her Mexican-American dad more than her white mom, Kelly's sister. But she could see the resemblance between Vic and her aunt now in their striking narrow features and soulful brown eyes. "Have you spoken to anyone about what happened?"

"You mean other than the doctor? No. The X-ray was pretty straightforward."

Kelly's forehead wrinkled into a V. "Didn't you have an incident at a club the other night? I read about it this morning, and Weston told me that you'd confronted—"

"No, no, the two are unrelated. Yes, I had a small encounter with someone the other night, but this had nothing to do with that. I slipped in the shower yesterday morning." Lie. Lie. Lie.

What was that look on Kelly's face? Skepticism? Pity? "And what happened at the club? There's a rumor that a man assaulted you?"

"It wasn't like that."

"Are you sure? You have a light inside you, Emma. It will draw people's attention and attract them to you, not because they want to bask in it, but because they want to snuff it out."

Emma didn't know what to say. It was so kind and . . . astute. Unless it wasn't?

"You never have to tell me anything, but remember that you always can," Kelly added.

The combination of Kelly's kind tone and perfume stirred up a memory from an event during the second season of *My Valentines*. A prop light had slipped and crashed into Emma's face, giving her a bloody nose. After the nurse had cleared her, she'd gone back to her dressing room to find her dad sitting at the table in her dressing room, his jacket across the back of the chair. He didn't come by the set much anymore, but Emma wasn't even twelve, and she still craved her dad's affection and attention. His showing up now, after such a silly accident, meant the world to her.

"Daddy!" she cried before throwing herself into his arms.

"Emma." He caught her in a hug. "I wanted to surprise you and hear about how things are going. Let's take a walk, and you can tell me what's new."

Before they could leave, the door to her dressing room opened and a production assistant slipped in, looking back at the hallway before closing the door. "Let's do this qui—"

"You're in the wrong room," Emma said, her arm still around her dad's waist.

Her dad's grip on her shoulder tightened.

The woman spun around, looking like a cat caught eating a pet bird. Her neck was red and splotchy, and she kept looking at Emma's dad. "Whoops, I must be turned around."

Emma pushed back from her dad. "You came to see her, not me."

"Don't make a scene." He didn't even have the grace to act sorry. She bit back a torrent of screams and ran from the dressing room, down the hall, and crashed into Kelly, who was visiting Vic on set, as she so often did. Kelly looked around at the empty hall before putting an arm around Emma and leading her through the studio and outside, to a quiet, shaded table. Emma hadn't said a word.

"Are you okay?" Kelly had paused, her voice soft and soothing. "You don't have to tell me what happened, but I'm here for you if you ever want to."

The words and tone were so similar, but Emma had forgotten how calm and focused Kelly could be back then, right after her last bout of rehab for her eating disorder. And now, over ten years since Kelly had fainted from near starvation at that party in Beverly Hills, she was as jobless as the day it had happened.

This business could be so cruel.

"Thanks, Kelly," Emma said.

Vic's door opened. "I don't think I can take another—Emma." She stopped, sliding her phone into the pocket of her boyfriend jeans. Vic had an effortless style. Emma had it, too, but she made sure hers looked effortless. She got the impression that Vic's look was authentic. "I didn't realize you were coming by."

"I thought it would be nice to catch up for a bit. I have a meeting with my trainer in the gym in ten minutes, so while I was debating stretching before meeting him, I decided seeing you two sounded like more fun."

"'More fun than adding ten minutes to your workout.'" Vic smiled. "It's the kind of ringing endorsement we like around here." She looked at Emma's hand. "How's that feeling?"

"Meh. Like dead weight. My trainer probably won't go easy on me.

He's mad enough that I can't seem to gain"—stupid Emma!—"more stamina. All those hours of squats and deadlifts, and you'd think I could handle taking the stairs, am I right?" she rambled. She could kick herself for complaining about weight gain to Kelly, of all people.

"*Deadlifts*?" Kelly asked, mercifully oblivious to Emma's blunder. "That's a violent term for an exercise, isn't it? Where do they come up with these names?"

"Good question," Emma asked before looking at Vic. "So, how are things going with your big return to Hollywood?"

"Well, I'm not sure that's really the direction I want to go, but my manager is keeping his ears open for me."

"Your manager. Is that the man who saved you after you went overboard?"

"Yes." Her head dropped enough for a glorious sheet of black hair to fall in front of her face. "Jerry. He's wonderful."

"He really is," Kelly gushed. She had a way of shifting her audience as she spoke that made conversations with her almost dizzying. "Such a wonderful man. When Victoria was first starting out in LA, Jerry was reluctant to take her on, because he didn't like working with musicians too young. He thought they lacked the spirit and wisdom necessary to make it, isn't that right? He's worked with all the biggest names. But after meeting with Victoria, he changed his mind, didn't he? He told me she had an old soul."

"Wow, that's incredible. That must have been exciting that he took you on in spite of his reservations. You must have really convinced him in that conversation."

"It was more of a heart-to-heart than anything," Kelly said. "They were both in tears when they left, which makes sense for Jerry, of course, considering he lost a sister to leukemia when he was Vic's age.

He saw something special in her, and how could he not? He even let her live in his guesthouse up until a few months ago, when she moved out."

Victoria held out her phone. "Sorry, I need to take this. Emma, I'll catch you later."

"I should be going too. If I'm late, I'll never learn how to do a burpee with a cast."

Kelly laughed, following Emma to the door. "*Burpee?* Oh, quit it. You just made that one up, didn't you?"

"You got me," Emma said as she waved goodbye.

Emma's training session was brutal. Her trainer wasn't as angry as her dad had led her to believe, but *she* was. She exercised to the point of exhaustion, but even then, she wasn't satisfied. She left the session with the link to an app that the two would share. She was to enter the nutritional information of everything she ate so her trainer could monitor her macros. Just the idea of shoving more food into her mouth made her feel sick, but she was done complaining. She was swimming in privilege, not a victim of it.

So instead of raging against the protein shake, she asked Brittany to add an extra raw egg and scoop of flaxseed. "I have your masseuse coming by later this afternoon," Brittany said over the pulsing blender. "And you've had six more interview requests come in." Brittany poured the shake into a glass and gave it to Emma before bottling two up for the fridge. "*People*, the *Today* show, *The View*, *New York Times*, *USA Today*, and *The Guardian*. Oh, and Drew called, asking if you've rehearsed the story yet. How do you want me to respond?"

Emma sat at a kitchen stool and rubbed her temples. "Talk to Drew, and we'll hold the interviews for now. Have her say something about how I'll tell the story soon, but I'm recovering from a training accident and respectfully request a few days to regain my strength. She'll know how to spin it."

"Drew will want you to call her directly."

"Tell her I'm taking a nap."

Emma drained her shake, walked to her room, and did just that.

Avoiding Drew—as always—proved a mistake. Because when she woke up, Emma realized that Drew had sent reinforcements.

"Dad?" He was sitting on the foot of her bed, like he had when she'd been so sick with the flu when she was six. But this wasn't a fatherly visit. Emma sat up, rubbing her eyes. She'd only been asleep for an hour—not long enough to touch the pounding headache that encircled her head like a crown. "What are you doing here?"

"Drew and I were talking. We're concerned that if you don't get ahead of this nightclub story, this Layton punk will find someone to tell his side to, assuming he doesn't sue. We both know there'll be plenty of tabloids paying for a story like that."

"I don't know, Dad. I've been thinking about this. He wants to tell a story about grabbing my crotch and getting his own butt handed to him as a result?" As much as she loved to upset him, she still struggled to curse in front of her dad, who had always expected "more" of his kids. He raised them to be famous like the Harry Potter stars—funny, thoughtful, dedicated to their craft. His kids would be actors with long, storied careers, actors who handled the pressures of their careers with grace and humility. What they were never, ever to be was those tacky teen stars who partied late and flamed out early. No way. Not his kids.

And the pressure wasn't making either of them crack or anything.

"You underestimate what people will do for money," her dad said with dazzling irony. "Either you tell it, or he will."

Emma stared at her dad's dirty-hazel eyes, tan, perfect hair, and the dimples he shared with Harlan beneath his trimmed beard. How could her friends have ever found him attractive? How could anyone? He just seemed so . . . oily.

"Okay, I'll tell the story. Who do you and Drew want me to talk to?"

"Let me hear you tell it first. Tell it well enough, and we'll offer an exclusive from the highest bidder."

She wanted to argue. No, she wanted *him* to argue and insist that no one got to treat his daughter like that and swear to take Layton down. She wanted him to hug her tightly and say how sorry he was. But the fact that he wasn't even a little protective made her wonder if there was even a reason for him to be. Because even her a-hole dad would care if she'd actually been assaulted, right?

She got into character. "So there I was in the club, minding my own business and getting my shimmy on . . ."

CHAPTER TWENTY-FOUR

Emma's management team decided that the talk-show circuit was the best way for Emma to tell her story. It was in such high demand that Drew had no problem getting other guests bumped so Emma could go on a full morning-and-daytime circuit the following week. She went from talk show to talk show, getting the applause and laughter she knew she would. There was one thing Emma Crawford could do better than almost anyone: turn it on.

If the details were a little off, it didn't matter. Emma's attorney spoke to Layton, and he signed a nondisclosure agreement in exchange for Emma not naming him publicly or filing charges. So the Layton threat was neutralized entirely. The story belonged to Emma.

She owned the hell out of it.

Brittany accompanied her on every interview, as did, surprisingly, Aleki. He'd told her he was eager to peek behind the scenes of more shows than just Weston's, but she wondered if there was more to it than that. Their flirtation had reached an all-time high at the club last week, and although it had calmed a little, their interactions were still charged. They weren't intense and soul-shaking the way they were with Liam. But Aleki wasn't a flight risk either.

Her last interview Friday was on a popular daytime show, and they wanted her and Harlan both. Daytime shows filmed in the morning, so Emma had missed an entire week of workouts at Riverside Motion that week. The adjustment to her schedule meant she was buzzing with unspent energy.

Backstage, Aleki squeezed Emma's shoulders and brought his

gorgeous face close to hers. "Remember, you are Emma Hotpants Crawford. You don't take no crap from nobody, got it?"

"It's Emma Hot*stuff* Crawford, if you must know."

"Yeah, it is. You got this, Hotstuff. Now go knock 'em dead," Aleki said.

Emma furrowed her brow in hesitation. The stage manager was flagging her attention.

"What?" Aleki asked. "What's wrong?"

"I was just . . . I was expecting one more cliché to really bring the pep talk home, all right?"

"Girl, I would slap your butt and yell 'Good game!' if I didn't know what you'd do to me."

"Maybe you don't know *exactly* what I'd do to you," she said, winking and walking out with Harlan when the crowd started cheering. She glanced back long enough to see Aleki grinning.

The hosts—Chloe and Ty—stood and gave them both hugs. Emma was instructed to sit in the first chair, next to Chloe. Emma and Harlan were always vying for the first seat, but as much as she hated to admit it to him, Harlan was the bigger star. Other than Weston, Emma had never gotten the first chair.

She flashed him a gloating look. He flicked her when they sat down. The Crawford sibling love language.

The usual banter ensued, with congratulations about their upcoming movies, questions about what it's like to live with a sibling, and jokes about who does the cooking (Harlan) and who does the laundry (dry cleaners). Ty complimented Emma on her cast before asking Harlan about getting blocked by Zac over their recent Twitter fight.

"I like to think of what's going on between us as a feud, like a classic rap beef, you know? It's good for both of us."

"You're both white boys," Ty said, "and those feuds aren't exactly 'good' for both parties. Some of them may be publicity stunts, but some are all too real and scary, bro. You never heard of Tupac? Biggie Smalls?"

"Not a bad point." Harlan scratched his head and looked at the camera. "Hey, Zac? I'm sorry, man. I suck sometimes."

"More than you know," Emma muttered loud enough to be heard and to get generous laughs.

"Let's talk about you, Emma. What happened in that club?" Chloe asked.

Emma told the story probably the best she had yet, with the right pauses, eyebrow movements, head whips, and gestures. Her timing was perfect and earned big laughs and bigger cheers. People in the audience held "Girl Power" signs and had T-shirts with her face on Rosie the Riveter's body. After one encounter with a creep in a club, she was a feminist icon.

It felt amazing. Addicting. Like a rush of endorphins and adrenaline all in one. When Chloe asked her about her plans beyond acting, Emma explained how she was mentoring a young female actor now, explaining how she wanted to help up-and-comers learn how to navigate the precarious world of Hollywood. That earned her another round of applause. And when Chloe asked if Emma was seeing anyone, Emma smiled.

"I'm not seeing anyone, per se. But I've been hanging out with a guy a lot lately who I wouldn't mind seeing more of."

Oohs scored her announcement. Ty leaned in. "Is it me? I'm flattered, Emma, but you should know I'm taken."

Chloe smacked Ty's leg. "Shush. You're scaring our guest. But, Emma, you know, if you want to give me a little exclusive info, I wouldn't mind."

Emma laughed. "I promise: if something happens between us, I'll let you know."

"Can you at least tell us anything about him?"

"I can tell you that he's kind and funny and good at talking me up exactly the way I need. He's not an actor, but he's familiar enough with Hollywood and comfortable enough with himself not to be intimidated. We actors can be a little overbearing."

"Speak for yourself," Harlan said. "I'm a damn delight."

Half of the crowd laughed; the other half screamed Harlan's name.

When the interview was over, Emma felt like she was flying. Aleki high-fived her. "That was awesome. You are a natural up there, girl."

"Thanks. And thanks for the pep talks. I wouldn't have been able to channel my inner Hotstuff without you."

"Psh. You'd have slayed without me, and we both know it." Aleki looked at their little group. "So what next? We need to celebrate a week of successful talk-show appearances, right?"

Harlan was talking to Sean. "Actually, I was thinking the exact same thing. I had Sean rent out a club for the night. It's time to celebrate."

Brittany squealed. "What can I do to help?"

"Why don't you help Sean arrange catering? Then you two can start on the guest list," Harlan said.

Brittany bounced off to start making calls.

"Wouldn't tomorrow be a little easier to manage?" Emma asked. "Oh, wait. The team has an away game this weekend, don't they? Let me guess: they leave tomorrow?"

"Bright and early for Miami."

She pinched her brother's cheek. "You and Liam are the cutest couple I've never shipped."

"Shut up," he said, though he was smiling.

———————

Harlan managed to pull the party off as though he'd had a month to plan instead of a day. He, Sean, and Brittany worked all afternoon making everything perfect, and when they all showed up at the club, it was proof of how well the effort had paid off. It was also proof of Harlan's and Emma's star power that so many people showed up so last minute.

There were only a couple hundred people there—friends and friends of friends, mostly. Former castmates and favorite crew members. Stylists and trainers. People Emma and Harlan had grown up with. Liam and half of his team were there, several with plus-ones. Misha and Jamal. Vic and Kelly, of course. Weston, Marcus, and some of the writers and crew from the show. Most of Weston's students from Riverside Motion, including—yuck—Bryce and KeyAra. Somehow, Sean and Brittany had maintained a precise balance of friends and obligatory guests.

On the dance floor, Emma spotted Harlan's favorite photographer, Julien. He was always friendly to the Crawfords, and she was in a magnanimous mood, so she pulled him out to the floor for a group photo. When he was finished snapping them in their glory, he leaned in.

"So, where's the guy you were talking about in your interview earlier? Is he here?" Julien asked over the music

"Jules, stop. Nothing has even happened yet." She looked from left to right. "But yes, he is. Look for the hottest age-appropriate guy here, and you'll be onto something."

"Mm, I love a challenge. I'll be back with theories."

"Which I will neither confirm nor deny."

"You're terrible, and I hate you," he said, snapping her picture.

She blew him a kiss and watched him move on to another group.

Why had she wanted out of the spotlight again? This was the life. Lights and parties and friends. Millions of fans who cared about every single thing she did, fans who cared so much about what happened to her that she had entire websites and fan accounts devoted to her, hanging on everything she said and did and wore.

How had she ever felt alone?

"This is the best night ever!" Emma yelled to Brittany.

Brittany whooped. "At least top ten," Brittany agreed.

The song ended, and Emma and Brittany took a break over in the VIP lounge. Emma dropped to the couch and kicked off her heels. "Okay, so what was your absolute best night ever?" she asked Britt.

Britt fell back against the burnt-orange leather couch and deposited her heels next to Emma's. "Homecoming, my senior year of college. Santino and I went together, of course. He was already interning at the station, and . . ." She fiddled with an earring, a simple pair of diamond studs that she almost always wore. A gift from Santino, if Emma had to bet.

"And he told you he loved you?"

"Oh, we'd been saying that since high school. No. H-he told me he wanted to marry me."

"What? Britt, I didn't know that. Wow. That must have been hard to let him down, huh?"

"He didn't actually propose. It was a *someday* discussion. He talked about how happy he was, about how the only thing that could make his life better was knowing that I would always be in it. It was the sweetest thing I'd ever heard."

Brittany's wistful look tugged at Emma's heart. "And that was the happiest night of your life? Britt, I'm so glad you came to New York, but . . . why? Why did you do it if you were so happy?"

"Everyone said we were too young. My roommates, some of my friends, even my own mom. They all liked Santino, but they said only a fool commits their life to one person without knowing what else is out there. My best friend told me that it would be like the only food

I ever ate in my whole life was pepperoni pizza: it's great, but to not know if something else is actually my favorite food would just be depressing. That's what she said. And the more everyone talked about it, the more it made sense. Shouldn't I try other foods? What if sushi is the best thing ever?"

Emma didn't want to say it, but she had to: "Well, sushi makes you vomit for, like, a day, so maybe another food would work better in this analogy, right? Like . . . steak. Thai food. Waffles."

"I do love waffles." Brittany gave Emma a weak smile. Emma could see the shadow of Brittany's doubt across her flawless skin.

"It's okay to mourn what you miss. And I'm guessing you still miss him."

Brittany spun her left earring around and around. "Today would have been our anniversary. He sent me flowers. The note said that he's proud of me for chasing my dreams."

"Good for him," Emma said. She had to admit: Santino sounded like a class act in every way. But just because he was a dream boyfriend, didn't mean Britt would have been better off with him. She was exploring her options and expanding her horizons. Where would Emma be if she hadn't been willing to try new, scary things? "It sounds like he's a good friend to you."

"The best."

"I'm glad you still have him, then. But I understand how much it hurts to leave someone you love," Emma said, her thoughts turning to Finley. In time, Emma and Brittany would both move on, but it was okay that they were both still grieving. Sacrifice meant giving up something that mattered for something that mattered more. Her relationship with Finley for her relationship with Harlan. Brittany's life with Santino for her dreams.

It wouldn't be much of a sacrifice if it didn't leave a scar.

CHAPTER TWENTY-FIVE

Aleki joined Brittany and Emma shortly after their talk about Santino, and his presence was like a light in a dark room. He told them a story about getting stung by a jellyfish that had them both laughing.

"Pee is the only thing in the wild that you can readily find to neutralize the sting. And between you and me, I've never had such a hard time peeing before," Aleki was saying over their laughter. "Seriously, if you haven't had to find a way to pee on your own bicep in the middle of Turtle Bay, you haven't lived."

"Stop it!" Emma was laughing so hard she could barely breathe. "You did *not* have to pee on your arm!"

"I swear on my honor as a Boy Scout!"

"That's not how it goes," Britt said, holding up three fingers. "It's 'Scout's Honor.'"

"No, that can't be right. You're making that up."

"Britt was definitely a Scout. Am I right?" Emma asked.

Brittany nodded.

"Told you!" Emma pumped her fist, and Aleki blew a raspberry in her direction.

More people joined them as the night continued. Hours into the night, the dance floor was lighter and the tables heavier. Groups had formed across the club, and people were talking, laughing, drinking, making out. Harlan and Liam, Misha and Jamal, Vic, KeyAra and Bryce all joined them, with other friends making the occasional appearance. Weston, Kelly, and Marcus were at their own table, while Sean sat with some of Liam's teammates at a table maybe ten yards away. Julien was wandering through the ranks, telling people to smile and taking pictures even when they didn't.

"I still can't get over how you karate chopped that dude's face off," Misha was saying between sips of her drink. She sat with her legs flung over Jamal's, and he was stroking her calves, which were works of art, so Emma got it. Their PDA was nothing compared to KeyAra, who was sitting on Bryce's lap as he nipped at her shoulders. "It's almost as awesome as what we did to Kleinfeldt's pervy nephew. Do you remember that?"

"Ugh, Mish, don't bring that up now. There are children present." She covered Harley's ears, and he bumped her hands away with an eye roll.

Aleki looked around at the table. "Are you going to leave us hanging? What happened?"

Emma shook her head, so Misha started telling it. "So the producer on *My Valentines* was Bob Kleinfeldt, right? Good guy. No problems. But he had this nephew. What was his name? John?"

"Josh," Emma corrected.

"Right. Josh. Creepy Josh was thirty if he was a day."

"I think he was twenty-three," Emma said.

"Exactly," Misha said. "Too old to be hanging on a bunch of fourteen-year-old girls, can we all agree?" Everyone nodded. "Well, he was a huge fan of Emma's. That last season, he'd just graduated from some fake college and was working whatever job Uncle Bob could find for him. And that job was as a production assistant on our show. So a couple of months before the season finale, he finally makes his move, right, Ems?"

"This is your story, babe," Emma said. "I just lived it."

"Okay, so he kept knocking on Emma's dressing room door, asking if she needed anything. Half the time I was in there—I was a regular on the series by then. So I'm in there, hanging with my girl, and Creepy Josh just keeps showing up. Well, one day, Ems and I decided to play a trick on him. I hid under her desk, and the plan was that when he started getting creepy, I'd come out with my camera, right? But, no. Emma had a better idea."

Emma looked around the table. Aleki, Jamal, and Harlan were eagerly waiting the story. Bryce was oblivious, too enraptured with KeyAra's flesh, though KeyAra herself was listening. Vic was staring at the table while Liam was looking right at Emma. She couldn't read his expression, but it was heavy enough that she had an idea. He wasn't looking forward to where this was going.

"So we're in the dressing room, and we hear Creepy Josh's signature knock—a calypso beat, of all things. I hide, and Emma tells him to come in. So in he comes, right? I don't know everything he's doing, but he's talking about what a great actor Emma is, how she's so beautiful and poised and a bunch of total crap—"

"Okay, he was a creep, but all of that was true."

"Ems, you told me he kept scooching forward until his knee touched yours. Maybe don't defend the guy for complimenting you?" Misha said. A few people chuckled.

Aleki was still watching them eagerly, and the powerful high she'd felt all week while telling a story to an engrossed audience swept over her. She cut in. "While Misha was hiding, Creepy Josh sat at the table with me, his knee touching mine. My character had just gotten glasses, and I didn't want Creepy Josh to get too carried away, so I decided it was time for the endgame. I asked him how he liked the glasses, and he leaned in and said that he liked me better without them. So I asked him how he liked the dress, and he said the same thing: 'I'd like you better without it.' And he put his hand on my knee. I wanted to stab a knife through his hand, but instead, I grabbed the necklace I was wearing and said, 'This is going to be so good to watch back later.' He took his hand off my knee and was like, 'What? What do you mean?' I pointed up to a dome on the dressing room ceiling—it was a light or carbon monoxide sensor or something, but he didn't know that. So I said, 'You mean you don't know? My dad has cameras set up all over the dressing room and on set. He even has one in this stupid necklace. Calls it his predator provision. I call it the killjoy cam.'

"So I took off my glasses all sexy like, but Josh jumped out of his seat and backed away, yelling, 'No, no! I'm not interested in that. I'm just a friend! An assistant!' and he ran out of the trailer." She pointed at Brittany, who looked like she hadn't blinked in minutes. "Always be prepared for the pervs, okay? Rule number one."

Alcki, Harlan, and Misha were laughing uncontrollably. Misha was wiping her eyes. "So I crawl out from under the desk, and Ems and I just bust up! We never even needed the recording. You'd better believe he left us alone."

The reaction wasn't exactly what Emma had expected. Liam was staring at Emma like he didn't know if he was in pain or in shock. Vic was shaking her head. Jamal looked disgusted and kept saying how messed up that was. Meanwhile, KeyAra was unimpressed. "You know what my dad always taught me to do if a man was trying to get on this?" She held out her hand and balled it into a tight fist before wrenching it to the side. "Squeeze and twist. You get me? You should have made him pay. I would have."

"But then you would have had to touch him," Misha said, laughing again. "No thanks."

KeyAra flipped her bone-straight black hair. "It's worth it. I will seriously mess up anyone who touches me. Or my man."

Julien showed up in time to hear KeyAra. He'd missed the story—and seeing the reactions around the table, Emma was glad of it.

"Has that happened, KeyAra?" Julien asked, taking a picture of her and Bryce. "Is someone trying to get at your man?"

She shot a quick glance at Brittany before leaning forward and smushing her cleavage in Julien's profoundly disinterested direction. "Listen, I'm a classy ho, and I'm not going to sit here and woman-bash, okay? But if you already had your chance and couldn't land him? Move the hell on."

Bryce looked across the table at Brittany long enough for Julien to connect all the dots. "She never had a chance, baby. I may eat organic, but that doesn't mean I want to visit the farm."

KeyAra and Bryce shared a laugh while Julien snickered and took some more pictures. Shock froze Emma momentarily, but the sight of Brittany's eyes welling with tears snapped her out of it. Before Emma could launch herself across the table to carve Bryce's heart out, Liam was on his feet, standing by Britt.

"Britt, would you want to hit the dance floor with me? Be warned: I will embarrass us both. But if you don't mind, I'd love to dance with you."

Brittany's eyes were pools of gratitude. "I'd love that. Thanks." She held up her hands, and he pulled her to her feet, holding her steady while she put her heels back on. Emma watched them walk back to the dance floor, her heart every bit as warm as she knew Brittany's must be.

Julien sidled up to Emma, fanning himself. "Isn't he that big soccer player on loan from Europe? Gabriel Price's son? Twelve-year-old Julien is in bliss right now. Tell me everything."

Harlan shifted toward them. Not exactly subtle. "Liam's great," Emma said. "He's become one of Harley's closest friends, right, Harley?"

Harlan slid across the booth to sit next to Julien. "Yeah, he's helping me train for my next role, and we've gotten tight. He's the best. Super dedicated and level-headed."

Julien cocked his head at Harlan. "I am grossly unsatisfied right now. When I said, 'Tell me everything,' I wasn't playin'. Spill your guts."

Emma put on her heels, slipped out of the booth, and walked over to the restroom. She passed Aleki and Vic talking. They were standing close, and Aleki was gesturing brightly while Vic wore a small smile on her lips. Maybe Aleki would sign her, after all.

On her way back from the bathroom, Emma wandered the room. Weston and Kelly were talking over glasses of champagne. Brittany was still dancing, but Jamal, Misha, and several of Liam's teammates had joined them. Emma walked over to them and heard Brittany and Luis conversing in rapid Spanish while they danced. Luis looked interested. Brittany just looked happy. When Emma caught Liam's eye, he nodded his head to the side of the dance floor, and Emma nodded, following him over to an empty set of couches.

It was late enough that some of the guests had already left, and it meant that the music felt too loud for the cavernous room. She and Liam sat opposite each other at first, but when they tried—and failed—to successfully communicate, Liam laughed and crossed over to Emma. He sat right next to her, inclining his head toward hers so he didn't have to yell. Emma mirrored his pose. She put her feet up on the table and leaned her head until it was almost touching his.

"That was a nice thing you did for Brittany back there," she said.

"I didn't just do it to be nice," he said. "That was part of it, but I also wanted to shut up Mr. and Mrs. Elton. They suck. Brittany is so much better than Bryce; she'd have to lose her soul to date that loser. And KeyAra. I don't—I have no words."

"No, of course not. You're a *classy ho*."

Liam and Emma laughed so hard, they were both in tears. Their shoulders bumped, and Emma clutched her side, which was aching from laughter. "That may be the best description I've ever heard," Liam said when he had recovered enough to talk again.

"And I appreciate now having something to aspire to." She laughed again. They both sat slumped down in the couch, their sides touching. Her body tingled wherever her skin touched his.

"Emma," Liam said, breathing out. "I'm so sorry that happened to you. Josh Kleinfeldt belongs in prison."

"Don't. Don't paint me as a victim, Liam. Nothing actually happened. I made sure of that." *Like I always do*, she wanted to add. But she still didn't know if that was the truth. It wasn't that she always took care of herself, but that no one else did. She'd made the best of bad situations, but no one could control everything.

"But . . . what if he hadn't believed you? Or what if he tried that on someone else who doesn't have your . . . your—"

"Ovaries? Chutzpah?"

"Both. Did you tell anyone?"

Her laugh was bitter. "Liam, who in my life do you think would have cared? My mom, who woke up with a glass of Chardonnay? My dad?" She didn't say what he would have done, because she already knew.

"What about Kelly? You two were closer then, weren't you?"

"Yeah, we were closer. But she was Vic's. She didn't belong to me."

"Weston then?"

"We weren't tight then like we are now. I still had too many daddy issues to talk to a father figure about things that mattered to me," she admitted, though if that were true, why hadn't she told Weston what really happened with Layton?

"I wish I'd known you back then. You could have told me."

She blinked away the stinging in her eyes. "Thanks."

"If you could go back, would you have done things differently?"

"You mean, would I have spoken out against Josh? I don't think it would have done much. The guy went on to work in finance or something, anyway."

"I'm not disagreeing with you, but can I play devil's advocate for a sec?"

"As long as you admit that you're working for the devil by doing so."

He smiled. "What's the point of having a platform like yours if you don't use it for good? If your career suffered, but you knew you'd helped someone else avoid a worse fate, would you have done it?"

The question hit a nerve. What happened then, what happened with Layton the other night . . .

"Liam, I told my dad what happened. I laughed with Misha about it, but I still knew it was wrong."

"You told your dad? What happened?"

"He told Kleinfeldt about it. Creepy Josh quit—although I hope Kleinfeldt fired him—and my dad took a settlement from the studio. I doubt he gave me a penny."

Liam put a hand over his mouth, and he looked like he was holding something back. She hoped it wasn't tears. *Please don't be disgust.* "Emma."

She didn't want him to say anything. She'd told herself that the assault in the club and what Creepy Josh had tried to do didn't matter, but her dad had found ways to leverage both into bigger paydays. The truth was clear: both mattered to him.

She didn't.

"I know you're disappointed in me, but you can't understand. Who was going to believe a fourteen-year-old starlet over a twenty-three-old college graduate and nephew to one of Hollywood's biggest execs? I told someone I should have been able to trust, and nothing happened. I know what Josh wanted to do was wrong, but he didn't technically do anything. I protected myself."

Liam grabbed Emma's casted hand and looked down at it. "I don't blame you, and I'm not disappointed in you. You're right. I can't understand what you've been through, then or now." He traced over some of the writing on her cast, but it was too dark for her to see which words or images. "A couple weeks ago, you asked me if I ever just let myself hate anyone. I *hate* your dad. I hate him. Why do you put up with him?"

How could she explain it? "He's always been our agent. He's the best in the business."

"But he's your dad. I don't care about his job; that relationship should have come first. I don't understand how he could hear what Josh did and not want to kill the guy. Why haven't you guys fired him after everything he's put you through?"

No, he didn't understand. When he walked away from a bad situation, people still loved him. Even when she'd fled halfway across the world, she'd clung to the circumstances that drove her away. When Harlan came knocking, she returned willingly.

That was why people loved her.

What did she have to do to earn the kind of unconditional love Liam took for granted every day? What more did she have to sacrifice?

"Do you think we could put aside all our personal drama and just enjoy ourselves for a change?" Emma asked.

"The two have never been mutually exclusive for me," Liam said, the club's lights dancing across his eyes and face. The beat morphed into a slow song, and the lights slowed with it. "But I think I can accept your terms, if you can accept one of mine."

"Which is?"

"Dance with me?"

Her first thought was of Harlan: where he was and how would he react if he saw them.

Her second thought was of Liam: he didn't seem to think less of her because of what had happened with Josh, no matter what he thought of her not firing her dad. He still wanted to be around her.

Her final thought was of herself.

"I accept your terms."

Liam stood and pulled Emma up. She liked the feel of his hands. They were strong and callused, but not rough. He kept her hand in his as he led her to the dance floor. They were away from the crowd, protected by a large pillar that shielded them from some of the bouncing lights and inquisitive eyes. She took a slow, unsteady breath as Liam's hands slid around the small of her back. It wasn't the risk that made her hesitate. It was the fact that she didn't care about the risk. Not right now.

She put her good arm around Liam's neck, and he held her cast against his chest and closed the gap between them. There was enough space that Julien wouldn't be able to write anything too scandalous if he caught a peek of them. Enough space that Emma doubted Liam could feel the steady thrum of her heart beating against him. It was too much space. Was he thinking the same thing?

She looked up to see him looking down at her. His gaze . . . She would never get enough of that gaze. The way he looked at her as if he saw her to her core.

It was too intense. She was drowning in his eyes. She looked away, but instead of coming up for air, she felt like she was going further under.

She was a mess. Worse, she was a fool. Liam was going back to Europe at the end of the season. He would escape her and Harlan and the drama they'd embroiled him in the last few months. So why didn't that knowledge make her want to back away and protect herself? If anything, she wanted to hold him tighter. She was such a fool, and she had no intention of stopping herself.

With her heels, she was tall enough to rest her cheek against his when he leaned down. The smoothness of his skin robbed her of her ability to think. His hand tightened against her back, pressing her closer to him. Close enough for her to hear him humming softly in tune with the song over the thundering speakers. Close enough for her to feel the muscles in his chest and abs against hers. Close enough for her to finally breathe.

And they danced.

CHAPTER TWENTY-SIX

Brittany bounced into Riverside Motion on Monday morning with more energy than anyone should reasonably have at 5 a.m.

"Well, someone had a good weekend," Emma said.

"Did Aleki tell you what happened?"

"No, I haven't seen him since the club. Why? What happened?"

She began rocking from side to side, warming up her muscles. After a little over two months, Brittany's thin body had become muscular and beautifully toned. Weston knew his stuff. "I'm shocked he didn't tell you. He told me he was going to the Highbury Saturday."

"I must have missed him. So spill before Weston gets here already!"

Brittany explained that after the club, she and Aleki had shared a cab home. "Aleki was so sweet. Even though he had to double back to get home, he insisted on seeing me to my apartment first, because he said that he'd binge-watched all of *Daredevil* recently and knew how rough Hell's Kitchen could get."

"Sure. *Daredevil* is notoriously reliable on the state of Hell's Kitchen."

"It must be, even though Marcus's complex has always seemed so safe. I've walked that neighborhood late at night and never had a problem. Until Saturday morning, when we were coming home from the club!"

"Wait, seriously?" Emma did a boxer's shuffle to warm up.

"Seriously. I'm shaking just thinking about it," she said, holding out her hand to show Emma how it was trembling. "I got out of the cab, walked up to the stoop, and was looking for my keys. Suddenly, I felt something cold and heavy against my back! I screamed, and this man told me not to fight or else it would 'end very badly for me.' He told me to give him my wallet, and I was just about to pull it from my purse, when suddenly I heard a thud and didn't feel anything against my back anymore. It was Aleki! He'd seen the man mugging me, and he'd left the cab quiet as a mouse—didn't even close the door so he wouldn't tip the mugger off—and then he grabbed a brick from the ground, crept up the stairs, and smashed it against the man's head. He fell like a . . . well, like a brick. I couldn't believe it. I've never seen anything so brave in my entire life." Brittany's doe eyes were half terror, half awe, and she was almost panting.

"How terrifying, Britt. Are you okay?"

"I don't even know. It was all so fast that I still can't believe it really happened." Her voice carried a tremor, and she was jumping in place with a nervous energy. "I can't believe the man had a gun. I've never even seen a hunting rifle up close! It was terrifying. But Aleki was so calm under pressure, and he's been kind to me since. I don't know what would have happened to me if he hadn't been there."

"I'm so glad you're safe. Do you need some time? Do you want to talk to a therapist about what happened?"

"I don't think so. It's nice to stay busy, and I'm going home soon."

"Well, let me know if you need anything. I'm so sorry that happened to you. It's just unbelievable," Emma said. And it was. For Brittany to have been held up at gunpoint? For Aleki to have done something so careless and so brave? The risk was enormous, for both of them. The man could so easily have heard Aleki and fired on him and Brittany both. BAM, BAM.

Emma shuddered. Weston came into class, telling them to step it up, but even with her mentor yelling in her ear, she couldn't shake the idea that was taking root in her mind.

Aleki had proved that he was willing to protect Brittany. Brittany was handling her trauma surprisingly well, thanks to him. He was the perfect person to represent her.

When Aleki made plans to come to the Highbury later that day, Emma was eager to set her plan in motion. She expected him around two, but he showed closer to three thirty that afternoon. Harlan had a few members of the team over after practice, and they were playing video games and talking about the loss in Miami. Emma kept waiting for Liam to take a break from the game, to make his way to the kitchen, where they so often found themselves able to talk.

But he didn't.

Maybe he was just playing it cool. Maybe he didn't want to make too big of a deal of that night, in case Emma wasn't. Which she wasn't, of course. They'd just danced for, oh, thirty minutes. An hour. Until the house lights had turned on and they'd slowly drifted to opposite ends of the club, looking for their respective roommates, with the occasional glance back at one another.

But why wasn't he making it a big deal? Maybe he regretted dancing with her. Maybe he couldn't stop thinking about how Creepy Josh had come on to her and how she hadn't done anything more than a practical joke. Maybe he couldn't stop thinking about how shallow and stupid she was for keeping Josh's predatory practices to herself, no matter what her dad did, for being the kind of girl so many guys tried to take advantage of . . .

Emma walked into the bathroom, slowly, calmly, but when she closed the door, she leaned toward the mirror and stared at herself.

He's not dad. He doesn't think like that.

It was true. She knew he didn't think like that. She'd had enough proof of that to know that she was avoiding the real problem. Liam wasn't a jerk. He was a runner. When things got tough and overwhelming, he bolted.

He wouldn't run because of disgust. She knew that. If he ran, it would be because he didn't feel equipped to handle her baggage on top of his. She didn't want him to run. She wanted to be enough for him to stay.

A signature on her cast caught her eye—one so small she hadn't noticed it before. She looked down from her reflection to the scrawl right above the inside of her elbow. It was what Liam had written right after coming to her rescue at the hospital. She'd forgotten to check, hopped up on painkillers as she'd been.

You're worth the fight.

She rubbed her temples. It was such a perfect message. But did it actually mean he wouldn't run? And was it even running if they both knew he was returning to England after the season ended?

A ring at the doorbell pulled her from her thoughts. She headed for the front door and opened it to find Aleki. And Vic.

"Look what I found in the elevator," Aleki said, gesturing to Vic.

"The more the merrier," Emma said, letting them in.

"Thanks, Emma," Vic said.

"You should know that half of NY United is currently occupying our main room, so find a spot, make yourselves at home, and try not to choke on the overwhelming stench of dude. Oh, and Britt is on the patio," she added for Aleki's benefit.

"How is our girl?" he asked as the three walked into the main room. "She told you about the other night?"

Vic took the armchair that Harlan had vacated. Liam and she greeted each other, and he asked her if she wanted to play. She gave him a bright smile that he returned before handing her a controller.

Emma watched all this while she and Aleki stood next to a wall of bookshelves featuring biographies that, as much as she tortured herself, she knew she would never actually read. She pulled her eyes from Vic and Liam. "About the mugger? Yeah, she told me. Aleki, I can't believe you risked your life to save her. Was it terrifying?"

"Horrifying! I'm glad I didn't know the guy had a gun. I'd never have tried to get the drop on him, otherwise. But don't tell Britt that, okay? Let her think I'm every inch the courageous hero she thinks I am?"

Emma squeezed his arm. "Your secret is safe with me."

Liam's eyes flashed to Emma and Aleki at the very moment that she was touching him, and because she'd been sneaking glances since the moment he'd walked into the apartment, she saw Liam's brow wrinkle and his mouth draw tight. He returned to the screen, looking like he wanted to do real harm to Wario and Toad. Was he jealous? Or was he regretting Friday night that badly already that he couldn't help the tortured look that had come to occupy his face?

Shut up, brain.

"I knew I could trust you," Aleki said. "Hey, come with me outside. Britt and I have been chatting, and she showed me her headshots. I have some news for her." Emma grabbed a blanket and wrapped it around herself, and they walked out to the patio. Brittany was bundled in a puffy white jacket, and her breath came out in small white tendrils. She had her phone out, but her eyes were on the sky and she was twirling an earring. The sun was hidden behind a thin sheet of clouds that weren't quite gray but that gave the city a dull pallor.

"Is a storm coming in?" Aleki asked.

"Hmm?" Brittany said, looking at Aleki and Emma as they joined her on the patio.

Emma shivered beneath the blanket and moved under one of the patio heaters.

"No, these are stratus clouds. They look gloomy, but they're a little too thin to produce much of anything."

"Good. Now are you ready to hear the news?" Aleki asked.

Emma looked from one to the other. Brittany's eyes opened wide in curiosity.

"I got you an audition for *East Side*, and I talked to the producer over at *So the Night Falls*, and they'd be interested in you coming back for a ten-episode arc. Apparently, people liked the guardian angel vibe you had with Bryce. Isn't that great?"

The excitement that had blossomed on Brittany's face withered at the rest of Aleki's news. "I couldn't act with Bryce. Not after . . . no. I'm flattered, but—"

"But while she appreciates the offer, she owes it to herself to explore opportunities that don't come with a built-in end date," Emma filled in. Brittany gave her a thankful smile.

"Cool," Aleki said. "How about the *East Side* audition? It's this Thursday."

"I want it," Brittany said. "Are you kidding? I've watched *East Side* since my sophomore year of high school. Santino's grandma is obsessed with it. She said it's how she learned English, and Santino and I used to joke that it's the reason she always speaks like everything's a life-or-death situation." Brittany laughed to herself. "She would flip to see me on *East Side*."

"Then I think we have some strategizing to do." He looked at Emma. "You mind if I steal your assistant?"

"I'll leave you to it."

Emma watched their smiling reflections in the patio door as she pulled it open. As she went to the kitchen for water, Alexa sounded out a reminder: "Time for a snack, Ms. Crawford."

She growled. Brittany was nothing if not dedicated.

Emma pulled a plate of salami-and-cream-cheese rollups from the fridge and shoved one into her mouth. She had finally started gaining more weight, with only five pounds left to go in less than two months.

She ate the rollups as quickly as she could, chewing minimally and swallowing the biggest chunks she could get away with.

"Mind if I have some of those? I'm starving," Liam said from behind her.

Emma choked on a piece far too big for her throat. She leaned forward, smacking the center of her chest and coughing with as much forced as she could. The piece dislodged before Liam needed to save her. Thank the stars. She spit the piece into the sink and ran the water.

"This isn't embarrassing or anything," she said.

"No judgment. I choke on salami at least twice a week," Liam said. He was beside her with a napkin as she stood up. She took it and wiped her streaming eyes and mouth.

"I'm counting that bite on my food log, and you have to take that lie with you to the grave, okay? My trainer keeps track of every macro."

"I get it. I've had intense trainers before." He grabbed one of the salami rolls and took a bite—a reasonable bite that wouldn't choke a child.

"So I saw that you tried some exciting foods in Miami over the weekend," Emma said.

"You looked for me on Instagram?"

"Of course. How else would I know where to find the best *chapulines*?"

Liam shuddered. "It was between those and the gator bites. What would you have picked?"

"Alligator, because it's an animal and not a bug." She nudged him in the ribs. "You ate grasshoppers, pal."

"Yeah, well, if the guys told you that gator bites were testicles, you'd probably have picked the grasshoppers too." He took a much bigger bite of the salami roll this time.

Emma hopped up on the counter, and a moment later, Liam joined her. "So, Aleki," Liam said before pausing.

"What about him?"

"Do you—are you guys—?"

"Friends? Yes."

Liam nodded, eating another salami roll. "So it wouldn't bother you if you found out he liked someone else. Like, say, Vic."

"Vic?" Emma laughed. "No. She drives him bonkers."

"Yeah, but I think it's because he likes her. Think about it: They walked in together."

"That's because he saw her on the elevator."

"So he was going up, and she was going down, and she just decided to go back up and come here, instead of wherever she was planning to go?"

"Maybe they met in the lobby then. But trust me: He's not interested. Not a chance."

Liam paused again. His brow was creasing, but Harlan's voice interrupted them from the main room. "Liam, where are those snacks, dude?"

Liam looked at the empty plate. "Um . . ."

"It's cool. We have snacks for days." She hopped off the counter and opened the fridge, grabbing a cheese-and-meat plate that Sean had had delivered that morning with their groceries. She handed it to him.

He bowed his head a little and walked back to the main room with the plate. Emma waited for a few minutes, wondering how Liam could be so certain that Aleki liked Vic and why he even cared. He had to be jealous of Aleki. It's not like Liam liked Vic. Right?

Oh, crap. Did Liam like Vic? Is that what he was getting at?

She didn't want to think about this. She pulled out her phone—the best numbing device she knew of—and looked at the press clippings Drew had been sending her all day. She was annoyed that her manager was bypassing Brittany, but at least it was all good news. The images Julien had posted from the party were positive, too, although the very first image was of Aleki and Emma sitting at a booth, Aleki's arm around Emma's shoulders as she leaned into him. It was completely out of context and missed the fact that Brittany was two feet away. But Julien had risen to the challenge, and considering there were already rumors about Emma and Aleki, this came as no surprise to the shippers online. Had this prompted Liam's question?

She kept scrolling through the pictures. There was one of Harlan chatting up a makeup artist, one of Aleki and Weston with their arms around each other, and one of Vic and Liam.

Vic and Liam.

They were sitting in a close tête-à-tête. Really close. He was whispering in her ear, and she was smiling. It wasn't her usual reserved smile either. It was a knowing, secret, intriguing smile that Emma had never seen on Vic before.

Of course Julien hadn't been able to find Emma's love interest. Because her love interest had been chatting up Emma's nemesis.

One dance, and you got ahead of yourself. Again. Look at that picture: He could just as easily like Vic as you.

Freaking Vic.

CHAPTER TWENTY-SEVEN

Emma passed Vic talking on the phone in the hallway on her way back to the main room. She took the seat that Vic had vacated, near Liam and the team. Aleki and Brittany were talking by the bookshelves at the far end of the room. Brittany looked so interested and animated, and Aleki so obviously loved the attention, judging by his larger-than-life gestures.

When Vic returned to the room a few minutes later, Emma watched Aleki's eyes follow Vic in naked curiosity. Vic joined their conversation and started explaining something. Then Brittany clapped and bounced, and Aleki hugged Vic. She looked so humble, even in the midst of this happiness. She'd had a terrible childhood, but if she had any baggage to speak of, it was a carry-on. Meanwhile, Emma had to check the entire Louis Vuitton set.

If Liam was running from Emma, why wouldn't he run straight to Vic? Why wouldn't he choose someone so low maintenance and well adjusted?

She risked a look at Liam, who was looking at her with that stupid wrinkled brow that she wanted to smooth out with her thumbs. He couldn't like someone else, could he?

Aleki jumped up on the coffee table like it was from IKEA instead of Fendi Casa. "Everyone, great news! Tomorrow, we're going on a little field trip to the Appel Room, where our very own Victoria Alba will be opening for Arcade Fire!"

Emma watched Liam's eyes pop. He walked over to give her his congratulations.

"Arcade Fire?" Liam gave Vic a hug that made her smile bigger than

Emma was used to seeing on Vic. "Congratulations! I know how much you wanted this. I love it when good things happen to good people."

"Thanks, Liam. I wish I had earned it instead of Tinker canceling last minute because of the flu, but it still feels good that they thought of me next."

"That means you still earned it. Congrats." His smile was so warm, and Vic's answering smile reached her eyes, making them look like puddles of melting chocolate that Liam couldn't possibly be insensible to. When had they talked about Vic's hopes and dreams? How did Liam know this event was even a possibility?

The guys on the team offered their congratulations, although it was clear that half of them didn't know who the indie rockers were. After Harlan congratulated Vic, it was Emma's turn. She held out her hands. "Vic, this is so exciting! Congratulations!"

"Thanks! I can't believe it's happening. You probably don't remember, but—"

"Season three, when we thought Weston had cancer for that episode and we were writing our bucket lists in case anything happened to him? I remember I just scribbled on my piece of paper, because they weren't going to show it. But you wrote down, 'Open for Arcade Fire.'"

"Yeah. I'm surprised you remember that."

Because she was so self-centered and shallow? "Well, I did. Congratulations."

Vic thanked her and said her goodbyes so she could rush downstairs to tell Aunt Kelly the good news.

Brittany immediately started making arrangements to obtain VIP passes, and Liam went back to the couch, which left Emma, Harlan, and Aleki to sit in the armchairs by the bookshelves.

"Is it me?" Emma asked. "Am I so distasteful that she can't even have a damn conversation with me? She is impossible."

"Not gonna argue there." Aleki blew air out of his mouth in a huff.

"Aleki, you know her. You've talked to her," Harlan said. "Why is she here? What's she actually after? I don't buy that she wants to return to acting. She could get an agent in a snap. What does she want?"

"If I could tell you that, I'd have cracked the female code, my man."

Harlan had his "celebrity beef face" on, the face he always got right before picking a fight online with someone. Normally, Emma tried to head it off. But right now, she was too frustrated. Too upset. Too worried that Liam . . . Liam . . .

"I bet her manager was into her," Harlan said. "Maybe she found out, and that's why she moved. Or maybe they had a thing. Maybe that's how she got him to sign her in the first place."

Emma could have laughed, but Aleki was wearing a mischievous smile. "What if it's not Vic? What if it's Kelly who had a thing with the manager, and he took Vic in as a favor to his secret lovah? We've all seen pictures of her back in her Calvin Klein days. Girl was fire."

Emma snorted. "Well, now we're officially off the rails." She was fairly certain Aleki was kidding, but Harlan was nodding, getting carried away with the idea.

"I can see it, man. Kelly would do literally anything for Vic's happiness. Do you know how many times she's stopped me in the lobby to tell me about Vic? If I see Kelly in a day, I can tell you everything Vic has had for breakfast for a month."

Aleki threw his legs over the armchair. "Dude, I know. Vic could trip and break a priceless vase, and Kelly would say how vases were a sign of bad luck in ancient Mesopotamia, and Victoria's always been so intuitive about what the universe wants that she probably felt the spirit of a Mesopotamian crying out for the bad luck to be destroyed."

"She wouldn't say that," Emma argued. "Kelly would say that it was her own fault for buying a new rug three years ago, because if she'd had the old rug, then Victoria would have still remembered what it felt like to walk on it, but the poor girl has been through so much in her life that how could Kelly have been so foolish as to expect Victoria to be able to thrive in an environment with a new rug, and this is the reason why coconut milk is the superior alternative for the lactose sensitive who eat the occasional bowl of ice cream."

Harlan and Aleki burst out laughing.

Aleki high-fived Emma. "Nailed it."

That night, Emma and Aleki helped Brittany rehearse for her upcoming audition. Aleki had scripts ready for Brittany, and Emma walked her through the audition process, talking about the value of getting into character over memorizing the script. When they finished up, Brittany ran into the kitchen to make Emma a protein shake. "You should come with us to Britt's audition," Emma said. "And you should officially represent her, because she's going to be great."

"I'm thinking about it. And that's a good idea. I'll come. I have some client calls, but I'll fit them around her audition."

"Thanks. I think you two are a really good fit, for what it's worth."

"She's so open to feedback. If I could fill my list with clients like her, I'd be the happiest agent in Hollywood."

Brittany returned with Emma's shake, and Emma grimaced before taking a quick breath to psych herself up. "Bottom's up." She tipped back the glass and downed its contents.

When she finished, Brittany and Aleki were sharing a glance. "It's a fine line between dedication and masochism, but you're walking it," Aleki said.

"Hell yeah, I am."

Aleki and Brittany headed out together, and with Harlan out at a poker night with the team, Emma was left to check social media as she got ready for bed. She looked back through Julien's pictures from the club and focused on the one of Liam and a laughing Vic. In the comments, hundreds of people were talking about how cute they were together, how they didn't know who Liam Price was, but they shipped the crap out of them. Emma couldn't keep looking at them. She looked through the dozens of pictures Julien had put up from the night, including one of Weston talking with Kelly. The comments under the picture of Kelly were enough to make Emma sick.

"Can you believe Kelly used to be hot? Her neck looks like an elephant's."

"The only chick I know who can go from Oscars to an Oscar Mayer eating competition."

"She looked hotter when she was fat."

"Not bony enough."

"Still would."

"What happened to Kelly Bates's career? She was my favorite actress for years. Does anyone know why she disappeared? Don't tell me it's the eating disorder. Lots of stars have had those."

That comment had dozens of replies, including a theory about how she'd been sleeping with a major studio exec and things had ended poorly when the wife found out, filed for divorce, and took half of everything the exec had. The commenter said before the exec's divorce, Kelly had been cast in three of the last five Oscar-bait movies that the studio had put out. The two crappy movies she'd done were with another studio. But as soon as things fell apart with the exec, her weight loss spiraled, and she passed out at the big party. After that, rehab, a few years of yo-yoing weight, and another bout of rehab, her career was history.

Emma tried to reconcile that theory with the Kelly she knew. She struggled to imagine the woman who bought her a unicorn notebook for her eleventh birthday offering quid pro quo for better roles, as Aleki and Harlan had joked. But who could say that Kelly hadn't had an affair with a married studio exec? Or with Vic's manager, for that matter? Emma didn't judge, but she wasn't so naïve as to think it couldn't happen. Everyone had skeletons in their closet.

CHAPTER TWENTY-EIGHT

Standing backstage at Vic's concert, Emma had to give it to the girl: she was born to perform. The acoustics in the room sounded like they were designed to amplify her rich alto voice, and if Emma had any remaining affection for Vic, she would have been transported by the performance.

Like Liam was. Like everyone else was, even Harlan, although she knew he'd deny it.

After the set, they went back to a lounge inside the performance hall for a small get-together. It was casual, with couches and chairs set up around the room and an impressive spread of food against one wall. Too bad for Emma, she could only eat the meat, cheese, and nut plate.

It was a good thing that basically all of her friends were athletes and actors, because at least she didn't have to see anyone eating the pineapple. She couldn't remember the last time she was hungry, but even on a full stomach, pineapple would taste like a friggin' dream.

A music journalist was listening to KeyAra and Kelly wax poetic about Vic's countless virtues. KeyAra was explaining how she and Vic had become best friends so quickly because Vic was the most open-minded and accepting person KeyAra had ever met, not to mention the hottest and most talented. It got a little weird. But Kelly was elated to hear someone talk with nearly as much passion for Vic as she had. Every time KeyAra said something about Vic, Kelly acted like a hype man.

It was a relief watching the spectacle with Harlan, because while she got annoyed, he got deliciously mean. He mimicked Kelly. "Oh, KeyAra is absolutely right. Victoria wouldn't let a butterfly fall from the sky without trying to nurse it back to health. In fact, she has the largest butterfly infirmary in her kitchen at home. You wouldn't believe all the notes she's received from the butterfly population thanking her for saving their lives."

Aleki joined them. "Is Kelly at it again?"

"What do you think?" Emma said, double-checking that Weston and Liam weren't in earshot. "Did you know that Vic is single-handedly saving the entire homeless population by always carrying boxes of granola bars and bottles of water?"

"That's actually really nice of her," Aleki said.

"No, it's not," Harlan said. "It's naïve and reckless. It keeps them from going to shelters and using resources designed to help them."

"I can see what you're saying, but I still think it's cool of her."

The worst part was that Emma did too.

Liam came over then. "Can you believe that set? Vic killed it. She completely stole the show."

Aleki looked at Emma, the annoyance on his face reflecting the annoyance Emma had been internalizing all night. To Liam, he said, "Dude, sounds like someone has a crush."

"You weren't at the same concert I was, weren't you? I think everyone in that room fell a little in love with her after that," Liam laughed, but it wasn't a dismissal. Vic's drama-free life was probably looking better to him by the minute. Blood pulsed in Emma's ears, so heavy and loud, it was blotting out the sound.

"I know KeyAra did," Emma said, trying to sound light, like this conversation wasn't slowly sucking the oxygen from the room and suffocating her.

"KeyAra liking Vic so much is kind of redeeming, let's be honest," Liam said. "Maybe she has some depth hidden somewhere inside."

Harlan punched Liam's shoulder. "Or maybe Aleki's right and you have a thing for Vic. It's cool to admit it, man. You're safe here."

Liam's ears spotted red. "Whatever fits your narrative."

The rational part of Emma knew this night was a big deal for Vic. That same part of her wanted to be happy for the girl who she'd tried so long to be friends with. But the memory of too many rejections still stung her. So many efforts to talk to Vic on set or off, so many invitations to hang out that were rejected in favor of anything else more important: school, guitar lessons, voice lessons, studying scripts. On the rare occasion Vic had shown a tiny sliver of humanity—like when she'd written her bucket list during that episode—Emma had foolishly made another overture, just to have it thrown in her face.

"Who is Arcade Fire?" Emma had asked between takes. She'd only had a chance to see the first line on Vic's bucket list, but her curiosity had overridden the defensiveness that had developed over the last few years of working with the girl.

"What?"

"I saw your list—you mentioned you wanted to open for Arcade Fire. Open what? Who are they?"

But Vic didn't answer. She looked horrified. And why? Because Emma didn't know a band that must be so important to Vic and her elite crowd of super-cool geniuses?

Emma walked back to her spot. "You know what? Never mind. I don't need to know."

If Vic had looked guilty or the tiniest bit remorseful for her shaming reaction, Emma could have forgiven her. But she'd looked relieved. Relieved that Emma had walked away. Relieved that she didn't have to explain something as transcendent as Arcade Fire to such a basic loser.

Emma had left the set that day promising herself not to try anymore where Vic was concerned. Because Vic only cared about important things, and Emma was anything but.

And now, here she was at an after-party for the girl who had made her doubt her worth more than almost anyone since they were ten years old. Here she was, celebrating the accomplishments of some-one who spent her weekends reading Proust and practicing the piano and probably learning her sixth language, when she wasn't too busy curing cancer.

If that wasn't bad enough, Weston was talking to Vic, beaming at her, showering praises on her. The man Emma loved more than her own father was telling a reporter how the experience of working with Vic and Emma and becoming their mentor remained the greatest pride in his life. Vic and Emma. Not Emma and Vic. If Vic had a cast, would he write that she was his heart too?

And there was Kelly again, going on and on about how Vic was the greatest niece and human and singer and actor. Vic had been contacted by several different casting directors and was turning down roles that she hadn't even auditioned for.

Liam was defending his position of defending Vic, and Kelly was telling how Dear Victoria always made her breakfast in the morning, and KeyAra was telling Bryce how good Vic had been for her brand, and Weston was hugging her, and Kelly was saying how Dear Victoria did everything so thoughtfully and carefully and how she'd never made a hasty decision, which explained all of her accomplishments. Kelly even attributed her recent health boost to Dear Victoria's cheerful mood.

It was like a swarm of bees had been released inside Emma's head. And they were stinging.

Vic cleared her throat, calling all eyes to her in the center of the large room. Her red-rimmed eyes were the only sign of her emotion—she was the greatest actor of their generation, after all.

"Thank you all so much for being here with me. I've loved music since I was in diapers, and I've spent years trying to hone my craft, years where I probably isolated myself from real life and real friends a little more than was healthy." Why this earned laughs, Emma couldn't say.

Kelly said, "She did, the poor thing. She threw herself into her lessons and her studies, and she was so lonely."

Just not lonely enough to be friends with Emma.

Vic was still talking: "Being a last-minute replacement for a band wouldn't seem like a dream come true for most people, but when I was young and going through a hard time, I discovered a band whose music sounded as heart-wrenching as my pain felt. That sounds dramatic, but it's the only way I can describe it."

Kelly: "It's a beautiful description, and she really was in such pain."

Vic: "I wrote a bucket list several years ago for an episode of *My Valentines*. The very top item was to open for this band, Arcade Fire. And tonight, I've finally been able to cross the top item from my list."

Kelly: "She's crossed off other items, but she's too humble to mention those."

Vic: "I owe so much to the people in this room. You all have supported me and befriended me, even when I haven't made it easy. I'm not always the easiest person to love."

Harlan to Emma: "To put it mildly."

Liam to Harlan: "Dude."

Aleki to Liam: "Your crush is showing."

Liam: ". . ."

Kelly: "Oh, who could be easier to love than her?"

This torture would never end.

Vic was almost in tears. "But during all of these years where I've struggled to find myself and my place in the world, one person has stood by me and loved me unconditionally: my aunt Kelly."

Kelly held her hands over her mouth. "Oh!"

Vic's lower lip trembled as she continued. "Aunt Kelly, I don't know where I would be without you. Anyone with access to a tabloid knows the sordid details of my emancipation from my parents, but

I was in no place to take care of myself emotionally. And because of you, I didn't have to. You sacrificed so much for me. You made room for me in your life and in your heart."

"Nothing could have made me happier," Kelly said over Vic.

"You helped me change agents; you helped me get tutors and teachers who prepared me for this moment."

Aleki elbowed Emma and leaned in. "I think procuring those teachers was Kelly's favorite part."

"What's that supposed to mean?" Liam snapped. Why was he being so defensive about Vic? Why did he have to care about her at all?

Emma felt like the molecules in her body were forcefully trying to separate, pushing in opposite directions in their effort to rip her apart.

Vic's tribute continued. "The day I signed with my manager was the start of a new life for me, and it never would have happened without you."

Kelly interjected again. "It was never a sacrifice. Helping you was a pleasure. It was always such a pleasure."

Meanwhile, Liam was still pressing Aleki, whose jaw had become stone. The men were both flexing, looking seconds away from fighting. Over Vic. "No, seriously." Liam pushed. "What are you trying to say?"

Emma's breaking point shattered. "He's trying to say that Kelly's *pleasure* landed her more than a few roles. And from the sounds of it, maybe it landed Dear Victoria her manager too."

Emma winked at Liam, but she knew instantly it was the wrong move. Everything she had just done was wrong. Because as much as she had meant to whisper, judging by the horrified looks on most of the faces around her, she hadn't. And deep down, she knew she hadn't. She hadn't even tried. The fact that a few people—including the journalist—were smirking made it all the worse.

Harlan laughed.

Aleki hissed.

Vic froze.

Liam looked like he'd never seen Emma before.

Weston looked deeply, utterly betrayed.

And Kelly. She looked like she'd been cut open and her heart was weeping from the gaping wound Emma's words had left. She sputtered. "I didn't sleep with . . . I never wanted . . . Is that what he . . ." Weston walked over to Kelly and put his arm around her, leading her to the nearest door. "I love Emma. What did I do to make her think I would . . . What could I . . . How could she . . ."

Her voice faded as Weston pulled her from the room.

Vic thawed enough to act. She didn't look at Emma. Why would she have cared about Emma, who had proved in one moment every thought Vic had ever had about how small, inconsiderate, and inconsequential she was? No, Vic had no energy to spare on Emma. She ran after the woman who had loved her perfectly and the man who saw her as a daughter.

The snickering journalist turned back to another guest, already moving on from Emma's sound bite. KeyAra and Bryce continued their chatter. Aleki was biting the inside of his cheek.

"I know you were joking, but girl, you gotta learn how to *whisper* whisper, not stage whisper," he said. "That wasn't pretty."

Emma closed her eyes, the coating of shame in her throat and chest getting thicker by the moment. "I didn't think such a silly joke would get such a powerful reaction."

"Are you kidding, Ems?" Harlan asked. "Forget about it. They're acting like you murdered their dog and made them watch. It was a joke. They need to chill the hell out."

Harlan's words did little to soothe her, but looking around the room, no one else seemed too fussed about what had just happened.

Maybe her brother was right: maybe it wasn't that big of a deal. Maybe everyone else could take a joke. Maybe, in a few minutes, Kelly, Weston, and Vic would return and admit that they'd taken it too seriously.

But if that was the case, then why wouldn't Emma look at Liam, when he was a foot away from her and his heavy gaze was sinking her into the floor? If it really wasn't a big deal, why did she feel like an empty, worthless husk?

"Emma, can I talk to you?" Liam asked when Harlan and Aleki walked over to the food table.

Emma shook her head, her eyes fixed on a spot of tile that looked subtly darker than the rest, as if the original had cracked and been replaced by something stronger and more reliable.

"Emma." Liam's voice throbbed like her hand just after she'd broken it. "We need to talk."

CHAPTER TWENTY-NINE

In utter silence, Emma followed Liam to a small, out-of-the-way corridor, where he wheeled on her.

"I know what you think of my truth bombs, but I can't let this go. You are one of the cleverest, sharpest, most compelling women I've ever met, and I guarantee every person in that room craves your attention and your approval, *especially* Kelly. How could you say that? We don't know what happened to her or what she went through. But you know very well that she was chewed up and spit out by the very industry that you left because you've seen it turn people to monsters."

Emma folded her arms and gave a playful shake of her head. "You're taking it too seriously. It was a joke, Liam. And I know you pity Kelly—so do I—but just try to tell me she isn't one of the most absurd people you've ever met in your life."

"So what if she is? She's still a person with feelings! She's a woman who loves you and who, according to Vic, was there for you at a time when your own parents couldn't have cared less what was happening to you. Or is Vic wrong remembering the way Kelly used to come and eat lunch with you on set, even when Vic was filming? Is she mistaken in remembering the countless pieces of advice that I know for a fact you've taken to heart? Your Go to Hell Fund? That came from Kelly. Your rule to never be alone with a studio exec or producer or director? Kelly. Would setting up Josh the Pedophile have even occurred to you without Kelly's voice in your ear?"

Vic, Vic, Vic. How much had they been talking? Emma couldn't answer. She couldn't look at Liam. Guilt was spilling from her eyes.

If she hadn't already given him enough reasons to run, she certainly had now.

"That was wrong, Emma. Even if you'd been talking about KeyAra, it would have been wrong, but at least she could have fought back. That fractured woman crying with her oldest friend has been shamed in front of the people who mean everything to her by a young woman she loves like family. That was cruel, and it was wrong."

When Liam marched away from her, it should have been a relief. She should have been able to breathe now that the tremendous weight of his disappointment had been lifted. If only her own disappointment didn't weight so much more.

Emma went home, took a sleeping pill, and woke dutifully four hours later to drink a protein shake. She slept until her next alarm and her next protein shake.

She skipped limalama and kept sleeping until an angry, incessant buzzing from her phone roused her for good. Drew. She swiped and answered. "Yes?"

"Someone have a bad night? No, it's okay. Don't answer. Of course you don't want to talk about it. So let's talk about damage control." Emma didn't bother asking what Drew meant. "Your little sound bite from last night is incongruous with your image as someone who has so fiercely defended womanhood. Think about it: you accused Kelly of sleeping with powerful people to get roles. Now, some troll has gone out and found old pictures of Kelly from her Calvin Klein days and has a series of nasty memes that the media wants you to answer for. Every picture is associated with a different movie. It's not pretty. But I've been talking to the management team, and your dad has talked to Brittany about posting a very heartfelt apology from all of your accounts. I'll field all the press calls for now and explain it was a thoughtless joke and how deeply you regret it." She went on, saying that she'd left messages for Kelly and Victoria and had talked to Victoria's manager. Kelly didn't have one anymore, so Drew had talked to a rep from Calvin Klein, as well as several of Kelly's old directors, a few of whom had already made statements in conjunction with Emma's team about what a talent Kelly was. Drew's plan was layered and involved an upcoming PR stunt, assuming they could talk either Kelly or Vic into appearing with Emma anytime soon.

So far, that was the only wrinkle in Drew's flawless plan, but Emma's manager assured her that it would be taken care of soon.

"Drew?" Emma said, interrupting the woman. "How do you feel about what I said?"

"I think by tomorrow it'll be yesterday's news."

"Right, but what do you think of it? Personally?"

Drew's voice carried a hint of something cold and steely. "I don't get paid for opinions, Emma. I get paid for ensuring you have the best career possible. Right now, that means cleanup."

"Got it." Emma said. She ended the call, even though she heard Drew talking again. She didn't put down her phone, though. She looked at a text from her dad.

Too bad not everyone can take a joke, huh? Drew and I have this covered.

Emma turned her phone off and went back to sleep.

———————————

At noon, Emma crawled out of bed, downed a protein shake, and went downstairs for the worst training session of her life. Trying to lift with a cast was hard enough on a good day, even with modifications, but today, it was impossible.

"Come on, Crawford!" her trainer yelled as she lifted and dropped and jumped and pulled. "What is this? If I didn't know better, I'd think you didn't want it anymore!"

That wasn't it, though. She did want it. She simply didn't deserve it.

On the way back from the gym, Emma stopped on the fourth floor and walked to Kelly's condo. She knocked. No one answered. She knocked again, harder. Louder. Longer. A shadow moved across the peephole. She slammed on the door with her left fist. "It's Emma. Please come out. Please let me apologize."

They didn't answer.

That evening, Emma got a phone call from Aleki. "We missed you at the audition today."

"*Audition*? I didn't—" She hit her forehead with her cast and cursed. "Brittany's audition. I completely forgot. How is she? How did she do?"

"She must have done well. They kept her there all day and just had her rehearse a scene a couple of hours ago. They did wardrobe and everything. She didn't seem happy with it, but I assured her that it was a good sign."

"Why didn't she seem happy? Were you with her?"

"I was on a call in the lobby at the time. It was maybe fifteen minutes. Twenty, tops. I told her that nerves make everything feel worse than they are, but I don't think she believed me. You should call her and check in."

"I'll do that. Thanks, Aleki. And sorry I wasn't there. Was she upset I missed?"

"No, she knows how busy you are."

Emma dialed Brittany, but it went straight to voice mail. She left a message full of inspiration and affirmations and a bunch of other crap she didn't really believe at that moment but knew Britt would appreciate. For good measure, she found a floral shop near Brittany's apartment and sent her flowers. She wished they didn't make her feel like a neglectful boyfriend.

She tried Brittany again before bed, checked her phone for a missed message when she woke up for her 1 a.m. shake, and then again first thing in the morning. No answer, no messages. Brittany was still in town, right? She didn't leave for Cleveland till tomorrow morning with Liam and his team. Maybe her acting class had known about her audition and had taken her out for a celebration/consolation dinner last night.

Emma drank her shake and looked at the clock. She had time to get to limalama. And she really should go. But when she blinked, she could still see Weston's face twisted in shock and betrayal. It was a look that she had done everything in her power to make sure Weston would never give her. And one bad night had brought it in full force.

She skipped limalama and went back to bed.

A few hours later, she emerged from her room to eat (stupid reminder) and shower. Harlan was in the kitchen after meeting with his military trainer. He was still sweaty and smelled like the outdoors, whereas Emma smelled like stale humiliation. Sean was making him eggs and bacon. "Are you sick or something?" Harlan asked. "What is wrong with you?"

"Nothing." She opened the fridge and pulled out a carton of plain, full-fat yogurt and started eating.

"Did you see the memes about Kelly? The one where someone added the tattoo of the word 'pleasure'? Hilarious." He laughed, and the sound made Emma wince almost as much as the story. "Oh, don't tell me that you're still upset about that stupid joke. You're just as bad as they are, getting so worked up about it. No one cares. Move on."

Emma put the carton down. "Harlan, *you* care! You looked at the memes, just like everyone else! You're talking about it, joking about it, and then you tell me to stop thinking about it? How am I supposed to do that when you're doing exactly what everyone else in America is doing? I can't take this anymore." She walked out of the kitchen and went downstairs to the fourth floor.

Emma pounded on the door. "Please, Vic. Please let me in. I hate that I did this. I never wanted to hurt Kelly, you have to believe me. Please let me in." She pounded again. "Please!"

The door opened, and Vic stepped into the hallway, closing the door swiftly behind her. Her face was expressionless. "You've done enough, Emma."

"Vic, please, you have to listen to me. I wasn't myself when I said that. I was defensive and upset, and I was jealous—"

"Jealous of my aunt? Come on."

"Jealous of you! You are everything I'm not. I'm a starter; you're a finisher. You're always doing all of these smart, amazing, life-changing things, and I complain about having to gain weight for a role that most people would kill for. I couldn't hack college, and you graduated early. You're soulful and sing about things that matter, and I literally inspired a T-shirt by saying, 'I hate spending money on things that don't make me look pretty.'" Of course, her tears had to follow such a trivial, stupid admission. "Do you know what it's like to always be compared to you? And to know that my friendship wasn't worth your time when I was your only option? *It hurt*, Vic. It still hurts."

Vic's eyes were watering. "How dare you make this about you and me instead of what you did to my aunt? And what gives you the right to say any of this? Emma, you and Misha made fun of me for being a nerd! I heard you in season four talking about me!"

"Season *four*, Vic. You had three seasons before that to talk to me like a human instead of a bug. But you were too busy studying and being important—"

"Do you know what happened to me when I got home if I wasn't ahead in my studies? My dad locked me in a dark closet for hours. A closet, Emma! So yes, I avoided being friends with you because I was terrified of what awaited me at home. And honestly, I was intimidated by you. I'm an introvert. I'm self-conscious. I worry about every stupid thing I say. You've always been so self-assured, and I've felt awkward by comparison, okay? And it hurt me too. Do you know why I was so worried when you saw my bucket list? Because of the other things I had on there. 'Learn how to make friends. Stand up to my parents. Quit acting.' I hated acting. I'm not making a comeback. I was exploited every day of my life from four to fourteen."

She'd craved this kind of honesty for years, yet now that it was here, Emma didn't know what to say. She hadn't wanted it like this. The cost was too high. She whispered, "I didn't know."

"The show was already over when I was emancipated, or things may have been different. I hated having to put my safety over my life, but I made a choice, and I stand by it. I'm not the one responsible for your actions. You were hurt and feeling defensive? *Join the club.* We all have parental issues here, Emma. We're all scared, hurt little kids. My aunt tried to inoculate us both against this messed-up industry, and you threw it in her face in the most painful, public way possible. So, no, I don't accept your apology."

Tears streamed down Emma's face. "Vic—"

Vic put her hand on the doorknob. "I'll tell her you stopped by."

Emma nodded, not trusting her voice, not wanting to sob at the wrong time and make Vic feel any more upset or defensive than she already had every right to feel.

Emma walked toward the stairwell, hoping to punish herself and her already burning thighs, when she heard a ding from the elevator. Before the stairwell door could close, she heard a heavy knock and then Vic's voice, full of a fury Emma hadn't known she was capable of.

"What are you doing here?"

"Vic, please." It was Aleki's voice. "You can't honestly blame me for what Emma said!"

"Are you trying to tell me you *weren't* riling her up? I heard you cracking jokes, Aleki, and if Emma's good at anything, it's knowing exactly how to appeal to a crowd." The comment was as true as it was scathing.

"I didn't want her to say that. I didn't want her to make a joke at Kelly's expense."

"Because that's your territory, isn't it?" Vic's voice was cold. "Do you think I haven't seen the way you patronize her or bait her into saying outlandish things for your own amusement? She talks about silly things because talking about things that matter is brutally hard for her, as you well know. At least Emma was just being an ignorant, petulant brat. But you know exactly what Rogers did to her. How could you say what you did?"

"Vickie, please, I was hurt—"

"You don't get to call me that anymore. Everything was moving too fast between us even before we moved in together. I told you I wanted time to think about us when we both came to New York, and you punished me by turning to the one person you know brings out all of my insecurities. I have nothing more to say to you."

"Vic—"

The door slammed on Aleki. Emma heard a soft thud, and then she heard Aleki mutter something that sounded like "I love you."

CHAPTER THIRTY

Emma ran up and down the stairs twice before heading back up to the condo. Thoughts of Aleki and Vic and Kelly and whoever this Rogers person was swirled in her head, but the exertion wasn't clearing her thoughts like she wanted it to. She arrived home out of breath, her hand sweating in her cast. She was on her way to her room when she heard Brittany's voice. Emma ran to the dining room, where Brittany, Sean, Liam, and some of his teammates sat at the table. She heard Harlan on the phone in another room, but she didn't care about him right now. When Liam saw Emma, he gestured to the guys, and they went into the poolroom.

Thank the stars. She couldn't handle his disapproval right now on top of all of her guilt.

"Britt, you're here! I'm so sorry I missed yesterday—"

"Don't be sorry," Brittany said as Emma threw her arms around her. "You had an appointment with your trainer and back-to-back interviews and—"

"That's no excuse. I meant to cancel everything. I should have. I'm sorry I wasn't there for you." Emma sat next to Britt. "How did it go?"

Brittany's smile was bright but didn't reach her eyes. "Aleki called me a bit ago. I was offered the part."

"That's amazing! I'm not the least bit surprised. How are you feeling? Are you excited?"

Her eyes were tight, not as wide and open as Emma knew to expect from a truly happy Britt. "I think so. Aleki is going to tell them I need a few days to weigh another option."

Emma grinned. "Just let me know when to find another assistant.

I'm so proud of you. Look at you, coming to New York and making your dreams come true faster than most people can find a job at Starbucks. You're an inspiration." Brittany looked away, and now Emma knew something was wrong. "But we can talk about that later. Right now, I need wardrobe advice for next week's interview. Help me pick?"

Brittany followed Emma into her room, leaving Sean to work in peace. Emma was telling the truth—she did have a late-night interview scheduled, but she'd planned to woman up and finally text Weston about outfits. "Britt, I get the sense you're upset about something. Is it the audition or the job? Or something else entirely?"

Brittany was looking at the outfits on their hangers, fingering the luxe fabric of a simple black dress. "I just want to make you proud, Emma."

"What? Of course I'm proud of you. How could I not be?"

Brittany's hand was trembling. "I broke a rule. I know I shouldn't have, but Aleki wasn't around when they asked me in for the scene, and I kept thinking how much time and effort you'd sacrificed to get me to that point, so I went in without him."

"Okay—"

"They had me read lines with an actor, and I knew I was in the character's head because the actor was really responding. The director said he wanted to see how I did on camera, so he told me to change into a cocktail dress to really get into character." Britt's chin quivered, but she held Emma's gaze. "I asked him where the changing room was, and he laughed. He said I must be from the Midwest to be such a prude and said that no real actors uses a dressing room for quick changes between scenes. His assistant was there, and she was laughing with him, so I thought it must not be a big deal or else she would tell me, right?"

Emma had changed shirts off to the side of a scene or a photo shoot countless times, but no one had ever pressured her to do it or paid attention, and she was sure the people she worked with would have respected her choice to use a dressing room. Brittany's story didn't feel the same.

"He made me feel like some pathetic prude. The wardrobe stylist pointed me over to a corner that was several yards away from everyone, so I pulled a rack of clothes in front of me and turned my back on them. I stripped down and put on the dress before realizing that I couldn't wear a bra with it. So I took the dress off again, took off my bra, and that's when I realized the director followed me. There was a mirror set up in the corner, and he was watching me in it. His phone was out, and . . . I think he was recording me. He'd followed me over to the corner and was recording me naked, Emma." She squeezed her eyes closed. "When I made eye contact with him in the mirror, he didn't even look away. The pervert *smiled*. So I pulled the dress back on, grabbed my clothes, and told him to go to hell."

Brittany held her head high, as she should have. Tears streamed down both of their cheeks. "I didn't mean to swear at him, but I'm not mad at myself for that. The only thing I'm mad about is that I let him talk me into doing something I didn't feel right about." Brittany let out a small sob. "I shouldn't have let him take advantage of me."

The ache in Emma's chest was too much to contain. She threw her arms around Brittany, who started crying in earnest. "Britt, I have never been prouder of anyone than I am of you. Do you hear me? Nobody gets access to your body unless you give it to them, and you didn't give it. He tried to take it. You stood up for yourself with more courage and strength than I ever could. You followed your conscience, and you made yourself clear. No matter what else happened, you have every reason to feel proud of yourself." Emma cried. "You are my hero."

Brittany sniffed and pulled back from Emma. "I couldn't have done that without you."

Emma's chest felt like it was cracking open and flooding with shame. "No, Britt, you wouldn't have been in that position if it weren't for me. I pushed you to turn down your dream job. I pushed you to stay in New York and to act and to audition. *I* did this to you," she said, her voice breaking, "and I'll never forgive myself for hurting you."

Brittany's face changed in an instant. "Don't you dare say that. You've done everything you could to help me and to show me how much more there is to the world. *He* did this, not you."

Emma's shoulders shook as she sobbed and pulled her friend into a hug. She couldn't open her mouth to speak, couldn't tell Brittany how much her faith in her meant, couldn't tell her how sorry she was for pushing her into a life Brittany had never wanted in the first place. All she could do was hug this brave, wonderful girl and wish that she could take away the pain and shame the director had tried to create in her.

"Who was the director, Britt? We should report this, if you think you can talk about it."

Brittany dropped her arms from Emma and clutched a silver tear-drop necklace with a large, black gem that Emma had never seen her wear before. "I remembered what you and Misha did to Creepy Josh and how you said your dad had bought you a necklace with a camera in it. So I wore this on the day of the audition, and after I caught him watching, I told him I was recording him. He was pretty upset. I think that's why he offered me the role."

"Good for you for thinking on your feet," she said, even as she felt sick that Brittany thought she was serious about the necklace.

Brittany's eyebrows pulled together. "No, I was telling the truth. As soon as Aleki told me I had an audition, I kept thinking about your dad's 'pervert provision,' so Marcus helped me find a tech shop that sells hidden cameras. There are quite a few in Hell's Kitchen."

Emma grabbed Brittany's hands. "Britt, are you telling me that you actually recorded the whole audition?"

"Yes. I already saved the recording to my laptop and to the cloud. I saved it to a thumb drive, too, but Marcus said I've watched too many spy movies."

Emma wanted to cry again, but for a completely different reason. She looked her friend in the eye and willed her to understand what she was saying in her very core. "Brittany, you genius girl. You are the most amazing woman I know."

"I was just doing what you taught me to do."

"You surpassed anything I could have taught you long ago. Can you send me the recording? If we can blur out your face and breasts, are you comfortable talking to my lawyer?"

"I'm comfortable telling the whole world what he did. I didn't give him access to my body."

Emma covered her mouth and tried to keep from weeping again. She failed. "You are my hero, Britt. I mean that."

A tear rolled down Brittany's cheek as she smiled.

The girls finally emerged from Emma's room two hours later. Brittany hugged Emma tightly before going home, where she and Marcus had a movie marathon planned while she packed for her week off. Emma felt a pit in her stomach as she watched Brittany leave. No matter how Brittany had acquitted her, she couldn't forgive herself for her part in what had happened. And she didn't deserve to.

The guys were watching a movie in the main room, so Emma sat at the kitchen bar with her laptop and a protein shake. There were a few mentions of Vic's slaying it at the Appel Room, but the memes about Kelly weren't trending. The story from Vic's party hadn't gone viral. Kelly Bates simply wasn't someone people knew or cared about anymore.

The name Vic had mentioned tugged at Emma's memory: *Rogers*. Emma knew a few people with that last name—a big actor from the '80s and '90s, a studio exec who had come out a few years ago, and a critically acclaimed director. A quick search showed that Kelly had worked with all of them, but . . . This was odd. Kelly and Dashiell Rogers had been seen at dinner a month before she fainted. One tabloid reported that she'd gone with him to his room. Then, a month later, she fainted at the party . . . which was at Dashiell Rogers's house. Emma looked at the timeline of Kelly's dangerous weight loss. She must have lost twenty pounds between those two events.

Emma looked at more tabloids from the time. One of them was linking Kelly to the studio exec with whom they said she was having the affair. But there was no evidence of the fact, just a photo of Kelly and the exec at a party that the wife had been cropped out of. It was more conspiracy than theory, even. Another picture from that time was with Kelly and her "adorable niece, Victoria," when Vic was filming a commercial. And then the party.

Emma combed through stories about the party. There wasn't much information, and most outlets reported the same thing: Calvin Klein model and actor Kelly Bates fainted at a party and was checked into rehab for an eating disorder. But one tabloid suggested that Kelly had crashed the party and fainted after causing a scene. The website had a grainy picture of Kelly standing on a table, and it looked like she was holding a drink in one hand, gesturing with the other. Her mouth was wide open, as if she was screaming. None of the guests had made a statement, except of concern or support. Rogers had never made a statement at all.

Two weeks after Kelly had checked into rehab for anorexia, Rogers cast a Kelly look-alike for a major role in a film that went on to be a commercial success, despite the actor's lackluster portrayal. The critics of the time had lamented the casting, saying the role had required a Kelly Bates-style charisma that the lead hadn't possessed. Yet, the woman went on to star in two more of Rogers's movies, while Kelly was never seen again.

Emma replayed Vic's words to Aleki in her head: *You know exactly what Rogers did to her.* And the pieces of the puzzle clicked together. Kelly's skittishness during to the discussion at Weston's dinner party. Her intuitive concern about what had really happened to Emma at the club. Her shell-shocked reaction to Emma's cruel, careless comment at the after-party.

Dashiell Rogers had—at the very least—assaulted Kelly. And Emma had thrown it in her face in front of everyone who mattered to her.

She closed her laptop and dropped her head in her good hand. She was all cried out, but she still had plenty of self-contempt to spare. How could she have said that about anyone, let alone a survivor, someone who had looked out for her and had tried to keep her from suffering her same, awful fate? Of course Vic and Kelly hated her. Of course Weston and Liam were disgusted with her. All this time, she should have been thanking Kelly, paying her kindnesses forward, but instead, she'd mocked and shamed her before pushing Brittany into a similar fate.

"Am I interrupting?" Liam said from the opposite side of the counter. He looked wary. "The movie's over, and Harlan just got a text from a girl he met at the club, so he's on his way out. The guys and I are clearing out too. I just didn't want you to wonder if we're still here for a minute without Harley."

"That's no problem. You can stay as long as you like, though I understand why you wouldn't want to," she said, taking a drink of her shake with a side of self-loathing.

Liam put his elbows on the counter, closing some of the distance between them. "Why wouldn't I want to?"

"Oh, come on, Liam. I'm a trash fire. You should run as far and fast as you can."

"Is that what you think I'm going to do?" Liam's words sounded sharp.

"I'm saying you *should*. I hurt everyone who matters to me. I abandoned Finley to spare Harlan's feelings, and I pressured Brittany into a career that's already seriously harmed her, but she's so forgiving that I'm only more disgusted with myself. Do I need to remind you why Kelly's too betrayed to talk to me and Vic is too furious to look at me?" An angry tear spilled down her face. "Are you ready to say 'I told you so' yet?"

"No. I just wish I knew how to help."

She wiped her nose. "I don't deserve help. I deserve to be left behind. I'm a monster."

"You're not a monster, Emma. You're human who made some mistakes. A monster would revel in them, not try to make them right."

"If you knew the half of it—"

"So tell me everything. Whatever you want me to know. I promise, nothing you say will change how I feel about you." His eyes stayed fixed on hers, and the look was so personal, so intimate. She wanted to ask him what he meant, exactly. How he felt, exactly. She wanted to trust him with the depth of her self-hatred, with her greatest shame, the way he had trusted her.

But what was the point of unburdening herself? He was already leaving in January. Anything she told him would only send him packing faster. The truth was, Emma didn't get to have him. The sooner she accepted reality, the sooner she could move on. So she said the only thing she could say. "That's really nice of you, Liam."

Harlan and the guys came into the kitchen while Liam was still leaning toward her. Harlan put an arm around Liam and pulled him to a stand, but Liam held Emma's gaze. "Come on, bro. Chastity awaits," Harlan said.

"Are you sure you know what that word means?" Luis asked.

"It's her name." Harlan smirked at Luis. "You know, she mentioned she has some friends who'd love to get to know the esteemed players of NY United better. You guys interested?"

Kelechi and Luis declined, while another teammate said he was interested. Harlan squeezed Liam's shoulders. "You in?"

"No, I have to go home and pack for the road trip. Don't cause any trouble, man," Liam told Harlan. "Chastity seems sweet. Maybe you guys could just hang out. Watch a movie or something."

Liam looked serious, but Harlan laughed and started walking out. Emma followed them to the door, watching them walk out to the elevator. "Night, sis," Harlan said as he stepped onto the elevator.

"Good night." She was closing the door as she heard Liam say, "Shoot, I forgot something. Go ahead. I'll catch up." He ran back to the door, and Emma held it open for him.

"What did you forget?" she asked.

He was breathing quickly, and his eyes looked wide. "To say goodbye," he told her. His arms moved a fraction, like he wasn't sure if he should hug her or not, but Emma launched herself at him. She wrapped her arms tightly around his neck as his wrapped around her back. He held her close, and Emma clutched him like a life preserver that would save her from drowning. She closed her eyes, breathing in the smell of his detergent, memorizing the way her cheek felt against his, the way they fit together. This could be the last time they held each other. She didn't deserve it, but she couldn't stop herself from reveling in the feeling of his body cradling her. He smoothed her hair down and rested his forehead against hers. "Bye, Ems."

Her throat creaked. "Say hi to Finley for me, okay? And travel safely?"

"I will." They let go, but Liam took her casted hand and brought it to his lips, kissing the skin of her two exposed knuckles. "Be good to yourself. I'll see you when I get back."

CHAPTER THIRTY-ONE

Emma couldn't remember the last time she was nervous before an interview. Talk-show interviews were planned and discussed in advance, but even if they weren't, she'd done enough that they were second nature by now. She knew better than most actors ten years her senior how to read an audience and tailor her reactions and energy accordingly. Nerves hadn't been a concern for her in ages.

Drew and her dad were standing around her, as if this interview was somehow more significant than the others she'd had lately. But it was just coincidence. Emma's dad was hoping to sign an up-and-coming comedian who was performing later in the show. Drew . . . well, Drew was paid to make Emma's career the best it could be. Given that Emma's life had been a little more dramatic than usual, Drew's presence was designed to make sure things went according to plan.

"The way you told the story on *Chloe and Ty* was perfect. Tonight, give them that same energy, but why don't you play up the chemistry between you and your date a bit more. Keep him nameless, but night-time viewers like things to get a little heavier and sexier than daytime viewers. Don't be afraid to get a little more raw."

"Not too raw," her dad said—not for any fatherly reason, she knew. "You're nineteen. If the story gets too heavy, people are going to expect a meltdown or scandal in your future. No one wants that."

"It's all about balance," Drew said.

"And your brand," her dad said. "Your drama has to be accessible to keep your fan base happy."

"Excellent point. So let's be a bit sexier, but keep that charm up. That's your signature," Drew said.

"Your whole strong, powerful female look is new and untested, so don't let it dominate too much," her dad said. "That plays better to a daytime audience, because all the sad housewives at home want to feel empowered. A nighttime audience wants to be entertained, so dazzle them."

Emma "All Dazzle, No Depth" Crawford.

She gave them both her most winning smile as the host announced Emma as his first guest. "I'll do my best."

The stage manager pointed at Emma, and she walked onto the set, smiling and waving at the exuberant audience. Her cast had come off that morning, but a splint was strapped over her hand in its place. She was glad of it. It felt like armor. Emma hugged the host, sat in the armchair, and away they went. She stuck to the plan at first—the upcoming *Valkyrie* movie and her role, jokes about going to school in Paris. He asked if the rumors about French hygiene were true and what she missed most about living overseas.

Then, the segue. "Everyone is talking about what happened to you at a club recently or, should I say, what happened when someone tried something on you at a club." The audience laughed. The story wasn't new anymore, but it was nowhere near old. "What is wrong with this guy that he thought, 'You know what will probably impress a girl? Me groping her.'"

"Well, let's be honest: it's never about the victim. It's about what a guy like him wants. What he thinks women owe him."

This wasn't what they had discussed. That was supposed to be Emma's opportunity to launch into the story. The host tried again. "So what happened? He went in for a grab, and what did you do?"

Emma mentally shook herself. *Get with the program!* She looked at the eager host and then at the audience. So many amused faces waiting to be entertained. And this was her chance to do so spectacularly. The audience was perfectly primed, ready to gasp and laugh and pump their fists at her takedown. She could read it in their faces, the way they leaned forward and sat on the edges of their seats, almost as if they were filled with helium. They were ready to be dazzled by the most dazzling girl in Hollywood. And the story was on the tip of her tongue.

Then she spotted a college-age girl with an older woman—her mom, probably. The girl was rapt, but she wasn't smiling or sitting forward. Her shoulders were hunched, her arms wrapped around herself. Her eyes were both wide and pinched, the way Brittany's had been. The way Emma's own eyes had looked in the mirror after the club. The way Kelly's eyes had looked a hundred times over the years.

She looked wounded. Hurt. She wasn't here to laugh with the crowd; she was here to know that she wasn't alone.

Emma turned back to the host and put her hand on his desk. "I know everyone wants to hear the way I wiped the floor with that creep, but do you mind if I monologue for a moment? Go off script?"

The host looked at one of the producers, who shrugged. "Yeah. Go for it."

"I defended myself physically. I kicked the crap out of the guy, and I'm proud of myself for it. But I'm not proud of myself for not filing charges. I signed paperwork saying I wouldn't, so that I could use the story without fear of *him* suing *me* for any so-called damages he received when I defended myself. I've downplayed the story to make it work for me, and in doing so, I've trivialized assault. So he gets his anonymity, he gets no consequences beyond a handful of bruises that have already healed, while I have to live with the knowledge of what he did to me and what I should have done to him. It's not right. I'll be calling my lawyer about this tonight and talking to the NYPD. I want to file charges."

This earned a huge round of applause, and Emma felt courage swell within her. The host told her that was amazing, how more women need to have their voices heard. "You're exactly right," Emma said. "Women are still being taken advantage of every day in this business and in all businesses. I was taught by the amazing model and actor Kelly Bates, to whom I owe the deepest, sincerest apology for a thoughtless joke I made at her expense," Emma said, her eyes wet. She could cry on command, but it turned out she couldn't *not* cry. "I love and admire Kelly, and I owe her so much."

"Like what?"

"Kelly taught me to always have backup everywhere I go. Auditions, meetings with studio execs and directors, wherever. She told me never to be alone with someone I wouldn't put in my will. That advice has served me my whole life when people have tried to take advantage of me. But, let's be honest: I'm absurdly privileged. I have a platform, I have a voice, and more, I have resources to fall back on for the rest of my life if I ever have to choose between a job and my body. But few women have such privilege. I read an account last night of an undocumented immigrant who works on a construction site. Her boss told her that if she didn't sleep with him, he'd report her and her family to immigration. What is she supposed to do? Who is her voice?"

"Wow," the host said.

She silently thanked him for going along with her instead of cutting to commercial early.

"And just this week, I found out that a dear friend of mine was being spied on and recorded by a director while she was in wardrobe. He took footage of her against her will and tried to buy her silence by offering her a part."

His eyes popped. "What? You found this out? How?"

"My friend took Kelly's advice too. She couldn't have someone with her for the callback, so she bought a wearable spy camera and caught the whole thing on the recording. She's already talking to a lawyer, and they're in the process of filing charges. We'd planned a big *60 Minutes*-style exposé, but she's authorized me to spare you all the suspense. It'll be live on my social media immediately following tonight's episode."

The *oohs* in the audience were as loud as any applause. The host was shaking his head, his mouth agape. "Wow. Wow. How is this kind of thing—"

"Abuse."

"Yeah, how is this abuse still so rampant? Who are these men?"

"They're the gatekeepers to our industry and throughout too much of the world. They're the men—and women—who've made power more important than people. Until we see a change in the gatekeepers, this abuse and harassment won't end."

The house band stood up, then, mostly men and women of color. They applauded. The audience gave Emma a standing ovation. Even the crew was clapping. She covered her mouth with her bare hand and her splinted one and fought back tears with all the grace she could muster. This wasn't about her. She wasn't here for the spotlight. But she'd be lying if she said the support of the people in that studio didn't feel pretty damn good.

When the show cut to a break, the host gave her a frazzled look. "Well, that took a turn, huh?"

"I'm sorry I didn't give you any warning. I didn't know I was going off script until right before it happened."

He gave her a suspicious look, but it was a good-natured one. "I'm not sure I believe you, but I'm not mad at you. That was great. It was important. Call me if you want to talk more about any of this, okay? I got your back."

They hugged, and Emma walked through the studio, waving at the audience in thanks. Her eyes landed on the girl she'd noticed earlier, and Emma ran up the steps to where the girl sat on the edge of the aisle. Her chin was quivering. Emma crouched beside her and grabbed the girl's pen and ticket, making it look like she was just signing an autograph. "Are you okay?"

"No."

"Do you have anyone you can speak to about it? A friend, a professor, a therapist?"

"I don't know."

Emma wrote down her personal number under her autograph. "Now you do."

The girl took the ticket and pen back with shaking hands. "Thank you."

Emma smiled at her and walked back down the stairs and out of the studio to the backstage. Drew and her dad were waiting. Her dad looked apoplectic.

"What were you thinking?" he demanded as they marched her to her dressing room. "This changes everything. This affects sponsorships, future roles, upcoming interviews . . ." He was still ranting when they reached the dressing room and closed the door "Not to mention the fact that the Vikings producers will have some serious reservations about you doing the same thing to them. Spy cameras, Emma? What were you thinking?"

"I was thinking about Josh Kleinfeldt. Ring a bell? The twenty-three-year-old pervert who I managed to keep from assaulting me by convincing him you had installed spy cameras in my jewelry and dressing room? Not that you would ever have cared enough to make such an effort. I went from daughter to cash cow so fast, I still have whiplash."

"What are you talking about? I threw a fit to the studio when that happened."

"Right, for a cool million-dollar settlement. It's nice to know what my safety's worth to you."

Her dad sat on the couch, crossing his legs. "You've always been so dramatic."

"Considering how disinterested you've been in my well-being, I think I've been positively restrained."

He shook his head and pulled out his phone. The conversation was over.

Except it wasn't.

"Dad, do you know I convinced myself that what Josh did was just creepy? It wasn't creepy. It was an attempt at statutory rape. What if I hadn't convinced him to stop? Has that ever occurred to you? Did that keep you up at night for months afterward? Because the sick thing is that you were so dismissive, it *didn't* keep me up, and it should have. I've been so turned around for so many years thanks to you that I couldn't have defined 'sexual assault' with a dictionary."

"You're being absurd. Of course it kept me up. Why else would I have fought the studio so hard? I ended Josh's career."

"No, you shifted it to the world of finance. At least there aren't too many minors working in corporate settings." She wanted to spit. "He should be in prison, Dad."

"Is that what you want? You want me to break the nondisclosure so we can get sued over something that never actually happened? You weren't raped, Emma. You make light of victims every time you claim to be one."

Drew shifted on the other side of the room, but Emma didn't pull her eyes from her dad, who was practically swimming in contempt and disinterest as he looked at his emails. He wouldn't even meet her eye.

And she realized—finally, truly realized—that it wasn't because she wasn't worthy of his attention. It was because, deep down, he knew he wasn't worthy of hers.

"Dad, I tried to do this once before, but Harlan convinced me not to, so I went along with what he needed because it felt more important than what I needed. But I'm done making everyone else's needs a priority over mine. You're fired."

His head snapped up. "You are an immature child. Give me a break."

"I'm not giving you anything anymore. You don't get my career or my time or any part of me. You would sell me to the highest bidder, if it were legal. We're done, Dad. You're fired. I'll have Drew send you the paperwork to terminate. Right, Drew?"

Drew nodded hurriedly, her mouth sealed shut.

"Get up and get the hell out, Dad, or I'm calling security."

"I *made* you, you ungrateful brat. You would be nothing without me!"

Emma looked at Drew. "Do you mind calling security?"

Drew grabbed the desk phone, and Emma's dad shot out of his chair. "I still own all your contracts," he said as he shoved his phone in his pocket. "I'll be getting paid for years for the work I've done to make you what you are today."

Emma yawned.

"Security?" Drew said into the phone. Instantly, Emma's dad stormed from the dressing room and slammed the door behind him, leaving the wall shaking. Drew put the phone down with a grim smile.

Emma looked at the woman. "Thank you, Drew. I've always liked you. If you're not on board with who I am today, I understand and will find new management."

"Are you kidding me?" Drew looked fiercely proud. "I'm more than on board. I wanted all of this for you, including you firing that miserable ass. I had no idea you were capable of such fire, or I'd have pushed you to take a stand months ago. You're strong, Emma. You have a voice people need to hear. And maybe I need to hear it a bit louder too. So if you think I'm not listening, speak up."

"Believe me, I will."

CHAPTER THIRTY-TWO

Emma got home late that night. She'd gone with Drew back to her office, where they had a long talk about strategy and what Emma wanted before setting up the video of the director who'd harassed Brittany. Marcus had a friend who was able to blur out Brittany's face and body when it showed in the mirror, but everything else was there. Drew had filmed Emma saying a few more words about the need for change throughout Hollywood and the world. She'd burned through too much energy on *The Tonight Show* to channel quite the same fire in the video for her social media. She was angrier, sadder, more world weary.

Drew told her it was perfect.

She didn't have the mental energy to watch the show that night, and Drew was going to have one of her assistants look through the comments while Brittany was on vacation to spare both Brittany and Emma getting sucked into the comments. But before bed, she checked her texts while she sipped on her protein shake. She quickly moved through texts of support from Misha, Jamal, and a few other friends, responding with hearts and thanks. She had one from KeyAra (how had she gotten Emma's number?) about what a great job Emma had done and asking if she wanted to partner up together to discuss makeup and women's rights. She'd get to that one later. She deleted several messages from "friends" who urged her to be cautious or careful. A text from Aleki said, *Hat tip, girl. That was fierce and important, just like you.*

Harlan texted, *Couldn't be happier to be a Crawford right now. Love you.*

Her aunt in Chicago left her a teary voice mail, saying how proud she was of Emma. Her uncle shouted his praise in the background.

She had a Marco Polo from Weston. He was sitting with his Great Dane on his lap and looked serious. "Come to class tomorrow. If you're not there, I *will* come to Highbury Lane and drag your butt all the way to my studio, and it will not be pretty."

Emma replied with a thumbs up to his video, not sure how to interpret his tone, not sure if she was forgiven or in hot water or something else entirely. She'd find out tomorrow.

She lay in bed, staring at the faint city lights that fought through the blackout curtains to cast long, dull shadows on her ceiling. What she'd done tonight hadn't made up for all the pain she'd caused, but it was the first step. Hopefully, she'd get the chance to finish what she'd started.

The next morning during limalama, Weston was impossible to read. He didn't smile or frown or treat her any differently than usual, which made her sweat extra all through class. KeyAra and Bryce were there—Emma had to admire the Eltons' commitment to fitness—and KeyAra bounced over to Emma when class was over, gave her a sweat-soaked hug, and told Emma to think about her offer. Emma gave her a strained smile, but no answer. Bryce held back when his wife went into the changing room. He kept rocking from foot to foot and darting glances at Emma. When most of the class had cleared out, Emma snapped. "If I'd wanted to hit you, Bryce, I would have done it months ago. Or is there something else you wanted to discuss?"

Bryce looked pained, and he walked over, probably to keep her from making their confrontation public. "I—I need to apologize."

"Come again?"

"I had no right to ambush you with that kiss, let alone to try again."

She did not see that coming. "And?"

"And I'm sorry."

"Good. Thank you for acknowledging what you did. What caused your change of heart?"

"KeyAra was really upset about what you talked about last night. She told me she was assaulted on a date a couple of years ago, and when I asked questions about it, evidently I asked the wrong ones. She's . . . not speaking to me. So I've been doing some soul-searching, and I realized what I did probably really sucked for you."

"Pretty much."

He nodded, his shoulders slumped forward.

"I'm not sure I forgive you yet."

Anger flashed on his face, but then his better angels seemed to take control. "I understand. That's your right."

"Are you planning to apologize to Brittany?"

"Brittany? No. I didn't do anything to her."

"You ghosted her and mocked her in public. You owe her an apology."

His nostrils flared. "I'll talk to my wife. If she thinks I should apologize, I will." He left for the changing room.

"What was that about?" Weston said from behind her. They were the only two people left in the room, although the next group of students would file in soon enough. She debated holding back, keeping her drama from dragging him down. She didn't want to drive him away too.

Yet, wasn't she doing exactly that by keeping him at arm's length? Wasn't her fear of abandonment precisely what was isolating her? Weston wasn't her dad. She owed it to herself to be real with someone who had always been real with her.

"Bryce came onto me pretty aggressively a few months ago, and he's been a huge jerk to Brittany. He apologized for hitting on me, but I told him to apologize to Brittany if he wants us to be square."

"Oh, Emma. I wish I'd known so I could have stopped throwing him in your path."

"I didn't want you to hear me talk badly about him."

"It only would have reflected badly on him, Nutmeg. Never on you. I'm sorry for what happened," Weston said. He stood beside Emma, and they both looked at the changing room, where Bryce had retreated. "But I don't think you should hold your breath for him to apologize to Brittany. He doesn't feel bad for what he did to her because it doesn't hit home like what he did to you."

"I think you're right." She turned to face her mentor. "Are we . . . are we okay?"

He put a hand on her shoulder, no hint of a smile in his eyes, but no hint of judgment either. "We should talk. Why don't you go change and meet me for breakfast after my next class?"

Emma did just that. She waited in their little nook at L'Orange, safe from prying eyes and cameras. For a while, she waited with her thoughts. But then the memory of what she had said to Kelly hit her, and she went online to see if anything was being said about Kelly now. The vicious memes came up on the first page of Kelly's search.

Weston showed up while she was looking at the images. He sat down across from her before she could turn off her phone. "Why are you looking at those, Emma?"

"I'm punishing myself, I guess."

"Why would you do that?"

"Because I don't deserve to move past what I did to her."

He kept looking at her, waiting for more. He had never asked for an explanation, and even though she'd kept her darkest secrets and shame from him, he'd always seemed to know her better than anyone. He had loved her and accepted her for years, and she had let her self-doubt keep him at bay. But that wasn't enough for her anymore.

She told him everything: her fear that letting someone in would make them run faster than her own parents had, her isolation, her years of self-consciousness around Vic. She told him about how she'd always felt surface-deep and how she'd never felt like enough for the people in her life, no matter how much she gave or how much she did. She told him about Josh Kleinfeldt, about what really happened in the club, and even her fears about Harlan and the way he was slowly becoming their dad. She told him that she didn't know how much more she could sacrifice to save Harlan.

Weston let her talk without comment, but the sad wrinkles in his face told a story of their own. When she finished, it was with a shrug. "None of this is an excuse for what I said about Kelly. I just want you to know that my head hasn't been right, but I'm working on it now, and I'm trying to fix things with her. I didn't tell you any of this because I was afraid that you wouldn't like what you saw."

"Emma Miriam Crawford, I like what I see just fine. But you're correct about one thing: your head has not been right. You don't understand love if you think that it's calculated on a tally sheet. Real love isn't conditional, and it can't be taken away just because someone does something boneheaded once in a while, or else we'd all be screwed. There's no shame in being self-conscious or scared. But . . . Nutmeg," he said, tears welling in his eyes, even though he hated crying in public. "What have I ever done to make you think I wouldn't be there for you when things got ugly? How could you think I would turn from you *ever*? You think I don't know the layers and depths that belong to you just because you don't tell me every thought in your head? I've known you since you were a little girl, and as exceptional an actor as you are, you can't fool me. How could you think that *I*—of all people—can't see past your candy-coated shell to the rich goodness beneath?"

Emma's cheeks grew warm. "You make me sound like a Cadbury Mini Egg."

"Now we're talking. After you're done filming, we're going to my mom's for a binge week," he said.

Emma looked at her plate of eggs and bacon and held her fork out to Weston. He bumped it with his.

"I know you, Nutmeg. The good and the bad that you think you need to hide from people. And I know a thing or two about hiding your nature from the world. I tried that as a teenager, when I thought I had to fit in with everyone else. I tried that in my twenties and thirties, when I didn't know who I was allowed to be or love or not love. At every turn, someone tried to cram me into a strictly defined box so they could understand someone like me. It took a string of failed relationships for me to finally accept that it really wasn't them, it was me. I'm happier single than I ever was in a relationship, because I've finally accepted all of me. Do you understand what I'm saying? Hiding who you are doesn't lead to happiness, only to that isolation you already feel. If you want to feel embraced and loved for who you are, let it all out. Let people love you in your totality, because you are worthy of love."

Her nose stung, and she rubbed it. "Thanks. Love you, Pops." It was what she'd called him on the show at the end of the first season, before she'd felt comfortable calling him "Dad," before believing that any man could love her enough to be her father.

She believed it now.

"I love you, too, Emma." He wrinkled his nose, spearing a tomato onto his fork. "But I have something I need to admit to you now." He put the fork back down, and a wave of goose bumps swept across Emma's arms. "I know how well you and Aleki have been getting along, but he . . . he told me something last night, something I'm furious with him over."

Emma reached across the little vintage table and put a hand over

Weston's. "If this is about him and Vic, I already know, and I'm more than okay with it."

Weston almost slumped in relief. "Oh, thank the stars. But are you sure you're not hurt?"

"I'm sure. He's a good friend, but the feelings were never really there for either of us. I think I mostly liked the *idea* of him because it would have made us family."

"I'm glad you're not hurt, but we're already family." He looked at her intently, as if his words mattered to him as much as they mattered to her. Because they did. "Don't you forget it."

After breakfast, Weston joined her on a quick errand before they went their separate ways. He hugged her and whispered how proud he was of her. That hug—those words—filled her with love, gratitude, and healing. It was the kind of hug that would help carry any daughter through the tough times ahead, the kind of hug her own father should have given her when he learned what Josh had done. It was the kind of hug he should have given her when she went to France and when she came home, when she got a new role or a rejection, when she had her heart broken and when she broke her hand. She'd needed that hug after she fought off Layton and when her guilt over her cruelty to Kelly threatened to eat her alive. She'd desperately wanted it when she finally stood for what was right. It was the kind of hug that made her feel seen and loved and important. It was the kind of hug that she realized she'd deserved all along.

At Highbury, Emma stopped on the fourth floor with the bouquet of flowers she and Weston had picked out. She knocked, but there was no answer. She left the flowers with a long, long note that she earnestly hoped Kelly and Vic would read.

So it was a profound relief that when she got upstairs to Harlan's condo, she found Vic and Kelly waiting in her kitchen, talking to Harlan. His desperate smile when he saw Emma showed too many teeth. "Emma! You're here. I've just been talking to Vic and Kelly. They insisted that they needed to be here when you got back. So we've waited together. For two hours."

"Thanks, Harley," she said.

He made his excuses and left the room.

"I'd have rushed home if I'd known you were here."

Kelly jumped up and gave Emma a tight hug. "Oh, you sweet, sweet girl. Thank you for saying all of those nice things about me last night. I can't tell you how happy they made this old girl. And to stand up for your friend the way you did was wonderful. You were wonderful. You *are* wonderful."

"I'm working on it. I am so sorry, Kelly. I should never have said anything other than what a wonderful woman and role model you've always been. I have no excuse, only an apology. I hope you can forgive me and trust me again, in time."

"Of course I forgive you. All is forgotten, dear Emma."

Emma frowned. "No, it's not. And it shouldn't be. I'm not saying this to punish myself, but . . . Kelly. I think you've been trying to tell me something for a long time, and I wasn't listening. You always kept a close watch on Vic and me, and I hadn't realized how much it meant or what you knew about, well, everything. I don't want to bring up anything painful, but I'm sorry I wasn't listening more closely. Thank you for looking out for me and for caring about me."

Kelly looked down at her hands, with her long, pretty fingers that looked like they belonged to a concert pianist. She was giving tiny shakes of her head, and Emma knew that, while Kelly understood what Emma was getting at, she didn't plan to talk about it. Maybe she never would, and that was okay. But when she looked at Emma, she smiled. "You're welcome."

Emma smiled back. "I wanted to talk to you about something that my manager and I have been discussing. We won't do anything without your approval, of course, but you've been instrumental in my life and now my friend's. I'm interested in starting a nonprofit dedicated to women's safety. My manager and I have several ideas that we'd love your input on, if you wanted to move forward. For example, we want to petition all studios and networks to have an independent HR representative dedicated to prevention and to investigating claims of harassment."

"Just one?" Kelly's laugh was darker than Emma had heard before. Sharper. "Go on."

"We want to have online tutorials that go through some of the lessons that you've always talked about—and more too. We would have financial planners, lawyers, and agents explain basic warning signs and red flags for female actors, and we would want a dedicated hotline for victims—*all* victims—who've experienced harassment where they could speak to someone who could offer comfort, but who could also let them know their rights. I'm sure there are a hundred things we're not thinking of. But this is important to me, and I know how important it is to you, and if you'd be interested—"

"I'm interested," Kelly said, though it was muffled by her clutched hands over her mouth as she nodded. "I'm interested."

"Me, too," Vic said. "If you'll have me."

Emma's grin almost hurt. She let out a laugh—a wet, sloppy thing. "The Kelly Bates Foundation wouldn't have it any other way."

CHAPTER THIRTY-THREE

Emma spoke to Brittany on Friday after a couple of phone interviews and before her appointment with her trainer. They'd texted all week but hadn't spoken since the night after the video had posted. Brittany sounded happier and lighter than she had in months, and Emma was relieved that, in spite of what had been done to her, she could still find happiness. Brittany hadn't told her family what happened during the audition, but she had no problem talking to Emma about it, and her attitude spoke of a determination and awareness of her worth that Emma hadn't noticed in her friend before. It wasn't because of what had happened to her, Emma knew, but because she was proving to herself that she was worth fighting for.

"What he did to me was wrong, and it's not my fault," she'd said in her email to Emma's attorney, who now represented Brittany. The firm was in the process of contacting hundreds of other women who had auditioned or acted on the show, and already, two other women had stepped forward with similar stories both on social media and to Brittany's attorney.

That director was going down.

But Brittany wasn't talking about that today.

"Liam got me tickets to tonight's game in Columbus! He actually gave me enough that my brothers and dad and Santino are coming too. I hope they don't throw something on the field when Liam's team wins."

"Britt, you know the team. Win or lose, they probably deserve it. Luis definitely does."

Brittany laughed.

"So . . . how is Liam doing?"

"He seems really good. I took my brothers to his game in Chicago on Monday, and we sat with his sister, Finley, and her boyfriend, Oliver, and with her boyfriend's brother, Tate, who is probably the most gorgeous man I've ever seen in real life. Seriously. He's a living Ken Doll. Better, even, although he mentioned something about rehab? Never mind. I forgot that you know all of them. In fact, didn't you date Finley's boyfriend last year too? He's super cute. But why am I telling you this?" She laughed. "Anyway, they were all just great! Finley flipped out whenever I talked about you."

"*Flipped out?* Why? Was she mad?"

"Not at all! She begged me for more information anytime I said something about you. She was so happy to hear about you. It was like she couldn't get enough."

Emma felt another crack in the protective coating around her heart. The whole shell was starting to erode now. "So you liked her?"

"I loved her. She and Liam are the best people ever, aren't they? Liam is such a good big brother too. We all went out to eat after the game, and he was so sweet and funny with her. They had all these inside jokes that I couldn't understand, but her boyfriend and his brother seemed to get them, and everyone was laughing and happy. It felt like . . ." Her eager, upbeat tone slowed a little. "It reminded me of me and my friends from home."

"Are you getting to catch up with them?"

"Oh yes. I've spent all of my time with my family and friends."

"Santino?"

Brittany's voice was as warm as apple pie, but her tone sounded like a little girl caught eating it. "Yes."

"I'm glad, Britt." She wasn't surprised to find that it was the truth. "I hope you two have a wonderful time together."

"Thanks, Emma." She didn't sound caught anymore. "I think I'll go do that right now."

"Good for you. See you soon."

The call ended, and Emma pulled out her phone to look at Liam's feed. He didn't post to Instagram much, but when he did, it was a picture of him eating something unique on a road trip. He always tagged the Arsenal club page. It was a reminder that he would return to England in a couple of months, so any attachment Emma and he made would sever too quickly.

She looked at the picture of him in Chicago. He was with Finley, and the two were eating matching loaded Chicago hot dogs from a local food truck, even though she knew he hated tomatoes. They were both wearing New York United hats and scarves, and Finley's nose was red from the cold. She was looking at the camera with a raised eyebrow while Liam pretended to be oblivious to the bright-green relish on his cheek. The caption was a gimme: "What? Do I have something on my face?" Emma smiled, even though just seeing Finley's picture made her chest ache like it had been hollowed out with a rusty spoon.

Before she could stop herself, she texted Finley.

Hey, I'm a loser. And I miss you.

A few seconds later, she had a text that said, *I'm sorry, who are you and how did you get this number?*

That was immediately followed by: *KIIIIIDDING. I miss you, you big, famous jerk. You should come to Chicago. All the cool kids are doing it.*

As proof, Finley sent a selfie of her with Liam and Brittany.

Emma felt like her heart had just been punched. This was the worst. Worse than the worst. Because that should have been Emma with them. *Britt's fab, isn't she? I'm glad you got to meet her!*

She seems cool, but if you thought you were fooling me by sending someone who wasn't you, you were wrong.

Emma laughed. *Really? Dang it. How long did it take?*

Just one punch to the ta-tas, and I knew I had the wrong girl.

BAHAHAHAHAHA sucker

Now I owe you two punches. And a hug.

Got some dust in my eye over here, Fin.

Three dots appeared. Emma waited for the accompanying text for what felt like an eternity. *How's Harley?*

The last conversation of any depth that the two girls had had was about how badly Harley was struggling. It was sweet of Finley to ask about him, but Emma was done making her brother a part of this relationship.

He's Harley. He needs to get his head out of his butt. How are you? How's University of Chicago? I can't believe you're a fancy college student now.

I'm probably the fanciest person you've ever met. I wore two different sneakers to campus yesterday and didn't notice UNTIL LUNCH. #Fancyaf

The two continued texting throughout the day, moving from funny to serious to stupid. Finley was in awe of Emma on *The Tonight Show*. Emma told her about the Kelly Bates Foundation, and Fin asked if she could be involved. Each time Emma took a break from her phone and returned to a missed text, she felt like a piece of herself was being restored and she was being made whole.

When Harlan got home just before midnight, Emma and Finley were talking on the phone. Their hands were too sore from texting, and Emma realized that the awkwardness she'd feared existed only in her mind. Finley was complaining about one of her three roommates, who tended to rant about how stardom and wealth were inherently immoral and who had actually told Finley that her dad's fame before his death had stained his soul and, by extension, hers.

"What?" Emma shrieked. "How dare she! Who does she think she is?"

Harlan mouthed to Emma. "Who are you talking to?"

"Hold on a sec, Fin, I don't want to miss anything." Emma pulled the phone away from her mouth. "I'm talking to Fin. One of her roommates is the *literal* worst. Her name is Dusk, and we're so over her. She's rude to Fin *and* her roommates. She made Janelle cry by telling her that pets forget their owners two weeks after they're away from their scent, and she threw out all of Hannah's Lactaid milk, because she said that drinking milk is an unnatural human evolution, and the fact that Hannah's body rejects it is proof that she shouldn't drink it. She's basically evil."

Harlan had stopped so abruptly that if they were playing charades, Emma would have guessed "Struck by lightning."

Over-actor.

"You're talking to Fin?" he asked, visibly grimacing. "Finley Price?"

Emma nodded with a big grin and held up a hand to Harlan as she returned the phone to her mouth. "Okay, I love and support all women because I'm a classy ho, but I officially hate her." Finley laughed about the "classy ho" line. They'd already discussed KeyAra. "Please tell me you put her in her place."

Finley had put her in her place, all right: She and her other roommates had wallpapered the apartment with every theater and movie poster the campus bookstore had. Every wall except for Dusk's.

Dusk had already put in a request to move. Emma cackled with laughter.

Harlan sat on the couch while Emma kept talking to Finley. She didn't get up and go to another room. She didn't cut the conversation short or temper her happiness. She laughed and screamed and spent another forty minutes catching up with her best friend.

When they finally ended the call, Emma was happy. So, so happy. Harlan wasn't.

"Ems, I'm confused. You know how bad I've been doing; you know how bad Fin hurt me. I thought you'd . . . I don't know . . . moved on from her."

Emma looked at her brother, and instead of responding with the anger that flared in her gut at his manipulation, she answered him with all of the love she had in her heart. "Harley, I'm sorry that my friendship with Finley hurts you. But not being friends with her has hurt me. I've felt totally isolated not having her to talk to—"

"You have me."

"It's not the same. If it were, you wouldn't have Liam, right? I love you, Harley. I don't want to hurt you, but it's not fair to either of us for me to have to sacrifice so much for our relationship to be okay. And my friendship with Finley is nonnegotiable."

"So you're cool being friends with someone who's so judgmental and inflexible that she doesn't even let people change? You're the one who's always saying that everyone has skeletons in their closet, and yet somehow you can be friends with her? Doesn't that make you a hypocrite?"

"There's a difference between making mistakes and acting like you're immune to the consequences, Harley. You hurt her. It wasn't her job to take you back; it was your job to earn the privilege, and you didn't." She stood up, not wanting to have a fight before bed. If she and Harley kept this up, even her sleeping pill wouldn't be able to quiet her brain. "Let's talk about this tomorrow, okay?"

"Let's not." He got up, grabbed his jacket from the back of his chair, and headed to the door.

"Where are you going?"

"To find someone who doesn't mind some skeletons. Later."

Emma pulled up Twitter and went to her brother's page. His most recent tweets had been sent during the last forty minutes that he'd been home. They were all picking fights with celebrities.

"Wouldn't it be cool if the Knicks signed actual NBA players next year instead of rejects from European leagues? @MahonNBA, it's called a pick-and-roll. You should try it sometime. #Unwatchable"

"I see the new #JamesBondMovie is trending. You know what I like in a James Bond movie? The lead not sucking. #Worstbondever"

The next tweet had a picture of Harlan and another actor wearing the same outfit, weeks apart. "Zac, next time you want to steal my style, just come over and raid my closet, bro. Let's not pretend you thought of that look yourself when you saw me wearing it at RayRay's last month. Unoriginal is a bad look on you."

Zac had retweeted Harley's post with a message on top: "Cool to see they're making a new Trolls movie. Except it's just about Harlan Crawford. #Thirsty"

Emma couldn't look through more. She put down her phone, drank her protein shake, and took her sleeping pill.

It didn't do much good.

CHAPTER THIRTY-FOUR

On Sunday, she had a weigh-in with her trainer and was up two pounds. The brace wasn't holding her back from lifting anymore, and it felt good to hit it as hard as she could. And she was done complaining—for good, this time. She had earned this role, and she had decided to prove it every day—not to her trainer, not to the studio, but to herself.

After her morning workout, Kelly and Vic invited her to lunch and then for some shopping. If Emma wanted to forge a real relationship with Kelly, she would never be able to eat with her again. Because as Kelly obsessed over every item on the menu, Emma fantasized about sticking her head in the water pitcher. But afterward, when they all went shopping for an updated wardrobe for Kelly, she had a surprisingly good time. Kelly had gotten her start in modeling, and stepping into Barneys had a strange effect on her. She became sharp and confident in a way Emma had never seen. As she had outfit after outfit sent to a dressing room for her, Emma looked at Vic.

"Wow," she said.

"I know," Vic said. "Shopping with her is my favorite."

Kelly found outfits for them, too, things Emma would never have picked for herself but that looked amazing. She and Vic picked out a handful of items before sitting on the dressing room couch and waiting for Kelly to reemerge every few minutes.

"Can I ask you something?" Emma asked.

Vic nodded, albeit warily.

"I heard all about you and Aleki, the dating, the break, the breakup. Are you okay?"

Vic blew air between her lips like she was blowing through a straw.

"He's so sure of everything. He's been sure of me since the day we met at a party last year. But when you grew up the way I did, it's tough to believe that someone could really like you for you, you know?"

Emma did.

"We moved in together over the summer, after that boating accident. And it was great, but that made it so much scarier than if it had been a bit rocky. I kept waiting for the rug to get pulled out from under me. When it didn't, I pulled it out myself."

"So coming to New York was never about acting?"

"No, I told him I needed a break to think about us, but I was just running away. Of course, I came to the one place where I knew he could follow me because I *wanted* him to follow me and fight for me. But every time he tried, I pushed him further away."

"You know nothing ever happened with us, right? Neither of us was really interested."

Vic picked at a fingernail. "I know. I could see it every time I was around you both. He really likes having you as a friend. He used to show me your posts to each other all the time. He'd even ask me for help commenting sometimes. I wouldn't let him admit that we were a couple in public, but I should have stopped him from flirting with you."

"If saying how hot I am on social media is flirting, the whole world has something to answer for," Emma teased. "I was never hurt. But I understand why you're so angry, both about me and about what we said about Kelly."

"You were both performing for a crowd. I know it wasn't malicious for either of you. I used Kelly as a wedge between Aleki and me. Anytime he wanted to get closer, I would mention how much Kelly needed me and how it was time for me to put her first. I think I made him resent her a little. It doesn't make what he said okay, but what I was doing wasn't okay, either."

"So what do you think will happen?"

"I'm not ready to go back to LA, and neither of us is ready to get back together. I need to learn to open up, and he needs to learn to shut up."

Emma laughed. "I really wish we could have been friends growing up, but I'm glad it's happening now."

Vic smiled, and they *oohed* when Kelly came out in a stunning navy pantsuit. The Kelly Bates Foundation had its leader.

Emma returned to the condo that afternoon, eager for her friends' return. Harlan was home, and they studiously avoided each other while she caught up on some work instead of watching the clock like a desperate loser.

Drew's assistant had sent Emma plenty to do: she needed to review a press release about the foundation; Jacques Clothing had sent a proposal to make Emma the face of their Young Professionals line; she had a dozen new companies wanting to pay her for sponsored posts.

She'd intended to address all of it, yet somehow, her fingers wandered to Instagram and Liam's profile. She saw his post from Columbus on Friday before the game, which showed him holding a chocolate-glazed, peanut-butter-cream-filled donut. He had a spot of cream right on the tip of his nose, and he was looking cross-eyed at it. The caption said, "Peanut butter has protein, right? So the Buckeye Donut is practically health food?"

She didn't care about the silly caption. She couldn't get past the fact that his face was a mirror image of hers from so many months ago. How carefully had he studied Emma's picture to get the goofy cross-eyes and the twist of the mouth just right? And what did it mean that he'd done it at all?

The doorbell rang, and Emma ran to the door before Harlan could beat her to it. She threw it open to find Brittany. "You're back!" Emma said, trying to bury her disappointment beneath the very real happiness she felt at seeing her friend. "How was your trip? You haven't texted me since before the game—how did it go?"

Brittany blushed and followed Emma into the main room. Neither of them sat. "It was . . . it was amazing, actually."

"Really?"

"I know this is the last thing you wanted for me, but I can't keep it from you anymore: I still love Santino, Emma. I've known for a few weeks, and I know it was wrong to keep it from you, especially because of everything you did for me with the audition. I'm sorry."

She hated the worry pinching Brittany's lips, hated that she had given Brittany so much reason to doubt herself. Emma grabbed Brittany's hands. "If Santino helps you feel your happiest—if a life with him is what you want—then I am one-hundred percent behind you." Emma's throat grew sticky. "I had no right to make you question your choices. You should have felt empowered to chase your dreams from the second we met. I don't know if I'll ever forgive myself for making you doubt yourself."

"Stop it." Brittany squeezed Emma's hands. "My choices are mine—they always have been—and I'm proud of them. I wouldn't trade the last few months with you for anything."

"But the audition—"

"Doesn't define me. I wish it hadn't happened, but I'm proud of myself for the way I handled it, and I'm proud to be a part of bringing a little more justice to the world. Your friendship has helped me figure out who I am. I'm stronger because I know you." Brittany's eyes glittered like jewels.

Emma dropped her watery gaze down to their hands, where a

diamond ring rested on the fourth finger of her friend's left hand. "Um, are you engaged and you didn't tell me? BRITTANY!"

Britt blushed like a campfire. "About that. I need to put in my two weeks' notice."

Emma laughed and pulled Brittany into a tight hug. "Tell me everything."

An hour later, Brittany and Emma were sitting outside on the patio under blankets, the heaters blasting as the first snow of the winter fell softly around them. The heaters melted most of the snowflakes before they could reach the girls, but every once in a while, a hearty flake would persevere and land on their blankets or noses.

"I'm so happy for you, Britt."

Brittany sighed, her breath a long, whimsical tendril in the frigid air. "I still can't believe Liam helped arrange for Santino to propose at halftime. It's a little cliché, but the station manager flipped over it, especially considering the weatherperson they hired got a DUI last week. They've asked me if I'd reconsider the position."

"And?"

"I told them to talk to my agent. Aleki's already on it. We have a five-year plan for me to take over the Chicago market."

"Winter White will take the world by storm, huh?"

Brittany scrunched her nose. "I think 'Brittany Smith-Ortiz' has a better ring to it, don't you?"

"Much better."

Brittany left soon after with a promise to talk more tomorrow . . . and to introduce Emma to Santino. He'd flown out with Brittany and Liam. He was taking a few days off next week to see New York and experience some of the life Brittany had come to love. Emma liked him already.

She had followed Brittany to the door and then returned to the main room, where Harlan was watching *SportsCenter* and Sean was working. She hadn't even realized her brother's assistant was there. She was about to head back outside when Harlan's eyes caught hers and lit up. Emma almost sagged in relief. She hated fighting with him. All she wanted was for them to support and accept each other. For him to support and accept her. The expression on his face made her hopeful.

She sat on the couch with him, just to see him rewinding the program he was watching.

"I gotta show you something," he said.

"What? Were you at a game yesterday or something?"

He didn't answer, just kept rewinding with that same spark in his eye. Clips of various sports flashed across the screen until Harlan slowed the rewinding. NY United was on the screen, the players she'd come to know so well running and sliding and jumping backward as video of a reporter speaking cut in and out of the games. One jersey was featured more than any other: number 11. Liam Price.

"Stop," she said a split second before he did.

"That's what I wanted to show you."

Clips of Liam's most spectacular goals and assists since his mid-summer loan played on the screen while a reporter explained that representatives from NY United were interested in extending Liam's loan for at least another year. However, a representative from Arsenal said the team was more eager than ever to have Liam rejoin the squad.

"And with a season like Price has had, who could blame them?" the reporter asked. "Rumor has it, Price will be on a red-eye tonight for London to discuss more opportunities with the storied team."

"What?" Emma pointed hard at the TV. "But it's the middle of the playoffs! He can't just go back to the UK right now."

"Sure he can," Harlan said. "United's next game isn't till Friday.

If Arsenal or his agent want him back to discuss sponsorships or his role on the team next year, why wouldn't he go?"

"But—but . . ."

Harlan's voice softened, and his understanding tone made her feel like the floor was plummeting. "Emma, I told you: this is what he does. When things get hard, Liam looks for an exit."

She felt a familiar stinging pain in her throat and behind her eyes. "What could he need to run from? What's been so hard for him?"

"Emma . . ."

She squeezed her eyes shut, wishing that he'd stop using that awful, pitying voice. "Don't, Harley."

"I warned you. I was worried this would happen."

"What?"

"That you'd like him. That you'd get attached to him just to have him leave and hurt you. I never wanted your heart to be broken like mine was." Harlan's hand patted her shoulder. "I'm sorry, sis."

She looked at him through tear-filled eyes. After the countless disappointments and hurts she'd felt lately, she hadn't known she could hurt anymore than she already did. She hadn't known that she could still be cut open, torn apart, and live to see her heart beating outside of her chest. Leaving for London.

"I don't agree with what he's doing, but think about all the drama you've had lately—Kelly, Brittany, Vic, Aleki. With everything you know about Liam, can you really say you're surprised he'd leave?"

Every glance and touch and conversation they'd shared entered her mind. Every time he'd avoided her, every time he'd disappeared out of nowhere. Every time he'd come back, come clean about what was going on. Every truth he'd confessed, every time he'd trusted her. Every time she'd trusted him back. Every time she hadn't, even when he'd asked, even when he'd hoped . . .

She jumped up. "No."

"What are you doing? You just said you're not surprised."

Emma started for the front door, Harlan on her heels. "I don't know if I'm surprised, but I don't accept this."

"Where are you going? Think about what you're doing, Emma. You're just going to make him run faster. Is that what you really want?"

She was pulling the door open when she looked at her brother. His eyes were wide and desperate. "I want him, Harley. I don't know if he wants me back, but I'm done sacrificing the things that make me happy."

The wideness of his eyes turned tight, and his tone turned sharp. "And what about what that does to me?"

"I guess you'll have to figure that out, won't you? You have enough skeletons in your closet, Harley. I won't become one of them." She ran into the hallway, slamming the door behind her. She pressed the elevator button, but it was too slow in coming, so she darted for the stairs, jumping the last several steps on each landing as she propelled herself around each corner. She sprinted through the lobby, nearly knocking down a resident in her haste to get to the street.

Snow fell in small puffs as Emma hailed a cab. She had forgotten a coat, but she was too hyped to feel the cold. When a yellow cab stopped in front of her, Emma patted her jeans to realize she didn't have her wallet. "Do you take electronic credit cards?" she asked after throwing the door open.

The driver's look suggested that tourists would be the death of him. "Of course."

She exhaled as she slid in and gave him the address.

The Sunday afternoon streets were busy—as always. Emma tried calling Liam, but it went straight to voice mail. "Dammit," she said, slapping her braced hand on the seat. She winced at a twinge of pain where her hand was still tender.

The driver made eye contact with her in the rearview mirror.

"Sorry," she mumbled.

The progress was slow into Harlem, but faster than running would be. Barely. When they got within a few streets of Liam's townhouse, though, there was a detour due to road work, and Emma knew exactly what that meant: delays. Long, stupid delays that would have her ripping her hair out in her anxiety to reach Liam before he left.

She tried calling again. Voice mail. The cabbie was just about to follow the detour, but Emma couldn't afford the time. The reporter had said Liam was taking a red-eye out tonight, but it was an international flight. If it left at 6 p.m., he could already be on his way to the airport.

"Stop here!"

The cabbie pulled over, and Emma pressed her phone up against the scanner in the back. A moment later, the machine beeped, Emma punched in a tip, and she ran out of the cab with a "Thank you!" She had already crossed the street and run two blocks when she realized that the worst was just ahead. Liam's street.

Construction.

Her pulse spiked as she looked at the long block of sidewalk sheds before her. Blue plywood platforms that were as iconic to any New Yorker as the Statue of Liberty rose above the makeshift sheds, their crisscrossing metal frames of poles and girders promising destruction, peril. Death.

Why had she watched that stupid documentary? Falling beams, collapsing platforms, crushed bodies . . .

"Shut up, brain," she whispered.

"Freak," a woman said, eyeing Emma as she passed her on the crosswalk.

Emma let out a shaky laugh. "Hell yeah, I am." Then she balled up her fists and made a run for it.

She passed Fat Bob's Burger Palace on the corner before being swallowed by the sidewalk shed. The bright-gray skies disappeared, and the air was instantly heavier and damper, making Emma feel claustrophobic. She focused on breathing in through her nose, out through her mouth, in, out, as she ran by shops, dodged pedestrians, and jumped cracks in the sidewalk.

You're not going to die. You're not going to die.

The power of positive thinking.

Soon, something small and white fell onto her eyelashes. With a breath of relief, she looked up at the clouds. The scaffolding was behind her. She'd made it!

She was alive!

She took the stairs up to Liam's townhouse two at a time, slamming a fist on the door. "Please be home. Please be home."

Luis answered. "Emma, what's up?"

"Liam," she said, panting. "Is he home?"

"You just missed him," Luis said, and emotion constricted her throat and burned the back of her eyes and nose. "Two ships passing, am I right?"

If she had the energy to spare, she'd want to punch him in the throat for his jaunty tone. "But you guys are still in the playoffs, right? Do you think he'll be back before Friday's game?"

"Uh, yeah. Unless you're planning to keep him."

"Huh?"

"What?"

"What are you talking about, Luis?"

His eyes shifted left to right, as if she was the one making literally zero sense. "What are *you* talking about?"

"ESPN said that he's going to the UK tonight, you bozo! To sign some stupid contract!"

Luis's head shook. "Huh. I guess that makes sense. Honestly, when he said he had to leave, I assumed he was going to your place. He seemed upset about something, and whenever he's upset, it usually has to do with either you or Harley."

She turned from him with a scream and caught the first cab back to Manhattan. She cursed the whole way home. Cursed with the fluency of an entitled movie star. Cursed with as much anger and bitterness as she could muster, because if she could stay angry and bitter, then she wouldn't have to face the heart-sinking disappointment that was making her insides feel like lead.

Leaving the cab, she went inside Highbury Lane, but instead of going upstairs, she sat in the small café in the lobby and asked the server for the most calming tea on the menu. While she waited, she texted Finley.

I have to tell you something.

She pressed send, but she didn't wait for Finley's response before sending another one.

I think I'm in love with your brother, and I think it's probably too late, and I think my heart is going to break in two and I'm going to bleed out and die.

Her tea came, and she escaped to a small circular table in the corner of the café. She couldn't handle talking to any of the other residents right now. The last thing she wanted was to smile and laugh and dazzle. She wished the earth would swallow her whole.

A buzz from her phone caught her attention.

Finley's response: *I think you should go home.*

Emma sent three question marks.

LIAM IS AT YOUR PLACE RIGHT NOW. GO HOME.

Emma ran.

———————————

Upstairs, she panted as she punched in the code to Harlan's front door. She'd taken the elevator, but she felt like she couldn't breathe for nerves. Why was Liam there? Was he saying goodbye before his flight? Was he catching up with his best buddy, Harlan? And could she really tell him how she felt in front of Harlan?

Yes.

She could. She had to.

The gesture—running through that effing construction zone—had felt so monumental and romantic that declaring her love felt almost easy by comparison. But now . . .

She opened and closed the door quietly, but she could have slammed it. No way they could have heard it over their yelling.

CHAPTER THIRTY-FIVE

"She doesn't want to see you!" Harlan was yelling from the main room.

"She's had her heart broken! I just want to be a good friend." Liam's voice was loud and shaking in a way she'd never heard before. He sounded hurt. He'd never said as much, but she was positive that not being heard was a trigger of his. After years of being yelled at and not being allowed to answer back, not being allowed to say how he felt without fear of violent repercussion, how could it not be?

"The last thing she needs is to rehash this. Just go already."

"So you're saying I can't even make sure she's okay?"

"I'm saying she doesn't need you to be okay. You gotta move on, man. Don't you get it?"

"No, I don't get it! Harley, I swear, I've tried to respect your wishes, but there's something there, and I'll never forgive myself if I don't see it through."

What? Emma held her breath for fear that she'd miss something.

"And I'll kill you if you hurt her. It's time for you to leave!" Harley yelled.

"I'm not leaving until I see her!" Liam said. "Does she even know I'm here?"

Emma took a deep breath, walking toward the main room. "I think they know you're here in the penthouse." Her pulse was a runaway train. Liam had said her heart was broken. Why? Because he was leaving? But he'd also said something was there. *Something* something?

Harlan stepped in front of Liam, his face red and his nostrils flared. "She's been through enough already, man. You need to let this go and leave now."

But Liam stepped around Harlan, just enough for him and Emma to make eye contact. "Emma, I'm not trying to stir things up, but I'm sorry about Aleki—"

"*Aleki?*"

"Just go," Harlan was saying, grabbing Liam's arm.

Emma put a hand on Harlan, stopping him. "Liam, what are you talking about? Did something happen to Aleki?"

The compassion on Liam's face was so pure and real that she would have fallen in love with him for it, if she didn't love him already. "Wait, you haven't heard?" He looked at Harlan in shock. "Emma, I'm sorry. Aleki and Vic have been lying to everyone. I hoped he'd come clean—"

Emma gave him a wry smile. "You mean about how they've been dating and living together for months? Yeah, I know."

"And it's been hard enough for everyone, so just drop this," Harlan said, still trying to silence Liam.

"*Hard?*" Emma looked at Harlan. "You know I never liked Aleki like that. What are you talking about?"

"You never told me that," Harlan said, but his voice was weak and feeble, especially with the way Liam was looking at him.

"How could you?" Liam asked him.

Harlan didn't respond.

Emma had filmed a scene a couple of years ago in an old, worn-down cemetery. Between takes, she and her costar had walked around the graveyard and looked at the headstones and statues. One statue was of a young angel, its face severely weathered and cracked. Emma had worried parts of the face would slide right off if they even breathed on it wrong.

Harlan had just breathed on Liam wrong.

She watched as the mask of Liam's belief and trust in Harlan crumbled piece by piece. His mouth was open, his eyes wide until the mask was gone. Liam looked bare.

"You really never liked Aleki?" he asked her.

"No," she said. Liam was watching her mouth, hanging on her words.

"I told you we were just friends," she insisted.

"I thought you were just saying that until you two made it official."

"What? Why would you think that?"

Liam looked at Harlan. Emma looked at Harlan.

Harlan looked at the floor.

"Harley?"

He didn't meet her eye.

"Look at me! How could you?"

"I didn't want to see you get hurt," he whispered.

She had never known such betrayal. It carved into her, but it didn't hollow her out. She was done giving him that power. "You liar. You've been manipulating me—*gaslighting* me for months. And for what? So you don't have to be alone? So I have no one but you to rely on? How could you do that to me? I thought you cared about me."

"I do!"

"No, you only care about yourself. You've used the people around you until they're empty shells that you can discard. You're exactly like Dad."

"I'm not—I haven't—"

"You have. You are."

She looked at Liam, who was watching their exchange carefully. Emma closed her eyes, shook her head, tried to keep her emotions in check. As much as she wanted to cry, scream, rage against Harlan, this wasn't about him. This wasn't even about Liam.

This was about her.

When her eyes opened, Harlan was gone. She heard the front door close a moment later. Nothing remained between her and Liam but an ocean of unanswered questions and unspoken tension.

He looked at her the way he always did: with trust written into the corners of his eyes and the set of his mouth. He wore a curiosity and a certainty that told her that whatever she said next would matter to him, just as he knew that what he said would matter to her too.

"Did you really come over because you thought Aleki broke my heart?"

"Why did Harlan say he didn't want to see you get hurt?"

"Is that the only reason you came over?" she pushed.

"Why would Harlan lie to you? To us?"

"You've avoiding my question."

A ghost of those flirty smiles he gave her months ago crept over his face, making her stomach flip. "Yes, I am."

Oh, that puckish smile. Her lips tugged up of their own accord, matching his. She cocked an eyebrow ever so slightly. "I ran all the way through Harlem's most dangerous construction zone to get my answers. You took a cab. Speak."

"I took a bus," he corrected, smiling bigger.

"Answer me, Liam."

Liam stepped closer. Closer. So close that she could taste the mint on his breath, that she could count his freckles, that she could watch his lips and replay their movement in her head in slow motion. "I needed to know if you were hurt over Aleki and Vic," he said.

"I'm not. My heart wasn't his to break."

"That makes me very happy," he said. Now that she'd noticed the curve of his lips, not even his eyes could keep her attention.

"Why is that? You owe me, Price. Construction zone, remember?"

"Why did you run through the construction zone?"

"Liam Price—"

"Because I love you." He was beaming now, his smile radiating with an almost painful intensity. "Wasn't that obvious?"

She felt like the power of the sun was bursting in her chest as she bit her lip. "*Obvious*? No. I don't think so. ESPN said you're hopping on a red-eye to London tonight."

"I'm not. I'm done running. I told my agent that I want to extend my contract here, if the team will let me. They're negotiating." He wrinkled his nose. "And I talked to Fin when I was in Chicago—told her everything. She answered exactly the way you said she would. I realized I've spent so long trying to run from my weaknesses and from anything that felt too hard to handle alone that I didn't realize how much stronger I would feel with people on my side." He placed his hands on her waist, and the heat in her chest dropped low in her belly.

She put her arms around his neck, running her fingers through his hair. How had she ever thought Aleki had great hair? It was too long, too wavy, too . . . not this.

"Now, Emma Crawford," he said, leaning in so that his lips touched her ear.

She shivered and held on to him tighter.

"About that 'running through a construction zone' thing. Did you conquer your greatest fears for me?"

"Nope. Sorry, pal. I did it for me. I deserve to be happy, so I decided to fight for it. Or . . . run for it, if you will."

"I make you happy?"

"I mean, I'm super in love with you, so yeah. Wasn't that obvious?"

He shook his head in a playful "no" while his mouth said, "Totally obvious." And then they closed the absurd, stupid distance between their faces, and their lips met, and hot damn.

Hot.

Damn.

Liam's mouth answered her remaining questions with a sort of diz-zying efficiency. His mouth. His unbearably edible mouth. He clutched her to him, pulling her closer and closer until they were bending the laws of nature and occupying the same physical space. Her hands coiled around his neck, slid into his hair, and tugged. When he groaned, the fire roaring in her spread to her whole body in a wave. She had never in her life wanted anything more than she wanted this. His mouth on hers, their limbs entangled, their bodies breathing the same air.

"I love you," he whispered through kisses, making her want to burst into song. Their frenetic energy calmed into something slow, steady, and beautiful.

Emma had kissed her share of guys, but nothing compared to kissing Liam Price. Because it wasn't just that their mouths fit together so perfectly and effortlessly. It wasn't simply that the way he held her made her feel both totally wanted and totally safe. It wasn't even that she could finally dig her hands into his hair and feel the muscles in his shoulders or how delectable it was to kiss his jaw and neck and every inch of his face.

It was that somehow, without saying anything, she still felt heard. She felt important. Cherished. Loved.

"Your mouth is unreal," Liam muttered against her lips.

"I was thinking the same thing." She smiled and kissed him twice before pulling back and breathing deeply. "But as much as I'd love to talk about how hot kissing you is, I really need to find a new place to live."

"Do you think you'll go back to Weston's?"

She stroked the muscles in his arms. "Maybe for the short term. But I'm actually thinking of going back to college."

Liam's eyebrows jumped. "Yeah? Good for you. Any idea where?"

"I'll probably apply all over, but I'm kind of hoping for Chicago." His arms tightened around her. "My aunt and uncle are awesome—we've been in touch a bunch lately, and they're planning a visit to check up on me. Of course, Finley is in Chicago, so you know I'd mastermind a way to become roommates. I love the city. It's close enough to everywhere I need to be but far enough for me to get some space from everything that's happened here."

"Chicago. Huh. I can get behind that."

"It's just a thought. But maybe we can save the planning for later? I need to pack, and I haven't had any protein in hours, and my trainer will probably kill me."

"Okay. Let's get you some protein, pack, then make out."

Emma tilted her head up and kissed his jaw. "Nah. Let's make out first."

He was smiling when his lips touched hers. "I like it when you're the boss."

She kissed him back, relishing the feeling of his smiling mouth on hers. "Then we are going to be very, very happy."

EIGHT MONTHS LATER

Emma and Finley sat in the stands a few rows up from the center of the Chicago Fire stadium. They were yelling "Foul!" as they watched one of the Chicago players slide into Liam before he could score. He fell to the ground, clutching his ankle and rolling in the grass, his face contorted in agony.

"I wish I could say I taught him that," Emma said, "but no one can fake emotion like a soccer player."

"He's been using that move all his life," Finley said.

The referee issued the player a red card—having already burned through two yellow cards for being an aggressive douche—and Liam was awarded a penalty kick. Emma and Finley screamed and jumped when it went in. NY United was up two to nothing.

"That was an amazing kick," Finley's boyfriend, Oliver, said as he sat down next to Fin. He handed Finley a hot dog and soda and gave Emma a bag of peanuts. Her appetite had all but disappeared since she'd wrapped up filming *Valkyrie* in March, but she still got shaky if she didn't get enough protein and fat in her diet. At least she didn't have to down raw eggs and flaxseed oil every ninety minutes anymore.

"Everything Liam does is amazing," Emma said.

Finley reached into Emma's bag and threw a peanut at her. "Gross."

Oliver's brother, Tate, and his girlfriend, Alex, sat down on Oliver's other side. Where they had found milkshakes, Emma had no idea. But it was their thing, and it was cute.

Emma leaned down to look past Finley and the guys. "You missed Liam looking super hot," she told Alex.

"Dammit," Alex said. "Did he do that thing with his hair after he scored? It kills me."

"Yes, and it was glorious and you should be furious with yourself for missing it."

"Tate, I should throw this milkshake in your face for making me miss it."

Tate kissed Alex's cheek. "Alex, you're a torturous beast, and I accept, because it sounds kinky." Alex grinned at Tate and kissed him back.

Emma smiled at the two. They were an odd pair, in some ways, but she couldn't imagine either of them fitting with someone else. They had an energy and a tension that would have driven anyone else away but that drew them together like magnets.

Finley had told Emma that it had taken her a few months to get used to Alex, but Emma and she had hit it off instantly. All three girls had grown up with pretty messed-up lives, but while Finley had risen above her circumstances, Alex had been buried by them before she learned how to dig herself out. Emma respected that, respected Alex. She also had rarely been around anyone who made her look tame by comparison. The novelty had yet to wear off.

When the game ended, the group waited in the team parking lot for Liam to come out of the stadium. He appeared quicker than usual, his hair still wet from his shower. He shook it out as he ran over to them.

Alex looked at Emma. "That hair," she mouthed.

"Just remember," Emma said, "you got a man."

"Can you two maybe stop lusting after my brother?" Finley asked. "It makes it difficult to look at you."

"Then look away, sweetie," Alex said. "Cuz Mama likes."

Tate put an arm around Alex and pulled her toward her car. "Okay, Mama. You're getting a little creepy." He looked back at them. "Meet you at Gino's?"

"See you there," Oliver said. He hung back as Finley ran over to her brother and hugged him.

Emma's thoughts turned to Harlan, who had just texted her a few days ago for the first time in months. He'd finally fired their dad and was wondering if Drew could give him any recommendations. After telling him how proud she was of him, Emma had gotten a list from Drew that she'd passed on with a note of support. He hadn't texted again after sending his thanks, but she felt hopeful.

"So, Emma, are you two happy?" Oliver asked, pulling her back to the present.

She smiled at him. She and Oliver had dated for a hot second at the same time as Finley and Harlan. The memories felt like they were from a different lifetime. She'd cared deeply for Oliver, but it had never been love, and it had never been long-term. They didn't fit the way he and Finley did or the way she and Liam did.

"I've never been so happy in my life," she said. "I've finally found myself."

"I'm glad. And now that you've been at U of C for a whole month, do you have the rest of your life mapped out?"

Liam and Finley joined them, and Liam put his arm around Emma, kissing her temple. "You know, I'm thinking business wouldn't be the worst thing. Can you imagine me in a boardroom? I would slay." Finley high-fived her. "But I'll keep acting. The world needs a little Emma Crawford."

Oliver and Finley laughed and held hands over to the car. Emma and Liam followed behind. "You may not be the actor we need, but you're the actor we deserve," Liam said.

"*The Dark Knight*, Gary Oldman, 2008," Finley said before Emma or Oliver could spit it out.

"Long live the queen," Liam said to his sister. To Emma and Oliver, he said, "You two should be ashamed of yourselves."

"Show-offs," Emma said while Liam nuzzled into her neck in a way that made her wish they weren't going out with anyone. The other couple walked ahead of them.

"I missed you," Liam said.

"Me, too," she said. "Three weeks is too long."

He nipped at her ear as they walked, and her knees buckled. "I have news."

"If it's not about how we're going to ditch these losers to go make out in that alley, I don't care."

He continued, undeterred. "You remember how it's the transfer window? Well, my agent called me right before the game: I've been transferred."

Emma stopped and turned to face him. They were almost to the car, but still close enough to the exit that the other players who were leaving called out to them. Emma waved them off. "Tell me. Now."

"I know how happy you are in Chicago. And it's been nice that I've been so close in New York. We've been able to see each other a ton—"

"Okay—"

"But you have to promise me you won't get sick of me . . ."

She grabbed his shirt by the collar. "Please tell me you're saying what I think you're saying."

"I just signed a five-year contract with the Chicago Fire."

"Yes!" Emma squealed and planted kiss after kiss on his face. "Yes, yes, yes!"

Finley ran over to them, a look of alarm on her face. "Did you just get engaged?"

Liam and Emma laughed. "Um, no. I'm not even old enough to play a high school senior," Emma said. "We'll tell you in the car."

Finley prodded her brother for information as he kissed Emma's face again. Emma and Liam slid into the back of Oliver's car, and Liam told them the news. Finley squealed as loudly as Emma had.

A smile split across Emma's face, and she settled beneath Liam's arm. Tomorrow, she had three classes, a meeting with her adviser, and a conference call with Kelly and Drew about the foundation. Next week, she had a photo shoot in New York for Jacques Clothing, and she and Weston were taking the weekend to go on a marathon shopping spree. They'd meet up with Vic and Aleki for dinner. Her assistant had just forwarded her an invitation to Brittany's wedding and needed her to RSVP. Somehow, Emma had made a new life for herself, one where she was surrounded by people who loved her and who sacrificed for her, just as she loved and sacrificed for them.

It was hard, learning how to balance being a college student, girl-friend, friend, actor, and so much more. She was making mistakes and making up for them. She was busier than she had ever been in her life, but every choice and every challenge was hers.

She wouldn't change a thing.

ACKNOWLEDGMENTS

This was the hardest book I've ever written, and that's saying a lot, considering I have a shelved fantasy trilogy of over 300,000 words that took me five years to write. But until this book, I never knew what imposter syndrome really felt like. Telling Emma's story didn't always feel like a labor of love, but more a labor of duty—duty to the women who trusted me with their stories, women who will not be named but whose fingerprints are on these pages and whose faith in me will hopefully not be in vain. To them, I say thank you for sharing your experiences with me and helping me shape Emma's story. Any mistakes I made are my own.

Readers, thank you for joining me on another journey. Your support means the world to me.

As always, profound thanks to Kelsy Thompson for understanding the core of this story and helping me flesh it out and turn it into something real and (to me) beautiful. My appreciation to Mari Kesselring, Megan Naidl, and the whole team at Flux for giving this story a home. Thank you, also, to my agent Dawn Frederick for continuing to advocate for me and my work.

My sisters are a part of every story I write, and I owe a special, huge, squishy hug to Susannah Ortiz for listening to my fears and doubts almost on loop while giving me the pep talks I needed to keep going. Sissy poos, thanks for listening to me and for putting up with me. I love you dearly.

Writing can be a lonely and difficult journey, so my heartfelt thanks to the writers who make this wild ride a little more manageable, including Gina Denny, Katie Nelson, Emily King, Breeana Shields, Caitlin Sangster, Rosalyn Eves, Jolene Perry, Katie Purdie, Sara Larson, Erin Summerill, Darci Cole, Anna Priemaza Abigail Johnson, Amy Trueblood, Kelly DeVos, Stephanie Elliot, Joanna Meyer, Kara McDowell, my Storymakers, Class of 2K17, AZ writer friends, and more. You can't know the impact of your kindnesses and friendship to me. My sincere thanks to the spectacular bloggers who read and support my work, including Krysti Meyer at YA and Wine, Sarah Cleverley at the Clever Reader, and Christy Jane at BookCrushin.

To my Teen Brain Trust—Chloe Bikman, Emma Bikman, Emily Hale, Hayley Boblett—thanks for answering my questions and keeping me emotionally honest to today's teen experience. Y'all are pretty fab.

To my fabulous(ly funny) friend, Lauren Caputo, alt 3 forever. Thanks for talking to me about what it's like to be a female comic, and thanks to you and Lindsey for all the support. Billy Zane will one day tell stories about filming with you.

To my entire Bikman/Cooper-Leavitt family, thank you for your love and encouragement. To Nana/Mom and Poppy/Don—I don't know that I could have written this book without your help. Thank you for watching and loving my kids when my deadline loomed extra super large and for trading houses and responsibilities with me. And thank you for raising such an outstanding son. I love you!

Elsie, Hugo, Archer, and Etta (hey, girl!): I love you with my whole heart, and with each of the extra hearts I've grown to accommodate my love for you. You are special and divine and of infinite worth, and you have added so much more to my life than I could ever add to yours, but I'm doing my best. I love you more than everything.

Jeff, I am tremendously blessed to have you. You have let me debate with you for years, you have listened to me rant vehemently about things that—ultimately—don't matter, and you have helped me become more open-minded, thoughtful, considerate, and loving. Thanks, babe.

Lastly, my profound and eternal thanks to my God, for everything I am, have, and can become.

ABOUT THE AUTHOR

Kate Watson is a young adult writer, wife, mother of four, and the tenth of thirteen children. Originally from Canada, she attended college in the States and holds a BA in Philosophy from Brigham Young University. A lover of travel, speaking in accents, and experiencing new cultures, she has also lived in Israel, Brazil, and the American South, and she now calls Arizona home. *Off Script* is her fourth novel.